LAYERS OF LIGHT

46. ASCENDING

S. R. CRONIN

Cinnabar Press, Black Mountain, North Carolina 28711

ISBN-13: 978-1-941283-36-3

Cover design by Deranged Doctor Design
Original Editing by Joel Handley
Editorial assistance and expertise provided by Dhivya Balaji and Shree Janani

This book is a work of fiction and, with the exception of news items, public figures, and cultural information, the events, characters and institutions in it are imaginary, as are the organizations c^3 and x^0. No individual character, organization, or group of people included as part of the fictional narrative is intended to represent any real person or group.

A version of this book was published in 2014 under the title c^3. It was designed for an electronic reader and included numerous links to photographs, articles and music. A later iteration was published in paperback. In Layers of Light, all text supplementing those links has been removed, and the story has been shortened and updated.

Dedication

This book is dedicated to my youngest daughter, who fills my life with hugs and fuzzy blankets and songs that make me cry. I thank her for always asking about my writing, I love her for her passionate spirit, and I cheer her on as she fights to make this world a better place. I have no doubt she will.

It is also dedicated to every sort of traveler: to those who wander, to those who seek, and to those who choose to answer a call.

Author's Note

This story is not erotic. It deals obliquely with the disturbing subject of human trafficking and forced prostitution, and therefore contains occasional mildly mature content and crude language. It's intended for an audience with sufficient maturity to handle that.

Along with its several other story lines, the novel celebrates those who find ways to light a candle in that particular kind of darkness, and how the resulting light they produce makes its way outward in every direction.

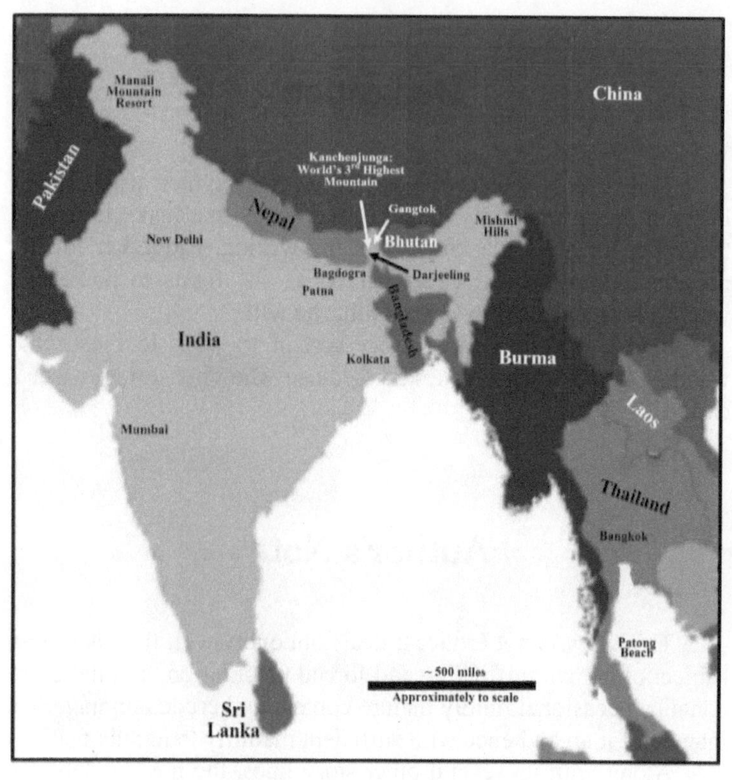

A Map of Southern Asia

Table of Contents

Little Birds

Leaving the Nest to Touch the Sky

c^3

The Abode of Light

A Thousand Ways to Soar

Little Birds

December 1999

1. Being Brave

"Where's your little sister? If she sees you, she'll tell on us."

"Relax." Thirteen-year-old Zane Zeitman held the portable phone between his neck and shoulder while he fumbled with the cork on the bottle of exotic liqueur he'd slipped out of his parents' liquor cabinet days before. As the top came loose, it smelled like coffee and paint. He hoped it tasted better.

"She's been asleep for hours, and she knows better than to come into my room."

His best friend Bhadra was an only child, and suspicious of siblings. She sat alone five miles away in her family's upstairs game room, staring at an unopened can of beer. She wished she'd been able to sneak something more appealing, but her parents didn't keep much around. They'd probably be home right after midnight, even on such a special New Year's Eve. She and Zane needed to get this party going.

"I can't believe they made me stay home on the biggest night of the whole world's life." Bhadra popped open the can.

"Yeah, well I'm here watching my little sister. Here's to outsmarting the adults, who think you have to be together to party. Happy New Year." He raised the glass of noxious brown liquid high.

"Yeah. Here's to a millennium filled with freedom for us." Bhadra closed her eyes and made herself take a swallow.

Zane coughed, and Bhadra gagged, but neither complained.

"I say the year two thousand deserves a second sip."

"At least." The second and third gulps weren't as awful.

“There’s a lot of cool shit gonna happen this next century,” Zane said, starting to feel more adult and philosophical. “I bet we see amazing things.”

“Yeah. Next thousand years, who knows what the human race is gonna do.” Bhadra giggled as a giant burp escaped her.

Zane giggled too. This whole party-by-phone thing was damn clever. The fourth gulp was easier, and by the fifth Zane was thinking he might enjoy coffee. Maybe even paint.

The mental image of him chugging a can of paint made him laugh, which made Bhadra giggle uncontrollably. They drank more and laughed louder and felt very grown up and like, well, actually the truth was Zane was starting to feel like he was about to throw up.

******

At the eastern edge of the mighty Himalayas lies a place called The Land of the Dawn-lit Mountains. Constant cloud cover hides the sparsely inhabited region from satellites. Tourism is banned due to ongoing border disputes, as fiercely independent nomadic tribes fight in a world that barely touches our own.

Za huddled with her four-year-old twins under fur blankets as the December winds howled off of the nearby peaks. She neither knew nor would have cared that she sat where the borders of China, India and Burma all met. She cared only that these children, her first, had grown strong and healthy.

Yesterday a winter storm stopped the small group of foragers, but tomorrow Za would bundle the boy and girl against her strong body and ride with her family to a more protected valley. Her husband and his brother stood outside, guarding against the many thieves from other tribes who would prey upon them if they were found.

Za looked down at her two sleeping firstborn and thought she had never seen faces so beautiful. She brushed each cheek in turn, wondering what future the spirits intended for her twins.

Then she heard a harsh war yell, and knew they'd been discovered.

******

Four-year-old Teddie Zeitman was a light sleeper cursed with an overactive imagination that saw creatures in the laundry basket and heard moans in the air vents. Her big sister Ariel said her bed was a fortress, impermeable to monsters as long as she stayed in it. She trusted Ariel, who was a wise eleven-year-old.

Big brother Zane laughed at Ariel's theory, but that didn't matter because Zane laughed at everything lately. Turning thirteen had changed him. He wouldn't play games and he treated Teddie like she didn't matter. He was probably wrong about the bed fortress thing, too.

She'd been woken by the sound of Zane talking to a friend on the phone. As she snuggled her head full of black curls deeper into her pillow, she pulled the soft green quilt tight around her body.

She wanted to go sit with Zane. Teddie hated having her own room and liked how Zane used to let her come sleep on his bed while he played video games or whispered on the phone with his friends. But now, he wanted his privacy. Teddie wasn't sure what privacy was, but she wasn't a big fan of it.

She'd almost worked up the courage to go knock on Zane's door when a shadow flickered across her floor. She cringed. The tree monster again? It probably was. So much for getting out of bed.

She pulled the covers higher over her head. "Please be right, Ariel. Please be right." Then she heard the unmistakable sound of Zane throwing up.

Is he okay? Mommy and Daddy aren't here. Ariel is at a slumber party. What if Zane's dying? But what if the tree monster is waiting for me to get out of bed? I'm pretty sure tree monsters scratch your eyes out.

Teddie huddled into a tinier ball, not knowing what to do. She was tired and her bed was warm. She drifted to sleep, hoping Zane was okay. Then she heard Zane retching again.

Teddie rolled over towards the side of the bed, while her body stayed safe under the covers. It was weird. She didn't stand up because she didn't have to. She floated up, without thinking about it, and then she floated through the opening in her door and down the hall. Worried for Zane, Teddie didn't hesitate when she came to his closed door. She floated through it and felt a funny fuzzy sensation as she passed through the wood. It tickled and made her giggle.

She moved to a vantage point below his ceiling fan, and watched him through his open bathroom door as he pushed away from the toilet and stood up. He looked awful as he wobbled toward his sink. He picked up his toothbrush and swirled it around his mouth and Teddie felt her worry ebb. She didn't think people who were dying bothered to brush their teeth.

Then it hit her. She was floating in Zane's room and her body was back in bed. How was that possible? As she turned to the door in panic, she saw a thin sparkly green cord running from her floating self back down the hall. She reached for the pretty cord and felt herself snap back into her body, no floating required. Just, zap. She was back safe inside of Teddie, who was under the covers safe inside her fortress bed. She hugged herself tighter as she pulled the soft green quilt up over her head.

Now that was scary. She'd never do that again. Unless, of course, it was an emergency like this one. Then, well, maybe.

******

It was easy to kill the two poorly armed men guarding the tents and then slit the throats of the others. The problem was the young children. These two were rosy and strong, likely to survive the rough ride back to the village. Women could be found to care for them and they'd have some value before long.

"Keep them?" the younger brother asked.

"Yes. They're ours now. We train the boy to fight. If he's weak, we kill him or sell him. The girl will be worth money, more if she's pretty."

"Maybe she can be of use to us." The younger brother made an obscene gesture to clarify the sort of use he had in mind.

"Idiot. This little thing's too small for that. I know of a man who buys them young, though, and for good money. We'll get plenty for our trouble."

So each brother bundled up a sobbing child and placed it in front of him as he mounted his horse.

******

January 1, 2000, wasn't the start of a new millennium but nobody cared. It was the day the nines rolled into zeroes on the odometer of time. It was the day on which the world might end.

On New Year's morning, a billion people turned on their television sets to watch the Pacific Island nation of Kiribati be the first on earth to greet the year 2000. Viewers learned with relief there had been no bombs and no apocalypse while they slept, and the open beaches of Kiribati had remained devoid of aliens, computer bugs and vengeful angels throughout the night.

Teddie sat with her brother eating cereal, watching as Zane ate without much appetite. He looked like he still felt sick.

"Way to go, humanity," one reporter gushed as she blocked the view of the dancers with flaming torches. "This day has dawned peacefully the world over. For one night, humans have done each other no harm."

April 2009

2. Being Helpful

Teddie thought her parents treated her too much like an adult. True, most other thirteen-year-olds would die to have that problem and she knew it, but those kids didn't understand. Adulthood wasn't about freedom as much as it was about getting your homework done and then making dinner, too. Teddie was all for being treated like a kid.

The problem with having two siblings seven and nine years older was your parents forgot how young you were. So here her dad was, asking her again to act like an adult.

"Your mom could use some play time, Teddie. She works hard. I've got a chance to take her on a canoe adventure she'll love, but I need to know you're safe for the weekend."

"I don't see why I can't just stay at the house."

"You won't be able to call us while we're on the river. We're not taking expensive cell phones in a canoe and we have to know you're okay. Come on. Shawna's family invited you out to their cabin for the weekend. Can't you put your differences with her aside for a couple of days so I can do something nice for your mother."

Shawna had been a childhood friend and there were a dozen good reasons why Teddie no longer wanted anything to do with her, but none of them were things any right-minded teenager would tell her parents.

"We were friends in fourth grade. We've grown apart."

"So, grow back together for a weekend. Shawna's dad said he'd be happy to have you; he said he missed your pretty face and wished you girls still played together."

Yeah. Shawna's creepy dad is one of the reasons we grew apart.

"Fine. It's just for a weekend. I'll go."

******

Amy Levitt liked to wear flowing foreign-looking clothes and bright tropical prints and she had a passion for wanting to help her sisters who'd suffered violence. She couldn't explain why. Her fervor didn't come from trauma or abuse, but was fueled by some internal sense of justice that was outraged by monsters she'd never personally encountered.

Her master's in social work gave her parents pause. "Maybe hospital administration would be more useful? Maybe more lucrative?" But no. Twenty-two-year-old Amy knew what she wanted to do, and it didn't involve administration of anything.

At twenty-six, she worked for an NGO dedicated to stopping human trafficking. She'd already spent two years at a hotline encouraging desperate women to get help. People kept asking if she was burnt out yet. Burnt out? No, she was just getting started.

At twenty-eight Amy accepted a promotion from the NGO. She was something of an expert in her field, in part because so many of her compatriots had left to take jobs with more money and less emotional demands. She was being sent overseas to be an administrator.

"You're going to run an office?" Her mother seemed amused at the news.

"Well, there's only six of us, and three are local volunteers. It's not like I have a big staff to manage."

"You'll do great, dear. I know you will."

Amy hoped so. Right now Darjeeling, India seemed far away, and the human trafficking problems of such a different culture appeared impossible to understand.

******

Jampa walked up to his favorite rock to meditate. No, it wasn't his favorite rock. He wasn't supposed to have a favorite rock. All rocks were fine. This rock was an effective place for contemplation and, as a young monk in training, Jampa knew meditation was important.

He slowed his breathing and slipped into the deep trance for which he was known. Those far older than he marveled at the discipline with which Jampa could let go of the chatter in his mind. The truth was, no one had taught him the technique. He'd been doing it for as long as he could remember.

Jampa had little memory of living with the traveling caravan that dumped him at the monastery door, but he thanked them every day for their mercy. He was told he was six or seven at the time, and had been purchased by the caravan to fetch water and do chores. The men complained that once they started their journey westward the little boy was useless because he'd go into deep trances. They offered him to the monastery as a gift. The monks accepted and made the child one of their own, giving Jampa his name, and making him a Buddhist and citizen of Bhutan before he was eight.

For five years now, he'd hidden the real secret behind his meditative abilities from the monks, who believed his trances indicated a powerful religious zeal.

******

Vanida curled up on her sleeping palette and hoped tonight she'd get to see her friend again. She'd known him since before she could remember, since before Pim and Noi had become her mothers and her owners.

Vanida had little memory of the man who sold her to Pim and Noi when she was little, but she remembered the two women saying they preferred older girls who would not cry at night for their mothers. Even though Pim and Noi were strict, they fed her every day and gave her a soft place to sleep, and that made them kinder than the man who'd sold her. Vanida tried from the start to not cry at night, so Pim and Noi wouldn't send her back.

She and her seven new sisters lived in a camp outside of a marvelous city called Bangkok. She'd never seen it, but Pim and

Noi told her over and over that it was full of wonders and one day she'd get to live there.

In order to have this fine life, though, she had to work hard. Soon after they bought her, the women did something quick and painful to her between her legs. After she stopped bleeding she was told she could practice with the other girls. Vanida was shown how to insert small things inside and use her muscles to control them. She and the other younger ones worked at using straws to blow out birthday candles. They got very good at it, because those who couldn't do the exercises well did not get fed.

Vanida was talented at inserting the special pen into her private parts and holding it tight while she squatted over a table and wrote. Most of the girls barely managed a scrawl, but Vanida had a knack for the writing trick. She was told she would make lots of money in tips if she got better at it.

She liked having this special talent because she was able to persuade Pim and Noi to let her practice writing with her hand, and to practice her reading as well. Otherwise, how could she compose notes that would make the men want to tip her more?

Then, Vanida got the women to let her practice words in English and French and Japanese. She moved on to phrases, her eager young mind learning all three languages with a speed that surprised her owners. Maybe she was providing herself with too much education? Vanida was smart enough to insist she wanted to be a better entertainer, and knowing more languages would make her worth more money. After all, how many of her customers were going to be Thai?

Noi finally began to give her old paperback books in all four languages. The books were always about handsome confident men who ravished beautiful women who secretly wanted them. She loved the books and by the time she was thirteen, she could read and write well in Thai, English, Japanese and French. Even Pim admitted she could see how Vanida was going to bring a high price once a buyer grasped the value of an exotic dancer who could write personal notes to clients in four languages with her pussy.

So while the other girls practiced the common, well-known Thai barroom tricks like shooting Ping-Pong balls across the room and cracking eggs inside and spitting out the contents, the mothers let her focus on her penmanship.

******

Amy's first impression of India was the airport in Delhi where the colors overtook her. Clothing, signs, and foods had a brightness to them, a passion that made Amy blink in happy surprise. A fair number of women wore the bright saris of India, and some of both genders sported Buddhist robes, many of plain cotton, but others of ornate brocades.

She looked down at her own neon-colored clothes and smiled. She'd always stood out in a world far too tastefully beige. Perhaps here, she'd find a home.

She ended up at the luggage carousel next to a tall, muscular man in a basic Buddhist robe, and she couldn't help but admire his well-toned physique and its contrast with the simple clothes he wore. He noticed her attention and smiled back as he studied her lime green, orange and fuchsia paisley top with its batwing sleeves. There was amusement in his eyes.

His shaven head and eastern Asian features made it likely he came from nearby Nepal or Bhutan. Amy was trying to think of something to ask him, a way to make conversation, when he reached past her for his bag and was gone, the paleness of his robes swallowed up by the cacophony of color around him.

I really have traveled halfway around the world. She grabbed her own two bags and made her clumsy way into the line for customs. *And I have no idea what I'm doing.*

April 2009

3. Being Quiet

Friday morning after she was dropped off, Teddie found out Shawna's family wasn't going to the lake cabin till Sunday, and she'd have to stay at their house till then. Shawna was nice enough as the two of them watched movies from an impressive collection of chick flicks. Teddie's parents allowed mainstream movies in their house, but Teddie was surprised by the R-rated material Shawna had access to.

"I get movies from my brother and his friends. He's a senior. Remember him?"

"He and his friends like chick flicks?" Teddie recalled a shy fourteen-year-old with bad acne who kept looking at her chest and had been too embarrassed to talk to her.

"No," Shawna giggled, "but his friends like to buy me things. I do know how to be appreciative." She blinked her eyes seductively. Teddie didn't reply.

Saturday morning Teddie discovered Shawna had persuaded her parents to let her have a slumber party out at the cabin that night. Shawna's dad agreed to drive Teddie and Shawna out there and drop them off. Okay.

Teddie listened to the guest list as Shawna called friends and helped them arrange for rides to the cabin, located forty-five minutes out of town. By mid-afternoon it looked like every girl in the eighth-grade class who drank, smoked weed or otherwise partied was going to be there.

So. She could do this if she had to. Smoking made her cough and alcohol tasted gross, but she could walk around with a drink in her hand and look cool.

No problem, right, dad? You did plead with me to go with these people, remember?

******

The girl almost always joined him when he entered his trance. Sometimes Jampa arrived first, and he called out to her. Other times, he felt a tug and dropped into a trance without meaning to. Those were the times he found her waiting for him. Every once in a while, they arrived together.

They never spoke. Sounds would not form in this world of their second bodies, so Jampa had no idea what the girl's name was. All he knew was they'd played together as long as he could remember. They'd chased birds and butterflies through the air and played hide and seek in the trees. These second bodies were so versatile. They could float and fly and move straight through solid matter if they chose. These bodies never got injured or tired or cold or had any other problems. Jampa and the girl always met in their second bodies, but he guessed she must have a regular one, too, like his back at the monastery.

They grew up playing together without clothes. Jampa never paid much attention, then the last time they met he'd noticed his nakedness. Embarrassed, he'd snapped back into his real body.

Now, he was afraid he wouldn't see her again. The last couple of times he entered a trance, she wasn't there and she didn't come when he asked. He was sad, thinking his nakedness had bothered her.

As he meditated on the rock like any other, he found his special body traveling into a clearing in the woods. He thought it was in the mountains because there was snow on the ground. He looked down in the twilight and saw he was dressed in a lightweight black robe. It fit him well and clung to him during his every move.

She was in the clearing, kneeling in the snow below, naked and shivering. He saw she was crying and he was confused. She'd never been cold, or anything other than happy, before.

He had a second robe in his hands. He'd never held or moved anything in this world before, so he reasoned the robe must be made of the same substance as his floating body.

He stood beside her and placed the robe around her shoulders. She accepted it, and pulled it tight. The robe fit her perfectly. She looked up and smiled in gratitude. He hugged her and he was sure then that she was not the female the monks had warned him he would crave and need to resist. Rather, he knew she was of him, somehow. Like him.

The two of them went back to playing together, exploring the snow-filled valley in the dusk and racing along the top of the nearly frozen little mountain stream that sparkled in the evening's glow. It was only later, when he returned to his first body, that he found a name for the feeling she evoked in him and knew what he must call her. She was Noom, the Bhutanese word for sister.

******

Shawna's older brother Blake had cured his acne and it looked like he'd acquired a nasty attitude to go with his clearer complexion. He was still as scrawny, but a certain belligerence made him seem larger. He also seemed to have acquired a group of older friends.

About three-dozen girls and almost as many boys from school had shown up over the last hour for the "slumber party." Most were driven out to the cabin by older siblings, some of whom stayed as well. Some beer had come with them, but the group didn't have the makings for a real party until Blake showed up in his four-door pickup truck with three other guys. The back was filled with beer and the sweet wine coolers most of the girls preferred. They were greeted with a cheer.

"We've made a generous contribution to your party," one of Blake's friends said to Shawna. "Get your girlfriends out here and lined up. Gonna take two of them to pay for tonight's generosity."

Shawna rolled her eyes. "You always want two." Then yelling out towards the crowd. "Okay ladies. Who's it gonna be tonight? Somebody's got to pay for the booze. Everybody out. Let our benefactors take a look at you."

Most of the girls came forward, primping like they understood exactly what was happening. A few hung back, a couple of girls looked confused and one looked frightened. Some gave helpless what-else-can-I-do shrugs towards their boyfriends.

Teddie was incredulous. *Surely this isn't as bad as it looks.*

The one girl who appeared frightened must have known more. She began backing towards the cabin, to where she'd be out of sight. Her ankle hit a log, and twigs snapped under her feet as she regained her balance. Blake looked at her.

"You're Nicki's cousin, aren't you? You moved to Dallas last year, but I remember you. You had breasts when you were in fourth grade. I used to fantasize about touching those titties of yours. Looks like I'm going to get to."

"No." Shawna spoke up. "She's off limits, Blake. She's here visiting. Pick someone who's part of this. You know the rules."

"No, I don't *know the rules*," Blake said, mimicking his sister's voice.

"Take three girls. But leave outsiders alone."

"No. But because I'm reasonable, we'll take one. That one." He pointed at Nicky's cousin. Shawna glared at him.

"We can have cops all over this place in minutes, while you and your little friends here without wheels try to explain what you're doing out here with all this alcohol. How does getting kicked off the cheerleading squad sound? You guys want off the football team?" He turned to the eighth-grade boys. "I didn't think so. Come on, Miss Dallas. Me and my friends are going to show you how real women have a good time."

Teddie wanted to do something, but as she opened her mouth she felt her entire body go ice cold. She was dizzy with fear and her legs felt like they weighed a million pounds. What could she do to change the horrible direction this situation was headed?

******

When Vanida saw the three men waiting for her as she came out of the camp shower, she knew what would happen. It happened to all of the girls around her age. She'd heard Pim arranged it so her girls wouldn't be inexperienced in the ways of the world. As far as Vanida knew, the other girls accepted the inevitable and pretended indifference.

Perhaps all the reading Vanida had done over the years affected her, filling her with ideas the others didn't have. She thought any man who ravished her would be handsome and secretly care for her. She didn't think his breath would stink.

Whatever the reason, she was surprised by how much she hated every second of it. She marched off when they were done, and stayed furious the rest of the day.

That night, she'd been comforted to find herself in her special flying body. She expected to escape the awful feelings the men had left her with, but when she saw the boy, she gasped. He was naked. Had he always been that way? With her gasp he looked down in surprise, then vanished. After that, Vanida refused to join him, even though she could feel the tug of him almost every day.

Pim must have been dissatisfied with the outcome of her plan, because she arranged for it to happen again. This time, it was two men who were gentler and slower. It didn't matter. Afterwards, Vanida curled up in her bed and cried and wouldn't get up for dinner.

She dozed while the other girls ate and then she was in her special body again, this time in a clearing in the woods. She thought it must be the mountains because she was kneeling in the snow and she was crying and naked. She felt cold, which she didn't understand. She'd never been uncomfortable in this body.

Then she saw the boy stood next to her, wearing a robe and holding one for her. He placed the garment around her shoulders, she put her arms through and pulled it tighter. It covered her completely. Vanida smiled at him in gratitude. He hugged her and she was sure he'd never hurt her. She hoped there were others like him.

The two of them went back to playing, exploring the snow-filled valley and racing along the top of the nearly frozen little mountain stream that sparkled in the approaching evening's glow. It was only later when she returned to her first body that she found a name for the feeling he evoked, and she knew what she must call him. He was Pêe chaai, the Thai word for brother.

After that, she was never attacked in camp again. She learned later that Noi had insisted to Pim she be left alone, so she wouldn't come to hate men and lose her value.

******

Teddie was in the woods, and she had no idea how she'd gotten there. She was watching tiny, bright blue bird's eggs in a nest high up in a tree. It was probably high in the tree to keep the birds safe. She was higher than the nest, which was odd. She wasn't usually floating up in the sky like this.

All four of the eggs were covered with tiny fissures, and Teddie watched as the point of a little beak poked through one of the cracks. Teddie cheered the baby bird on as two more of the eggs started to break apart.

She watched the little creatures labor until they managed to break the shell around them and emerge, each one shaking its damp little body as it tried to stand.

"You can do it. Yes, you can." Teddie whispered her encouragement to each bird. She felt herself grin when the last one stood. Then she looked down and saw the ground twenty feet below her and gasped. With a snap she was back at the camp.

She looked around in panic. Where was she? What had happened? She was inside the cabin, on a couch, shivering under a blanket, feeling nauseous and ice cold.

"Teddie?" Shawna was in the doorway. No one else was there. "Are you okay?"

"I don't know."

"You, like, passed out, right in front of everybody. Worse than passed out. Your body was freezing cold and nobody could revive you and it looked like you were dead or something."

"I've no idea what happened." Teddie's voice became shrill as her strength came back to her. "What the hell were you thinking bringing me here?"

"Hey, this wasn't my idea." Shawna was defensive now. "My dad insisted on doing your dad a favor. What was I supposed to do?"

"You could have warned me."

"Right. Like this is an arrangement I want to explain. I figured they'd go with a couple of their favorites and you'd either be cool with it or you'd be oblivious. You know, some of these girls enjoy getting chosen. Leave it to Blake to be a creep tonight."

"Did my passing out at least put a stop to things. You know?"

"Yeah, it put a stop to *everything*. People thought you were in a drunk coma and we were all gonna be in trouble. I told them it wasn't possible, you hadn't taken a sip out of your drink, but everyone left scared anyway. A lot of them probably won't even come back next time."

Shawna seemed more upset about the blemish on her status as a hostess than anything.

"Whatever. I'm just going to sleep here on the couch." Teddie turned away from Shawna and didn't say another word.

Sleep wouldn't come, though. She couldn't stop thinking about what really scared her, which was that Blake could just as easily have noticed her instead.

Shawna's mom showed up early the next morning to take Teddie home. She chattered away in the car about how worried she was about her sick guest, but Teddie hardly listened. She kept thinking about how the woman ought to be more worried about Shawna's frequent slumber parties at the cabin.

No way a kid is supposed to tell on another kid, but Teddie was considering it, even though it would destroy her social life for years. Would it do any good? Probably not.

With a sigh, Teddie stared out the window and said nothing. She could barely manage a thanks for the ride as she got out of the car.

That night, Teddie found out her own mom hadn't even had the glorious adventure Teddie's dad had planned. Instead, she'd gotten thrown from the canoe, trapped under it and almost drowned. The first night home her mom seemed haunted, like she was still half under water.

Teddie wanted to talk to her mom about the party, but as the days wore on, she didn't notice Teddie's attempts at conversation. She spent all her spare time planting flowers on the porch and every time Teddie came outside, Mom was drinking wine. Teddie couldn't stand the smell of alcohol now, and as time passed she grew infuriated with her mother.

She shouldn't have needed to go on an adventure. Not while she had kids at home, kids who shouldn't be packed off for the weekend with dangerous people. She should be there for Teddie now, not acting like a zombie who cringed every time she heard running water. She hadn't drowned, so what was the problem?

Sometimes Teddie's dad would go out on the porch with chips and guacamole and he'd drink a beer as he sat next to his wife. The smell of the beer and the wine together was worse than the wine alone. Other times, her dad would fall asleep on the couch waiting for her mom to come inside. Then Teddie would get madder at her mom for not being there for the people who needed her.

She was glad Zane was coming home for a visit in a week and Ariel, who'd just finished her junior year at college, would be home for the whole summer. There would be normal people around soon, and Teddie couldn't wait.

May 2011

4. Moving Forward

Teddie didn't want to go the graduation ceremony. She was finishing her sophomore year in high school, and she didn't want to have anything to do with the place. She couldn't understand why her dad didn't feel the same way. Mr. Zeitman was a physics teacher at the school and over the past year he'd led an effort to curb the increasing racism on the part of the school's administration. Teddie sided firmly with her dad, and she was proud of the part he'd played, but so much about this last school year was embarrassing beyond belief.

If a kid she was close to wasn't giving a speech and walking across the stage, Teddie would absolutely not be going. As it was, she was going to clap as loud as she could for him, then stare at the floor for the rest of the time and pretend she was somewhere else.

******

Amy's organization focused on aiding former victims of human trafficking. Obviously, preventing human trafficking was part of their mission too, but Amy was realistic about what the small office could do against a world-wide cash cow for those with no moral scruples.

She worked with safety education for local girls and parents. When she got calls asking her to help locate a missing daughter or friend, she referred the desperate callers to authorities and groups more suited to finding missing people. Every once in a while, though, she got more involved than she should have.

Twice in the past two years, she'd charged out of her office with mace and a stun gun in response to girls who'd called begging her to keep someone from driving off with them. One of those times harsh words had worked until the police arrived. The other time, she'd ended up using the stun gun on a boyfriend, and driving the beat-up girl to a local emergency room.

It had given her a reputation; she was now the crazy American who charged in to save girls. Apparently you didn't have to do it often for people to notice.

This third time was different. A desperate mother had called Amy early in the morning, sobbing for help. The woman claimed a man marched in her front door, walked upstairs, picked up her unconscious fourteen-year-old daughter and walked off with her.

It was an incredible story. Amy was skeptical, but she went to the address thinking she could calm the woman down. She was surprised to find a large, well-protected home with a lavish yard, ample fence and a fine security gate.

"My husband's out of town. We have one child and she was asleep. It's the maid's day off so I'm in the kitchen making coffee and this man drives up. I watched him punch in the security code and just drive in. Big guy with muscles. He walks into the house without knocking." The woman was outraged at this insult.

"He never says a word. Walks upstairs like he knows what he's doing and comes down with my daughter. He has to have given her something because she doesn't stir even though I scream at him to put her down. He walks by me like I don't exist. I grab at him, but he swats me away like a fly. Puts her in his back seat and drives off. What could I do?"

Amy didn't know what to say.

"That's incredible." She tried to think of something to ask.

"How did he seem? Like he was doing a job or like he knew your daughter? Was he rough or gentle with her?"

The woman thought. "I suppose he seemed angry, but not at my daughter. He handled her with care."

"My guess, then, is this is a kidnapping for money. Was he angry because it's money he thinks he's owed?" The woman made no comment.

"You've got to call the police. Once a ransom demand comes, they'll work with you. If you like, I'll stay till they come."

"Please."

"Can you tell me more about the man?"

"I can do better than that. Let me pull up the security footage for you."

"Oh." Amy had to laugh. "Well, that will go a long way to help the police identify him. Let's look."

The woman knew how to operate her security system and soon she had a view of a tall muscular man with a shaved head and features Amy had learned to recognize as Bhutanese. She had a sinking feeling she'd encountered this kidnapper before.

She'd seen him for the first time two years ago at a luggage carousel when she first arrived in India. She'd considered making conversation with him and the memory stuck because her innocent bad judgment still made her cringe.

A few months later a photo was circulated by her organization showing the same man with a young girl in a Muslim headdress. The photo was taken as the two checked into a hotel in Jakarta. This man had not only been seen there with the girl once a week for months, but he'd also been observed with under-aged girls and boys in compromising locations throughout Asia. He was presumed to either be a fervent consumer of children for sale, or to be part of the machinery that turned them into products.

"Why would that man kidnap my daughter?"

Odd as the break-in had seemed, Amy was afraid she knew the answer. It saddened but didn't surprise her to learn a ransom note never came and the girl was never heard from.

******

As Teddie's friend stood up to speak, she thought he wasn't nearly as scared as he should be. She was nervous for him and squirmed in her seat.

"I'm a time traveler," the boy began. It was a good intro, and Teddie knew it because she'd help him write the speech.

"I began my time travels in nineteen-ninety-three and I've been moving forward through time ever since." Teddie's mind wandered as he went on with the words she knew by heart. "For with time travel comes change, change every single second, whether I like it or not."

It does. It really does.

She knew she'd come a long way since that horrible party two years ago. She'd made better friends in high school and learned to direct her anger towards those who deserved her fury. She'd forgiven herself for blacking out and convinced herself it was okay to have fun with people she trusted. That night had changed her, but she'd moved on.

It was part of why she'd told her best friend Michelle she'd join her as a foreign exchange student for the first semester of their junior year. The idea of being in in a different country, far away from her home, sounded pretty terrifying, but it would only be for four months. Michelle really wanted to go, and had begged her to come along.

The speaker's voice intruded on Teddie's thoughts.

"We must keep moving. We don't know what kind of world we are moving into, but we do know we *are* going into the future. And there, together, we'll all find out what happens."

The warm applause seemed like a sign to Teddie, a sign that she needed to move forward into her own tomorrow. Fine. She'd gotten her assignment in the mail that morning, and put it aside till later so it wouldn't take away from her friend's big moment.

Tomorrow, she'd share the news with her parents that she was going to move forward all the way to Darjeeling, India. It was at the foot of the Himalayas and supposed to be a beautiful place. What could be safer than a high school that was named The Lord Peartree International Academy for Exceptional Students?

She was exceptional. She was going to live at a boarding school. She was going to go trekking with kids from around the world, some of whom would have delightful British accents, while birds sang and mountains sparkled in the background. What could possibly be the problem with that?

Leaving the Nest
to
Touch the Sky

August 2011

5. Traveling

Michelle was far more excited than Teddie about this *adventure*, as everyone kept calling it. Maybe that was why she'd slept through three out of the four bouts of wailing from the babies on either side of them during the eight hour flight.

Now, Michelle was wide awake and eager to explore the Frankfurt airport before the girls boarded the second plane on to Delhi and then a third on to some town Teddie couldn't begin to pronounce. That would be followed by a three-hour car ride.

Teddie just wanted to sleep in a bed, preferably her own soft cozy bed, but at this point any real bed would do.

Wandering around the Frankfurt airport in a daze, the girls paused to watch a photo shoot in an area full of shops. The model, a tall girl with long honey-blonde hair, couldn't have been much older than they were, and she looked as tired and irritable as Teddie felt. An older woman kept trying to coax the girl into donning various backpacks and holding hiking gear while two men passed a giant camera back and forth discussing angles and light. Teddie felt sorry for the girl and hoped she got to go home soon and get some rest. Speaking of getting to go home… Teddie felt the tightening in her chest that occurred every time she remembered it would be four freakin' months before that happened.

The flight to Delhi was full too. Teddie had been warned to expect crowds of people crammed into less space than she was used to. India, only about one-third the size of the U.S., had over three times as many people. It was going to be part of the cultural adjustment that would make this *adventure* so enriching.

As Teddie arranged her things to get comfortable for another eight hours in the air, she noticed the honey-blonde model doing the same about eight rows ahead. Interesting. Teddie hadn't expected to find a model flying coach. The oddest thing, though, was the change in the girl's face. She had a wide smile, with all trace of irritation gone.

Teddie glanced up and the down the plane. The prop lady and two photographers were nowhere to be seen. Maybe the girl was grinning because she'd escaped?

******

When Usha's teacher encouraged her to apply for the scholarship to the English boarding school last year, she'd hesitated. Her father was ill, and her mother needed help with the younger children. So the teacher had called her home, and her teary-eyed mother, Ashmita, made the decision.

"You must do it, Usha. The doctors won't say it, but I know it doesn't look well for your father. Without him, others will think I shouldn't send you to school. You are so smart, that would break my heart. Darjeeling is not nearby, but it's also not so far from Patna. You can take the bus home on weekends and help me. We'll manage. You, and your future, they are my hope."

So Usha had not only applied, she'd worked harder than she'd ever worked, to get into this international academy for exceptional students. Exceptional. To think someone from her family could be considered *exceptional*. After she'd gotten the scholarship, she was so proud some days she could hardly sit still.

Her mother had been right about her father; he only lived until the summer. Then her mother found herself facing horrible bills, depleted savings and no income. Usha knew her father had managed their money. Although he was a loving husband, he'd failed to prepare her mother for how dire her situation would be.

Usha's maternal relatives were a thousand miles away in Mumbai. More traditional Hindus frowned on a widow living alone or taking a job, and in Patna there were plenty who held traditional beliefs. So late in the summer of 2011, Ashmita moved herself and her five children into the home of her husband's wealthy older brother who lived nearby.

The man made the offer kindly enough, which was odd, because in Usha's memory her Uncle Jeet had never been a kind man. He surprised Usha and her mother by insisting he would not only care for his departed brother's family, but would assume their debts as well.

Usha worried Uncle Jeet was not acting entirely out of compassion. He and her father weren't close and Usha suspected her father's marriage was part of the problem because Uncle Jeet and Aunt Riddhi had always been cold to her mother. So she wasn't surprised when, after they moved in, the uncle wasted no time in locating her mother and the younger children in his servants' quarters, and informed Usha she would join her mother in working to pay back her father's debts.

Her mother would serve as a maid in the brother's household to cover the cost of their food. Usha was to live and work as a servant for a nearby family. She'd be given room and board and her meager salary would go to Uncle Jeet. Usha would be free to return to school once her uncle had been repaid for his generosity.

Then something incredible had happened. Usha's mother, who had never before stood up to anyone, much less to someone as overbearing as her brother-in-law, said no. Usha would do no such thing. Usha would honor her dead father by using the scholarship she'd been awarded. She'd attend the school in Darjeeling and do well there. She had the capacity to be a doctor or a teacher. At this comment, the uncle laughed aloud but her mother ignored the laugh.

"I'll work in both households. I can do it and the younger children will help me. You'll see. You'll lose nothing by letting her go, and perhaps you, too, will gain honor one day from her accomplishments."

Something about the firmness in her mother's tone convinced her uncle he was better off not arguing.

"Very well, foolish sister. We will see. Show me you can keep my house clean and my neighbor's house as well. Show me your daughter can do well in her classes when placed in an environment so far above her. If any of it fails, be warned. I will want interest on the money I've lost while waiting for you to regain your senses."

Usha's mother nodded, like she was agreeing to a plan the brother-in-law had suggested all along. That night Ashmita dug deep into a jar and gave Usha her last rupees.

"Use this to take the bus to the school, first thing tomorrow morning. You'll be a few days early, but tell them you had to come now, you couldn't wait. You don't have money for uniforms and supplies, but pretend like you thought the scholarship covered it all. They'll help you, I think, or let you work there to earn it. They're good people at this school and won't send you back here. Plead with them if they try."

Usha guessed what her mother was going to say next, and she didn't want to hear the words.

"Usha. Don't come back here. No matter what. Some day you'll be with me and your sisters and little brother and we'll be a family again, I promise. But not now. If you can't stay at the school for any reason, don't be where your uncle can find you. Do you understand me?"

Her mother gave her a serious look, the look she got whenever she talked to Usha about her body and female things. Usha understood. This uncle could consider himself justified to sink to lows worse than forcing Usha to clean houses. She nodded with as much adult understanding as she could, then gave her mother the longest hug of her life. Usha left at dawn, with a bag of clothes slung over her shoulder, almost one hundred rupees in her pocket and tears in her eyes.

Once she was on the bus, though, the sheer joy of what she was doing came to her. She'd work so hard at this school and someday she'd come back and get her family and they'd have all they needed. Then her mother could spit in Uncle Jeet's eye if she wanted to. Usha hoped her mother would.

******

Vanida liked it best when her brother Pêe chaai called to her, because then they got to play in the cold fluffy snow he seemed to take for granted. The amazing white softness came with the frozen water that made lakes and rivers glisten in the light. Her brother seemed happy in either place, enjoying the snow but intrigued by the ferns and birds of her rainforest.

It had been years now since Pêe chaai had given her the wonderful robe. It was still as soft and warm and it never stopped following her every move while she romped in the snow. Every time she met Pêe chaai she was wearing it.

But Vanida's other life was about to change. Pim and Noi had new little girls they needed to train. Noi told Vanida she and several of her sisters would be taken from the camp soon. They had been good girls and would be sold to fine gentlemen, who would take good care of them and give them nice lives. The girls would perform for audiences that would appreciate the rare talents they'd worked so hard to develop.

Vanida was excited about her upcoming grown-up life in glorious Bangkok, but she was also sad to leave Pim and especially Noi. The women had raised her, and the camp had been her home for as long as she could remember.

What would become of her relationship with Pee chaai? Vanida wished they could talk. She wanted to tell him to come see her in the city once she became a rich performer. Then they could play in the streets of Bangkok instead of the forest. She wanted him to know that no matter where she lived, she'd always come visit him in his abode of snow.

******

Teddie and Michelle's parents had hired a car to take them to the school. Teddie was ready for a nap during the three-hour drive, but she could tell Michelle wanted to talk.

"You probably wonder why I pushed you to come. Teddie. I know I should have told you what was going on."

"Are you okay, Michelle?" No matter how sleepy she was, Teddie couldn't ignore a pal in trouble.

"I'm working at it. You know my older sister leaves for college next week. Well, I decided I couldn't stay home alone with my parents this year. No offense, but you don't have a poker face. I knew if I talked to you about this before we left, they'd figure it out. Maybe they wouldn't let me go." Michelle looked at her friend for understanding.

"Your parents fight a lot?" Teddie had already gotten that impression.

"Sometimes." Michelle shrugged. "It's more like my mom tries hard not to piss my dad off, but sooner or later she does some random thing that infuriates him."

"What are we talking about? Is he jealous?"

"No, it's a pride thing. If she does or says anything implying he's less than perfect, it insults him. Like if he tells her we have plenty of milk and she checks the refrigerator just in case, he's furious.

"He beats her?" Teddie was surprised.

"Oh no. You'd have heard about that, believe me. He goes into this offended sulk, and won't speak for days. She asks for his forgiveness; he ignores her. She used to cry and beg him, but now she says she's sorry once, then ignores him too. He gets over it."

"I hope she tells him to shove it then."

"She doesn't dare or he'll punish her by getting upset with me or my sister. He knows that hurts her worse and she won't intervene."

"So he beats you guys?" Now Teddie was angry.

"Nothing that unacceptable. He'd ground us for no reason, or takes away things that matter to us. One year he threw my birthday cake on the floor and stomped on it."

"Anger control issues. What was your crime?"

"He wanted my help moving a bookcase. I was on the phone with you and asked if we could do it when I hung up but that showed insufficient respect. I knew it was coming. He hadn't spoken to mom since she reminded him to pick up my cake. He is *not* an idiot; he doesn't need reminding."

"That was your fourteenth birthday, wasn't it? I knew something was wrong that day. I asked you and you said nothing. Why didn't you tell me?"

"It was just a dumb cake," Michelle shrugged with embarrassment. "My dad was such a creep and your family was so nice. I wanted to pretend my family was nice, too.

Teddie looked out the window, trying to think of something comforting to say. They were climbing higher into the foothills, leaving the poverty of the cities behind.

"Your mom's a sweetheart."

"She is, but I lost respect for her the night she didn't stand up to him when he burned my sister's prom dress. My sister stayed home from her senior prom and cried all night."

"I thought she got sick?"

"That's what we told everybody. My mom downloaded a different kind of anti-virus software than the one my dad picked and suddenly my sister's gorgeous dress was too promiscuous and she needed to be taught a lesson. Mom said he was our dad and had the right. I decided I'd be halfway around the world come fall when my sister left. So here we are."

Michelle finished with a weak smile, then she looked up at the view outside the car. "Oh my. It is turning gorgeous out there."

"It is. This might not be so bad, Michelle. How did you get him to let you leave?"

"He got a lot of praise for my getting into this program. *It's so impressive your daughter is doing this.* Only I wasn't quite brave enough to do it alone. Teddie, please don't be mad. I'm so glad you're here."

"I'm not mad." Teddie took a long look at the vista opening up ahead. It was more spectacular than the last. "I think I'm starting to warm to this *adventure*. What do you think?"

"Me too."

August 2011

6. Arriving

Pictures hadn't prepared the girls. They knew the school was painted blue and yellow with burgundy trim, but didn't know it was surrounded by a jumble of other buildings brighter and more oddly shaped. The girls stood on the street in front of the irregular explosion of color and looked around.

Michelle reached over and gave Teddie's hand a squeeze. "I appreciate this more than you know."

"I know you do." Teddie picked up her backpack and followed the porters inside with her luggage.

"I arrived a few days early so I had to pick a bed. I hope this is okay with you?" The girl from India who was one of their other two roommates greeted Teddie, speaking slowly with a strong accent that was British and something else. She had a long dark ponytail, big solemn eyes and a serious face. Teddie noticed the girl had almost no possessions in the room, and few clothes except for her two school uniforms in the open armoire.

"Hey, all these beds look pretty much the same. No big deal." Teddie shrugged, as she eyed the four small, brightly painted wooden beds, each one crammed against a different wall. She tried to loosen the girl up with her warmest smile, but the girl didn't lose her serious expression.

"After I unpack a little, maybe you can show me around."

"Oh no. I cannot do that," the girl said.

"Oh. Okay." Teddie wasn't sure how to respond.

“I have just arrived here myself. I have never been to a school this magnificent. I am Usha, the top winner of the Central Board of Secondary Education Scholarship for the most deserving girl from a surrounding district. Who are you?”

Teddie tried not to laugh at the seriousness of the introduction. “I’m Teddie, a high school student from Texas who lets people talk her into things much too easily.”

She said it without thinking, but Usha finally gave her a smile back. “Then we are much alike, Teddie from Texas. I let people talk me into things much too easily also.”

“You’re never going to guess who our other roommate is.” Michelle had been dawdling outside and now poked her head around the door.

“We know her?”

“Her private car got her here ahead of ours,” As Michelle spoke, the honey-blonde model from the Frankfurt airport came into the room.

“What?! We thought you were some sort of supermodel,”

“No, but how my mother wishes I was.” The girl laughed and Teddie noticed she had an unusually large mouth, made all the wider by the smile dominating her face. “I’m Haley, from Denver. My parents set this school thing up for me while they drum up more sponsors for my climb next spring.”

“Climb? You’re going to climb a mountain?” Michelle asked.

“A very big one, I hope, and I'm going to do it while being photographed. A lot."

“Do you wish to do this?” Usha asked.

“Yes, in that I love to climb. It’s my whole life and I’ve been doing it forever. No, in that I hate having my picture taken.”

Hmmm. That and the overnight flight from the U.S. explained the girl’s bad humor at the airport.

“So how many other exchange students are here?” Teddie asked.

“I was put into this quad with you because all the other girls in our grade are returning from last year, and rooming with friends or previous roommates,” Usha said.

Teddie gave Michelle a wary look. “I thought this place was part of an accredited exchange program.”

“It is. It’s part of a larger program that places American students in English-speaking boarding schools the world over,” Michelle said.

“Maybe this school wants more foreign students and is just getting started?” Usha said.

“Maybe. We might be their first Americans.”

“Even more fun.” Teddie had to laugh “Not only do we get to wonder what we’re doing here; we get to watch everyone else wonder the same thing.”

******

After more than two years in India, Amy knew Darjeeling was her home. It didn’t hurt that the city boasted a thriving artistic community, the climate was wonderful and the view of the mountains astounding. The preponderance of spoken English helped, as did enough variety of ancestry in the area for her to blend in and not always appear the outsider. It helped that she’d embraced much of the region’s culture, dress, cuisine and style.

There was only one noticeable lack in her life, as her mother had pointed out on her last visit home. Amy was, after all, almost thirty.

Amy explained it was hard to have a relationship when she was married to her job, but they both knew that was only half the story. The other half was that she lived in a culture where dating opportunities for older single women were slim, and Amy was too much of a free spirit to be good marriage material for any traditional local male of any background. She couldn’t help but notice that no matter how free thinking they were on other matters, the local men she’d met were all looking for a traditional woman. That, or a one-night stand. There wasn’t much middle ground.

Maybe she’d move back home in a couple of years, she assured her mother, and get a desk job. She’d buy normal-looking clothes, and develop habits other women had. What were they? Pilates? Baking? Antique shopping? Whatever. She could make somebody a regular girlfriend. Someday. She just wasn’t ready yet.

Besides, the trade in virgins in the area was on the rise again, and local girls lured into prostitution were now being shipped to Thailand to provide variety in the brothels. Amy had caught a glimpse of a man she could have sworn was the kidnapper at the house she had gone to last May. Perhaps she could be part of apprehending this creep. Everywhere she looked there was so much to do. Normal would have to wait.

******

The first night made it clear dinners were more formal than anything Teddie was used to. The three American students were introduced to the rest of the school before the meal began, and Teddie was relieved to find these particular boys and girls friendly and curious. She had some adjusting to do regarding personal space, but while her new classmates were different, they weren't unlikable.

Some, however, were unintelligible. Teddie was fast discovering that just because someone spoke English didn't mean she could understand them. She'd been told her ear would acclimate to the accent and to give it time. Teddie hoped she wasn't flunking all her classes before this magic acclimation occurred.

The first night Teddie ate the rice and a few little pieces of chicken and left the other, harder-to-identify items for another day. Nodding and smiling, she pretended she understood what was being said around her. Judging from the blank looks she got when she talked, she guessed her classmates were having as much trouble understanding her. Would they acclimate to her speech too over time? She hoped so. The idea of being essentially mute for months was frightening.

She decided to finish unpacking while she could have a few minutes alone, but Usha was in the room already. She pretended to read while Teddie unpacked.

"Why do Americans have so many clothes?"

"I was asking myself the same thing, and also why I brought them. Especially since it looks like I'll be wearing a stupid uniform most of the time. No offense."

"None taken. I did not pick the uniforms. But don't you wear uniforms in the U.S.?"

"Some schools do. Just not the public school where I go."

"You, a rich American, do not go to a private school?" Usha seemed crushed to learn this news.

"I'm not rich, not for where I live, Usha. My dad is a teacher at a public school, so I go where he teaches."

"He could not find a job at a private school?"

He didn't want one. He says he likes teaching all kinds of kids." Then, looking for something positive to say about her school, she added "It's out in the country."

"Oh." Usha didn't say anything for a few minutes while Teddie set up a few pictures on the small dresser by her bed. Usha studied the pictures.

"I think your father must be noble to want to educate the children of all people, no matter how poor."

"I don't know if I'd go as far as noble." Teddie laughed. "But he's a good guy. I'm sure your father is too."

"My father is dead," Usha said, and she went back to reading.

The girls huddled together on Michelle's bed after lights out, sharing their stories the way teenage girls do the world over. They were unsure how strict the rules were, but guessed newcomers would be granted some slack on the first night. Teddie's pale skin glowed in the bluish light of her flashlight, and her thick head of black curls disappeared into the darkness around her as she spoke.

"Last year at my school there were some problems, and a boy who was, I don't know, who ran around with a violent and hateful group decided he liked me. A lot."

"A gang member?" Haley asked, her eyes widening.

"No, more of a self-styled skinhead. He's gone now, but this seemed like a good semester for me to be somewhere else."

"Did your family like him?" Usha asked, her brow wrinkling.

"Thankfully, no. They hated him worse than I did."

Usha nodded with relief. "So you have a real boyfriend now?"

"No. I've dated some, but, I don't know, I just seem to attract the jerks."

"I'm the other half of the reason she's here," Michelle offered, the olive tones of her face and the straight black hair Michelle had inherited from her Vietnamese ancestors blending into the shadows as she set the farthest from the light.

"I had this perfectly nice boyfriend freshmen and sophomore year and then, well, it ended kind of messy."

"He dumped you?"

"The opposite. He decided he owned me. By last spring I thought I was going to have to get a restraining order to keep him away from me." Michelle winced.

"So you came all the way to India to get away from him?" Usha sounded impressed.

"Well, him and few other things."

"I'm not trying to get away from any boy," Haley said. "Something about being a climber seems to scare them off. Hopefully that changes as I get older? Meanwhile, I've got a dad who's taught me mountaineering, and a mom who thinks I've got the looks and body for a supermodel."

"She's kind of right, Haley. You do." Haley's long-legged athletic stature was a world away from Teddie's ample curves and Michelle's petite slender body. Only Usha seemed to have an average girls' shape.

"Too bad my mom didn't get a daughter who shared her interests," Haley said, "but I'm an only child. She carted me off to kid's beauty contests, but I just pulled the bows out of my hair. She'd still be a frustrated stage mom if my Uncle Steve hadn't gotten involved."

"What's your uncle got to do with this?"

"Oh, he's always working on ways to get rich, and I'm his latest idea. He's decided my parents are both right and he can monetize me. He talked a cosmetic company into sponsoring my climb if I get accepted. Dad's got me on a list to be considered for a team ascending Kanchenjunga in May.

"Ascending Con Shen what?" Teddie asked. Usha laughed.

"Con shen JUNG ah," Usha said. "Look out the window tomorrow. Remember those beautiful mountains you couldn't stop marveling about at dinner?"

Teddie knew she had gushed on a bit about the gorgeous mountain range visible from everywhere in town.

"Kanchenjunga is the highest peak in the range," Haley said. "Over twenty-eight thousand feet. It's the third highest mountain in the world."

"Can I just call it Junga?"

"If you must. The name means 'five treasures of snow,'" Usha said. "The five peaks are sacred. Few groups are allowed to climb it, and it's harder for a foreigner to be included." She looked at Haley.

"That's why I'm here. My dad has contacts with climbers in Darjeeling and he thinks if I study at the climbing school in town then my chances of getting a spot on the expedition are good. I've already climbed thirty peaks over fourteen-thousand feet, and I'm only sixteen."

"And if you do get a spot?"

"Then I'll be the youngest person ever to climb Kanchenjunga." Haley had pride in her voice at the possibility.

"Wow." The three other young women said it in unison.

"I do not have such adventure in store for me," Usha said "but I need you to know I, too, have to work hard and I am hoping you, my roommates, will support me in this."

The girls listened as Usha told of her father's lengthy illness and her mother's plight. The three young women nodded as Usha talked of how sad she and her siblings had been, and how scary it was to move into her uncle's home. The outrage at her uncle's stinginess and the praise for her mother's courage were unanimous.

"Can your mom do this?" Michelle asked. "Can she take care of four kids and clean two houses?"

"My closest sister is eleven, and she will help clean, but probably she will not get to go to school anymore, which is sad because my father believed in education. Neither will my seven-year-old sister because she will be watching the five- and three-year-olds while the other two clean. So you see, many have given up much for me to be here."

The weight of the responsibility made for a harsh expression on Usha's face. "If my mother fails, I pay a high price. My uncle will take me from this school and put me back to work."

"Usha, that's ridiculous. No one will let him do that." Even as Teddie said it, she realized she had no idea if she was right. Maybe everybody would be perfectly happy to send Usha home to pay off her father's debts. What did she know?

"But that's not the worst possibility. I can clean houses, but my mother is afraid the money will come too slowly for my uncle's tastes. She is worried he will find ways for me to pay the bills faster."

No one wanted to say it, but when Usha would not say more, Teddie did.

"Usha, do you mean your own uncle would expect you to, like, turn tricks to pay your father's medical bills?"

"He would probably sell my virginity instead. That would bring a higher price. He has no fondness for me, so it is perhaps to his credit he did not turn to that option right away."

"You need to be careful when you go home to visit," Michelle said.

"No. My mother has asked that I do not come home. If my grades are not high enough my uncle will pull me out of school anyway."

"Is your eleven-year-old sister in danger?"

"Not yet. But my mother said she will send my sister away soon, before she is viewed as having earning potential."

The girls sat in silence for a minute.

Teddie thought one's junior year in high school was supposed to be a fun time. This conversation left her wishing she could go home, crawl into bed and pull the covers up over her head. Once you turned sixteen, were you too big to do that?

As each girl settled into her cot, Teddie felt the oddest tingling sensation pass through her body. She'd had that sensation twice before, once when she was a small child and made a mysterious trip down the hall to check on her brother, and once before when she passed out at a party she should never have been at.

Surely her body wasn't going to add to the weirdness of this situation by doing *that* again. Teddie couldn't imagine anything she needed less. She was glad when the sensation passed and she fell asleep.

September 2011

7. Wandering

At night, Teddie took refuge from the strangeness. The collage of colors, faces, and smells that permeated her world by day subsided into the comforting greys of darkness. She lay in her bed and thought of how much she missed boots. Western boots, and pickup trucks. Country music and dead armadillos in the road. Now wasn't that stupid? Pine trees and Tex-Mex food and churches everywhere even though her family didn't belong to one. It was her world, and she missed its familiarity.

In fairness, this place wasn't all bad. She could understand people better each day. The classes were challenging, but she was a good student, and doing well in class earned respect here, not disdain. Teddie knew she was surrounded by sixteen-year-olds from India, Nepal and Bhutan, who came from wealthier and better-educated families. They kept mostly to themselves, but no clique was rude to her. It made Teddie sad that a girl from India would not have fared as well at her own high school outside of Houston.

Haley spent most of her free time at the mountaineering school, and Usha clung to Michelle and Teddie more than they would have liked. She was having the most difficult adjustment, at a loss to understand many of the things her American roommates talked about, and yet separated from others at the school by a chasm born of upbringing and money. Teddie could only imagine how lonely it would be to have no home to go to, so she tried to show patience as Usha's serious dark eyes followed her and Michelle's every move.

One of the biggest adjustments was not having a cell phone. Teddie was surprised to discover texting was a big part of her life. However, the school was adamant; no students were allowed to have cell phones. At least she had her laptop, and today she had gotten to video chat with her parents before class. The sight of the two of them sitting on the geranium-filled porch in the Texas evening had left her yearning for surroundings she was used to.

That night, she starting sleepwalking.

She didn't remember getting out of bed, or walking down the hall or going out the door of the school. Didn't they keep it locked at night? She thought they must. Maybe she had climbed out the window? Could she do that in her sleep?

Yet there she was, walking down the street in front of the school in the middle of the night. Lights were mostly off and half a moon was high in the sky. A group of older boys stood huddled together a couple of blocks away, smoking cigarettes. If they noticed Teddie they ignored her.

She looked around. The mountains in the distance glistened with snow and she took the time to enjoy the view without people jostling into her. The boys down the street all wore jackets, and Teddie wondered if she'd thought to grab a coat. She glanced towards her arm, and the next thing she knew she was back in her bed, with no memory of how she got there.

Well, sleep-walking was supposed to be an odd phenomenon. It had probably been set off by homesickness, to be honest. Good thing her subconscious found ways to navigate her in and out of the school. This time. Hopefully it wasn't going to become a habit.

One thing Teddie liked about Lord Peartree Academy was the emphasis on enriching their students. The schedule of guest lecturers included artists, musicians, a politician, a doctor and even a Bollywood movie star. Tonight's speaker, however, was only for the girls at the academy, and Teddie wasn't terribly enthused.

Well-known local activist Amy Levitt was going to speak about the realities of human trafficking. The school was concerned organized crime was getting more involved and the demand for virgins over twelve had risen dramatically. They would learn how to be observant for girls in need of help, about resources they could direct victims to, and of course how to avoid scams and claims that could result in their own victimization.

Teddie considered faking a stomach ailment and having a precious night alone in the room before she noticed how quiet Usha had become once the evening program was announced.

This is part of her world. She lives in fear of this. Perhaps a caring roommate ought to learn something about local resources?

When Ms. Levitt entered the auditorium, Haley could hardly conceal a smirk. The woman was petite and a bit on the wrong side of chubby by American standards, and she accentuated both issues by wearing the most outrageously gaudy paisley print Teddie had ever seen. Her clothes overflowed with layers of chiffon, and although her hair was a soft brown, she sported wild unruly curls.

"Unique style," Michelle said.

Apparently Amy Levitt was a local figure, and the rest of the school wasn't surprised by her appearance, or by her shocking opening.

"In Bombay, girls as young as nine are sold at auctions to men who believe sleeping with a virgin cures STDs. This, girls, is the world we live in."

She spoke of the problems in India, from females driven to prostitution by poverty, to the smaller numbers sold by their own families, to the rarer, yet still significant, problem of kidnapping. She cautioned against job offers too good to be true, helpful strangers offering rides and good-looking boys offering party invitations.

By the time Ms. Levitt finished talking, Teddie had forgotten about the lady's outlandish appearance and was focused on her words, words that left Teddie slightly nauseous.

******

Lhatu came to India often, and he had become adept at absorbing the noise and chaos without allowing it to warp his inner peace. He tried instead to gain energy from the surroundings, energy to do the bidding of those he served.

His large size made travel harder on him, but he recognized it also made him an unusually capable operative on behalf of his group's needs. At thirty-one years old, he was tall and physically strong by the standards of any race. He could see over the crowds to find others, and thanks to clearly visible muscles he was seldom a target of the pickpockets or scammers who preyed on those who traveled. The simple robes he sometimes wore brought him respect from those of any faith.

Today he arrived in Bagdogra, and had been told to take the train to Darjeeling. He liked Darjeeling; it had a certain spirit about it. There was a girl attending a school there, a young woman whom he'd been asked to observe. Do not make contact. Just bring back information.

Very well. Lhatu was used to odd assignments. He did not question the wisdom of those who directed his life.

******

For decades the mountaineering school had offered classes for women, and, in this modern age, it also offered mixed classes. However, most of the courses were still for men only.

The mountaineering school had been adamant that, in spite of Haley's extensive climbing background, she must take their two basic courses before she could get into the advanced class that would increase her chances of being allowed on the Kanchenjunga climb. This wouldn't have been a problem, except the only basic classes open to women were offered too late in the year for the advanced class. So the school agreed to let Haley into the all-male introductory trekking class in early September, but only if every registered male had no objection.

Of the twenty-three signed up for the course, five expressed reservations, but they agreed to meet Haley before blackballing her. The meeting was tonight. Haley was trying on clothes in her room.

"Just wear what makes you comfortable," Teddie said.

"No." Michelle shook her head. "If she really wants to get into this class, she needs to show up looking good. These are young guys; they're not going to turn away an attractive female they think they can hit on."

"It's not right for her to do that," Teddie said.

"Come on. She's already at a disadvantage having to plead to get in, in the first place. She's a way better climber than anyone in this class is gonna be. She should use any advantage she can get." Michelle was as adamant.

"It might work against her," Usha said. "Attractive women make some men nervous, and it doesn't help that she's foreign and underage. I think she should look as ugly as she can, so they think of her as another male."

"I don't think she should try to look anything," Teddie said. "She needs to ignore the fact that she's female."

"How the hell does she do that?" Michelle answered with a gesture at Haley's long shapely legs.

"This is just stupid," Haley spoke up as she pushed the entire pile of rejected outfits onto the floor. "I want to climb mountains, not play inane mind games. Did you know slime mold has over five-hundred different genders? Right now, it would be easier to be slime mold."

"You wish to be mold?" Usha was incredulous.

"She's joking, Usha."

"Jeans and a flannel shirt. No cleavage, no makeup." Haley had made up her mind.

"Good hair and tight jeans?" Michelle suggested.

"Good hair and my normal jeans which aren't exactly unflattering."

"And your best smile," Teddie added. "When they see how bad you want this, who is going to deny you?"

Three of the men were.

Haley had tears in her eyes the next morning as she explained the verdict to her friends at breakfast. Three boys reported afterwards that while Haley seemed a delightful young woman and they wished her the best, they preferred the camaraderie of an all-male group.

"I don't think I could have said anything that would have convinced these guys. Without this stupid class, I don't think there is any way I can climb Kanchenjunga now."

"Can you spread this out over another year?" Usha was trying to ask in a reasonable tone when one of the women from the kitchen came running to get Haley and bring her to the office for a phone call.

"The climbing school has called you back," the woman explained, and a hopeful Haley left the rest of her breakfast to run and take the call. She was back in minutes, beaming.

Someone at the climbing school agreed this was nonsense. Upon reflection, they'd declared her class as co-ed and moved the three objecting men to another all male session. Haley would spend the following week in the mountains, with the remaining twenty men. Her wide lips were in a grin that shown through her hazel eyes and filled the rest of her face as well.

******

Over the next few days Usha became as withdrawn as Haley was effervescent. At first Teddie thought it was homesickness, but by the middle of the week she was certain something had changed. Usha avoided conversation, and Teddie became concerned the American girls had excluded their roommate once too often. When Teddie stopped back at her room to drop off books and found Usha crying, Teddie was certain of it and tried to apologize.

Usha actually laughed through her tears. "You think it matters to me that I do not always understand your jokes? You don't understand mine either."

True. Was there a boy maybe? A teacher hassling Usha? Other girls picking on her?

"It's my mother. She is sick."

"Oh dear. I'm so sorry Usha. Heart problems? Cancer?"

"No, a bad cold."

"You're crying because she has a cold?" Teddie was baffled. Then she got it. "She's too sick to clean for your uncle?"

Usha nodded. "She has a fever and has not gotten out of bed for three days. My sister Diya called. She is trying to do everything my mom did, but she has her own chores already, and now the next sister is sick too and so she cannot watch the little ones."

"Wait. Your seven-year-old sister is too sick to watch the three- and five-year-old?"

"Yes and Diya has a sore throat and is afraid if she gets sick then my uncle will send for me to come take over. Teddie, I am not as lucky as you. Too many people are having to give up too much for me to be here. I cannot stay."

"Usha, don't be ridiculous. Your mother doesn't want you to come home and clean houses. You know she doesn't. Your father didn't want that for you either. Look, how much does it cost to hire a maid for a week? I'm serious. I'll help you hire someone to replace your mom till she gets better. How much can it be?"

"This is not a good idea, Teddie. You are not rich enough to buy every friend you make here a way out of their problems. You are better off not starting." Teddie knew it was true. She'd been cautioned by the student exchange group that the differences in relative wealth would make it tempting to try to do exactly that. In the groups' experience, the end result of such help by well-meaning Americans was often more requests for money than any student could meet, and then hurt feelings all around. Don't start, she'd been told.

But there were times to ignore even good advice and Teddie was sure this was one. She figured she could do without snacks and spending money while she was in India. Mostly. She didn't want to involve her folks because she knew they'd disapprove, but maybe she could write Ariel and get a little cash from her sister.

"I have an allowance for the semester. I won't take no for an answer, and we're both going to pretend like I did no such thing, because I do understand you are right. Okay?"

Usha's hug was answer enough.

******

Jampa worked to clear his mind, to fill it with the lack of attachment those who seek enlightenment must strive to attain. He knew from experience that before he could empty his thoughts, sometimes he had to let a few of them run their course.

The girl. She was his only point of contact with his earliest years, and something in him longed for his missing childhood memories. He wished to have known a mother or a father. That was understandable for a child. He embraced the knowledge of this wish and forgave himself for the desire. He recognized it was why he had chosen to make this childhood playmate into a sister.

Jampa did *not* understand how he occasionally left his earth body immobile and found himself in his second, lighter body with the girl, but this had occurred for as long as he could remember. When something has always happened, you don't question it. It had taken years for Jampa to deduce that others at the monastery had no such playmates and no such experiences.

Jampa had no trouble believing in multiple realities. In fact, layers of existence were part of the foundation of his religious beliefs. So while his partnership with this girl was unusual, it was. It simply was. He had no problem with that. It was his duty to accept his situation, and to experience compassion for this girl and for others with whom this second body might put him in contact.

So he would. Jampa focused on his breathing and let lack of thought take over.

******

The next time Teddie went sleepwalking, it occurred to her she wasn't walking. She was floating and she was pretty sure she was headed towards the train station. It was the middle of the night and this was no time to catch a train. What was she doing going there?

This felt a lot like the time when she had gone to check on her brother Zane, when she was only four years old.

She was moving faster now, almost like she was in a car, and certainly like she knew where she was headed. How did she know where she was going?

She thought maybe she should go back to bed when it occurred to her that if she got to the station, she could take a train to the airport. If she could get to the airport, she could get on an airplane and fly to a place where eleven-year-old children didn't have to be scared when their mother got a cold, and girls didn't have to plead to get admitted to classes for men only, and high school juniors from Texas didn't have to cough up their entire allowance to keep roommates from getting taken out of school by evil uncles.

Was the uncle really evil? He must be.

Then she felt the uncle grab her arm and she jumped. But it was Usha grabbing her arm. She was in bed.

"You were making noises in your sleep. You were having a bad dream?"

"I didn't think I was dreaming at all." Teddie turned over, and then she felt confused. So she wasn't going places in her sleep? She was having dreams about going? Why?

******

Uncle Jeet began to make a few discrete inquiries. Clearly something had to be done. The medical bills, which had been a fortune to Ashmita, were still substantial to him, and his wife Riddhi's spending went up every month in spite of how he beseeched her to rein it in. The most frightening aspect of all was the four daughters themselves. How had his brother Chakor allowed this to happen?

Both brothers were raised in the traditional manner. Granted, Chakor had turned to modern ways, starting with his unwise choice of that woman for his wife. But even a modern father must feel some obligation to provide a small dowry for his daughter, and to provide a wedding worthy of the family's name. Not even a wealthy man could afford four daughters!

Jeet had been generous over the years. He'd given Chakor money to help with the last pregnancy, once they learned it was to be a boy. Even now, he'd tried to mitigate the situation by securing the oldest daughter a position cleaning homes. Only Ashmita had been too foolish to embrace the opportunity, insisting instead on educating the girl.

Knowing Chakor and Ashmita, Jeet was pretty certain he had a sixteen-year-old virgin on his hands. He needed to know what that was worth. A man at work knew someone who knew someone who put Jeet in touch with an oily-looking little man named Nandi. When they met for tea, the small man had quick nervous gestures and wore an expensive suit. He swallowed the hot liquid in two gulps.

"Is she attractive?" Nandi asked him. Jeet supposed so. She wasn't ugly.

"Could you provide a photograph?" Of course he could. Ashmita must have pictures of Usha somewhere. "Several would be better." Okay, several.

"How would you describe her?" Jeet rolled his eyes in frustration. What was there to describe? She had her nose in a book all the time. Why all these questions? Surely her personality did not matter.

But Jeet was wrong. Nandi, who had been kind enough to gather information so he would have the facts, pointed out that while an auction to the highest bidder could bring in a lot of cash, often there were discrete markets for this kind of thing. Men with specific tastes. The value of the girl could go up considerably if she was of interest to one of Nandi's high-level clients.

Jeet was not aware of this. He supposed he was uninformed in the ways of this slice of the world. Okay then. This girl was serious, studious and kind of naive. Did anyone like *that* kind of girl? He saw Nandi nod and smile. Very well. He would bring photos tomorrow.

September 2011

8. Fleeing

Most of humanity over time has thought of the earth as a mother who provides for the vast array of life she is proud to have nurtured. “Look at me,” she says to the other planets within earshot. “Look what I’ve grown on my surface now. Aren’t they magnificent?”

“This last group is a little aggressive, dear,” Venus replies.

“Maybe you need to get a spray to keep them under control,” Mars adds.

“Oh no, I’m sure they’re harmless.” Earth laughs. “I love the way they build stuff. Aren’t these teeny things they call trains adorable? Look at them go.”

Earth moves slowly, for she is a large, gentle creature. Every once in a while though, she gets an itch and has to shake. It happens; she means no harm.

The 6.8 earthquake hit the hills of Sikkim at six p.m. on Sunday, September 18. Teddie and Michelle had just gotten off the Darjeeling Himalayan Train, after an optional school trip for students to enjoy the picturesque ride.

The girls were leaving the station, still gasping about how beautiful the scenery had been, when the ground under them began to shake. As the tremor changed into a discernable roll, people screamed and children ran to their parents. The ground rose and fell like waves on the sea. Several buildings cracked, and a few crumbled like they were made out of cookies.

Teddie grabbed Michelle's arm and looked around in panic for the teachers and the other students. Her eye caught an unusually tall, well-built man in a monk's robe. He was noteworthy not only because of his size, but also because he was standing still in the middle of the chaos, undisturbed by the earthquake. He was staring at her and Michelle.

******

The uncle was offended by the offer to hire a maid for a week. Did Ashmita think he wanted an unknown woman in his house cleaning? She needed to remember her place. If he wanted someone to fill in for her, he'd handle it.

Ashmita was feeling better when she made her offer, so she hoped her strength would return fast enough to make the disagreement about hiring a maid moot. Ashmita guessed what really bothered Jeet was that Ashmita had other resources. He told her any pittance she could raise would not affect her family's obligations to please him. Then he'd left to meet some man for tea.

By the next day the uncle began talking about what a mistake it had been to allow Usha to go to school. Surely her mother could see the girl was needed here. His voice became softer. Perhaps in a year or two she could return to her studies, if all went well. He and Ashmita could work together to make that happen, if Ashmita would bring the girl home now.

By the way, he'd noted Usha was shy, more interested in her books than boys. Her father had elected not to look into an arranged marriage, but Jeet thought the possibility should be considered. Not to be indelicate, but was her mother sure the girl was a virgin?

This last question disturbed Ashmita. She often looked at Usha's pictures in a small album she kept, and this morning, several pictures of Usha were missing. Ashmita felt a chill inside as the pieces came together. She made a grim decision.

Later that Sunday afternoon when Jeet and Riddhi were being entertained elsewhere, she called the school and insisted on talking to Usha in person. She told her daughter to get out of Darjeeling as soon as possible, and offered as many helpful options as she was able.

Then after the phone call, she thought about her daughter living at the mercy of acquaintances and strangers. Perhaps she'd over-reacted. Maybe Usha would be safer staying at the school.

Ashmita picked up the phone, thinking she would tell Usha to wait a day. But the earthquake had struck moments before, and there was no way to reach Darjeeling by landline or cell phone or any other means.

******

The school received minimum damage, but electricity was out when the students made their way back from the train ride. There was no phone service or internet. Teddie hoped her parents weren't listening to the news and she'd be able to contact them before they heard about the earthquake. Word was it was bad in parts of town and several people had died, crushed by the rubble. Many were worried about aftershocks, so the school gave reluctant permission for anyone to sleep outside if they wished.

Usha was scared and insisted she would sleep outdoors away from the buildings. Teddie supposed the girl had experienced earthquakes before. Haley had left Saturday morning for her week of training with the mountaineering school, and Michelle was too nervous about bugs to sleep outside. Teddie wasn't crazy about it either, but between Usha's pleading eyes and Michelle's assurances she'd be fine indoors, Teddie agreed to a night on the lawn with Usha. The two girls found a spot near the edge of the yard designated as the girls' side, and Usha curled up and fell asleep.

Teddie, of course, tossed and turned with only blankets between her and the hard cold ground. She was worried about aftershocks, bugs, and everything else her imagination could dredge up. It was an impressive list. She accepted she'd get no sleep at all when she was surprised to be dreaming.

At least she assumed she was dreaming, because she felt like she was sleepwalking again, and even in the dream she remembered the sleepwalking wasn't real.

So why was she going to the bus station? She was positive that was where she was going. Was she trying to go home again? She really had to stop this. No wait. She was following somebody,

somebody with a long dark ponytail running down her back. The girl was walking fast, not gliding through the air like Teddie, and her hunched shoulders made it clear she was cold and scared.

It was Usha. What was Usha doing going to the bus station? There was no bus until dawn, but Teddie saw a faint bit of light in the east and realized dawn was close. Would the bus even be running after the earthquake?

Others hoped so, for the station was already busy with those needing to leave town for one reason or another after the disaster. Teddie watched the restless people, and realized she didn't hear a sound coming out of their mouths. Had all these dreams been silent? It seemed like they had.

Teddie made it around to Usha's side and saw the relief on her face as she surveyed the crowd. Numbers meant safety. Usha was fingering a wad of money in her hand; it looked like the collection of bills Teddie had given her. Was Usha taking it to her uncle? That sounded like a bad idea. If not, where was she going?

Teddie watched Usha make her way to the front of the line and use most of her money to buy a ticket. As Usha grasped her ticket and moved into the waiting area, Teddie decided to confront her friend.

"Usha, what's going on?" Although Teddie formed the words and felt her vocal chords move, no sounds came out of her mouth. Weird. Worse yet, Usha didn't glance her direction.

"Hello." Teddie waved her hand up and down. Usha turned her head but pretended like Teddie wasn't there. Well, this was rude. Teddie tried jumping up and down, but the world stayed silent and Usha continued to stare through her. So did everybody else in the bus station.

Teddie realized her friend not only didn't hear her, but she also didn't see her. In fact, all the people at the bus station were unaware of her.

I'm dreaming about being invisible. It's bad enough I can't stop dreaming about sleepwalking, but now I'm dreaming about being a sleepwalking ghost.

She started to turn away from Usha, when she noticed one person was having no trouble seeing her. The large muscular man was here too. He was dressed in normal street clothes, standing in the middle of the bus station staring at her. As she noticed his gaze, he nodded to her and gave her a slight smile back. Teddie was at a loss to explain why, but nothing in her entire life had ever scared her as much.

Teddie knew something was wrong as soon as she woke up. She was chilled and lying on hard ground, the many blankets above and below inadequate for the task of keeping her comfortable. Others were already up and talking, made boisterous by the novelty of a night of camping outdoors on school grounds.

There was an element of giddy relief in their laughter, and Teddie remembered. The earthquake. Of course. Usha's fear of being crushed during an aftershock while sleeping. Teddie turned to her friend but saw Usha was already up and gone.

Probably headed off to breakfast. Being cold sure gives you an appetite.

She gathered up the quilts and headed into the school. Teachers were starting to herd the rest of the students inside, and in the rush of people and noise Teddie took the bedding back to the room and went to the dining hall.

She was sitting alone eating a piece of the pan-fried bread when Michelle joined her.

"Where's Usha?"

Teddie shrugged. "I figured she'd be here in the dining hall. She's probably in the bathroom."

"She never came back to the room."

"Odd." Then Teddie remembered the dream about the bus station.

"What's wrong?"

"Nothing. I had a weird dream about Usha and you just reminded me of it, that's all"

"Well, if she isn't in class, we better tell somebody,"

******

Usha felt terrible about using the money her new friend had offered up for the maid, and she hoped if she paid it back someday it would keep Teddie from hating her. At first she was only going to take what she needed for bus fare, then she realized that was foolish. She'd need to eat, and her friend would be no more angry if it all was missing.

The bus ride to Gangtok wasn't long, and she was going north, away from her uncle. Her mother had given her the name of a woman who lived in Gangtok and with whom her mother had once been friends. Surely this kind lady would take Usha in and help her.

******

The mountaineering school went out of its way to send a female instructor along on the trek. Haley felt bad about the special accommodation, but it was nice not being the only girl among so many males. Not that ability was an issue. The basic outdoor skills this class covered were things Haley's dad had taught her before she was eight.

Many of her classmates were young Indian men in their late teens and early twenties. They were boisterous, and many of them stared at Haley a lot. She avoided eye contact and kept her shirts buttoned all the way up to her collar. She didn't want to socialize; she had brought plenty of schoolwork with her.

Once word of the earthquake made its way to the group of trekkers, the mood calmed down as others became worried about family and friends. Haley was relieved to learn her school had survived with little damage.

The instructors were kind. Once it was clear she was appropriately humble, but had little to learn from the class other than specifics of the culture and the mountain range, they left her alone. As the week wore on she retreated further into her books. By the time she returned to school she was caught up in all of her classes.

******

A search for Usha began midday, but it was hindered by the many missing students and teachers, as families in town struggled to recover from the earthquake. One more missing girl was a problem, but as bodies were pulled from the rubble around the city, the urgency of Usha's situation lessened.

The school concluded the seismically active hills had spooked the girl from Patna, who'd probably stolen bus fare from her friends and headed home. Only Michelle and Teddie knew how unlikely *that* was, and they could think of no effective way to search for their friend.

However, when Haley made it back to campus a few days later, she had an idea.

******

The home office had reprimanded Amy for becoming too involved in matters of individual missing girls. She was there to provide support for former victims, and to address global problems of safety. There was a fine line to walk with runaways who chose prostitution and with families who were complicit in the sale of their own female relatives. Amy promised every time to be more sensitive to local cultural and economic issues. Every time she held her fingers crossed behind her back in the childish gesture that meant she didn't mean it.

So when the three American girls came to her office begging for help in finding their friend, Amy knew this had all the markings of a case that would get her in trouble with the agency. The involvement of three American students only made it more probable this would reach the press and the ears of Amy's superiors back home. A savvy woman would give these girls the brush off.

"What did you say her name was?" Amy asked.

"Usha." It was the tall confident girl with the long blond hair girl who spoke first. "She's really smart and so happy to be in school, and she has these beautiful big trusting eyes and you've got to help us find her."

The girl with the East-Asian ancestry jumped in. "The school's been busy with the aftermath of the earthquake all week. Last night they got a hold of her mother who says she has no idea where her daughter's gone and so the school now says she's a runaway who couldn't handle the advanced classes and they're washing their hands of it!"

The pretty one with the head full of black curls picked up the narrative. “We know better. There’s no way that’s true. Usha was doing great in her classes. She has to be in real trouble.”

“Okay,” Amy said. “Start at the beginning and tell me everything you know. No holding back.”

The three girls starting talking all at once. Amy smiled at their vehemence, their innocence and their concern for their friend. There was an uncle from another city, and huge debts to be paid. The girl wasn’t even from Darjeeling so there was no one local to help her. Amy looked at the photo one of the girls had on her laptop. She sat for a minute in silence as she studied Usha’s face.

A young hopeful human being, full of potential. Just as all young people were. Was that reason enough to get involved? Of course it was.

September 2011

9. Accepting

Amy started her day out by cursing the earthquake for making it impossible to trace how a young girl had left town. For days after, roads were damaged, transportation was erratic and communication out of Darjeeling was almost nil. Amy suspected Usha had hoped to get away unnoticed and grabbed the opportunity. The chance to sleep outside and leave the school unsupervised under cover of darkness had been a gift.

Earthquakes were part of living near the Himalayas, caused by the subcontinent of India shoving its way under the rest of Asia. India would run out of steam in a few million years and the Himalayan Mountain Range would extend another thousand miles north. Would any descendants of humanity be around to see what the finished product looked like? Amy wasn't betting on it.

Here she was, trying to track an intelligent young person who had much to offer the human race, but her own kin had decided they'd rather devastate her to make a few bucks. Amy knew too well that a host of other humans would be happy to participate in the girl's destruction and would feel no remorse about doing so.

Ashmita, the girl's mother, continued to insist she had no idea why her daughter had left or where she'd gone. Amy was pretty sure that wasn't true, but Ashmita seemed too scared to trust anyone and was sticking to her story.

While Amy could only plead for information, the uncle had Usha's siblings to threaten. Amy was sure the uncle would use them to find a way to learn whatever Ashmita knew. So, what was the best thing she could do? It seemed to be to make sure Ashmita would contact her after the uncle knew Usha's location.

******

Having to flee from the school she loved seemed like a bad dream to Usha, starting with the nightmarish dash through dark streets, looking over her shoulder, hoping no one was following her. She had no idea how she would have escaped without the earthquake, but there was no sense worrying about that. Her mother had been clear. Your uncle will come for you if I refuse to call you home. Leave now.

It was lucky her mother knew someone in a direction no one would guessed she'd go. The bus going north was filled with those from Sikkim anxious to get home to check on loved ones, and there was much worry that mudslides and damage from the quake would prevent them from making it to the city of Gangtok. Usha didn't care. She felt safe on the bus. If it took days to reach her destination, all the better. Difficult road conditions only meant she'd be harder to follow.

Her mother's acquaintance turned out to be an elderly woman named Bela, who'd once been a close friend of Usha's great aunt. Decades ago, this woman had married a man from Ashmita's home city of Mumbai, then lived in Mumbai for years. Bela had moved back to Sikkim once she was widowed.

The old woman who greeted Usha seemed perplexed by the request to house her, and confused by much of what Usha said. She asked what her plans were for traveling onward. Oh dear. Usha took a chance.

"My great aunt thought perhaps I could be of use to you. I could do your shopping and a bit of cleaning and cooking for you and, of course, go to the local school during the day. She sent me to help you. Did she not explain?"

The woman looked thoughtful for a minute. "I don't remember every conversation as well as I used to, dear. Did I tell her it would be okay?"

Usha felt so bad lying to Bela, but her other choices were so much worse. "You said it was a fine idea. I'm sorry, would you rather I left after all?"

"No, no of course not. Let's get you in school, and let's go over your duties. I'm sorry, dear, but you'll have to remind me of things from time to time."

Usha smiled with gratitude. "That's no problem. I'm happy to." She promised herself she'd help Bela more than enough to make up for her deception.

******

Haley tried to enjoy the two weeks back at school even though they were filled with worry for her missing roommate. Usha, who had sometimes been annoying, felt like a true best friend now that she was gone. Haley recognized the irony; it was how friendship worked sometimes.

Haley tried to get ahead in her classes, knowing her next stint in the mountains, with yet another group of two dozen men, would involve more strenuous physical climbing and a more challenging social situation. She was actually relieved when she got word her Uncle Steve would join her for part of the class in late October.

He wouldn't be doing any climbing, of course, but had gotten permission to come along to photograph her. Normally that prospect would have Haley cringing in dread, but nothing had been normal lately. It would be worth posing for the man's endless vignettes just to have a familiar face around.

******

Teddie admitted she could be over-emotional at times, but she always calmed down eventually and dealt with reality. That, of course, presupposed she knew what reality was.

As the dry, cool month of October got underway, she had no more episodes of sleepwalking, or of dreaming about sleepwalking, but she couldn't get the mental picture of Usha at the bus station out of her head. If it was a dream, it was so unlike a normal one.

Let's face it, my dreams are about me. It's my subconscious after all.

Yet this dream had been about Usha, from the girl's nervous escape down the dark streets of Darjeeling to her frantic purchase of a bus ticket to Gangtok. Wait. Teddie froze mid step. She'd forgotten that detail. No question, she'd seen Usha buy a ticket to Gangtok, a city to the north, in Sikkim. Usha was from the south, so she hadn't been going home.

Should she tell somebody? Why? It wasn't real. If she'd been really sleepwalking, then everyone in the bus station would have seen her. Usha would have talked to her. So she hadn't been there, and had no idea of where the real Usha had gone. Best keep these dreams to herself. They were of no use, and with any luck she was done with them.

Then that night she had another one. She was in a place filled with snow, and she had no idea how she'd gotten there. She remembered the word Himalaya means "abode of snow," and she thought she was somewhere in the Himalayas. Interesting. She felt warm and welcome, as though she was answering an invitation, or even responding to a physical tug. Had her presence been requested? By whom, and why?

She looked around and saw a boy and girl about her own age not too far away, playing like younger children would. She approached them. They both wore soft black robes made out of some sort of fuzzy material. Teddie loved fuzzy clothes. She reached out to touch them and saw the boy and girl both had a luminescence to them that made Teddie wonder if they were human.

They smiled at her and waved. It felt a little like when the big monk had acknowledged her in the bus station. Like she was a ghost and they were ghosts too, except this felt less creepy.

The boy moved a few feet back, gave her a grin, and then leapt into the air and executed a perfect double forward somersault. *A gymnast.*

The girl, not to be outdone, waited until her partner landed. She took a step back, only to leap higher than the boy and perform a double backwards somersault before landing on her feet. They both bowed and gestured to Teddie.

She shrugged. They wanted her to do gymnastics? She noticed she was wearing a robe similar to theirs, just as soft, but of the light, mint-green color of the blanket she had on her bed as a child. Nice. It covered her perfectly as it moved with her.

She'd always been good at cartwheels. She leaned right, thinking she'd join in by doing two of the best cartwheels she could manage, only to find the slight effort sent her careening over and over into seven or eight perfect turns before she could stop.

She stood amazed while they grinned at her and clapped silently. That was fun.

Then Teddie was back in her bed, wide-awake and sure she hadn't been dreaming. Or sleepwalking. Which posed the question: what was it she was doing? And why did it feel like she'd been invited so she could discover how much fun it could be to do this?

******

Haley was doing push-ups, grunting as she worked her way into the higher numbers.

"You really go after that stuff, don't you?" Teddie said, thinking she might go wash her hair until Haley was done making noises.

"I have to," Haley panted, then came to some acceptable number and stopped. "Seriously," she said between heavy breaths. "When you climb, how good a shape you're in can make the difference between surviving and not." She started in on sit-ups, but seeing her two roommates staring at her, she stopped.

"I'm sorry. If this is too intense for you guys, I can do my workouts when you're not in the room. I get this is kind of weird."

Teddie felt bad for staring. "Don't worry about it, Haley. Do what you need to."

"It's no problem in my book," Michelle added. "If being in better shape can save your life, work out twice as much."

******

Pim took the older girls aside to give them instructions. "You leave here in a few weeks. Our agent will find you good homes. Remember, you must do what your new owners say. Always. Life stays good if you don't be a problem."

Pim looked happy, like she was proud of the girls.

Vanida was confused. She thought nobody was going to own her once she moved on to her fine adult life in Bangkok. She was going to get to do what she wanted.

"Aren't we going to be free women?" she asked Pim. The other girls looked at her with surprise, and Pim gave her a narrow glare.

"I don't know where you got that idea. Did Noi talk nonsense to you when you were little? Girls like you aren't free. We get you good owners. Ones who feed you, and who won't hurt you if you behave, and who buy you nice things if you do a good job. You be grateful for that."

Pim turned her gaze to all five of the girls who would be leaving next month. "We have a good reputation. We count on you girls to make us proud."

******

No female instructor was available for Haley's second one-week course. Haley again had the requisite proficiencies and more, but culture and gender left her on the far side of a divide with these new classmates. She did her best to be no trouble. Damn the school for making her do this before she could get into the advanced course, which started in two more weeks.

She'd hoped having her uncle arrive on the second day would improve her situation, but it was soon obvious Uncle Steve in India was different than Uncle Steve in the Unites States. While Haley's dad had acquired some cultural sensitivity by climbing with others, Uncle Steve only got louder and more obnoxious when he felt uncomfortable. Not having much to brag about on his own, he turned to bragging about Haley instead.

To one uninterested group he waxed eloquent on how Haley had been a child prodigy on the peaks of Colorado. To another he boasted about Haley's looks and how she was going to have a great future endorsing beauty products when she returned from this venture. Haley overheard him actually discussing her figure with a group of men from Japan whose command of English was fortunately rather poor. At least she hoped it was.

By the third day Haley began to notice occasional sympathetic glances from a few of her classmates. Uncle Steve's bad behavior seemed to be buying her a bit of understanding, as most people had at least one relative that made them cringe.

On the fourth night, the evening before the group would scale a beautiful cliff, her uncle began avoiding her gaze, and went quiet with everyone. Haley learned from an instructor that Uncle Steve had gotten permission to photograph the climb the next day if he would supply a set of the photos to the school to use on their website and in their advertising.

So that is why they let him come along.

Once they were in their shared tent, Uncle Steve was more willing to talk.

"Honey, this whole thing is expensive, you know? Do you have any idea what my airfare was to come over here?"

Haley knew how much airfare to India was. Her parents had made sure she'd known.

"Good thing I've got some great news. I've kept it from you until now, because, well, I wanted to wait till the right minute to tell you. I have a another potential sponsor for you and they are big. These guys, honey, these guys make this whole thing work. If I bring them back the photos they want, they'll use them in an ad campaign they're about to launch and will consider sponsoring your entire climb. This is it, the break we need."

"I thought the cosmetic company already was our big break?"

"Chump change compared to this. Oh, don't get me wrong, we're glad to have them too, because they got this whole thing started. Luckily, the lingerie folks don't see a conflict, so we can do both. And it's gonna take both to pay for this, for sure. But it'll be worth it. Once you climb that mountain, you are going to be golden. As in the golden goose. An ATM machine on legs. I just need this one photo from you tomorrow. Okay?"

"Sure, Uncle Steve." Haley was tired and wanted to end the conversation. "I promise to give you my best smile and even wear a little make-up and not be grumpy about it. Okay?"

"Uh, I'm going to need a little more from you than that, dear. This is a lingerie company. The biggest. They want you in your beautiful smile *and* in the new sexy yet versatile bra they're introducing to the market in a few months."

"You want me to wear their bra while I climb?" Haley found the request almost funny. So that's what Uncle Steve had been embarrassed to ask her. "Sure. I need to wear somebody's bra. Why not wear theirs?"

"No dear. I want you to wear their lovely bra, and once you get to the spot I picked out today, I need to photograph you in it. I'm sorry honey, but that would be without your shirt."

"What? Hell no." Haley didn't say it; she yelled it.

"Shhh." For once it was Uncle Steve asking her to lower her voice. "You can just unbutton your shirt all the way really fast and pull it open. I'll try to time it so most of the guys have moved on. Haley. No photo, no sponsorship. No paying for my expenses to come here. No nothing. Come on, it's fifteen seconds of your time. You'll look great in this bra. It covers everything like a swimsuit, so what's the big deal?"

"It's my underwear and everybody knows it, that's the big deal. Why can't somebody just Photoshop in the damn bra?"

"They told me to not even think about that. This whole ad campaign is about authenticity. Sexy clothes for real women who do exciting 'real-women things' like climb mountains. They don't want anyone from this climb seeing the ad and posting on the internet about how it was faked. Kind of kills the authenticity thing, you know?"

"So you're saying I have to not only be photographed in my bra, I have to be seen by my fellow climbers doing this, and, let's be honest, the company hopes these guys will post on the internet about how hot I looked in my bra while climbing a mountain?"

"Yeah, sort of. It doesn't have to be a lot of them." To her uncle's credit he looked ashamed. "Hey Haley, I didn't design this world, I'm just trying to get by in it."

Haley wanted to tell him to get by without her, but she knew already she'd agree to do it. That's how badly she wanted to climb Kanchenjunga.

******

Pavel studied her pictures and read the report. She was pretty enough, with her big eyes and the long ponytail, but pretty wasn't what mattered. He had all the pretty girls he wanted whenever he felt like it. Here, he was looking for something special. A treat. Not just a virgin, but an innocent who he could make his own.

It said she was studious and smart. Those were plusses. Hindu was good, he liked them pure Indian. Soon to be seventeen? That was perfect. No children for him; he wasn't a pervert and he liked a woman's curves. Older virgins were becoming rare. It was sad what the world was coming to.

He studied the pictures some more, and then he nodded as he made his decision. He got the special box from the back of his safe, and fingered the other photos of things he'd made totally his. The rare white lion killed ten years ago. The dead elephant lying on the ground with its beautiful long white tusks. The extraordinary Ming vase he'd cherished for months before he allowed himself the joy of smashing it into a million pieces.

He studied the giant male baboon he'd killed with only a bow and a poisoned arrow. Now that had been a worthy challenge. Here was the girl from eight years ago, the first time he'd purchased his own virgin from Nandi. What a revelation it had been, to discover he could own a girl.

He studied the picture of the second one, bought four years ago. She'd amused him for longer, although both virgins were younger and more compliant than he'd have liked. Even so, they'd each been great fun, before he took his final pleasure with them.

Now this new one. She would have more substance to her, more fight. He could feel it already and laughed at how his manhood responded with its own anticipation. He dropped her picture into the box. *You will be mine.* He turned the small combination lock closed.

He took the phone off mute. "Yes, Nandi. She'll do. In fact, I'll pay ten percent over asking price if you don't show her to anyone else and get her to me no later than Saturday noon."

Pavel sat back in his chair and smiled. Some men liked to go fishing when their wives went out of town. He'd never seen the charm in trying to catch a dumb little fish.

October 2011

10. Seeking

After meeting with Amy the first time, Teddie and her friends figured out how easy it was to ride the bus over to her office, and they discovered the school would let them do so. It didn't take long for the woman's wild clothes and barrage of potted plants occupying every bit of extra space to seem normal. At least, it seemed normal for Amy, who impressed them because she took time to listen to whatever theories or facts they had.

The second time they came, it was because one of the younger boys told Michelle he had woken up in the middle of that night outdoors, and when he couldn't go back to sleep he'd snuck off to play with an electronic game he wasn't supposed to have. He had seen Usha leave by herself.

This was good news, Amy assured them. At least she hadn't been kidnapped from campus.

"You don't really think her uncle would have driven up here and grabbed his own niece in the middle of the night, do you?" Michelle asked.

"Possibly. It depends on how he intended to, uh, monetize Usha. In some cases, he'd turn the job over to someone more experienced at this kind of thing. Do you think Usha is a virgin?"

The girls all nodded.

"We talked about boys a little. Usha was shy and her parents were strict. She had a boyfriend in ninth grade, and they kissed at parties, but her parents put a stop to the relationship."

"The cultural norms for teenage experimenting are different here," Amy said. "My working assumption is her uncle has been looking for someone to buy her outright for a large fee. His part of the deal is to provide her whereabouts and make sure the family won't cause trouble. Then he lies to Usha's mother and the authorities."

"So, there are organizations out there that buy and sell girls? Teddie was nowhere near ready to accept this with the cool nonchalance Amy had acquired over the years.

"Yes. They're not lurking around every corner, but there are places, in the US and everywhere else, where they operate with little trouble."

Teddie shuddered inside.

A few days later, Amy called the school and asked if the girls could come to her office. By then Haley was at her second mountaineering class, but Teddie and Michelle were happy to oblige.

"I was thinking," Amy said, "if Usha ran, something must have spooked her. I found someone at the school today who told me Usha spoke with her mother minutes before the earthquake. I was hoping you girls could look into this. Maybe someone was in earshot and overheard part of the conversation."

Teddie and Michelle nodded, eager to help.

"It sounds like the earthquake couldn't have had worse timing," Michelle said.

"That timing could be the thing that got your friend to safety," Amy said. "If that's the case, and I hope it is, we need to find Usha to let her know the men her uncle sold her to may keep trying to track her down, particularly if money has exchanged hands. She, and the people hiding her, aren't safe, and Usha may think they are."

"We'll do everything we can to find out more," Teddie said. She knew for a fact girls at the school eavesdropped on each other all the time. Usha was widely regarded as odd; maybe somebody had been curious enough to listen in. Teddie hoped so.

******

Uncle Jeet threw his morning newspaper down next to his breakfast plate and gave a snort of derisive laughter. Ashmita kept cleaning on the other side of the room, trying to attract no attention.

"What is it, dear?" his wife Riddhi asked.

"This feminism thing has gone entirely too far."

"Of course it has, dear. But what now?"

"Now, we are so worried about the self-esteem of girls that we are letting them rename themselves."

"You mean the government is taking away the names given to them by their fathers?" Riddhi was indignant. She and Jeet had one grown son, and she would have been fighting mad if anyone had dared to change the name Jeet had given him.

"Yes. Apparently the name Nakusa is no longer acceptable. Dozens of girls in the Satara district are being allowed to pick their own replacement names. What will be next?"

"Doesn't Nakusa mean unwanted?" Ashmita asked, then regretted opening her mouth.

"It does. The girls probably were unwanted," Jeet said. "Now we have to pretend otherwise? Why?" Jeet glanced past Ashmita and saw her five-year-old daughter standing in the doorway.

"I tried to convince your husband to name that fourth one Nakusa, you know. Fourth daughter in a row? I couldn't think of a better name. In fact, I think I'll start calling her that now."

He looked hard at the little girl. "Your new name is Nakusa. If you answer to anything else, I'll have you beaten. Do you understand?" The little girl ran from the room crying while Ashmita glared at her brother in-law.

"Riddhi, I need to speak to my brother's wife privately about some other family matters. Would you run along, dear?"

"Of course." Riddhi took a last little sip of her morning tea, gave Ashmita a sort of vague smile, and hurried out of the room. Ashmita supposed she was going shopping.

"This whole nonsense with renaming girls reminds me, there is virtue in the blunt speaking of truth. Don't you agree, dear sister?"

Ashmita looked him in the eye but said nothing. Jeet gave another snort of a laugh.

"You're smart enough to hold your tongue, I'll give you that." Jeet paused a moment, long enough to enjoy watching the first glimmer of fear creep into Ashmita's eyes. Ah yes. Now she realized where this discussion was going.

"Ashmita, you owe me far more money than you can possibly repay. You and your brats require more out of my pocket every day than you put back into it, and as your daughters approach the age of marriage they will cost me more. This puts me in a foul temper, and I fear I will slip at times, like I did now, and take it out on your children. A man can't help himself."

He took the last bite of his crumpet. "This is a bad arrangement for everyone. If only there was a quick and easy way for you to repay your debt to me. It could even be a way that would allow me to give you a stipend so you could travel back to your family in Mumbai. If only such a situation existed." He gave Ashmita a long look.

"Don't even think of it."

"Of course, I could just sell Diya. They do buy them that young, you know. Poor Diya wouldn't even understand what was being done to her, would she?"

"She's eleven. You wouldn't."

"Of course I would. And I probably should and just be done with it. But I've learned recently that a sixteen-year-old virgin will fetch considerably more money than an eleven-year-old. I could sell them both of course, and maybe together. Some men like sisters, I can't imagine why."

Ashmita was staring at him aghast.

"But you are family, and it is lucky for you I have a sense of honor. I would rather not sell a child. On the other hand, Usha is a young woman. She is entirely capable of doing what young women do and I rather suppose she can learn to do it reasonably well." At the thought, Jeet made a little face of pleasure. Ashmita charged across the room at him. He grabbed her wrist before she could strike him, and then he laughed.

"Don't get hurt, dear sister. You've four more brats to care for. Usha already has a buyer and the deal has been made. He paid handsomely for her and he wants her immediately. He's impressed with her age and virginal status, and intends to treat her well. It will be almost like having a rich husband, really. Meanwhile, you can thank me for arranging this, and take your other children and make a safe life for them in Mumbai or wherever you choose. This should be an easy decision."

Another pause for a bite of food. Then Jeet dabbed at his lips. "Or you can defy me and pretend like you don't know where Usha is hiding, and let me sell off each of your other daughters instead. They'll be sold one by one, to far less savory buyers. Usha would have a good life. Do you know anything about the kind of men who like five-year-old girls?"

At the last question Ashmita thought she might faint. She sat down hard in a chair and put her head in her hands.

"This buyer is not patient. I told him Usha would be easy to retrieve from her school. I never guessed she would take off on the run for no reason." Jeet gave Ashmita a meaningful look. "Now I need to find her fast or the deal may fall through. So, by tonight, you and I will have an arrangement, one way or another. Oh, and get me some more tea. This cup has gotten cold."

With that, Jeet picked his paper up and went back to reading.

******

Darjeeling celebrated the holidays of most of the world's religions, but none more fervently than Diwali, the five-day Hindu celebration of the victory of light over darkness. Teddie had heard of it back in Texas as the Indian Festival of Lights, and in 2011 the lunar based holiday occurred at the end of October.

Houses were decorated and even the school created rangoli, the beautiful traditional designs made out of colored sand and flower petals, in their main hallway. Most students from India went home for the holiday, and all students who remained on campus were given time off to enjoy the festivities. Teddie had heard the fireworks displays were amazing.

Amy suggested the girls join her on Friday, the main central day of the festival. Haley would be back from her class on Thursday night, and the four of them could tour the town and go out for a dinner. Teddie had been a picky eater back home, but she'd gone from being suspicious of the local food to becoming a big fan, and the chance to eat off campus was a coveted privilege. The girls agreed at once.

They ended up at a small crowded restaurant, hoping to finish before the fireworks displays began. They'd found a place to sit when Teddie looked up and felt a chill of fear. The tall, well-muscled East Asian man who'd been the only one able to see her at the bus station the night Usha ran away was sitting twenty feet from them and looking right at her.

Teddie's first fear was that she was dreaming again. *I'll go crazy if I can't tell when I'm awake or asleep.* Then she remembered she'd also seen the man as she and Michelle were leaving the train station, and that time she'd been awake. So okay. This guy existed.

Amy must have seen Teddie's look, for she followed the girl's gaze and muttered. "No. Not here. Not today." Teddie felt a flash of relief. Amy saw him too. That was good.

"You mean the dude over there who looks like muscle for the Buddhist mob?" Haley laughed.

"Yeah, him. He's not from Darjeeling, but he's made his way onto my radar twice before." Amy thought for a minute. "Once in a bulletin involving an underage girl and a hotel in Indonesia, and another time when I saw taped footage of him as I was dealing with a local girl who had gone missing."

"He doesn't seem menacing," Michelle said. "I mean, he's just sitting by himself, eating food like we are." Michelle shrugged, then looked right over at him and gave him a little wave.

"Don't do that," Teddie said.

"Chill." Michelle responded.

"I've seen him twice before too, Michelle, and once, well, Usha was there." Teddie hoped she could get away with leaving it at that.

"Did he pay attention to Usha? Say anything to her?" Amy perked up at this last piece of information and, of course, persisted with the questioning.

"Sort of. I mean, he paid attention to Usha. He didn't say anything." Teddie was trying to walk a fine line between raising appropriate suspicions about a guy she thought deserved it and not giving information that would make her sound crazy.

"Where were you guys? Was I along?" Now Haley was curious, too.

"Uh, no you weren't. We got permission to run out and buy me a couple of things I needed. We were just off campus for a few minutes. You were doing some mountain thing."

"When exactly was this Teddie? Tell me every detail you can remember." Amy was concerned.

Great. I am such a lousy liar. I should have kept my mouth shut.

"It was a few days before Usha disappeared. I don't remember much about it." Teddie knew she sounded defensive but she couldn't help it.

"It's okay, Teddie. No one's accusing you of anything," Amy said. "But if there's a concrete way to link this guy to Usha's disappearance, then I need to have it."

"There's nothing concrete. Just, well, he gave me the creeps. I don't remember much about it and I'm sorry I can't tell you more." *There, that was honest and safe to say.*

"Okay," Amy said. "He's already a suspect in the world of trafficking, but if I call the police now, in the middle of holiday, he'll be long gone before they get here. So let's just leave and go see some fireworks."

She turned to Michelle. "Please stop smiling at him."

******

Usha was fond of Bela. She was usually confused but always kind and generous. Over the past three weeks, Usha had fallen into the role of a younger female relative, scrubbing Bela's back for her when she bathed and braiding her long hair faster than Bela's own arthritic hands could. Many times the woman called Usha other names, names of the woman's own daughters, Usha guessed, or maybe of her sisters too. Usha never corrected Bela; she replied with soothing words and cared for the woman as best she could.

So Usha was torn when a new friend at school invited her over to spend the night and to celebrate the main feast of Diwali with her family. How wonderful it would be to do something so normal. But how could she leave Bela alone on such a holy day?

She broached the subject with Bela early in the week, and it was clear the elderly woman had no idea what time of year it was. Bela's own children were too far away to visit her. Would they at least call her? Usha hoped so. She decided to accept the friend's invitation for Friday night, and then to make Bela a special dinner on Saturday to celebrate the holiday with her.

She was horrified when she returned home on Saturday morning and found Bela crumpled on the front room floor. First

Usha thought the woman had fallen ill, and she was filled with guilt. But as Usha rolled Bela's body over she saw the bruises and marks. Someone had beaten Bela unconscious, and Usha had a horrible idea of who it was.

She looked around the small home. It appeared the place had been searched, but Bela had little of value, so it was hard to believe this kind of mess had been made by thieves. Bela moaned and Usha hugged her with relief. She had to get the lady medical help.

The good news, if it could be called such, was Bela probably hadn't remembered someone named Usha lived with her. The bad news was someone wanted Usha so much they came all the way to Gangtok for her. If they were that determined, they'd find neighbors or classmates who'd verify she was here and they'd keep searching. She had to get out of Gangtok now.

Usha looked at the cabinet in which she knew Bela kept her meager money. God forgive her, she was going to have to steal again. What was she turning into, if she could be a common thief so often?

I am borrowing the money. The day will come when I pay every rupee back to everyone, with interest.

The way things were going, though, that could be a while.

******

Teddie was in bed, exhausted but still wound up from the Diwali celebration and the odd occurrence over dinner. Usha's bed, the one closest to Teddie's head, lay empty. It was unlikely the school would have reason to fill it for the rest of the semester. Haley's bed, the one across the room, had been empty for the past week but Haley was back and snoring softly. It occurred to Teddie that Haley had said little about her second week of training. Teddie hoped it had gone better than the first. Michelle was sound asleep in the bed nearly touching Teddie's feet.

Usha, Usha where are you? Are you safe?

As the words made their way through her mind, Teddie thought she heard Usha's voice in the hall. She stood up to go see, happy her friend might have returned. As she got to the door she noticed all sound had stopped and she was floating.

Damn. Not this shit again.

With that thought she almost snapped back into her body, which she could see huddled under her covers. But she didn't. She stopped, although she had no idea how.

Okay, I do have some control over how this works. That's good.

Teddie tried to think as she concentrated on hovering inside her bedroom door. She looked back towards her still body and saw herself breathing. Breathing was good. Better yet, it looked like she was sleeping, which meant no one who came upon her would have any reason to worry or be suspicious.

So what would happen if someone tried to wake her? She remembered the times she'd popped back without warning. Maybe one reason for quick returns was her body thought it needed her back. Good also, because it meant she wouldn't be leaving herself in danger if she went exploring.

Teddie wondered if she could open the bedroom door to go out into the hall. Would her ghost hands, as she thought of them, work in the real world? She didn't think so. She remembered little four-year-old Teddie giggling as she passed through Zane's bedroom door. That was the way to do it. She moved up to the door, nervous. It was as impermeable as ever. Great. Did she need fairy dust or a magic feather to pass through walls?

Come on. If you could do it at four years old, you can do it now. The next thing she knew, she was on the other side of the wall. *Note to self. Don't over analyze.* Teddie kept moving.

She passed two teachers in the hall, and wasn't surprised when the two women looked through her. One of the young teachers must be from around Patna, because her voice reminded Teddie of Usha. That was who she'd heard in the hall. At the sad realization that Usha wasn't there, Teddie almost snapped into her body again. She caught herself. *No. As long as this is safe, I wish to learn more.*

It sounded like a command when she said it, and it occurred to Teddie she'd never commanded anyone or anything. Yet, whether she was issuing this edict to herself or the universe, it was listening and obeying. So far, so good.

I want to go to Usha and see if she's unharmed.

It was a simple command and Teddie had no idea what to expect. She began to move, not by force, but by what felt like her own choice, down the hall and out the door and down the street. Teddie had never been comfortable with heights, so she was relieved that while it felt like she was flying, she was flying in the manner she'd have chosen. She was skimming really, maybe ten feet above the ground, close enough that if she fell she'd be okay. She made her path down roads rather than over buildings, but she was picking up speed as she went. It seemed like she was guiding herself, that a part of her knew Usha's location and was leading the rest of her to where she wished to go.

She was headed north towards the mountains, speeding now over the major road out of Darjeeling into the Himalayas. Weren't those some of the renowned tea fields off to the left? Teddie looked closer, and the next thing she knew she was standing in the middle of the tea field, examining the beautiful green tea leaves up close. Great. She was stuck in a field and had no idea what to do next. She felt herself about to snap back.

No. If my body is safe then I want to go to Usha and see if she is unharmed.

With that, she was back on the road and moving again. This time she concentrated on not becoming distracted, and she picked up speed as she went. After a while, she slowed down as she entered a large city. Gangtok? She made her way through streets to a far edge of the town, where she found herself standing next to an old pick-up truck parked outside a roadside hotel. Usha was sleeping in the back of the truck. Oh dear. Her friend was homeless, and had stopped to sleep in the soft hay lining the back of a stranger's vehicle.

There was barely a sliver of a moon in the sky, but the east was beginning to glow over the green hills. Teddie knew it was nearly dawn. Had she traveled most of the night? She watched Usha start to sit up and rub the sleep out of her eyes.

A man came out of the hotel and headed towards the truck. Teddie looked around for a way to warn her friend. Was there anything she could do that Usha would see or feel or hear? She didn't think so.

Wait. The man's mouth moved as he gave Usha a friendly wave. He seemed to have expected to find her there. Behind him came a woman and three sleepy children wrapped in blankets. The man carefully placed each child in the back of the truck next to Usha.

The woman, holding an infant who was nuzzling to get fed, smiled at Usha in appreciation as she got in the front of the truck. So Usha was working as a nanny to get passage somewhere? Where? Teddie studied the plates on the vehicle. They looked different from those in Darjeeling. BP4. Wasn't that Bhutan? The truck took off heading east. Usha was going to Bhutan.

Teddie felt an unmistakable need to return. This time she knew not to object. She woke up in her bed, swatting off a fly on her nose. She was wide awake as the sun rose, and she knew she had to find a way to tell Amy what was going on.

November 2011

11. Doing

As November began, it seemed to Teddie everybody had issues. Haley had said little about her second mountaineering class, but after the Diwali celebration she said little about anything. Michelle finally got a chance to video-chat alone with her mother, and after that conversation she was as withdrawn as Haley.

Teddie had problems of her own. She was willing to accept she had the capability to do something unusual, maybe even remarkable, but it would be nice if she had some idea of what *it* was.

Teddie liked to think if one of her friends came to her and said, "Guess what I can do?" she'd listen with an open mind. She wasn't sure Haley or Michelle would be so receptive, so she spent a lot of time staring off into space, wondering what made her able to take these odd journeys.

The three girls avoided conversation for days, until Michelle and Teddie dawdled over dinner one night and came back to the room to find Haley crying into her pillow, trying to muffle the sounds. As they entered the room, Haley covered her head with another pillow and told her friends to go away, which of course they knew better than to do. Her laptop was open and they took a look.

Haley had been reading an angry blog post from a German college student who'd been in Haley's second climbing class. A quick glance showed the boy was being pissy because a lone female had been allowed in and had to be accommodated for all sorts of privacy issues. His post went from annoyed to outraged as he described how said lone female contributed to the vulgar commercialization of climbing by doing something as crass as posing mid-climb for a lingerie ad. Dozens of others had responded with agreement, including other students from the course.

"The thing is I agree with these guys. I feel the same way," Haley choked the words out between sobs. "What they don't get is I didn't have a lot of choice. They get to show up and be in any class they want. They fit right in because they've all got the same body parts. They don't have to choose between being a nuisance and not climbing, and nobody tells them they have to raise money to climb by posing in their underwear. No one even suggests it."

Haley grabbed a tissue and blew her nose hard.

"Oh my god," Michelle said. "Your uncle made you pose in your underwear?"

Haley rolled her eyes and scrolled down to the pictures of her hugging the rock face in jeans and a shiny satin purple corset thing that could not have looked more out of place.

"Sexy underthings for real women. It's going to be the latest Courtship Closet ad campaign."

"You're modeling for Courtship Closet?"

"Yeah, but only if I'm willing to do so while trying to be a serious climber."

"This guy has a lot of nerve," Teddie said looking at the photos. "He took these pictures himself. He complained about your being there, then took several shots of you half-dressed, and then he posted zoom-ins on the internet and complained some more. I think somebody should tell him he has to go up a rock face like this in his jockeys."

Haley gave Teddie a grateful look. "Why does everything have to be more complicated if you're female?"

"Maybe because males make the rules."

As Haley turned to close her laptop, Teddie turned to Michelle. "So what's been bothering you? Nobody talked you into rock climbing in your undies, did they?"

"No. And I don't want to talk about it."

Haley chimed in. "You want to wait until we come back from dinner and find you crying? Come on Michelle. You've been as pissy as I have the last week. What gives?"

Michelle sighed. "My mom and I had a long talk. She and dad are doing better and she wondered if I'd consider staying over here for the whole school year."

"What's wrong with that?" Teddie said "You were thinking of trying to talk them into that."

"Yes, but," and Michelle's eyes started to tear up, "but I thought I'd have to talk them into it! I thought they'd beg me to come home. At least mom would." At this last bit the tears came harder. Haley put an arm around Michelle. Teddie, who knew the Tran family better, didn't know what to say.

Once Michelle calmed down, she turned to Teddie. "You're disappointed in my mom, aren't you?"

"Yeah, a little. But Michelle, we're not there and don't know the whole story. Cut your mom some slack. She could be like Haley here, going up the side of a mountain in her purple brassiere because, odd as it seems, it's the best choice she's got."

Michelle nodded and Haley laughed. "Why have you not been yourself lately?" Haley asked Teddie.

Teddie decided to stick as close to the truth as she could. "Me? I'm having these weird dreams about Usha. I think I have some issues with this whole get-sold-into-prostitution thing that I'm not dealing with."

Michelle knew about the party Teddie had been at a few years ago and how her best friend had blacked out. She'd kept Teddie's story quiet, and the two of them seldom brought it up, but Michelle could put two and two together.

"Maybe the school could give you something to help you sleep?"

"I'd rather not start taking stuff. Amy's trained in counseling, so I'm thinking about getting permission to go over to talk to her."

"That's a good idea.

"Did you know when honeybees mate, the male's sex organs break off?" Haley asked.

"What?" Michelle said, looking confused.

"Yeah and when praying mantises mate, the female sometimes just goes ahead and eats the male while they're having sex with each other. The funny thing is he goes right on humping her even after she's bitten off his brains."

"That's sick," Teddie said.

"That's nature," Haley replied. "Sex is messy for most species. We just happened to get stuck in one that makes it so much more difficult on the female."

"You want to be an insect?" Michelle asked.

"Maybe a seahorse. The guys have to carry the unborn seahorses in their pouches while the ladies get to go do whatever they want."

******

The ride into Bangkok while huddled in the back of a truck was not the glorious entrance Vanida hoped for. The girls had already been told they would be separated. Buyers preferred it that way.

Vanida was dropped off second and greeted with a scrutinizing sweep of the eyes by Khae, her new owner. Khae was a large, coarse woman, and Vanida would soon learn she was capable of acting harsher than Pim on her worst days.

Khae let her put her meager things in the upstairs room that housed all the girls. What could Vanida say? It wasn't exactly the living quarters she'd been led to expect.

******

As Amy strained to hear the words Usha's mother spoke, she realized she would say whatever she needed to her bosses back home, but this was one battle she wasn't going to walk away from. Ashmita was calling from the house of an old friend who'd let her use the phone and the woman could barely talk through her sobs.

"I tell you nothing or everything. If I tell you everything it's because I decide you are a good person who won't cause my brother-in-law to hurt my children."

"The last thing I want is to cause harm," Amy said, but she was wise enough to know harm could be done with the best of intentions.

"Don't try to help Usha. Promise me. You and I must accept this. I am so sad, but now I must think of her three sisters."

Out came the story of how Ashmita had been told to bring her daughter home from school but instead had sent her to a family friend in Gangtok. Because Ashmita dared not contact Usha, she didn't even know if the girl arrived safely. Her most encouraging news had come from Jeet when he pressed her for information on Usha's whereabouts. It meant Usha had gotten away from school and he did not yet have her.

Ashmita cried as she told the story of Jeet's threats to sell her other daughters, and of his assurances that a grown virgin like Usha would command an excellent price and be the prized possession of the man who planned to buy her.

Yeah right.

"What would you do? Save one child or save three?"

"That's a choice no mother should have to make." Amy tried to steer Ashmita back to the facts.

"After you told Jeet about this friend Bela, do you think Usha's purchasers sought her out in Gangtok? Do you think they found her there?"

"I have not heard otherwise. If she somehow did escape, I am feared for my daughter Diya's safety. I think Jeet will take her and sell her instead. Can you protect us?"

"Yes. Actually, we can." Amy was relieved to hear the request because she did have access to a safe house for those in danger. The rules were strict, but if Ashmita was willing to comply, Amy could get her and her children to safety.

"You'll have to leave Jeet's home, and promise to have no contact with anyone you know. I'll give you a phone number and an address. They'll take you and the children to a safe place, and once you're there, I won't be able to contact you."

Amy hoped she was conveying to Ashmita what a serious step she'd be taking. "You should go soon. Don't wait for news that Usha eluded whoever they sent after her. By then it will be too late to help Diya. Do you understand?"

There was a long pause. "I brought the children and a few things with me when I left the house this morning. In case. Give me the information. We'll go there now."

"I'll call ahead so they're expecting you. Once I've given you enough time to get to safety, I'll try to find Usha."

"That would be wonderful. If you do find her, tell her how sorry I am for telling them she was in Gangtok."

"With luck, Ashmita, you'll tell her yourself before long."

******

The man in the bright blue silk suit stopped every passerby to offer them a discount. Only two hundred baht, five dollars, to see at least eight acts from the laminated English menu he waived in their faces on the bustling sidewalk outside of the Sexy Lady Bar and Showroom.

"PUSSY TRICKS," it said in big, bold capital letters. Below, it listed two dozen acts starting with "PUSSY CRUSH EGG, PUSSY SHOOT DARTS, PUSSY LIGHT BULB, PUSSY DRINK COKE, PUSSY SMOKE CIGARETTES, PUSSY BLOW OUT CANDLES, PUSSY WRITE LETTER," and even "PUSSY OPEN BEER BOTTLE."

Elsewhere in world the reaction would have been shock or disbelief, but if people were walking through the Patpong district of Bangkok, they'd come to see some of the most extreme sex shows on earth, or at least to watch others go in through the doors.

"Tonight! We have new girl. Brand new, never on stage before. Very young!" the hawker yelled to a large group of Aussie offshore oil workers passing by and in danger of moving on to another bar. "She very good. Been training since six years old."

One of the men stopped. "How old is she now?"

"Don't know. Eighteen. All girls eighteen."

"Yeah, right," the man laughed. Then to his friends, "Let's check out the new girl. She might be fun."

******

Vanida was scared. For as long as she could remember, she'd trained for this day. Starting now, she'd be a woman, and unless Pim and Noi had lied to her completely, she'd be allowed some freedom with her new status.

All she had to do was dance a little in her thong bikini, then shove the crotch to one side and put her special thick-handled pen into her vagina. Squatting over paper, she'd write for the audience in her beautiful cursive, like she'd practiced so often. She'd write love notes using the flowery prose learned over the years, filled with phrases gleaned from the many romance novels Noi had given her. The men would love it. She'd collect the tips. Easy money.

Yesterday she learned that after her performance she would be expected to serve drinks in the bar, to give the audience the chance to ogle her and make comments. It was part of the entertainment. Okay, if she had to, she could do that, too.

Then today she'd been given the tiny bikini she was to wear. She asked about the tag with the number on it. Twenty-seven. What was twenty-seven? It was her number so customers could order her. Order her for what? Khae looked at her like she couldn't believe the question.

Didn't she understand the bar would rent her out to customers upon request? Of course she got an extra stipend when it happened. Vanida's heart sank. Noi and Pim had not mentioned this part of the job.

When she came onstage to dance for the first time, the audience was bigger than it was the day before, when she'd been allowed to watch. Yesterday there'd been a few curious Western couples and some shy young men. Tonight, there was a rowdy group of eight big, drunk males in front of the stage. Vanida walked out to their hoots and froze. She barely managed the slightest of dances while the men hollered for more. Khae gave her a steady disapproving glare.

Then came the pen. She squatted over the paper on the small stage while the manager turned to the audience for requests. "She writes in English and she has great penmanship. Two-hundred baht and she writes anything for you that you like. Anything at all."

"Have her write 'I'm a hot slut who can't wait to screw the guy in the red shirt,'" yelled a guy in a red shirt.

"Four-hundred baht for so many words," the manager said. She gave Vanida a gesture that said *start writing.*

Vanida tried, but when she finished with the word hot, the pen squeezed out of her vagina. She was mortified. That had never happened before. She stuck it back in and got as far as finishing the "s" in slut before it began to ooze out again. The manager started to come towards the stage. Vanida took a deep breath. She needed to do this. S. L. U. The pen started to come out again before she could begin the letter T and she broke into tears.

"I'm not a slut. I'm not a slut, you stupid man," she said looking at the guy who had made the request. Khae was standing next to her now, and she leaned down to slap Vanida hard across the face, sending her sprawling onto her back.

"Yes, you are slut," she said to Vanida in English. Then to the man in the red shirt, "No charge. So sorry."

Khae picked up the pen and paper herself and motioned to the girl who shot darts to come out on stage. Then she grabbed Vanida by the arm and pulled her back to the bar.

"I'll have you beaten later," she told Vanida in Thai. "Now go serve drinks." So a teary-eyed Vanida approached a sympathetic looking older couple to take their drink order.

When one of the men asked for number twenty-seven, Khae was surprised. Maybe the man thought it would be fun to punish the girl himself? Should she permit it? At barely ninety pounds the girl would pose no threat to the customer, but there was a chance she'd be harmed and her value reduced.

Khae shrugged. Best the new girl learn how to take care of herself now, otherwise she'd be of little use anyway.

******

In spite of their squabbling, the world's religions often transcend their differences to provide asylum to those of any faith who are fleeing danger. Thus, when the young Hindu woman knocked on the door of the Buddhist convent in Bhutan, she believed she would be granted shelter, and she was.

Usha waived to the Bhutanese family who'd insisted on driving her as far as they could up the steep dirt road to the side of the cliff where the convent sat. She yelled one last "thank you" down to them before she bowed her head to the nun who greeted her. She went inside.

Asylum has its costs, and Usha prepared herself for hard physical work, few comforts and more silence than she'd ever experienced. Nonetheless, she would be safe here. She'd stay till they asked her to leave or a better plan came along.

******

When Vanida was told her number had been requested, she was sure the man in the red shirt was going to take his revenge up close and personal. Would it be better or worse than what the manager was planning to do to her? Maybe she could screw the man really well and he'd go easy on her. She wasn't sure how a woman did that, exactly, but maybe he'd give her guidance. It was worth a try.

To her surprise, a different man had asked for her. They all sort of looked alike to Vanida, but this one wore a green pullover, and he had a gentler smile. Vanida allowed herself to hope she'd make it through the night unharmed.

The man took her back to his hotel room, but he didn't want to have sex with her.

"Jack was going to buy you, and he can be an ass when he's drunk," green shirt explained. "So I asked for you first. I have a nice girlfriend back home, I don't do prostitutes, and I don't do children. How old are you, anyway?"

"I don't know," Vanida said. "I can pay you back for the money you spent on me. In a few days. I'll have tips by then."

"Honey, in a few days I'm back on a drilling rig off the coast of Malaysia. You know what the really sad thing is? I paid less for you than I did for my dinner. Don't worry about the money; get some sleep."

"You, you did this to be nice?" Vanida was considering the concept.

"Yeah, and when I take you back I'll even tell your manager how great you were. Maybe she'll have cooled off enough to leave you be. Would you consider another line of work?"

"I can't. I belong to them and I have nowhere else to go."

Vanida sank into the softest bed she had felt in her life. She put a pillow under her head and giggled with pleasure. "Do you get to sleep in beds like this often?"

Green shirt gave her a sad look and didn't answer.

November 2011

12. Discovering

Teddie knew she should have called Amy first, but she was so excited to have a pass to leave school alone that she didn't want to wait. The constant monitoring and need to stay in groups was one more thing she hadn't considered when she signed up for this. She knew it was for her own safety, but some days all she wanted was to get into her little pick-up truck, turn her music up loud, and drive.

Ana, the employee at Amy's small office, apologized. Amy had left for the day.

"She's chasing a lead on Usha and made me promise to tell no one where she was going, for Usha's safety."

"Can you give me the direction she went?"

"No, but she's left the city. She won't be back until tomorrow."

As Teddie headed back to the bus, she realized the school expected her to be gone for a while. She *could* go shopping, or go visit some of the little art galleries along Nehru Road. Playing hooky for an hour would do wonders for her outlook.

She wandered around, enjoying the street art and small shops, and on her way back to school, she stopped at the mall for a soft drink. She was sitting at a little table in the food court when she saw him.

He was at the other end, staring at her. She looked away and pretended to look for something in her purse. Out of the corner of her eye she saw him stand up to his full six-feet-plus height. Her heart start to pound. He was walking in her direction. Teddie felt dizzy with fear and looked around for a stranger who could help. She got up to talk to an older woman to her left, but as she stood up fast she felt light-headed, and then she started to faint.

Teddie stood over her own collapsed body, confused. Was this *another* variation of these dreams? She looked up. Everyone else in the food court was ignoring her and looking at her unconscious body on the floor. The woman to her left, the one she'd hoped would help her, was gathering up her parcels to leave, not wanting to get involved.

Only the large man was looking into her awake and aware eyes. He gave a short, solemn bow, then jumped into the air and turned a perfect double-forward somersault, landing on his feet like the girl and boy had done in the snow. Not a soul in the food court noticed him.

As the strangeness of the situation sunk in, Teddie felt light-headed again. Then, she was lying on the cold tile floor, watching a security guard hurry towards her. The large man was gone.

******

Haley dreaded the final training session at the climbing school. This last class was the two-week advanced course, offered only to students who'd shown acceptable aptitude. It was open to men and women, at least, and would involve serious climbs she could learn from.

The bad news was the post of her in the purple lace climbing cami, as it was now called, had pretty much made it around the mountaineering circuit. Her dad had received dozens of comments from people he'd climbed with over the years, ranging from sympathetic to downright nasty. After one unpleasant email sent to both of them, he called Haley to make sure she was okay and to assure her he'd vet all of Uncle Steve's ideas point forward. Haley knew this promise was as much of an apology as she would get.

Her mom, on the other hand, called to tell her how gorgeous she looked in the photos. Haley appreciated the compliment, but wished her mom had more than a one-dimensional understanding of the situation.

The twenty-two men and three other women in the advanced climbing class were polite enough to not say anything to her about the incident. As Haley worked to prove she was a capable climber, most of them warmed to her. True, there was a group of four guys from Argentina who joked to each other about her in Spanish. She'd gone to school with enough Latinos to understand some of the crude slang, and figured out they were teasing each other about having sex with her.

Two of the women were cold to her from the start and got frostier as the rest of the group grew friendlier. The women's growing animosity bothered Haley more than the Argentinians' smutty remarks.

Diane, the fourth woman in the group, was taking the class with her husband and socialized with him and his friends. One evening after dinner she sought Haley out.

"Buy you a cup of tea?" she offered.

"Once I get back to Denver I'll be fine with not having tea for about three years." Haley laughed.

"Yeah, they do drink a lot of it here, don't they? Hey, I couldn't help but notice there aren't a lot of social opportunities in this group for a single woman. Wanted to let you know you're welcome over at our camp any evening."

"Thanks. A few of the guys have made the same offer and I appreciate it. I'm pretty good with being by myself though."

"Well, don't mind Leah and Charlotte over there," the woman said pointing to the chilly duo. "Some people are born with broom sticks up their butts, you know?"

"I know. There are so few of us that do this, though, that I'd like their respect." Haley realized it as she said it.

"You're not going to get it." Diane shrugged. "Just like you won't get the respect of those guys from Argentina who can't stop talking about your body parts and who think none of us speak Spanish."

Diane was a cute, petite woman who looked older up close. She squinted at Haley like she was trying to figure out if Haley knew something. Finally she said, "There are people, dear, both men and women, who don't like a pretty woman who's good at something. They only like her when she fails."

"I'll pass on that kind of friendship."

"As well you should. Beauty plays to deep insecurities in both genders. Add to that being a capable mountain climber who's never rude and looks good enough to model lingerie? Ha. Give me a break. You'd fare better if you acted bitchier."

"Oh, I can be bitchy, trust me, but my dad taught me people should be their best on a climb. Said it was dangerous enough without adding human drama."

"Sounds like a smart man. Too bad more people don't think like him." Diane nodded towards Charlotte and Leah. "Come over to our camp if you get lonely. Tomorrow, I'm going to start talking loudly in Spanish. Maybe yell comments to you about the Argentine guys' bodies." She grinned. "Listen for it. It should be fun."

******

After the incident in the mall, Teddie became determined to get some facts about what was happening with her. Normally she'd search on the internet, but the school monitored students' usage, and she didn't want to raise concerns. Too bad she wasted her time goofing off yesterday. It'd be harder to get a second pass today. Of course, if she hadn't been at the food court, she wouldn't be so antsy to figure out what her body was doing.

She was a bad liar, but she sucked it up and told the counselor she'd waited an hour yesterday for Amy and then been asked to come back this morning. The counselor looked peeved.

"We have nothing but respect for her work, but this is too much school for you to miss. Can't I help you with this?"

"You could, of course," Teddie said, "but she's cleared her schedule for me now."

So Teddie showed up at Amy's office again.

"I told you she wouldn't be back until late today," Ana said.

"I know. I was hoping I could use your internet to, uh, search on some sensitive female issues. I'd rather not do that at school."

"Okay." Ana looked dubious but let Teddie sit down at Amy's desk and connect her own laptop to the organization's Wi-Fi.

"Can I help you with some information?"

"Thanks. But no." Teddie gave the woman her best vague smile and waited for her to leave. Then she typed, "floating travel dreams" and up it came. OBE. Out-of-body experiences. *That* was what she was doing.

Apparently, there were websites and books devoted to the subject, and a few quick clicks revealed stories of hundreds of people doing this. Or claiming to do this. Or thinking they did this.

Teddie wasn't sure where reality ended and fantasy began as she skimmed accounts that ranged from believable, at least to her, to ridiculous. She was sure of one thing. This absolutely, positively described what happened to her. She didn't think she'd ever been so hungry in her life to learn more.

She found facts to keep her going. A lot of people called this astral projection, but astral projection was something else involving visiting other spiritual planes removed from this reality. Teddie didn't know if she even believed in other spiritual planes, but she was pretty sure she hadn't visited one.

There were several experts who wrote and lectured on the subject. Teddie couldn't tell from a quick look whether they were scam artists laughing all the way to the bank, or sincere but functioning delusional people. Or maybe they were like her. Then she found a well-designed website that claimed one out of ten people had some type of out-of-body experience, but it was, in fact, nothing more than a lucid dream. *Oh.*

A lucid dream was a dream so real the person thought it was happening. But it wasn't. The body was asleep and the conscious mind was awake, apparently a possible combination. That sounded plausible.

It raised important questions though. At key times in Teddie's life, including yesterday at the food court, had she slipped into some narcolepsy-type sleep? Out of the blue? If so, did she have some medical condition? Was her subconscious assigning bogeyman tendencies to a harmless man only because he was a large male with what Teddie's subconscious perceived as an exotic appearance? In that case, Teddie needed to be careful about making accusations.

It also meant that seeing Usha buying a ticket to Gangtok, and later riding into the dawn in a truck with a license plate that said BP4, were not clues to her friend's whereabouts at all. They were Teddie's subconscious mind trying to make sense out of frightening events. Understandable, but she shouldn't send limited resources in directions chosen by her dreams, because if this last website was right, they were just that. Dreams.

At the end of two hours of research, Teddie knew she had to get back to school. Now that she knew words to describe the experience, though, she could learn more. Look in libraries. In bookstores. Maybe she could get her sister Ariel to find books online for her. Teddie's sudden interest in the metaphysical would strike Ariel as odd, but Teddie thought her sister would help anyway.

Teddie left the office feeling better than she had in weeks. Maybe better than she had since she was four years old.

******

Amy got back from Gangtok later than she wanted, and as she parked her car to drop items off at the office, she was conscious, as always, of the need to mind her safety when alone after dark. Sometimes she wondered what it would feel like to live in a world where an unaccompanied woman didn't have to be afraid, especially at night.

She thought of the older woman Bela who'd given Usha shelter for weeks. The lady shouldn't have been living alone. Bela did remember two men coming to her house asking about someone named Usha. She said she tried to tell the men there was nobody there named Usha, but they wouldn't believe her.

Amy guessed the men must have thought, at first, the elderly woman was trying to be a hero. They beat Bela up seeking information, but she kept telling them her daughter was visiting. They must have realized, eventually, that Bela thought she was telling the truth.

The hospital said a girl called for an ambulance the morning after the beating but the girl wasn't there when they arrived. Amy guessed Usha had found Bela, called for help, and then fled. But to where? She was a young girl without means.

Bela's daughter had arrived the day after Bela was hospitalized. Before she left Gangtok, Amy gave her a list of local resources for her mother. One of Bela's sons was flying in tonight, and Amy hoped the family would come together and find a way to see Bela got the care she needed.

Amy was lost in these thoughts as she fumbled with the lock to get into the darkened office, and she jumped when she heard a noise behind her. Two men emerged out of the shrubbery, blocking her from the sidewalk. They were large men, older and well dressed. They didn't look friendly.

One reached out and grabbed onto her lower arm and squeezed hard. She gasped at the audacity of the stranger's uninvited touch.

"This is a warning," he said. "We choose to allow you to go about your business, because you're useful. You add to the illusion our business is declining. We prefer this illusion."

"Who are you?"

The man ignored her. "However, there are situations in which your involvement is inconvenient. This is one. Tell me you understand this message."

"What situation?"

"The girl called Usha. She's been sold to a powerful man, one who will accept no substitute. He gets that way sometimes, and then he must be accommodated. You won't interfere further. Do you understand?" He squeezed her wrist harder until it hurt.

"You've got to be kidding. I don't give up on anybody. Ever." She said it as she jerked her arm towards the man's thumb, pulling it free the way she'd been taught in self-defense classes.

The man seemed amused at her stunt. "That's a poor choice. Reconsider."

The two walked away before Amy could say more.

******

As soon as Teddie saw Amy, she was worried. The woman was subdued, and the normal electric-colored patterns were missing from her clothes. She shoved wilting plants off of her desk as Teddie sat down. Teddie felt silly intruding with her own trivial problems.

"I'll make this quick. I know you're busy. I thought you might have some ideas because I'm not sleeping well and I'm having these weird dreams since Usha left. I think I have more issues with this than I'm admitting."

"Let's start with the dreams. Weird, how?" Amy focused on the young woman in front of her as Teddie described dreams so real that she thought they were. Amy heard about Teddie's first guess that she was homesick and sleepwalking, and then heard about her pre-dawn trip to the bus station behind Usha.

"It was so detailed. I watched her take out a wad of rupees and buy a ticket to Gangtok."

"Why was she going to Gangtok?" Amy asked with a sharpness she hadn't intended.

"I've no idea. These dreams are like reality, except everything is silent. I can't touch or feel or move things; I only know what I see. She buys a ticket; I watch her buy a ticket. It's all I know."

"Did you try talking to her?"

"No one can see me or hear me. I'm like a ghost. That's how I figured out I wasn't sleepwalking."

"Okay." Amy seemed disappointed. "I agree. If no one could see you, it was a dream. So why Gangtok?"

Teddie shrugged. "I guess she had to be going somewhere."

"Not really. She must have said something to you earlier, or you overheard something and you forgot it. Maybe you didn't even consciously know you heard it."

"Why do you think that?"

Amy sighed. "Because she did go to Gangtok. That's where I was yesterday."

Teddie felt a tingle that passed from her feet all the way up to her head. "In that case, if my subconscious is that clever, would you like to hear about the dream I've had since then?"

Amy hesitated. What were the odds Teddie had more real information? Not high. Would she be helping Teddie or doing her a disservice by encouraging this? Maybe Teddie would benefit from thinking she was helping her friend, as long as the fantasy didn't get out of hand.

"Tell me."

Amy heard about the truck with the BP4 license plate driving into the dawn with Usha huddled into the hay in the back. The story made sense. Amy had to hope it was somehow true, even though she hardly believed Teddie Zeitman had prophetic dreams. Maybe the girl had overheard something twice.

Secretive, remote Bhutan had to be the safest place in the world for a young girl to be alone. Half the country would take her in as a guest and care for her, which was why the country let almost no one past its borders.

Maybe, in this case, a lone girl had slipped in. Amy could only hope.

December 2011

13. Seeing

Pavel sat alone in his office, finishing paperwork and thinking life hadn't had enough play lately. He took out his container of possessions and studied her picture for the hundredth time. She'd been in his special box weeks for weeks now, even though she wasn't yet his. Clever girl. She'd run off to where her uncle couldn't find her, and her own shrewd mother had gone into hiding as well.

Perhaps he should purchase another. Nandi had been keeping his eye out for a substitute.

He studied her big eyes and the long ponytail, thinking of the fun he could have using something as simple as her own long hair.

Hadn't he chosen to hunt the great baboon not only for its size and strength but also for its cunning? He liked them smart. This particular kind of prey came smaller, but an intelligent one could be hard to defeat. Pavel decided this little virgin was already providing him with entertainment. He didn't want another; he wanted to finish this hunt.

******

Amy invited Teddie and Michelle to meet her at the food court on a Saturday in early December. Haley was away at her final climbing class, but Teddie and Michelle were eager for the outing. When the girls' arrived, Amy was happier than she'd been in a while. She'd received final word that Usha's mother and siblings had been relocated by Amy's agency and their whereabouts would be secret for as long as necessary.

"Ashmita's family will welcome her in Mumbai and help her in her widowhood, but we will keep them hidden until Usha's Uncle Jeet has given up on the idea of trying to sell anyone."

"But what about Usha? Where is she?" Michelle asked.

"We don't know. I'm pretty sure she was promised to a particular man, and he can't find her either. We have to hope he'll give up and move on. I've circulated Usha's photo to colleagues to be on the lookout. Because she hasn't been spotted anywhere, there's a good chance she's found somewhere safe to hide."

"Like maybe a farm somewhere in Bhutan?" Teddie asked.

"Maybe." Amy smiled. "We're not ruling out anything."

Then the softness in Amy's eyes disappeared and Teddie saw anger flare as Amy looked past the two girls at someone behind them. Amy stood up and marched across the food court to the large man sitting where he'd been when Teddie fainted. He was watching them again.

"I don't know who the hell you are, but leave me alone." Amy spat the words out. Teddie was a little embarrassed, even though she felt the same way towards the man. "Stop sitting around and staring at girls. What you people do is despicable. I don't know if you are an advance spy, or what, but you should be ashamed."

The man watched her, surprised at first, and then looking confused. Teddie wondered how well he spoke English. Finally, he seemed to understand what she was talking about. He smiled.

"This is not amusing. You tell your people I'm not afraid of them and I won't back down. Do you understand?"

With a glare Amy turned and walked back to Teddie and Michelle.

"Sorry. I got some threats recently, and I've had it with being afraid, and with that man following me around."

Amy put her head in her hands and didn't look up for a few seconds. "I lost it with him, didn't I?" she asked.

"Yeah," Teddie agreed.

"But he did get up and leave," Michelle said.

“That much is good.” She laughed. “I’ll consider getting him out of this food court to be a small victory. So, how about some ice cream?”

******

The boy Jampa had seen others who moved in second bodies like his own. It didn’t happen often, but when it did they were always older and kept their distance, so he let them be. His sister Noom ignored them too.

A few weeks ago Jampa had called out for another playmate, wanting to make more friends. He wasn’t sure why, really. A Western girl answered his call and Jampa saw she had the same gift as he and Noom. The two of them had tried to play with her, but she was inexperienced and she left soon after she came.

Shortly after, something changed with Noom. Now when he called for his sister, often she didn’t answer. When she did, she didn’t want to play. Was she older? Sadder? Jampa couldn’t quite define the change, but it wasn’t a good one.

Tonight, he felt this Western girl’s tug. It was much like Noom’s, but less compelling. He was surprised another could call to him. Very well. He chose to respond, only to find that Noom had been invited and had come also.

The Westerner did a couple of cartwheels, showing them her new-found control, and then she gave them a friendly wave and left. It made perfect sense to Jampa that such an interaction was all she wanted. He waved back, then turned to Noom hoping they might once again play together. Up close, he saw shame in Noom’s eyes. Had she done something wrong?

They’d never spoken to each other, for there was no sound in the world where they met, and he’d never thought they needed to speak. But this night, he realized he had to find Noom. He had to find her in the real world, the one in which he could ask her what was wrong and he could hear her answer.

******

Haley returned from her two-week advanced mountaineering course in better spirits. In spite of bringing schoolwork with her, she was behind in her classes, but at least this course had brought no incidents. By the end of the two weeks she'd become friends with Diane, the older woman climber, and with Henrik and Hans, two climbers from Norway in their thirties who hoped to join the Kanchenjunga expedition as well.

Teddie and Michelle listened as Haley described the two American women who had continued to snub her and the group of Argentine men with their ongoing bad behavior.

"So did your friend Diane really start talking about them in Spanish like she said she would?"

"Sort of. When one of the men yelled up to his friend to help me up a rock face by pushing on my butt, Diane told him in pretty good Spanish that she thought *his* butt was cute and she'd be happy to give his hind quarters a push once they were climbing. Then she repeated the conversation in English for everybody." Haley laughed. "I wish I hadn't been hanging on to a cliff when she said it. I hear the look on his face was pretty funny."

"Oh good for this lady," Michelle said.

"Yeah, their whole tone changed after that. The guys backed off and one of them even apologized to me, saying they'd never meant any offense."

"They probably didn't," Teddie said. "I bet not one of them thought about how all their elbow-jabbing and pointing made you feel."

"Yeah, too bad it took somebody like Diane to cool them down," Michelle said.

"It's easier to act like Diane did when you're forty years old and tough as nails," Haley said. "Of course, if I was a blanket octopus I wouldn't have this problem. The females are about six feet long, and the males are only a couple of inches in size. He detaches his penis and sends it crawling inside her by itself and she doesn't even notice."

"Did you write some kind of a paper on bizarre animal sex?" Michelle asked.

Haley grinned. "I missed a lot of school because of climbing, so I was always doing independent study projects. Might as well pick something interesting, huh?"

"Did you get the grade you needed?"

"Oh I got an A on that project."

"No," Teddie said. "I meant from the climbing class."

"Oh right. I think so. I need an A, and they hinted to me I'd get one. They haven't posted the grades online yet."

Later that night, the grades were posted, and Teddie and Michelle came back from dinner to find Haley starring at her laptop screen with tears streaming down her checks.

"Oh no."

"Oh dear."

Neither of them knew what to say to her.

"No. You don't understand. It's okay. They didn't give me an A; they gave me an A plus. The only one they've ever given for this course."

Haley started to cry harder as she talked. "The instructor says my mountaineering skills are exceptional but more importantly my determination to work hard and ignore distractions has impressed the school greatly. He said any climb would be lucky to have me as a participant. Lucky to have me. Lucky to have *me*." Tears were streaming down her face by this point. Both Michelle and Teddie engulfed her in a hug.

"We promise not to tell all those tough guys you cried when you read this."

******

The luxury car was parked in front of the agency's door before noon. A small Indian man wearing a nice suit was at the wheel. Amy looked at him through the window. He showed no signs of getting out of the car as he alternated between tapping his phone and scanning a newspaper while drinking something out of a thermos cup. Amy decided to skip lunch and then to reschedule an afternoon appointment because something about the guy had her intuition on red alert.

Now it was getting near quitting time. She walked up to the window and looked at him again. He definitely wasn't the Buddha muscle man, and he was too small to be either of the goons who'd threatened her the other night. Well, there were plenty of other people in this town with reason to wish her harm. Maybe one of them had picked today to act on it.

Ana tapped her on the shoulder and Amy jumped. “Sorry. You startled me.”

“Is that man parked outside making you nervous? Do you want me to go see who he is?”

“You noticed him too? He's parked legally; we've no right to bother him.”

Ana laughed. “I’m not going to get near him, I promise. Watch.”

Ana picked her cell phone up off of her desk, walked outside, stood on the sidewalk about fifteen feet behind the man’s car and snapped a photo of the license plate. She gave the man a little wave and walked back inside.

“Why not make him nervous too?”

The police had asked Amy to call if she ever felt threatened and they seemed sincere. She reached for her phone to report the license plate, and jumped when the phone rang in her hand.

“Don’t call anyone,” the voice said as she answered. “You’re in no danger from me. I drove here from Patna hoping to have a conversation with you, and yet I don’t wish to come into your office. You are going home sooner or later, are you not?”

“I’m calling for a police escort,” Amy said.

The man laughed. “The police have better things to do. If you won’t come out, I’ll talk with you by phone while I watch you through the window. I have a business arrangement with a powerful gentleman who won’t give up on acquiring something he wants, although he is getting tired of waiting. He tried leaning on Jeet to produce the treasure, but it’s apparent Jeet has no idea where this gem is hiding.”

Amy’s heart sank. The buyer hadn’t gone away.

“Jeet and my client think you don’t know where the girl is either. We’ve seen the feelers you’ve put out. Clever child. Where has she gone? This particular client likes a smart girl and enjoys a good game of cat and mouse, if it doesn’t drag on too long.”

“There’s nothing I can do to help.”

“Oh, but there is. You’ve complicated the game in an unfair way and he’s asked me to fix that. You broke the rules when you hid the people who could provide my client with leverage over the girl. You do know where the girl’s mother is, don’t you?”

No, she didn't, but Amy decided to keep that information to herself for the time being. "The mother can't help you either. She doesn't know any more than we do."

"I believe that, but who is the first person the girl will get in touch with once she thinks it's safe?" the man asked.

"Well, it would probably be her mother, but her mother is in hiding and can't be reached."

"Exactly," the man replied. "Exactly. We need to remedy that. We need to make this mother easy for the girl to find."

"Go to hell," Amy said. She hit the red end call button hard.

******

Teddie was in bed, about to put her ear plugs in. She could tell from the sounds in the room that both Haley and Michelle had fallen asleep.

Ariel had agreed to buy Teddie books on out-of-body experiences, and promised to bring them with her when she came to India to visit for the Christmas break. Teddie's current theory was she was merely a lucid dreamer, because that was the easiest thing to accept. Nobody really projected their consciousness outside of their body. That left the whole Gangtok thing as somewhat baffling, but…

… but, Teddie was open to learning more. Although it was hard to share such a small sleeping space with two other girls, it had the advantage of eliminating the fear factor. You know, being scared of things going bump in the night. Teddie had pretty much outgrown that, of course, but if one was going to go messing around with metaphysical theories, well, it was nice to have two sleeping friends close by.

So here goes. She squirmed around in her small bed until she was comfortable, then she began the simple relaxation exercises she had read online. Really, it was a lot like the yoga class she'd taken with Ariel one summer. Start with your toes. Totally relax your toes.

Teddie had only made it up to her thighs when she started to feel the tingling she'd come to associate with this type of experience. *It's just a dream. I am in control. I can do what I choose.* She repeated it like the website suggested as she made the conscious decision to swing her dream body into a sitting position and then stand. Her real body, for lack of a better term, lay sleeping in her bed. Her dream body, however, seemed to prefer floating to standing, so she let it float, rising a little off of the floor but not too high.

She thought about her last journey to see Usha and how it had taken most of the night to get there. Usha was further away now, and Teddie didn't want to spend a whole night floating along mountain roads. Well, if this was a dream, there should be more options for travel.

"I'd like to go see Usha, and I'd like to get there fast."

She waited. Nothing happened. "Please." Still nothing.

"Let's go to Usha now," she said, summoning more authority.

With no transition, she was moving fast, really fast. Her body passed through the walls of the school and then began avoiding obstacles, only occasionally passing through the outer edges of objects she didn't completely miss. She couldn't hear or feel the wind on her face, but she had to be going faster than a car on a highway. It was like being in one of those flying cars in old cartoons about the future. That was it. She was in her own fast, and safe flying car, only there was no car and she wasn't driving. After a while, she slowed down.

Then she was standing outside of a lovely stone building, high up on a cliff, looking down on a pastoral valley in the moonlight. It was stunningly beautiful by any standards. Matter-of-factly she turned to the nearest side of the building and walked through the stone wall.

This lucid dreaming stuff is way better than real dreams. In a dream, who knows what weird shit would have happened when I tried that.

Filled with confidence, Teddie floated inside and kept going through walls until she found herself in a room with a handful of younger women all sleeping on the wooden floor. Assorted blankets lay over and under them, and they looked warm and comfortable. Along the far wall was Usha, sleeping peacefully.

Teddie wished she could wake her friend, give her a hug of comfort and tell her that one day soon it would be safe to go home again. But it wasn't possible, so she turned and floated back out.

The night and the view were so beautiful. She hated to leave. Feeling a little silly, she tried the cartwheel again that had set her careening down a road with two kids watching her in the moonlight a few weeks before. This time she held her dream body with more control. She turned two mid-air cartwheels and finished with a gymnast's pose. Whee. She wished those two kids could see her now. She tried it again. Yes. What a shame she didn't know how to find them. One more time. Then she turned and saw the two kids sitting on nearby rocks watching her.

What were they doing in her dream? She guessed it didn't matter. It was a big dream universe with plenty of room for everybody. She put her best effort into turning two final cartwheels, then gave them a friendly wave before announcing "I'd like a quick return home."

******

The winter winds forced Jampa to move his meditation indoors. He sat on the cold stone floor and let his thoughts work towards a natural stopping point.

The girl Noom. Obviously, she was experiencing trouble. As were billions of people in the world. Feel compassion for all.

Yes, Jampa wished to help everyone as best he could. Assigning Noom a greater importance ran counter to the teachings he embraced. Yet the Buddha taught that one must seek one's own path. Using wisdom in the seeking was recommended, but one needn't deny an impulse appearing to lead in a correct direction.

Jampa was sure his own correct direction included finding his sister. He needed to find her here, on this earth, and he needed to do it soon.

December 2011

14. Disappearing

Usha knew it was silly, but she was glad the nuns didn't make her shave her head. She was being housed now with the young women who were studying to be ordained novices. They would take vows to not kill, steal, have sex, lie, or drink, to avoid music and ornamentation, to sleep on the floor, and to fast after midday. Several of them had been eager to shave their heads, to show their commitment.

Usha was happy to join these girls in the chores, and to spend time each day in study and contemplation. She found the contemplation soothing. If learning about Buddhism made it easier for the convent to justify caring for her, it was a trade she was willing to make.

It still amazed Usha that a Bhutanese family had seen the fear in her eyes that night in Gangtok, and helped her. They'd taken her along the mountain roads of India into Bhutan, then headed east a long way before dropping her off at this convent. They insisted it would be the safest place on Earth for her.

Though she wasn't sure where she was, she knew enough geography to guess it was somewhere in the eastern half of Bhutan. Definitely remote. She was picking up more Dzongkha, the Bhutanese language, every day, while managing to get by with the English and Hindi spoken by some of the nuns and new girls.

Usha was pretty sure they'd let her stay for the rest of her life. The only problem was, Usha didn't want that. She was happy to be safe, but she was hiding here, not living. Life for her included noise, emotions and, well, boys. She wanted a husband and a family someday and the lack of boys was going to be a problem.

Wandering around homeless was never going to be a good idea either, so she needed a better plan than staying and a better plan than leaving. She wished she could talk to her mother. Her mother would have some ideas.

Usha wondered how many weeks she'd have to wait before her uncle would give up and it would be safe to go home. Would four weeks be enough? Six? Did the convent have a way for her to get in touch with her mother? How soon would be too soon to ask?

******

Amy went at the problem of helping Usha every way she could imagine. She asked her local law enforcement contacts to push the police in Patna to find out who Usha's Uncle Jeet had dealt with. The police in Patna were unhelpful, and Amy suspected someone in their ranks was protecting this procurer of young girls. Amy asked contacts at other human rights agencies to look into likely purchasers for Usha. As the fall months wore on, she'd got no helpful responses.

Once she provided the license plate Ana photographed, however, an agency came back with a name. A certain businessman from Patna named Nandi was suspected of being a high-end dealer in virgins for rich clientele. Nandi had stayed below the radar because he dealt in such low volumes and had friends in such high places. She studied his picture and was sure it was the man she'd spoken with while he sat in his car.

Amy was assured a case was being made against Nandi, but it would take time because he was so careful. He ran a one-man business, so the only ones who could turn on him were his already guilty customers. She wasn't surprised when the agency asked her to let this lead alone. Amy would put herself in danger if she pursued this, and anything she did would put the ongoing investigation at risk. In due time, her testimony would be used.

Amy sighed as she hung up the phone. No, she did not want to get hurt. No, she did not want to muck up the efforts to bring this pathetic man down.

******

His teacher smiled with understanding when Jampa entered the room, his shaven head bowed and his meager clothing items bundled together on his back.

"You have decided to leave us?" the old man asked.

"I am free to go, am I not?"

"Of course. I suppose you are off in search of your roots."

"Yes, teacher. It's clear to me I must make this journey before I'm ready to travel further down my spiritual path. I leave with gratitude for all you've done for me and hope I will return someday."

"You will be welcome if you do. We wish you well on your journey." The teacher waited for what would come next.

"Teacher, do you or the others know anything else about my history that could help me?"

The bald old man smiled wider, showing the many missing teeth inside his mouth. "You were brought to us ten years ago by a trading caravan from the east. You did not live up to their work expectations. But you know this already. They told us you were eight at the time, but we thought six was more like it. Did I mention to you they said you'd been a captive? Cared for by various women in a village until your captors could sell you? We asked about your family because we were worried you might cry for your mother."

No, Jampa had not been given this last piece of information and he was sure his venerable teacher knew it.

"You did not cry for a mother, but you cried for someone else. Often at first. It was a name we didn't know; in a language we didn't recognize."

Jampa had a foggy memory of this now. He'd cried for Noom in his sleep. By another name. Long ago.

"Do you think I would go east to find this person?" Jampa asked.

"What do you think?" his teacher said.

"I think I need to go somewhere with more ferns and greenery. South would be better."

"Then you should go south. Safe journey, Jampa."

"Thank you, venerable one."

******

Haley shared the good news with her family across the twelve-hour time difference, and two days later Haley's dad called the school back with better news. The team preparing to ascend Kanchenjunga in May had extended a conditional invitation to Haley to participate in the climb.

"Conditional?"

"Two things," her dad said. "The first one I kind of expected. It's my fault Haley. I needed to keep a tighter rein on your Uncle Steve. They asked you not to embarrass the sport by participating in any ad campaigns before and during the climb. Your Uncle Steve's visions of photographing you in lingerie at the base camp is totally out."

Haley breathed a sigh of relief.

"They acknowledged the need of all climbers to raise funds and went so far as to note that the sponsor pool for a seventeen-year-old girl is going to be different and they understand that. You are, of course, free to raise funds after the climb any way you choose. I thought they were reasonable."

"Can we afford to do it this way, dad?"

"Not easily," her dad said. "Your mom and I are looking into some short-term loans. Once you get off the mountain, we'll need you to take the lingerie contract if they'll still have you."

Haley said nothing.

"The other condition causes more concern," her dad said. "This started out as a traditional climb, with a full support team almost to the summit. Now some of the group members want to jettison the support early and finish it as an alpine climb, with less cost and less of a footprint on the mountain. You haven't climbed with oxygen before. It's a lot of weight to lug up there with your hundred-and-twenty-pound body. We'll accept the invitation, but I want to monitor the evolving logistics. You're not going up there unless this is something you can do."

"Dad, I've done alpine climbing all my life."

"Yeah, but not at twenty-eight-thousand feet. We'll talk more about this over Christmas, Haley. Which brings me to the last thing. That school over there isn't cheap and now that you've got the invitation, your mother and I don't see the need for you to stay.

We have better work-out facilities here too. So we'd like to take you out when you come home at the end of the semester."

"I don't want to come home, dad. I love you guys, but here I get to look at Kanchenjunga every day and she looks back at me. I know it sounds silly, but, I like it here." Haley realized it was true as she said it.

She could hear her dad's sigh. "I was afraid of that. You get attached to a mountain, don't you?" He said it with understanding. "I'll talk to your mom, but no promises, honey. This whole venture is on a tight budget. You've got to work with us."

Haley put the phone down and walked back to her room.

"What did your dad want?" Michelle asked.

"They want me to come home for good at Christmas and go to school in Denver."

"What? That sucks. You're giving up on the climb?"

"Oh. No. I should have told you the good news first. I got invited to join the climb."

"What?" Teddie gestured through the walls towards the peaks all three girls knew were on the other side. "You got your invitation? You're going up there?"

"I did. And I am."

******

It was the week before the semester break and the girls were almost done with tests and papers. Michelle had made arrangements to stay for the full year, and had mixed feelings about her three-week trip back to the U.S.

For months Teddie had been counting the days until her parents and brother would arrive from the U.S. and Ariel from London. Teddie knew there would be nice hotels, fancy meals out, and presents her mother would carry all the way over here. Then Zane and Ariel would go back to their lives as grown-ups, and Teddie would go back to Texas with her parents and be a junior in high school. She'd get to wear her jeans to school again, drive her truck to any fast food restaurant she liked, and blare her country music as loud as she pleased.

Now that the prospect of all those wonderful things was close, she wasn't as excited as she once had been. Indian spices, brightly colored weaves and silly school uniforms were a part of her now. She enjoyed the way her classmates made English sound so exotic. She looked at Junga every day, and even though she wasn't going to climb it, a piece of her was of the mountain, too. She didn't know how to say it plainer. A part of her had nestled into Darjeeling and gotten comfy, and now it wasn't so anxious to go.

The Tuesday evening before the break, students of the Lord Peartree Academy were offered a field trip to shop for Christmas presents, if Christmas was a tradition they kept. Back in October everyone had found a need to shop for Diwali. Now, everyone had a relative somewhere who needed a Christmas gift.

Teddie, Michelle and Haley didn't let the coming separation overshadow the fun of going to the local mall. The students arrived in buses, laughing and talking as they dispersed, while teachers shouted instructions about when to return and where to meet.

Haley took off to buy her father a t-shirt showing the Himalayas. Teddie and Michelle went looking for locally made earrings for their older sisters. Teddie found the perfect pair, but when Michelle couldn't find what she wanted, Teddie asked if it'd be okay if she joined Haley.

Michelle waved her on. "I'm trying to decide if I should buy my mom a pair too. I'll catch up with you guys."

Teddie found Haley, and they wandered off to get ice cream, figuring they'd run into Michelle at the food court. When she didn't show, Teddie started to ask other girls about Michelle. One had seen her in the earring shop, but that was all.

Teddie wondered if her friend was more bothered than she was letting on, disturbed about going home to visit parents who seemed happier when she was gone. Maybe the piped-in Christmas music and crowds of shoppers had gotten to her and she'd stepped out for air and some time alone. Teddie wandered over to the front door of the mall and looked out at the parking lot.

A rusted-out white van started its engine as Teddie walked through the main entrance. It pulled up next to her with the passenger door facing her, like they were going to offer her a ride.

Don't be paranoid. They're picking up someone behind me.

Teddie squinted into the van's windows and saw Michelle sitting in the passenger seat. Duct tape covered her mouth and her eyes were wide with fear. The van waited until it was obvious

Teddie had seen her friend. Then, as she reached for the door handle, it took off with a squeal, sending angry pedestrians scrambling out of its way.

Teddie ran after it as it picked up speed, weaving through open spaces between parked cars. As the van started to put distance between them, she screamed for help. Several baffled shoppers tried to catch up with her, not knowing what was wrong but hoping to assist. She kept running, but by then the van was at the edge of the parking lot, where it turned into traffic and was gone. As a last hope, Teddie looked for a license plate. The van had none. She screamed in fury.

Why would someone take Michelle?

Teddie tried to steady her breathing, to think clearly. She needed to get to the police. Notify school authorities. She didn't know where to start.

The first teacher Teddie found didn't believe her. Teddie kept insisting they had to get the police now because minutes mattered, while the teacher kept insisting the girl she saw probably wasn't even Michelle and to please calm down. Teddie took off in disgust to find mall security herself, and the teacher followed.

By the time the police started searching for the van, no such vehicle could be found. Michelle was confirmed to be missing from the mall, and Teddie was asked to come to the station to make a statement. She was happy to do so, and that's where she ran into Amy.

"Oh, Teddie, I'm so sorry." Amy was covered in a copious soft aqua gauze outfit that under other circumstances would have mesmerized Teddie, but all Teddie could see now was the worry on Amy's face. "This is my fault. I should have handled it better. I had no idea these people would stoop to this."

"What people? What are you talking about? This has nothing to do with you!" Then Teddie realized it probably did.

Amy explained how a couple of hours earlier a boy had hurled a brick through the window of her office, with a note taped to it saying, "Her mother. Now." Amy thought vandalism was the threat and told onlookers it would take a lot more than a broken window for Amy Levitt to put a young woman in danger.

The boy was identified by neighbors as a local kid. He admitted he had been paid to show off his cricket arm while two men he didn't know watched from across the street. Amy asked the police not to press charges.

Then Amy's office got a call from a different part of the police force letting Amy know a young American woman had gone missing. Given Amy's network of resources and the girl's nationality, any expertise Amy's group could offer was welcome.

"As soon as I got the call, I made the connection. I knew it had to be one of you girls. That's how they made it personal."

"We've got to get Michelle back." Teddie meant it more than she'd ever meant anything in her life. "We've got to find a way do it without giving them Usha."

"It looks like Usha has some crazy man after her. I got a threatening phone call a few days ago and I hung up on the man. Before I did, he told me capturing Usha has become a game to this man, a game he enjoys. Never mind that he has all the power, money and resources to do anything he wants, and she has nothing but her own wits. It constitutes some warped sport to him."

"Usha does have resources," Teddie said. "She has us."

Amy smiled at Teddie's naive optimism but the smile never made it from her mouth up to her eyes.

******

Michelle's father arrived in Darjeeling twenty-four hours after his daughter went missing. He'd already contacted the embassy, Interpol and several agencies in the State Department. His daughter would not become a statistic. He was angry, and Teddie suspected half the anger was directed inward. For all that the man behaved poorly, Teddie knew he loved Michelle. She'd spent enough time at the Tran household to see affection co-existing with the dysfunction.

Amy was candid with Mr. Tran about the friendship she'd developed with Usha's roommates and her suspicions that Michelle's kidnapping was directed at her.

"That's easy then. Get those scumbags in contact with the girl's mother and get my daughter back."

When Amy hesitated the man cut her off before she could start.

"I'm not asking you to trade another girl for my daughter. I'm not the monster here. I want to trade my daughter for the illusion this man is getting what he wants. Once we have Michelle safe, we can do whatever it takes to ensure her mother doesn't lead these men to Usha. If it's a matter of money, my family can help with expenses. We buy Michelle's safety by pretending to play along."

His pleas were not being heard. He could tell it from Amy's expression.

"Why the hell not? Wouldn't you do it if it was your daughter?"

"I would," Amy said. "I'd do it for your daughter too. In a heartbeat. That's why I don't know where Ashmita and her children are and it's been handled so I can't find out. Those emotionally involved in a case aren't allowed to know where a family is hidden. Too many variations of this happen."

"Well then get your agency to work with me on this."

"They won't. They can't. Mr. Tran, if they did, every time this nefarious underworld group wanted something, they'd just grab somebody's daughter. It's a sad fact. You get the behavior you reward."

"Oh for God's sake. This isn't *somebody's daughter;* it's mine. I want to talk to your boss."

"There is another thing you should know first. We have no reason to think Michelle is a hostage. There's been no offer to give her back if we comply."

Mr. Tran looked shook by that news. "But that makes no sense. What the hell is she, if not a hostage?"

"I think she's a warning, Mr. Tran. Of what they can do more of whenever and however they like, if we don't give them what they want."

"You mean she's just gone?" Mr. Tran said it with more sadness than Amy thought she'd ever heard in a grown man's voice.

"Gone for now, sir. We're going to do everything possible to get her back."

"Will, will they kill her?"

"I doubt it. That's the bleak good news, such as it is. I suspect they'll move her somewhere far away and put her to work."

"Work? Doing what?" As soon as Mr. Tran asked the question, he knew the answer.

"Oh my God. Oh my poor baby. How did this happen? Oh my God."

He sat down and put his head in his hands. Amy left him alone until he could compose himself. Then she would try to persuade him to go back home, because there truly was nothing he could do for Michelle here.

c^3

December 2011

15. Celebrating

The day Teddie's family showed up in Darjeeling was a blur. Ariel sent messages from her cell phone. "All in Delhi." "Boarding plane to Bagdogra." "Piling into hired car." "Really small car." "2 hours away!"

Then there they were. Hugging and laughing and pretending everything was alright for a few minutes, because, of course, they all knew it wasn't. It had been five days since Michelle disappeared from the mall parking lot, and Teddie had cried more than she had in years.

Teddie's parents' first thought had been to get Teddie home on the next plane, but she convinced them to let her take her last exam to finish out the semester. The school had been given extra police protection and no students were allowed off campus now, other than to go home for the break. She was safe.

They considered cancelling their own trip to India before deciding Teddie would be safest if she were traveling home with them. They'd do a short version of their planned vacation and then get their daughter home under their own watchful eyes.

The first night at the hotel with the mountain view, they ate in the hotel restaurant while security made several obvious passes by their table. The family had opted for a two-room suite with Mom and Dad in one room, Zane on the couch, and Ariel and Teddie in the other room. They had also opted to hire a car and a driver, rather than rely on random cabs.

The next morning, Teddie and her parents rode over to Amy's office while Zane and Ariel slept in. Instructions to not leave the hotel under any circumstances didn't set well with the independent older two, but the phrase "we don't want to be part of an international incident" had been persuasive enough.

Teddie was nervous about more than safety on the ride over. She wasn't sure if her parents would love Amy or hate her, and she wanted these important adults in her life to get along. She was glad to see her parents look past Amy's lime green and purple print kaftan as they were reassured by the woman's expertise and by the concern she felt.

"I know you're being cautious and I'm glad, but honestly the men hunting Usha are most likely to back off to give me a chance to comply with their demands," Amy said. "Soon enough, they'll realize I can't get the information they want no matter how much I want to."

As to what the kidnappers' next move would be, Amy thought a second kidnapping was unlikely. "I mean, if one kidnapping doesn't persuade me to cooperate, why would two?"

Amy figured her unseen adversary was smarter than that. He'd wanted to get her attention, let her know how seriously he took his little game. Now that he'd achieved his objective, he'd find another approach. She told the Zeitmans she wasn't looking forward to his next move.

As they talked, Teddie thought she should consider staying in Darjeeling until Michelle was found. Maybe she could remember helpful information. Maybe she could even do her out-of-body thing and learn something useful, if what she dreamt bore any relation to reality.

Usha buying a ticket to Gangtok had been real. Maybe Usha going to Bhutan and sleeping safe in a nunnery had been real, too. Why couldn't she do something similar for Michelle? She'd been far too agitated try, so far. Over time, she'd calm down. If it happened, she could tell Amy, and Amy could find a way to get the information to the police without making Teddie sound like a flake.

Of course, maybe she could do this from home as well. That would be safer, but Teddie was dubious. For reasons she could only guess at, her time in Darjeeling had focused and nurtured this skill. If it was a skill. She wasn't sure she could do it back home. What's more, there seemed to be a spatial component to it. She traveled, and even when she traveled fast it took time. She wasn't sure what her speed limit was, but she couldn't imagine going from Texas to Asia.

As the three of them climbed into their hired car, Teddie mentioned that maybe she should stay at Lord Peartree Academy until Michelle was found.

"Absolutely not!" Her parents actually yelled it in unison.

Her mother softened a bit. "Your friend Amy is a capable lady, and yes, I do like her. In fact, I love all the plants in her office." Her mother smiled. "But there is no way I'm willing to bet your safety on her being right about what some psychopathic crime boss will do. We'll have Christmas here, then travel to Delhi while not taking our eyes off of you. We get one side trip to see the Taj Mahal, that's it, and then we head home. All of us."

Alex was nodding. "If you left it to me, we'd can the Taj Mahal too, but I got out-voted on that one. Let me be clear, Teddie. I couldn't be more concerned about Michelle's welfare or more sympathetic to her parents, but there is no set of circumstances in which you stay in India and we go home. Do you understand?"

Teddie nodded, and knew she was relieved. Bravery wasn't her strong suit, and safe-at-home had a nice sound to it. Police and skilled agencies would do their jobs and get Michelle back, maybe even before Teddie left. She desperately hoped so.

******

"Wouldn't it be simpler to kill the girl?" Vasily asked, choosing to speak Russian both for privacy and because it was easier for him.

"Yes, and no," his boss replied. The two men were enjoying lunch at Pavel's favorite table, the one by the picture window with the breathtaking view of the mountains.

Pavel often left his home in the picturesque Indian resort town of Manali during the winter to vacation in warmer climes, but this year he'd preferred to stay put. The wife and children had been sent off to join his in-laws for two weeks of holiday in Turkey, where he'd make a quick Christmas appearance for the sake of the children. He was still hoping to get his hands on the Indian virgin while his wife was away, so he could give the delicious situation his undivided attention for a few days. Wouldn't that make for a delightful holiday?

Unfortunately, things weren't going as hoped. Against all odds, the clever girl had found a safe hole to crawl into somewhere. He'd have found her by now if that American bitch hadn't hidden the mother and sisters of his prize, removing his best leverage for finding the girl.

He thought he could solve the problem by sending two men to reason with the bitch, only to discover her agency had placed the girl's family somewhere using a double-blind system. That was smarter than he expected. Now, no matter how much he threatened her, she couldn't help him. He wished he'd known that before nervous Nandi decided to remedy his mistakes by kidnapping some Yankee Vietnamese girl and hand-delivering her to Pavel.

"What the hell did you bring her here for?" an incredulous Pavel had asked Nandi when he arrived in Manali with the girl locked in his trunk.

"I drove here to give you your money back in person, and give her to you as interest. I take care of my clients. Always. Enjoy her, and maybe she is leverage for you to get the girl you want."

Pavel had not been pleased. This boneheaded move brought too much attention to both of them. But what was done was done. Perhaps instilling fear into everyone would work to his advantage in ways he couldn't predict.

"So why not kill her?" Vasily persisted as they finished their lunch. "You don't want her. She's useless." He was talking about the American girl, of course, in which Pavel had no interest and who now sat bound, gagged and heavily sedated in a walk-in closet in a vacant rental home in Manali.

"If she's dead, we know she's useless," Pavel said. "If she's alive, it remains to be seen. I want her out of here. I do not—repeat, do not—want any trouble to come from this."

"You have a business in Bangkok. We could send her there." Vasily said.

Pavel was impressed. "That's perfect. She'll blend in. Make sure you don't lose track of her, though, in case she can be a bargaining chip down the road. Oh, and Vasily? I don't want you or your goons laying a hand on her before you send her off. I mean it. Your guys do not know the meaning of the word restraint."

"Plenty of others gonna lay hands on her where she's going,"

"Yeah, well, most of them don't do so many things that leave marks." His boss glared at him. "I mean it, Vasily. Get her to Bangkok where she can earn her keep and be out of our way. If we can use her, we'll bring her back."

"Yes boss."

Power did strange things to men, Vasily thought. There had been a time when Pavel would have okayed the kill *and* joined his men in the fun.

******

"Turn around and smile," Ariel said, tapping Teddie on the shoulder. They were at the town's beautiful sixty-foot-high Peace Pagoda, an obvious place for a great family picture. "That nice man offered to take it." Teddie turned, putting her arms around her sister and her mother as she posed with a happy grin.

Then she froze. The large, well-muscled man holding Ariel's camera was familiar, and he gave Teddie a little wave as he said, "Smile."

The other Zeitmans smiled and thanked the man, but Teddie stood, trying not to look terrified. Why would this guy not go away? It wasn't until she watched the man hand the camera back to Ariel and look deep into Ariel's eyes that Teddie's fear turned to anger.

She waited until her family moved on, then she strode up to him. "Don't you think of hurting my sister."

"I would never hurt your sister," he replied. "I'm a Buddhist. I don't even hurt insects."

"Then why do you keep following my friends? Why were you looking at her like that?"

"This has gone too far," the man said when Teddie's mom turned around and saw her daughter separated from them and talking to a stranger.

"Teddie!" Her mother screamed it, and half the people at the Pagoda turned to stare. "Get over here now!" She said it the way she would have if Teddie had been three years old and running into the street. Teddie wouldn't have guessed she could be so embarrassed and so angry at the same time, but apparently she could.

She gave the man a glare. She gave her mom a glare.

"I've had it. I'm ready to get out of here."

******

Michelle ached everywhere. She was hungry and thirsty, and she could smell her own pee. Her hands were taped behind her back, and there was duct tape over her mouth. A tiny line of light along the floor showed she was in a closet. She was groggy, like she'd been running a fever for days. How long had she been here? She sat in the dark for a while, trying to piece together what she knew.

A man had bumped into her at the earring store. He'd been a little guy in a suit. She'd felt something like a bee sting and then her muscles had stopped working. He'd caught her as she fell and slapped something onto her head. A hat? A wig? A veil? She had no idea. She remembered him half walking and half dragging her out the front door of the mall. She remembered him saying "My sister feels ill" to someone.

Then she was sitting in the front passenger seat of a van, hearing the man mutter, "Come on, come out and look for your friend" for what seemed like hours. It couldn't have been hours. After a while the van moved and Michelle's arm worked well enough to reach for the door to try to open it. She looked up and saw Teddie's horrified face not ten feet from her window, and heard her friend yell. Then there was another bee sting. She'd woken up here.

She ran over the facts six or seven times in her mind, looking for anything she missed. The better to help her escape when she had the chance. The better to keep herself calm now.

The closet door finally opened, and a new creepy man stared down at her. He shook his head and said something in a language Michelle didn't understand. It seemed to be an expression of regret.

Her insides went to ice. Did he find it regrettable that he had to kill her? But he only reached out towards her with a syringe, and the bee stung again. It was all she remembered for long while.

******

Acting on impulse has its charms, but December is a poor time to leave the shelter of a monastery in Bhutan and head off into the unknown. Jampa had not gotten far before a winter storm halted his travels and he was forced to seek shelter. The building high up on the cliff appeared to be another monastery, and he was hopeful he could undo the consequences of this poorly conceived plan by wintering with another group. Unfortunately, that was not to be.

Although they are rarer, women have their orders in the Buddhist world, and by tradition their convents do not welcome men. Understandably. In fact, had the weather not been life threatening, Jampa would have been offered a bit of food and water to consume outside of the convent walls and then asked, with kindness, to move along.

Under the circumstances, however, the nuns were willing to be more flexible. They offered him shelter in their small barn, providing blankets and food along with instructions to knock if he needed anything more. He was welcome to stay until the storm passed, and then they wished him safe journey.

As he settled in, Jampa realized he'd seen this particular convent before. His second body usually went where it pleased, playing and exploring. It occasionally went where it was called by his only true friend, Noom. His previous visit to this convent had been the sole exception. The Western girl, the one learning how to use her second body, had been here. She'd wanted to show them she could do a proper cartwheel, so he and Noom answered her call and came to watch.

Why in the world was the Western girl at a convent in Bhutan? Jampa didn't think he traveled over oceans in his second body. The monks had taught him geography. Even Noom, when she called him, didn't seem to be half a world away. Why had the girl been here?

Curious, Jampa waited until the next morning. Then he made his way through the lightly falling snow and knocked on the convent door.

"Yes?" The older nun didn't seem happy the young monk had accepted the offer to knock if he needed anything.

"I hope to leave tomorrow if the snow stops," he said, thinking that would please her. It did. "Before I go, I must ask. Do you have a girl staying here from far away? Not a Buddhist? Not from Bhutan? I seek her with a personal message. May I deliver it, if she is here? It will only take a moment."

The old nun looked dubious. "We have such a young woman. I'll see if she wishes to speak with you."

Jampa had no idea what he could possibly say to the Western girl who had a second body like his own, particularly under the watchful eye of this dour nun. He tried to bring the English the monks had taught him into the front of his mind and to think of something to say in it.

But when the nun came back, the young woman following her was someone Jampa had never seen before. She was a girl from India, with bright, intelligent eyes, who gave him a smile when she saw him.

"I'm so glad you came for me. Does my family wish for me to go with you?" she asked. The nun raised an eyebrow. Jampa saw the joy in the young woman's eyes. Perhaps he should keep options open until he learned more.

"Possibly, Miss." He turned to the nun respectfully. "I know this is irregular, but I have been asked to, uh, escort this woman safely to her family, if it happens she is ready to leave and if she wishes to go with me."

The nun was dour, but she wasn't stupid. "I don't think so. This girl should not be traveling on foot this time of year. She is ill prepared, and you seem a doubtful escort at best. Stay in the barn through tomorrow, until the weather improves, and give me a chance to learn more."

"Of course. May the girl and I speak?"

The nun pursed her lips. "Very well. Usha, you may walk with the boy to the front of the barn."

Usha had trouble containing her delight. Once they were outside they spoke at once. "Who are you?"

"I was looking for someone I met," Jampa said. "A girl from Europe I think. She was in this area."

"Oh." Usha looked disappointed. "I hoped my friends had somehow sent you. Why did you say you'd come for me?"

Good question. Particularly as I'm soon to take a vow to never lie.

"I guess you seemed so hopeful. I wanted to leave the door open for me to help you. If I said I didn't know who you were, they'd hardly let me do that."

Usha laughed, and Jampa liked the sound of her joy. "Perhaps your harmless deception will serve us both well. You should stay and enjoy the warmth of the barn until the weather improves. Who knows? Maybe you are the friend sent to escort me, but neither of us knows it yet."

"Maybe," Jampa said. "I'm willing to give it time and find out."

******

Teddie's mom invited Amy to join them for their Christmas feast. When Amy declined, Lola responded with, "Of course you have other plans. What was I thinking?"

"No, I don't. I appreciate your kindness, but I don't celebrate Christmas."

"Oh." Lola took a guess. "You're Jewish?"

"Yes. Christmas isn't one of my traditions."

"Would you join us for a meal then?" Teddie's dad asked.

They met at the best restaurant they could find. With the five beautiful Kanchenjunga peaks sparkling in the background, Alex raised his glass for a toast.

"Merry Christmas and Happy, uh, happy every holiday. Here's to…what the hell?" Alex's gaze shifted to two men at another table and his mouth dropped open.

"That's an odd toast, dad," Ariel laughed. She followed her dad's line of sight, as did the rest of the party.

"No!" Both Teddie and Amy said it in unison as they saw Alex looking at an all-too-familiar large muscular man sitting at a nearby table with another man. Each wondered how Alex recognized this person they'd come to fear.

"What's he doing here?" Alex said. Zane and Ariel both gave their dad puzzled looks, while Lola got up out of her chair and squealed with delight.

"Olumiji!"

The second person, a tall, thin black man, got up out of his seat and was moving to greet Lola while Alex watched him with mixed emotions. Lola ran to Olumiji and gave him a warm hug. "What are you doing in Darjeeling? Why didn't you tell me you were coming?"

"I couldn't Lola. I'm sorry. I had to talk to my friend Lhatu here first. Now we need to talk to you about your daughter. I'm so sorry to interrupt your feast, but I'm only in town for a couple of hours and this is important. It's about the missing girl Michelle. Would you, your husband and Teddie join the two of us in my car so we can talk privately?"

"Uh, sure. Of course we can. Let me have a couple of minutes to explain to my family," Lola said.

"Let's meet outside in five minutes."

Lola looked at her children and wondered where to start. They were preoccupied by something altogether different. Zane and Ariel were nudging each other, and looking at their younger sister and laughing.

"Let's see. Who was it who was complaining last year when we had to eat our Christmas dinner before breakfast in order to get Dad on a plane to Belize?" Zane said.

"Surely not the same person who was complaining the year before when we ate Christmas dinner late at night because we had to pick up mom at the airport?" Ariel replied shaking her head.

Teddie wouldn't take the bait. She was the one who'd complained both times, of course, but this was more than an interruption, and it wasn't funny. Her mother, her super-safety-conscious mother, was asking her to go get into a car with a known kidnapper after her own best friend had been kidnapped. As Olumiji and his nefarious companion walked outside, she tried to tell her mother so.

"Teddie. I would trust my friend Olumiji with my life. Actually, I have trusted him with my life. You're in no danger, I promise you."

"They have a video of the other guy kidnapping a girl, mom. Amy says he kept showing up at a hotel in another town with, like, a twelve-year-old girl. This man is around a lot when bad things happen. We saw him watching Usha and Michelle. You've lost your mind."

Amy chimed in. "Why not hold the conversation here? If you want privacy, we'll move to another table."

"Good plan. Teddie will feel better." She turned to her daughter. "We'll talk here, honey. Everything will be fine. You'll see."

Teddie would realize later that her mother never got out of her chair to tell Olumiji of the change in plans. Rather, he and the other man came back inside and waited while Amy, Ariel and Zane grabbed their wine and appetizers, preparing to scrunch together at the men's small two-top. Zane gave her a hug as they left.

"Don't worry about it, Teddie. We all get to screw up Christmas dinner once."

"Thanks Zane."

Amy whispered to her as she walked by. "Be open, Teddie. Sometimes partial knowledge is worse than none."

"Okay." Teddie nodded.

Then her mother's friend Olumiji and the dreaded muscleman sat down with them. Teddie couldn't help thinking her life would never be the same after this conversation.

December 2011

16. Recalibrating

Was it possible her mother was crazy? Could she have somehow suckered her otherwise sane husband into believing this story? Maybe love could do that; Teddie wasn't sure.

Watching her dad, she *was* sure he was convinced Teddie's mother was a telepath, and a good one. It tied into the time she spent with these Nigerians and the canoe accident when she'd almost drowned. To be honest, as Teddie sat in the restaurant that Christmas day, she felt too lightheaded to concentrate on most of her mother's story.

"I know you don't believe me, but honey, it's important you pay attention," her mother begged while Teddie picked at her food. As Teddie tried to listen, her mother explained she'd become friends with other telepaths who'd helped her develop her talents. She never intended to tell her kids about this, until her good friend, teacher and über-telepath Olumiji had shown up in Darjeeling during their Christmas dinner.

The woman was sincere. What choice did Teddie have but to think her mother could be telling the truth?

Then Olumiji told Teddie how he worked with hundreds of telepaths and kept track of thousands of potential ones worldwide. His ancient group had its roots in Bhutan, and the organization's modern name in English was simply "one"—spelled x^0. Her mother was a card-carrying member.

Then Lhatu began his own explanation, talking to Teddie in a soothing voice as he tried to erase her fears of him. He was not a telepath or a member of this x^0. He identified himself as the heir-apparent to the leadership of a much smaller sister organization originating out of Bhutan as well. His people, whom he called travelers, were more rare than telepaths and they had a skill all their own.

Only it wasn't "they" Teddie noticed. The pronoun he used was "we." We have a skill all our own. Later Teddie would realized this was the point at which she accepted it as true, because Lhatu understood exactly what she did and how it worked.

She felt relieved as she listened to Lhatu, and the light-headed feeling receded. It was going to be okay. Maybe her mother wasn't crazy and neither was she.

Lhatu explained how one of his duties was to seek out new travelers in the region who were attempting to come to terms with their abilities, somewhat like what Olumiji did with telepaths. It was Lhatu's responsibility to offer information and training to help young people. Unlike telepathy, which could show up at any time during a person's life, the ability to travel in what Lhatu referred to as a "spirit body" usually developed in young people, in the first few years after puberty. It caused caused a good bit of anguish when it did.

"I've been watching you, not your friends," he said. "You're becoming adept, spurred on, I think, by your own homesickness and the traumatic events around you. I wanted to come forth and help you months ago, but I'm not so used to Western girls, with their outward confidence and yet deep inner fears of strangers. I was checking on you, trying to be careful, considering if you needed my help and the best way to approach you. I only managed to scare you, and for that I'm sorry."

Olumiji took over. He said he was certain both Usha and Michelle needed to be rescued from dire situations they were unlikely to escape from on their own. Sadly, telepathic abilities were not well suited to tracking criminals or missing people, although in this case he intended to try.

Traveling, however, was often successful at locating someone, but only when done by someone else who was linked emotionally to the missing person. The traveler needed to be well trained, and it was helpful to be physically near the person being sought, as traveling had a spatial component to it.

"That's why modern travelers call our group 'c cubed,' instead of using its ancient Sanskrit name. You'd pronounce that as *Ju vaa laa lay ah*, and it means the abode of light. Most of us are well grounded in modern physics, and c represents light to us, as well as its speed, of course. To us, Jvalalaya is also c^3."

Teddie's parents weren't listening to what the name c^3 meant. Both of their faces had gone pale. They knew what Olumiji was going to ask next.

"Absolutely not," her dad said.

"I can vouch for her safety," Lhatu replied.

"As can I," Olumiji added. "I am prepared to put phenomenal resources on protecting your child. She'll be fine. However, without her, we have little hope for saving the other two young women. With her, my friend Lhatu is sure he can find and rescue both girls."

Olumiji looked down like he was trying to decide whether to say more. "Right now, I can't find Usha at all. Therefore, I believe she is safe at the moment, doesn't wish to be found, and doesn't know the danger she is in. I *have* found Michelle."

"What?" Teddie's dad gasped. "Let's go get her now."

Olumiji shook his head with a sad smile. "That's the problem with telepathy. I can only know what she knows. She is bound and gagged in a closet. She has no idea where. She hasn't been seriously harmed and isn't in immediate danger, but she's weak and she's terrified. That's all she knows."

A memory of wanting to help someone scared and powerless washed over Teddie and she did something she could never have imagined.

"I'll stay." She said it thinking of Michelle, helpless and scared. She said it like she knew what she was doing,

"What?" her dad said.

"No, sweetie," her mother intervened more softly. "There are other ways. These two men are talented. They can do this without you."

Lhatu looked at Teddie with admiration.

"No, we can't, and I think she understands enough about her gift already to know that." Then to Teddie he added, "So you must go back to the school, continue on with your studies as normal. Arouse no suspicions; say you are staying because you are clinging to hopes Michelle will be found and you want to be here for her when she is."

Lhatu eyed both of the parents before he looked right at Teddie and went on. "I know you want to save your friends now, before further harm or trauma comes to them, but this can't be done fast. I'll need to set other parts in motion, and will be back in a few days. Your training will start then. Be patient."

"How long would she need to stay here?" Teddie's mom asked.

"I won't mislead you. It could be weeks or even months," Lhatu answered. "You, her parents, must stay strong, too. She won't be asked to do anything before she's ready. For this you have my word."

Later Teddie replayed the Christmas dinner over and over in her mind, trying to make more sense of it. Had she been a fool to agree to stay? She shook her head. No matter how many times she replayed the scene, she couldn't imagine it ending any other way.

Teddie's family headed home a few days later without her. Before leaving, her mother explained to Teddie why she would need to meet and spend a few hours with the five telepaths who would join Olumiji in taking shifts monitoring her well-being, day and night.

"They can do a better job if they know you," her mother said. "I give you my word, they'll never intrude into your private thoughts; they'll only monitor you for fear. If something scares you, they'll listen. If it seems serious, they'll call the others. If the group deems you're in trouble," and at this possibility Teddie could see the distress in her mother's eyes, "then Lhatu has people in place to respond instantly. They've asked me not to be part of this, because I'm too emotionally involved to react rationally, and that's true. Olumiji and my close friend from Nigeria, Somadina, will lead the effort. Please be open to them and the four others and let them help you."

Teddie's dad gave her a long hug but said little. Zane seemed baffled by the half-baked explanations he was getting for her remaining in India. Ariel was mostly silent, and she grew more aloof than usual. Teddie hoped her big sister wasn't hiding something, too.

As soon as she was alone, Darjeeling turned overcast and cold. The school accepted her back with little question, and she spent most of her time in her room by herself, waiting for the rest of the students to come back from break.

The only interesting event occurred on New Year's Day, when an uneasy Teddie found herself spending the afternoon drinking tea and eating cookies at the spacious home of an elderly couple from Darjeeling named Mr. and Mrs. Dutta. As the two aging telepaths finished each other's sentences, Teddie couldn't help smiling.

Joining them was a housewife who had driven up from Kolkata, and who insisted on holding Teddie's hand for a long while after they were introduced, explaining to Teddie how the prolonged contact improved her ability to link with a stranger.

The other person there was a beautiful young Nigerian woman with her one-year-old daughter. Olumiji had gone to great pains to bring the woman from her small village, and she hugged Teddie long and hard like she knew her.

"Your mother is an incredible woman," Somadina said. Teddie gave her a dubious look.

"I understand," the Nigerian laughed. "Kids don't appreciate what their parents have done. It's the way of the world. But your mother risked her life to save my sister, and I want you to know I would do anything to protect you."

"She did what?" Teddie had trouble imagining a scenario in which her mother saved anyone's life, and she started to think there must be more to this story of her mother's telepathy than she'd been told.

"I thought there were going to be six of you watching over me," she asked, looking around at the four others in the room. Then she glanced at the little girl tottering on the edge of the coffee table considering taking a step, perhaps her first.

"She's not a telepath, too, is she?" Teddie asked Somadina.

"Oh, heavens no," Somadina laughed. "She could develop it someday. There is a mildly genetic component, we think, but it's not strong. Odds are she'll be normal."

"Do you think maybe she'll be a traveler like me?"

"I'd be delighted if she was."

Then Teddie noticed Mrs. Dutta was fooling around with the computer on the dining room table and had stepped back in satisfaction. She saw the face of a nervous young man on the screen, his head wrapped in bandages.

"This is Tariq," Mrs. Dutta explained. "He's from Pakistan, and he'll be your other guard. He couldn't travel here today, but we're going to include him as best we can by video-conference."

Teddie noticed that in spite of the injuries the boy was quite attractive, and the idea of having him watching her at random times without her being aware of it made her uncomfortable. She motioned to Somadina. "Can we speak privately in another room?"

Once the two of them were in the kitchen, Somadina said "No one will intrude on our thoughts here. Is there a problem with Tariq?"

Teddie hesitated. She felt kind of silly.

"I get it," Somadina said. "No telepathy needed. He's cute, isn't he?"

"Yeah," Teddie giggled a little. "Trust me, I've got nothing against attractive boys, but the idea of having one hover inside my head when I can't even tell he's there, well…"

Somadina nodded. "I told Olumiji this might happen. Occasionally, there are things the man does not get. Look Teddie, Tariq got included for two reasons. One, he's bedridden and he will be for weeks, if not months. We're all in pretty close time zones, and we're going to be taking shifts. We need people who can focus on you reliably in the middle of the day and Tariq qualifies."

"Aren't there any ugly old telepaths in nearby hospitals?" Teddie asked. Somadina laughed.

"He begged for this chance to help, Teddie." Seeing the look on Teddie's face, Somadina added "Not because of you. Because of how he got injured."

"Oh." Teddie felt bad she hadn't even wondered what had happened to the boy. "How'd he get hurt?"

"Defending his sister. Unsuccessfully. It was five against the two of them and the other guys had bats. His sister didn't live through the ordeal. Olumiji thought the chance to do some good might help Tariq heal. Only if you're willing, that is. If you're not, we'll replace him."

Teddie rolled her eyes. "No, it's okay. Given the situation, I'll deal with it."

Somadina gave Teddie's arm a squeeze as they walked back into the living room.

The hosts passed out more tea and cookies, and then Somadina led the group in asking Teddie questions, most of which had to do with how she felt about this or that.

"We're trying to calibrate your feelings," she explained. "I don't want to upset you, but if we can get a sense of anger and fear and sadness from you, as well as happiness, we can better look out for you."

So Teddie described how she felt about capital punishment and Broadway musicals, about gang warfare and birthday parties and extreme poverty. After two hours she felt drained and she noticed all five of the others were nodding.

"You are a wonderful young woman, with a warm and caring heart," Somadina said, "and I think we have all we need. Teddie, from this point forward, you won't know we're there with you, because you don't have the gift of hearing us. But at least one of us will always be attuned to you while we keep a respectful distance from your inner thoughts. If you call to us and ask us to pay attention, we will. All six of us are capable of sensing your emotions and, to some extent, framing those feelings into words. We may not get specifics, but we'll get enough to find a way to help you almost immediately. So," and here she smiled a bit, "don't hesitate to call. Okay?"

"Okay."

Teddie returned to her dorm, and true to Somadina's word, she had no sense anyone was watching out for her. She considered calling for help to see if it would work, but decided false alarms were probably a bad idea.

******

Vanida managed some days better than others, and over time she found more ways to cope. The rowdy oil workers were not typical, luckily. Many of the men, and even women and couples, who came to watch her write were merely curious. Sometimes shy. Often ashamed to find themselves there. Vanida learned that a bit of warmth put people at ease, and with their ease came tips. She began to work the market well.

Even then, these were not the grand get-rich tips Noi and Pim led her to expect. Nonetheless, it was money of her own. She noticed that Khae, the owner of both her and the bar, watched her tips closely. Vanida was pretty sure if she started to make more, she'd owe the bar a cut. So she kept her act short and friendly. She wrote notes like, "don't ask me where I got this," that brought chuckles from everyone, and she pocketed her money fast and watched it well.

None of the men who came in were anything like the men she'd read about in the wonderful novels Noi gave her; those troubled and mysterious men tormented by dark secrets, yearning for the right woman to bring out the gentle lover in them with her beauty and her strong spirit. No, the ones who picked the girls by number were usually drunk silly men, insecure and often mean. Vanida worked hard at being invisible to them, avoiding eye contact and blending into the shadows.

On the rare times a man chose her, she offered the work to one of the other girls. There was always someone who wanted the money, and bikinis were easy to swap. Not once did a man who picked Vanida complain that he didn't get the girl he selected. Either the men didn't notice, or didn't care.

Khae, however, knew what was happening, and she took Vanida aside. Khae spoke English with Vanida, and Vanida suspected the woman was trying to teach her to speak better.

"You don't like to earn extra money?" she asked.

"I'd rather not," Vanida answered honestly.

"Okay." Khae nodded. "But if a man complains he picked you, you have to go with him."

"I know."

"And if we run out of girls, you have to work," Khae added.

"I know."

"Shouldn't happen though," Khae said. "Got a whole truck full of new girls coming next week. They don't know pussy tricks; they just dance and screw. So I gotta keep you talented ones happy." She gave Vanida a big half-toothless grin. "You work the audience well. I like you now."

Vanida decided that was as much praise as she was going to get in this business.

******

It was a welcome sound when her door burst open the evening before classes started and a familiar voice yelled "Teddie!" In came a laughing Haley, with snowflakes on her parka.

"What are you doing here?"

"Providing companionship to a friend. Looking for my lost buddies." Haley was grinning. "Doing what I think is best."

"You escaped?" Teddie laughed.

"No, I acted like an adult and promised to help my parents raise the money it would take to send me back here. I explained that if I was going to make a dangerous climb in a few months, I needed to be here for lots of reasons. They listened. They really listened to what I wanted, and they worked with me on this."

"Why didn't you tell me you were coming?"

Haley fidgeted with her gloves. "I was worried about you when you wrote that you were staying on. It didn't sound like you were in a good place, you know, emotionally. I didn't want make things worse by telling you I was coming and then have it fall through. It came together so fast at the end and bam, I was on the plane. So I decided to surprise you."

Teddie gave her a look of thanks. "I could use a roommate. I'm really glad you're here."

As she said it, the new phone Lhatu gave her that the school allowed her to keep under the circumstances, chirped for the first time. She picked it up. The text was from an unknown number and said, "We start tomorrow."

January 2012

17. Beginning

Olumiji had two specialties within x^0. One was helping mature individuals who found themselves developing telepathic abilities later in life. Often such skills came on surprisingly fast, yet an older mind, set in its ways, struggled with how to cope. Olumiji would arrive to offer aid.

His other specialty involved search and rescue. Telepathy was more of an ability to sense emotions than it was a skill at reading minds, and as such, it was a poor tool for locating confused and distracted humans at a distance. However, those trapped by natural disasters tended to be close at hand and to broadcast mental pleas for help. This made them easy for a telepath to find.

Rescue workers the world over had come to know Olumiji as the tall, thin Nigerian man who showed up after earthquakes, mudslides and tsunamis to offer assistance, and who had an uncanny ability to find barely alive souls in the wreckage. He stayed out of their way and asked for nothing in return, so most wrote him off as a harmless oddball. Some speculated he lost a loved one in a natural disaster and in a way, they were right. Olumiji had never lost anyone, but he'd heard the cries of the desperate so often and so well in his own head that deep in his heart he felt connected to every human who had ever died yearning to be found.

He had one chink in his armor and he knew it. It was born of guilt. As a male in his home country, he'd grown up accepting the many casual ways young women were forced to have sex. From arranged marriages to gang rapes, from bizarre bridal customs to forced prostitution, the horror of lacking ownership of one's own body escaped him until his telepathy let him discover it. Then, he was outraged by the day-to-day fears endured by more than half of his fellow humans.

Don't dress that way. Don't go out at night. Don't talk to him. Don't meet his eyes. Any of it can earn you pain and humiliation and more fear, and people will tell you it was your own fault. Olumiji had been astounded.

For all the people he had calmly rescued and helped since, every time a case came his way where a young woman was put at greater risk, merely because she possessed a vagina, or worse yet, a hymen, he felt a deep burning anger at a world that called the situation unavoidable.

"No," he wanted to scream. "This is not unavoidable. We're better than that. We have to be."

He supposed this was part of why he had made the rescue of these two lone young women such a high priority. He knew that no other crime against the emotional well-being of humans was perpetuated with such frightening regularity. He couldn't begin to stop all of it. But these two girls? He would, by all the gods who were worshipped on this sorry planet, find a way to help them.

******

Amy and Lhatu eyed each other as they sat at opposite ends of Amy's small living room. Teddie sat awkwardly on the couch in the middle. It was Lhatu who'd suggested this first meeting take place in a home of someone Teddie trusted.

Amy was protective about her private life, as most social workers were. She'd never invited the girls over to her apartment, and probably never would have. She certainly didn't want Lhatu there, but she recognized she was the only friendly face Teddie had in Darjeeling with a living room to offer.

"I still don't get why you spend so much time lurking around young girls," Amy said as she served tea, not exactly starting the conversation out on a good note.

"I work with training young people. Turns out half of them are female. I observe, recruit, and provide help. That necessitates some lurking." Lhatu came across with an odd mixture of defensiveness and amusement.

"It was me he was watching," Teddie said, hoping to diffuse the tension. "I have a skill set he works with. He wasn't interested in Michelle or Usha at all."

Amy looked at Teddie, then turned back to Lhatu.

"I have you on tape kidnapping a young girl from this region," she said.

"You do."

"You don't deny it?" Amy spat the words back at him.

"To the contrary, I'm proud of it." He responded with similar venom creeping into his voice. "You have no idea what I rescued that child from or how she begged my organization for help. Happy homes are not always what they seem."

"Her parents were so upset when she was taken!" Amy was outraged. "They love her and they are still working with me to hunt for her."

"No, her parents miss abusing her and are worried she'll tell her story to someone and be believed. They are afraid their methods of raising their only child might be misunderstood. Both her mother and father found a hundred different horrible and creative ways to discipline her ever since she could cry and beg for mercy. They enjoyed her tears and pleas, and later they would bond sexually, each aroused by their cruelty to her. She didn't even know her life was unusual until she got older. She's safe now, and she has no desire to speak to either of them again."

"How would you even know about something like this?" Amy asked, curiosity beginning to mix in with her indignation.

"She found me, and I understood she needed help."

"Why in the world would she come to you?"

"Because at that moment, I was the only human around who could see her."

Lhatu swallowed hard. He had known before he ever agreed to do this that the next few sentences would be the most difficult part.

"Let me back up. Please. Amy, you see the world from inside you, so to speak. Our consciousness comes from inside of our bodies, inside of our brains. Some people imagine they leave their bodies and wander off while they sleep or even as they go into a trance."

"Sure," Amy said. "Astral projection. I've heard of it. You think it's impossible?"

"No, I'm saying in most cases the person is experiencing a lucid dream, or a creative daydream—harmless, maybe even illuminating. I've no quarrel with this, it just doesn't involve really leaving their bodies in, well, in the way that I do."

"Oh." The sarcasm was back. "So most other people can't do this, but you can."

"Yes." Lhatu said without embarrassment or pride. "I've been trained to do it since birth. I work for the people who taught me. I serve as their chief scout and trainer."

"Is this shadowy organization, known for sneaking around watching kids, run by a crime organization by any chance?" Amy asked.

"No. It's a sort of informal monarchy run by my grandmother."

"Oh." Amy didn't know what to say.

"Look, there aren't a lot of people who can do this," Lhatu said. "It's not as common as, say, telepathy, which, of course, isn't all that common either. Most travelers—we refer to it as traveling—most travelers start to have out-of-body experiences in their teens. Often some trauma encourages this ability. Feeling powerless, being powerless, needing to escape and having no other means to do so can set this ability in motion if the young person is prone to it to begin with."

Lhatu gave Amy a long hard look. "It shouldn't surprise you that more females develop this ability than males. Not that there aren't plenty of young males in this world trapped in awful situations, too. Obviously, most young people can't do this, no matter how desperate they become. Like everything else human, this ability seems to come from a combination of genes, environment and the very essence of the person themselves."

Lhatu turned to Teddie. "I'm right, aren't I?"

Teddie looked down embarrassed, and Amy got it.

"Teddie? Is that what this is all about? Your dreams? Seeing Usha at the bus station leaving for Gangtok? Seeing her flee into Bhutan? Now you think this all is real?" Amy asked.

"I guess so," Teddie said. "At least this good friend of my mom's thinks it's real because Lhatu told him so, and now I'm supposed to be trained so I can help them find Michelle and Usha.

I'm scared, Amy." The words popped out of Teddie's mouth before she could call them back. "I'm not sure I want to learn how to be a freak." She gave Lhatu a bit of an apologetic smile. "No offense."

"None taken," he said. "This is your choice, Teddie, and it will continue to be so. You may quit or pause the training any time." Then he added with his own small smile "We're all kind of freaks in our own way, you know? This will just make you a more talented freak."

"Talented freak. I kind of like that." Teddie smiled back more confidently.

For the sake of her young friend, Amy decided to put her own skepticism on hold. "I can attend this training with you, Teddie, at least until you get comfortable."

"We don't usually do that." Lhatu hesitated. The firm look of protectiveness on Amy's face reminded him there were exceptions to every rule. "If you'd be willing to let us use your apartment for the initial work, of course you could be present."

Another piece of the puzzle suddenly made sense to Amy. "So that's why you rented hotel rooms with the young girl in Jakarta?"

Lhatu nodded. "The hotel had their own theories, and every time we showed up I got chuckles and nudges that made me wince. But yes. Her name was Doddy, she was fourteen, and I had no other place to train her. This has happened more than once. Using your apartment would be a vast improvement."

"Consider it done."

"We'll do some initial work tonight, so Teddie has things to practice. I have to return home tomorrow." Lhatu paused when he saw the look of impatience on Teddie's face. "I promise it's only for a couple of days and when I come back I'll have lodging and transportation set up. Teddie, we'll meet and work every other night then until you're ready. Can you be patient for a couple of days longer?"

The girl nodded. "Sure. I'm not going anywhere."

Amy looked at Teddie. Was her young friend capable of out-of-body experiences? Could Lhatu do what he claimed? What if he was a fraud? That was a frightening concept. What if he wasn't a fraud? Amy sighed. That was even more frightening.

******

Vanida couldn't wait for the truck full of new girls to arrive. During the holidays the bars of the Patpong district of Bangkok had overflowed with tourists. Twice Khae had run out of girls to service the men who wished to celebrate the feast of Christ's birth by screwing a Thai whore.

The first time Vanida pleaded an upset stomach, but the second time she knew she had do her part. She sought out the drunkest customer she could find and made eyes at him. When he pointed to her and slurred out her number, Khae nodded at her and Vanida took the man upstairs.

She'd calculated well. After convincing him to let her rub his feet for a few minutes to heighten his pleasure, he fell asleep on the bed with a loud snore. Vanida curled up next to him on the cot, and took a short nap too. She'd tell him later how great he'd been. The other girls told her that was what all the men wanted to hear.

******

Darjeeling stayed dreary and cold as school started, and for days on end the beautiful mountains couldn't be seen. Teddie spent a lot of time avoiding other students so she wouldn't have to answer questions about Michelle. However, her dorm room was not the refuge she'd have liked.

Haley spent most her free time in the room too, using the impressive array of workout equipment her father had sent with her. She had weights and ab straps, rotating push-up bars and some sort of cardio jump device. She used them all like her life depended on it and Teddie supposed it kind of did. The net result was the room was filled with Haley's grunts and groans, and was starting to smell like a locker room. Teddie went out and bought fruit-scented air freshener.

She tried doing the exercises Lhatu had left with her, but compared with Haley's workout, they just seemed silly. Lhatu's few days dragged on to many, and Teddie spent more time curled up under the covers. She wanted to go home. She was supposed to be home. Why was she wasting her time here?

******

Jeet had looked over his shoulder since that horrible day in September when Usha disappeared from school. Who'd have thought his niece would take off on her own like that? He knew he should have waited before using the money to pay off the credit card debts, but those banks and their interest rates scared him.

Once the girl was located in Gangtok, he breathed a sigh of relief. The goods would be delivered. How could anyone have guessed she'd run away a second time and hide so well?

Then, of course, there was that meddlesome American woman who'd put Ashmita and her children somewhere Jeet couldn't find. He'd been so certain Ashmita would lead him to Usha. Now he couldn't even find Ashmita. And, they were right back up to their limits on the damn credit cards, so it had been for nothing.

"But these little statues are perfect in our living room, Jeet. Look how well they match the carpet?" His wife was home with her most recent purchase. As she began to arrange the statues, she pointed to the ornate Persian rug they complimented. Her face turned pale as soon as she saw the blood on the carpet.

"Who made this mess?"

Jeet didn't say a word, but held out his left hand to show the bandaged stub where his little finger had been. Blood was still seeping through the bandage.

"Oh my God. You couldn't have put a better rag around it?"

Then, as the situation began to sink in, "Was this the work of the man you sold Usha to?"

"No, this was done by the man he sold her to." Riddhi looked at Jeet and realized her husband was in shock. "Paying me before the girl was in his possession was a clerical error," Jeet said, a dull tone in his voice. "Nandi, the middleman, is a professional procurer. He's already paid this horrible man back with interest to avoid trouble. This disciplinary action wasn't about money, I was told, but about thwarted expectations."

Riddhi sat down and averted her eyes, disgusted and terrified. "Will this man who bought Usha be back?"

"I don't think so. He told me he'd happily cut off a finger a week if he thought I could find the girl, but he knew I couldn't and there was no point in making me fingerless. He wanted me to remember, going forward, not to make promises I couldn't keep." Jeet looked down at his hand.

"What about this Nandi man who paid him back? Is he going to show up with a knife as well?"

"He dropped by this morning," Jeet said. "He has influential friends, and he is quite interested in getting his money back. We discussed options."

"Could I do anything to help?"

Her husband nodded. "You can get the maid to clean the blood out of the carpet. It will bring a higher price if it's clean. Then, you can fire the maid. But first, drive me to the hospital."

******

Locating the feelings of a distant unknown person is impossible, so it didn't surprise Olumiji that his searches for Usha only brought back a sort of ambient white noise. However, once a telepath does forge a link, it becomes easier to find the person again. Olumiji suspected his ability to locate Michelle, as she sat bound in a closest on Christmas day, had been aided by Teddie's close emotional connection to her friend, and by Lola's acquaintance with the girl and adeptness with telepathy. In fact, Lola would probably have an easier time tracking Michelle than Olumiji would, and they both knew it.

Yet, they had a silent understanding that this would be a bad idea. It was important Lola remain supportive of her own daughter's efforts, and calm would be nearly impossible if Lola allowed herself to be part of whatever hardships and horrors might be forced upon Michelle.

So along with his duties of monitoring Teddie, Olumiji made a daily effort to reach out to Michelle to see if he could learn anything helpful. He wished the girl could hear him in her own head, so he could reassure her. However, Michelle had no nascent telepathic abilities and remained deaf to Olumiji's presence.

Worse yet, while all humans project emotions, Michelle was a self-contained young woman who held her feelings in check. In a world full of people transmitting screams about how they felt, Michelle barely whispered. So not only could she not hear Olumiji, but he could barely hear her either. When he got nothing at all, he assumed she was unconscious. Many days he picked up nothing, and other days he could only sense her fear.

Finally, he got that her situation improved. She was still held captive, but she was no longer restrained or heavily drugged, and food, water and toilet facilities were provided.

The most noteworthy event was when Michelle realized her captors didn't see her as human. Olumiji was present in Michelle's mind when she realized she was a commodity, a product being kept in a warehouse until it could be transported to market and sold.

Michelle was down-to-earth about the realization, thinking that understanding the perspective of her captors was useful. Listening to her clear-headed evaluation broke Olumiji's heart, but also gave him hope this girl could survive what lay ahead.

January 2012

18. Learning

Once they began, the practice sessions in Amy's living room were as tedious as Teddie feared. Lhatu had her tensing and relaxing muscles and using imaginary hands to massage her own neck. She took endless deep breaths focusing on candles and her belly. Then she took endless more, focusing on the tip of her nose. It all seemed pointless. Amy watched over her, interrupting with tea or lemonade and intervening when she thought the session went on too long.

Teddie wasn't sure what contacts her mother's friend Olumiji had, but they were impressive. The normally protective Lord Peartree International Academy for Exceptional Students not only allowed her to keep and use the cell phone from Lhatu, they also granted her unlimited permission to leave campus with him or Amy any time of day or night.

Haley soon became suspicious. Her own extra-curricular activities with the mountaineering club were at a minimum until winter lifted. Of course she wondered what Teddie was up to when she disappeared every other night. Teddie considered making up a story, or maybe a half-truth, but the best choice seemed to be to bring Haley into the situation.

One evening in late January she told her roommate about her walking dreams and the interrupted Christmas dinner and the shadowy organization called c^3 that reached out to the rare young person as they developed this unusual gift.

Haley shook her head and laughed. “I knew there was something weird with you. So this out-of-body stuff is real, huh? And you can do it? Wow.”

“You don’t think I’m crazy?" Teddie was relieved but surprised. "You accept this more easily than I did.”

“I’m from Denver.” Haley shrugged. “I bet I heard more strange metaphysical claims growing up. After a while, you start to think, well, maybe. So, what are they teaching you? Do you think you can get good at it?”

“Right now I’m getting good at a lot of stupid relaxation exercises, but this guy Lhatu insists I have to learn this so I can control my abilities. I’ll learn anything, if it means I can help Michelle or Usha.” Then she had to ask. “It doesn’t creep you out now, sharing a room with me?”

“Are you kidding?” Haley seemed baffled by the question. “It’s cool to know how to do things. Who knows, maybe if I need help going up that mountain you can bop by in your spirit body and help out.”

“I’m too scared of heights for that. I’ll be ecstatic if I can find our friends.”

“So will I. Let me know if I can help in any way.”

******

Michelle knew she’d been moved after her capture because she had memories of lying in the trunk of a car. After that, she’d spent what seemed like weeks in a large closet, with leering, creepy men giving her food, water and bathroom breaks. Yet no one harmed her.

Then, she was transported a second time, again waking up groggy in the trunk of a car. When she regained consciousness, she was at some sort of warehouse. Every muscle in her body ached and she had a thirst for water she couldn’t quench. She was in a room with several other girls who’d arrived at the same meeting point. They were given food and permitted to stretch and bathe. She tried to communicate with the others, but they only gave her wary or fearful looks, and she heard no language that sounded familiar.

After two days at the warehouse the girls were forced to remove their clothes. Most cried in fear and embarrassment. Michelle hung towards the back and was relieved to see the girls were barely touched as they were sedated and loosely bound before being thrown in the back of a van. When her turn came, she tried to cry no more or less than the others. Her first rule, she decided, was to avoid suspicion.

Michelle's main memory of this leg of the trip was waking up each time the van stopped to hand money over to men with guns. She counted nine girls crowded together on the floor of the vehicle. The trip went on for days, broken up by short bathroom stops along the side of the empty road and small rations of water and rice cakes. Finally, they were allowed out of the van at a big barn-like structure in the middle of nowhere.

For the next few days they got to move about the large interior room, under the watchful eyes of the guards. Michelle tried to inconspicuously massage her aching muscles to regain some of her physical strength.

Here the girls had access to all the water they wanted, and Michelle drank her fill. She kicked herself when diarrhea hit on day two. Damn, she should have guessed. If her problem became obvious it would mark her as an outsider. Luckily a primitive outhouse provided some privacy, and her body helped by recovering before the problem was noticed.

The food handed out to them from a locked pantry was more plentiful and varied, and there was ample straw for the girls to sleep on. Michelle guessed this giant shed served as a frequent way station for human cargo. What a sad fate for a building, and yet compared to her previous couple of weeks, this place was like heaven. More vans of girls kept arriving.

Michelle kept to herself, fighting to stay strong and aware. She thought she knew what the future was going to bring, and she was determined to face it with all the intelligence and courage she could find. She had facts. She was capable of self-control. If she played her cards well she need not be a victim in the truest sense of the word.

She kept her eyes open for scraps of anything useful. A reasonable opportunity for escape would present itself sooner or later, and she would be as prepared as possible when it did.

******

Lhatu was pushing her to practice later than usual and Amy wasn't objecting. Teddie didn't think she couldn't do one more breathing exercise, so she got up out of her chair and turned around, only to see herself sleeping in her chair. Oh my.

She caught the sense of panic as it began and soothed it down, the way Lhatu taught her. She held still and focused. Then she turned towards Lhatu. He was giving her a wide grin and a slow wave from a translucent body hovering a couple of feet in the air over his own sleeping self. He pointed back to her body, the way a diving instructor might point a student in the direction they needed to go. She understood.

In order for her to remember these first voluntary out-of-body experiences, he said they had to be short. If she didn't bring back a memory, then it would be to her brain as if it had never happened.

Teddie took a second to enjoy the lightness of this body. Lhatu had gone to great pains to reassure her it wasn't a spirit, or a ghost, but a physical phenomenon having nothing to do with religion or death. It was Teddie's body on another plane of existence, a real plane consisting of electromagnetic energy. It coexisted with the heavy solid plane she normally inhabited.

Teddie saw Lhatu's warning look and stern gesture back to her sleeping body, and she nodded. This was all she would get for tonight. She willed herself back and then sat up in her chair with a squeal of delight.

"I did it. I did it."

"Teddie, you've done it the last three times we practiced. The first three times you wouldn't listen to me and went flitting around the room, then the memories were too long for you to bring back. Tonight, you did it and remembered it, and that's what counts. Do you know how to ride a bike?"

"Of course." Teddie thought everyone knew how to ride a bike.

"Do you remember the first time you went some distance by yourself and didn't fall over?" Teddie cringed at the memory. Ariel had defied her parents' instructions and tried to teach her eager little sister to ride, with a lot of scraped knees and tears ensuing. But yes, she'd learned to do it.

"It wasn't easy the second time, but it was easier than the first, right?" Lhatu asked. Teddie nodded.

"Well, that's tomorrow evening. A longer ride and an easier one."

Teddie was looking forward to it.

Lhatu and Amy drove her back to the dorm, just as they had picked her up earlier. Lhatu now insisted on accompanying her any time she left the school, and Amy usually insisted on riding along.

Teddie suspected Lhatu considered himself her bodyguard, and Amy had assigned herself the role of chaperone. It was helpful that Lhatu willingly accepted Amy as part of his security team, and Teddie was grateful to both for their concern.

******

Jampa spent the month of January sleeping in the barn at the convent and went out of his way to earn the grudging respect of the nuns. He performed menial chores made easier by his youth and size, and he asked for nothing in return other than his mid-day bit of rice, and the use of their well for water and their barn for shelter.

Usha was allowed to speak more with him, as long as they remained outdoors in sight of the nuns. It was now acknowledged that Jampa was a friend of Usha's family and Usha was making the difficult decision of whether she wished to remain at the convent or return to the life she'd fled. At least, the nuns assumed it was a difficult decision.

In truth, Usha longed to leave the austere quiet of the convent so much that she was willing to travel with any decent person who would take her along. Jampa easily exceeded her minimum requirements. He'd shown himself to be resourceful and his day-to-day actions were filled with the kindness instilled in him by the monks who raised him.

She was seeking a safe place to live where she could find a means to get by and a way to make contact with her family. He was on a quest of his own. He was seeking the only family he'd ever known, a sister he had vague memories of and who he was reluctant to discuss.

Usha was sure she and Jampa were meant to travel together. Once winter began to creep back up the mountain, Usha intended to inform the nuns of her reluctant decision to return to the secular world.

******

When the truck finally arrived, Vanida was dubious these reinforcements were going to be useful any time soon. The girls looked scared, disoriented and untrained, and they huddled together while Khae walked around making her selections. Vanida decided Khae must be a regular buyer, as the two men in the truck let her take her time. She poked at some of the girls with a stick and gauged their reactions. Vanida wondered if Khae was looking for the most docile, or for the more alert.

In the end Khae bought five new girls, all of whom seemed sluggish, like they would be easy to train. Vanida sighed. Too bad for the girls, but their compliance would make her own life easier. Then, as Khae turned away, Vanida smiled when she saw one of the new young women become more aware once she was no longer being watched by her new owner. Ah well. She might have a sister-in-spirit after all.

The girl noticed Vanida's attention and whispered to her. "You don't speak English, do you?"

"Yes. French. Japanese. I'm learning Russian now." Her Thai accent was heavy, but Vanida knew she spoke well enough to be understood.

The girl's eyes widened. "Where am I?"

What? She didn't even know where she was? Maybe this one wasn't so smart after all.

"Where do you think you are?"

"I was in India," the young woman replied.

Vanida had to laugh at her own ignorance. She had no idea they bothered to truck girls in from so far away. Why? There were plenty to be had in the countryside around Bangkok.

"Well, you're in Thailand now, sweetheart," Vanida said, adopting Khae's manner of speaking without even realizing it. "You belong to one of Patpong's best floor shows and brothels."

To the girl's credit she expressed neither surprise nor dismay. "That's what I expected." The girl hesitated like she was weighing her options while Khae continued to dicker with the two men about price. "What can you tell me about surviving here?"

Vanida didn't mean to be unkind, but taking care of Vanida was a full-time job. She didn't need a second one. "Not much, unless you know something useful for me."

"I can tell you a lot about Western men and the rest of the world," the girl said. "My name's Michelle, and I'm American."

American? Those people had resources. How had one of them ended up here? This could be useful.

"Okay, worldly Michelle. I know things about this place. You look Vietnamese. Let people think you are. You'll be safer that way."

"I'm trying hard not to get any special attention."

Vanida nodded her approval. "Smart. Don't talk much. I'll teach you some Vietnamese words."

"I already know some."

"Learn more," Vanida said. "I'll get Khae to let me train you. She's nervous when girls become friends, so I'll be rude to you around her. You be rude to me back. Okay?" Vanida smiled.

"Okay."

******

Pavel could be a patient man, and he knew how to put his personal desires on hold. Contrary to what he supposed many people thought, one did not rise to a position like his by being ruthless, or even ruthless and smart. Self-discipline was essential. Pavel had seen too many men brought down, not by the law or enemies, but by their own vices.

With his wife and children now back from Turkey and school in session, his life was back to its normal routine. This particular winter was more dreary and cold than usual, and his wife wanted a getaway to somewhere exotic. She had her sights set on Thailand next month. The nanny could watch the kids. How about a romantic week on the beach?

Pavel sighed. He'd be bored to tears in two days. However, his wife and children were useful, and they could cause problems if sufficiently alienated. Occasional humoring was a piece of necessary business.

He had financial concerns in Thailand. Perhaps he could settle his wife into a nice resort, head into Bangkok after a romantic couple of days, look after some business, and return before their departure. She'd be miffed of course, but the lovely jewelry he'd bring back from Bangkok would sooth her.

Did he want to spend three or four days in Bangkok? The city had its charms. It also had the girl Nandi kidnapped before Christmas. He'd been too annoyed with Nandi to enjoy her then, but now that his anger had cooled, maybe he'd look her up as a consolation prize. It was also smart to check on his holdings. There was nothing like a visit from the boss to keep an enterprise running smoothly.

Then when he got back, he'd hire some additional talent to find his elusive virgin. There were men who specialized in this sort of thing, men who could find anyone. Vasily and his goons weren't up to the challenges posed by this clever girl. It was time to apply professional finesse to the situation.

******

After Teddie's first success, she approached her lessons with a new-found urgency. She wanted nothing more than to go find her friends, but Lhatu insisted this couldn't happen right away. He likened the process to scuba diving. Safe, but only if one knew what one was doing. Just because a new diver manages to go under water, breathe for a few minutes and emerge safely, hardly means the diver is ready to explore submerged wrecks at the bottom of the sea.

"Everyone's consciousness exists in both a physical body and a lighter body in a reality that matches the heavy one. I know you're not fond of physics, but you must accept that the two realities coexist in the same physical space and they're linked. When your two consciousness streams are split apart and each takes in different input, this is potentially dangerous. It requires great care."

"Doesn't my mist body have its own eyes and brain?" Teddie decided she preferred the term mist body even though Lhatu kept insisting it was misleading because no water vapor was involved. On this issue, Teddie ignored him.

"It does, sort of, but your mist body, as you insist on calling it, has inputs as temporary as the separation itself. To use Western terms, there is a physical entanglement between your mist brain and your solid one. When you travel they become separated, but in a real sense they still touch. Like two entangled electrons in particle physics. Einstein called it 'spooky action at a distance.'"

Lhatu saw Teddie's eyes glaze over at the mention of particle physics and he stopped. "The most important thing to remember is when the two brains are reunited, only one memory can be preserved. The default is the memory of your solid brain. That's everyone's default. We're working to change the setting for you, and one messes with the defaults of nature at some peril. Do you understand?"

Teddie nodded, but what she really understood was she had to keep working a while longer before Lhatu would let her go find Michelle.

February 2012

19. Unlearning

As far as Amy was concerned, the jury was still out as to whether Lhatu was a well-meaning kook or an adept with a rare and powerful talent he was teaching her young friend. Amy saw nothing but concern in Lhatu's actions. Everything he taught Teddie about relaxation and self-control was positive and healthy, and it served to keep the girl calm during a difficult time. So, true or not, Amy saw no reason not to be supportive of his efforts.

However, she also saw no reason not to be out there hunting for Michelle. She had considerable resources she *knew* were real, so she worked her networks hard.

Two sources came back describing a van packed with groggy young women, spotted a month ago traveling through the back roads of Burma. The driver provided lavish tips to any local police who stopped them. Neither of Amy's sources got a good look at the girls, but both had seen a mix of South Asian features and guessed girls from India, Pakistan and Nepal were being sent southeast to provide variety in the brothels.

The timing sounded right, so Amy tried to trace this van's route forward and backward—backward to confirm Michelle was in it, forward to find Michelle. Ten years in this field had left Amy well informed. If her expertise found Michelle before all this mist body travel did, she was sure no one would complain.

******

Vanida's only real friends had been the boy Pêe chaai, and possibly Noi who'd given her all the books to read when she was young. She didn't know her age was seventeen. She only knew she'd coped with the last year of her life by deciding she was a hardened older woman, looking out for herself in a harsh world. It was the worldview held by most of the women she knew who were surviving in the sex industry.

She hadn't seen Pêe chaai now for months. Perhaps they'd outgrown their need for each other? Perhaps. Or maybe she'd ceased to heed his calls. With a better understanding of her place in the world, perhaps she didn't feel worthy of his friendship.

She laughed at the idea. He was a silly monk, ignorant in the ways of the world. What did she need him for? Let him go turn somersaults in the air. She had a real woman's responsibility now and needed no one, certainly not him.

Except, she possibly needed this new girl Michelle. This improbable prisoner, who'd arrived in the last batch of scared country girls, was different. While the other new girls remained drugged and chained to beds upstairs until they acclimated to their new life, Michelle established herself as an experienced and willing addition. Only Vanida had seen her throwing up in the bathroom after her first trick, and suspected the bravado was an act designed to get her more freedom.

After a few days, Michele told Vanida she'd made a check list for her own survival. She was avoiding beatings to keep up her strength, and was giving her captors no reason to drug her, particularly by anything addictive. She wanted enough awareness in her encounters with men to try to entice them into condom use. She figured every time she succeeded was one less time she played Russian Roulette with her own health.

Vanida pressed Michelle for more information about these sexually transmitted diseases, a topic Noi had only mentioned in passing. Michelle was more than happy to provide details.

Her goals were pragmatic. She intended to escape soon, without becoming HIV-positive or pregnant, without a drug addiction and without permanent physical scars. She told Vanida she'd deal with emotional scars later. Vanida realized she'd never met anyone like Michelle.

However, the American lacked information about Thai customs and languages, and that was where Vanida could help.

Michelle was willing to trade her broader knowledge about diseases and drugs, and her contacts with some aid organization in India, for Vanida's local knowledge. They could escape together.

Vanida was all for the information exchange, but explained how a woman like Vanida gained nothing by escaping. She had no family, and no other life to turn to. Michelle disagreed.

"You can keep working your sex act in a bar if you want. That doesn't mean someone has to own you. No one should say you have to turn tricks and how often and with who. Earn money performing and go home to your own place when you're done. You could even learn other skills. You could get out of Bangkok."

"Khae would just hunt me down. She paid for me."

"She's more than made her money back. I know people who can help you. Once you get away, you could negotiate your freedom by paying her a little. Or, you go so far away that hunting you down isn't worth it. Trust me, Vanida, right now you live at the absolute bottom of the food chain, and it doesn't have to be this bad. Help me and I can help you."

Vanida considered the possibility. "You want to not go with the men who ask for you? You can give them to other girls who want the business."

A look of deep relief passed across Michelle's face as Vanida elaborated.

"We be careful about how we do it or Khae will think we're friends. Pretend you're watching me and copy. Okay?"

Vanida thought for a minute more. "Not turning tricks is easier if you're good at something else. You shoot anything out your pussy?"

"Hell no," Michelle sputtered out a laugh. "That wasn't something they taught at my school. Let's see. I was okay in drill team. I aced chemistry last year. In fact, I was so good at it I was thinking about pharmacy for a profession."

"You mean drugs? You don't want to touch that world here. What else happens in chemistry?"

"I don't know. You mix stuff up. In the right amounts."

"Really? You ever make fancy drinks? Like Mai Tai?"

"I used to make drinks in the blender all the time at home. Without alcohol. It was fun."

"Okay. I'll find a book in English on how to make drinks. You learn it. Convince Khae you subbed as a bartender on busy nights where you used to work. She thinks you've been in the business a while. A good bartender is harder for her to find than a scared girl to tie to a bed. On slow nights, you dance and serve drinks and give your business away. On busy nights, you're more useful behind the bar and she won't make you turn tricks."

"I like it. I like it a lot." Michelle smiled with relief.

So Vanida had a new friend, or at least a new business partner. And *this* partner didn't think Vanida belonged at the absolute bottom of the food chain, just because someone had sold her as a child.

******

Olumiji promised to give Lola ongoing reports, and she promised to use the greatest of wisdom in dealing with the information. Although Teddie video-chatted weekly with her mom and dad, Lola relied on Olumiji's weekly calls for the full picture.

In early February he was able to tell her that Teddie remained safe and in good spirits and she'd made some sort of breakthrough in using her abilities. Lhatu was hopeful she could start looking for Michelle in a few weeks. All six telepaths continued their round-the-clock surveillance and would do so until Teddie was back in Texas.

Usha remained off everybody's radar. Amy was working hard to learn the identity of the girl's initial buyer and was seeking assurance that he remained unable to locate her.

Olumiji made occasional mental contact with Michelle. He was certain she was in Southeast Asia at a brothel. She was an incredible young woman who had focused her impressive intelligence and courage into surviving this ordeal.

Along with that focus came a mental wall, one she'd erected to keep her own fears and revulsion under control. Unfortunately, the wall kept Olumiji out as well, making his glimpses into her world short and rare.

******

Lhatu began to spend more time on theory, much to Teddie's frustration. Teddie didn't care how out-of-body experiences worked, she only cared about having them so she could find Michelle and Usha. The more she resisted the information, however, the more Lhatu insisted she had to learn it.

"Ask people if an apple will always fall to the earth once it breaks free from the tree and one hundred normal adults will tell you it will," he told her at their next session. "But a child will say 'maybe not, because it could float into the hand of a magic genie.' A mystic will tell you he could levitate the apple if he wanted to. A physicist will begin instructing you on stronger and weaker gravitational fields and then move on to the oddities of warped space. If you are still listening, he might begin to discuss probability functions with you. They are all scratching at the same truth, namely that this universe is far more complicated and interesting than our day-to-day experiences would lead us to believe."

Lhatu did not often touch Teddie, but now he took her head into his heads and looked deep into her eyes.

"You are having to unlearn many of your assumptions in order to absorb this new material." He spoke slowly, trying to convey the importance of the concept. "This unlearning is as important as anything else we do. Just as a scuba diver can't afford to panic and respond as she would on dry land; in an emergency you can't afford to panic and respond as you would in your solid body. You must unlearn those responses."

He let go of her gently, and his eyes were pleading. "Please."

Teddie took a deep breath and tried to focus. She was going deep under water and had to learn the rules for her own survival. This could not be rushed. She opened her mind to learning.

By the end of the evening Lhatu was more pleased than she'd ever seen him. "When you come tomorrow night, you will choose to go traveling out of the building for the first time. I will go with you, even though staying together is difficult for travelers. It is like trying to move in a heavy current together. I think by the end of the week you'll be ready to be go on your own and start seeking your friend. You've done well tonight."

As had become normal for them, Amy and Lhatu took Teddie back to her dorm at school. It was late and Haley was already sound asleep, leaving a note about today's math assignment on Teddie's chair.

Teddie was so happy as she fell asleep that it never occurred to her she'd take off on her own, without Lhatu's okay.

******

She snuggled against her pillow, and then she was back at the convent where she'd found Usha months ago. She was floating above the ground, passing through walls with only a slight tickle. She didn't remember the trip there. Hadn't Lhatu taught her something about keeping part of her consciousness in her solid body during a return to a previous location?

She saw Usha sleeping on a pile of blankets in a room with four other women. Her friend seemed unchanged except for a healthy glow about her. Perhaps ample fresh air and more exercise had offered benefits to her city-bound bookworm friend?

Once she was sure Usha was fine, she felt a gentle tug to come outside. The boy was there, the one who'd done such creative somersaults. The girl was not. The most unusual sight, however, was the slumbering body of the boy inside the barn. He lived here? At least he was staying here for the night.

She longed to ask him questions, but at least she now understood why the world of the traveler was a silent one.

"Sound and light are different," Lhatu had explained. "Sound must travel through a medium that vibrates, like air. There is nothing to vibrate in what you call the mist world. Light, however, can travel anywhere, even through a vacuum in space. Your mist world is really an abode of light, not water vapor."

"So there's no way to talk?"

"Not like you mean," Lhatu had answered. "You can't make sounds and you can't pick up a pen because your hand passes right through it. Two travelers can use sign language, though, and most adepts learn some for this purpose."

Teddie looked at the boy and wondered if he knew sign language. She tried the motion for a military salute that meant hello to deaf Americans, then remembered the boy wasn't from her home country. Did he use a different greeting?

It didn't seem to matter. The boy mimicked her gesture with a smile, and then they looked at each other. Now what.

Teddie wanted to ask, "How do you know Usha? Is she okay?" She wanted to demand answers to questions like, "Why do you keep showing up here?" But she didn't know where to start so she looked at the boy helplessly.

******

Jampa had fallen asleep in the barn with the door open. It was a warm night, and as slumber approached he thought of how it had been months since he'd seen Noom in her second body. She continued to ignore his requests to meet him. Desperate, he'd sought out her solid body when she was asleep.

Several times he'd found her, curled up on a filthy cot. Each time he could see hardness growing in the lines on her face. What were these people doing to his sister? Each time he looked around, trying to learn where she was. He had no sense of temperature when he traveled, but judging from those there, the place was warm, uncomfortably so.

The house was filled with women, and Jampa had been horrified to find some tied to their beds. Their half-dried tears and bruised bodies made it all too obvious what was happening. Other than that, he saw much written in a language he couldn't read.

Tonight, he'd fallen asleep calling to his sister, but instead he was in his special body, greeting the Western girl he'd seen here months ago. She gave him a funny sort of salute and he saluted back. She seemed harmless, but frustrated by her inability to talk to him.

He was going to turn and reenter his sleeping body, at a loss for what else to do, when it occurred to him this girl must a have reason for returning to this convent. Usha had mentioned friends looking for her from some school in India. Maybe not all her friends were from India?

Jampa gestured to the convent. The girl seemed to understand and agree. She followed him, floating closer to the ground than he did, and moving slower. She was less experienced in her second body, he decided, but more confident than the last time he saw her.

They moved together into the room that held the sleeping Usha, and Jampa thought they now shared the same theory. Jampa pointed to Usha and nodded, then put his hand over his heart. The girl did the same. There was no more they could say. My friend. Your friend. Our friend. Jampa wanted to promise the Western girl he would work hard to keep Usha safe, but he had no idea how to do so.

******

Teddie followed the boy into the convent, happy he wanted to communicate with her. He pointed to Usha and she nodded hard as she could. He nodded back with the same enthusiasm. He was connected to Usha somehow. How? It didn't matter. It was clear the boy intended to look out for Usha, and Teddie felt better knowing Usha had someone on her side.

Teddie wanted to say to the boy, "Please help keep her safe," but she had no idea how to communicate something so complicated.

******

The next morning Teddie considered calling Lhatu, but decided this needed to be told in person. Now that she was making such progress, they were meeting nightly, anxious to get her hunting for Michelle.

Lhatu and Amy were waiting for her after dinner in front of the dining hall. As she began to describe what had happened, Lhatu was frustrated with her for going on this unauthorized adventure. How could he be? She hadn't chosen to do it.

But as Lhatu listened to her, he disagreed.

"On some plane, you chose to go, Teddie. Your mind has different levels and they don't always communicate consciously with each other. But they are all you. You need to develop the self-discipline to only go traveling when your conscious and logical mind deems it is safe."

"But it happened all by itself."

"I know that's how it felt. It's as much my fault for teaching you so fast. We'll work more on self-control. Meanwhile, we rejoice because you returned unharmed."

"We rejoice about more than that," Amy interjected with a bit of an edge.

"You bet we do," Teddie gave her an understanding look. "I know you don't totally believe me, Amy, but I'm sure Usha is okay for now and even has a friend who's looking out for her."

"I'm undecided about how much of this I believe," Amy said, watching Lhatu's reaction.

"I know this, too," he replied. "You care so much about these young women that you are willing to let me, a man you despised for years, into your home night after night, on the off chance I can provide a means to help them."

Then as Lhatu parked the car and they got out, he turned back to Teddie.

"Can you tell me more about this boy?"

"He kind of looks and dresses like you," she offered. "I mean he's younger and smaller and his skin is a little darker but …"

"But he is a Buddhist, from somewhere in or near Bhutan?"

"I think so. I don't mean to insult you, but shouldn't you already know about a Bhutanese monk who's good at traveling?"

"Yes, yes I should." Lhatu actually laughed. "That's why I'm asking about him."

The trio walked the short distance to Amy's apartment, and Lhatu talked while he kept his eyes vigilant for anything amiss. Any time he had Teddie off campus, he never forgot that "bodyguard" was in his job description.

"There is a sort of, what I think your culture would call an urban legend," Lhatu said. "Various travelers claim to have encountered two children over the years. Children don't often travel, and the experience is frightening to a child when it happens."

Teddie remembered floating into her brother Zane's room on New Year's Eve of 1999, and nodded.

"But these two children seem to be fearless. One theory is they were twins who were separated, and discovered traveling as a means to play together. Likely both of their lives were pretty bleak, and they were linked at the most profound of levels, having spent nine months in a womb together. Every so often an adept would run into the two of them. The children would wave and go back to their games as if what they were doing was the most natural thing in the world. Their solid bodies were never nearby, so we could never approach them and learn more."

They walked into Amy's apartment and headed to the living room. Amy normally let them be at this point, but tonight she sat down with them, also intrigued by Lhatu's story.

"Having a 'twin sighting' got to be sort of badge in my organization. Then a few years ago travelers noticed the children were becoming less childlike. Approaching puberty. It led credence to the theory these were real human children who traveled to be with each other. The group talked about ways to find their solid bodies, to reach out and offer them information and training. Once we got serious about it, no one has seen them since."

"So you think I saw your twins, all grown up?" Teddie asked.

"The age sounds about right. The problem is they were never seen separately. Some of us guessed they were unable to travel alone. Are you sure the boy who is with Usha is the same boy you saw doing somersaults with the girl months ago?"

"I'm positive. He was living at Usha's convent and he pointed to her and put his hand over his heart."

"He's in love with her?" Amy asked.

"Maybe, but it seemed more like a gesture of friendship than romance. I responded by doing the same thing and he nodded. It was like saying we both cared about her."

Lhatu looked troubled.

"Isn't this good news?" Amy asked.

"Possibly. There's a lot more theory to what I do, more theory than I could begin to explain in the time we have."

"Try a couple of salient points," Amy said with a hint of frustration.

"Such directness is part of your culture, not mine. But I will try to tell two Westerners why finding this boy alone worries me, and I will try to do so in the style of the West. Don't get frustrated with me when concepts requiring much groundwork sound silly when said to you in your famous few words."

"I'll allow ample leeway for that."

"Okay. Everything is interconnected physically, in space. It all touches, like the water in the ocean. You can pull out a cupful here or there but it's still part of the ocean."

Amy's eye roll was visible to both Teddie and Lhatu. "I like new age metaphysics as much as the next person," she said. "But..."

Lhatu gave her a smile back that wasn't entirely friendly. "The boy and girl are powerfully connected. These children, these barely grown children, don't understand their own strength. They are waves on the ocean. They are part of the whole but with a force of their own. Possibly a strong force. The boy has now forged a connection with Usha, so she is part of this wave as well. Where is the girl? The ocean, the universe will balance this out. Good and bad are terms we humans apply, not terms the ocean understands. Balance will happen. We humans will deem it good or bad, based on its effect on those we care for."

Lhatu stopped and looked at Amy. "Does this make any sense to you?"

Teddie could have sworn she heard a touch of condensation in Lhatu's voice, and she supposed it was understandable given Amy had pushed him to explain his deepest truths in a few sentences after he had told her such could not be done well.

Amy surprised Teddie with the kindness in her voice.

"Thank you, Lhatu. It makes perfect sense." She seemed to mean it, and Teddie noticed Lhatu looking at Amy with a new appreciation.

February 2012

20. Finding

Teddie wanted to hone her skills with actual practice. However, Lhatu began the next session with more information.

"There are three kinds of traveling. It matters which kind you are doing. If you encounter other travelers, it matters what type they're engaged in. Would you like to guess one of the types?"

Teddie didn't care to guess, but her participation was part of Lhatu's teaching technique.

"One kind would be just sort of wandering around."

"Exactly!" Lhatu seemed quite pleased. "The first type of traveler is a wanderer. The untrained do only this, and often their memories don't make it back into their stream of consciousness. Beginning travelers make about ten times as many trips as they recall. You did. If you encounter another traveler who is wandering, it helps to know they have a high probability of not recalling the encounter."

"So experienced travelers don't wander?"

"Oh, of course they do. It's relaxing and you learn things. It's like going for a casual walk. So what do you think is the second kind of traveling?"

"Uh, not wandering? I mean, traveling for a purpose."

"You've got the idea. We call it seeking. Looking for something or someone. Even though you are still learning about wandering, in a few nights we'll move on to seeking. It should be obvious why seeking matters to you."

She nodded. "What's the third kind?"

Lhatu smiled. “Let’s not get more than one step ahead of ourselves, okay?”

The first trip involved going out to the street and back, and, as promised, Lhatu tried to stay next to her as she moved through the apartment walls. Before they left, Lhatu reviewed issues about passing through objects that were impermeable in the solid world. Once they were outside, they traveled in and out of a few parked cars for practice. Glass, metal, brick and wood each had a different feel, and passing through a large living creature like a tree resulted in a slight exchange of energy, giving a light tingle Teddie could feel.

Upon return, Lhatu talked more about passing through objects. No wall was impenetrable, but psychological issues could make it seem so. Relax. Or find another, more creative way in. Drop down through the chimney.

Massive solids, like cliffs or the ground itself, should be avoided as they tended to leave one too disoriented to exit. Occupying the same space as a living creature should be quick, lest it begin to drain the life force of either being.

On the next night Teddie was instructed to do her best to stay with Lhatu. He didn’t tell her ahead of time where he planned to go. She tried to stay with him as he headed down the street, and she got her first appreciation for why travelers moved alone.

Afterwards, Lhatu reviewed speed and distance with her. Travelers couldn’t use feet to push off of the ground, producing the reliable direction and velocity one was used to in the solid world. Traveling in an energy body was like skydiving or swimming in a fast river. One focused on one’s own movement for safety and effectiveness. Adept travelers could stay together, but they seldom bothered because it took so much attention.

The third trip involved going upstairs to Amy’s bedroom, where Amy had agreed they could spy on her so Lhatu could deliver a lesson on proximity to solid awake people. This trip proved the most interesting. Amy was lying on her bed reading. A few feet away from her lay a large white poster board. She’d written in green magic marker, “Tell me you saw this and I will believe this is real.”

Teddie clapped her hands at Amy's cleverness, but Lhatu looked pained as soon as he saw the sign. He put his finger to his lips and shook his head.

Later, after they returned, he whispered to Teddie. "Let me talk to her about this alone, okay? It changes things, once a non-traveler knows what we do is absolute fact. Doubts have their role." He did not look happy about Amy's strategy, so Teddie agreed to not mention seeing the sign.

Instead, she listened to an explanation about life-force and how solid beings could sometimes sense a traveler. Getting the "willies" or the feeling of a location being haunted was often caused by nothing more than a traveler passing through a solid person.

After the three trips in succession, Lhatu insisted they take a break, and let Teddie get caught up at school.

They met again Wednesday night, February 29. Teddie had always liked this odd leap day stuck into the calendar. Even though she knew better, it felt like a bonus day added into her life. So she was in good spirits when Lhatu announced that it was time for Teddie to seek Michelle.

"You're willing to let me make such a long trip?" she asked.

"You finally have enough basics that I'm confident in your safety. I'll stay here with your resting body, and we'll see if your emotional connection allows you to find Michelle as easily as you found Usha. If so, sooner is better and tonight is best of all. If you can't find her, and even if you can, I'll teach you about learning to seek. But you don't need this knowledge for what you do tonight."

That made sense to Teddie. She noticed Amy was paying less attention to them; the woman seemed distracted and disappointed. Teddie guessed Lhatu hadn't talked to her yet about her big green note.

She must be worried all these travel attempts are nonsense. Teddie hoped Lhatu would set Amy straight soon.

As Teddie worked her way through the relaxation and concentration exercises, she was aware this would be her first conscious travel attempt over any distance.

Her thoughts wandered to the used black and white pick-up truck setting in her folks' driveway waiting for her. She felt a pang and spent some time thinking of all the places she and Michelle had driven in it before they left. Then she thought of all the places they hadn't gotten a chance to explore. She started to make a list of places to go once they were both home and then there she was, standing by her truck in the blazing sunlight. Of course. It was daytime in Texas. Her folks were at work, and she'd traveled again without remembering the journey.

"I'll be back in a few months." She mouthed the words to her truck. Then she added, "Now I want to go to my friend Michelle."

She began to speed down the sidewalk and then down streets. *Wait, I know this route. I'm on my way to Michelle's house.*

Teddie stopped on Michelle's front lawn, baffled. Had Michelle come home? She hesitated, feeling odd about invading the Tran's privacy even though her friend's safety was at stake.

The outside wall of the house was harder to penetrate than the walls at Usha's convent; it left Teddie with a feeling of passing through mush. Inside, it was deserted. Both Trans were at work, and Michelle's room showed no signs of having been used recently.

"Take me home," Teddie said in frustration. She felt a momentary confusion, as if on some level she was trying to decide if home was across town or across a world. That's when she realized she'd somehow covered thousands of miles and crossed an ocean and she had no memory of how she'd done it. She froze in terror.

There was no way she could float back across a whole damn ocean with giant waves under her. And there was no way she was going high up in the sky either. So how was she going to get back to her body? Shit. Why had she gone so far away? She felt the panic grow and fought for the calm Lhatu had tried to teach her.

"If you get into trouble, see the cord connecting you back to your solid body. It's not always visible, but you can make it so. It leads directly to a plane on which your two types of bodies always touch."

Teddie had been dubious, and she was more skeptical now. Then, she remembered four-year-old Teddie seeing a sparkly green cord and snapping back into her own bed.

Snap. Teddie was back inside Teddie, the solid Teddie, and she had never been more glad. Lhatu was holding her wrist, monitoring her pulse.

"I was wrong. It was too soon for you to try this, wasn't it?" he asked.

She gave him a fearful nod. "I thought I might be stuck out there, and never get back. I don't know how I got across a whole ocean without knowing it.

"You returned to Texas?" Lhatu shook his head. "I should have considered this possibility. On rare occasion, a traveler goes unconsciously and with great speed to a place they know well and miss. A place they call home. It never occurred to me..."

"I don't want to do this anymore." Teddie meant it as soon as she said it."

"Maybe you don't have to," Amy said as she walked into the room, a sense of purpose clear in her every step. She turned to Lhatu. "This has been interesting, but if it's scaring Teddie then it needs to stop."

"Please," he said. "She can do this. I just have to prepare her better."

"You don't have to bother," Amy said. "Teddie doesn't want to do this anymore, and I've just found Michelle."

******

One of the things Pavel liked best was how people jumped to please him. Waiters, store clerks and bureaucrats would fall over themselves trying to make him happy and none tried harder than his own employees. Being the boss had its perks.

His brothel in Bangkok was one of the more successful in the city, thanks to Pavel's heavy financial investment in it and his ongoing oversight. It was good to diversify, and a mutually beneficial arrangement with local businessmen allowed him to operate here without hassle.

His manager, Khae, ran the place like the business it was, with the bar and floor shows bringing in about half the profits and the girls bringing in the other. Khae was a big, half-toothless woman whom Pavel would have found disgusting in other circumstances, but she knew how to handle the girls, she knew what would please the clients, and she had a good head for making the enterprise work.

The new girls upstairs were almost all profit, of course, after the fair amount of overhead invested in procuring them. Pavel and Khae agreed that such girls, rotated out before they became too jaded, paid off well with a certain type of clientele. His brothel had a reputation for providing one of the best venues for that type of experience, and Pavel was pleased to learn that an underground publication for sex tourists had recently given his establishment a five-star rating in that category.

Of course, not all men wanted that kind of amusement. Some preferred willing girls, selected from the many bikini-clad cocktail waitresses. Others liked to watch the girls perform and then go back to their hotel rooms to masturbate, feeling like they'd broken no vows. Pavel didn't care what a man liked; he was happy to provide entertainment for all tastes.

Tonight was a Wednesday night, but the place was busy. Maybe people liked to go out and play on February 29?

The bar was scrubbed and the floor was freshly mopped. The best girls were onstage, hoping to impress the boss. Khae was running around barking orders, happy to show off how well the business ran. The bartender looked a little flustered as he poured Pavel his best single malt scotch, and Pavel noticed the drink orders were starting to pile up.

"You need a third bartender for busy nights like this," he barked at Khae and she gave him a thumbs-up.

"Got the perfect one, boss. She's fast, she's good and she dances and turns tricks when drink orders are slow."

"You're training one of the whores to bartend?" he laughed in surprise.

"Why not? You make better money if you don't let people sit around. So, thanks to you, I got a good back-up bartender, and I peddle her ass when I don't need her to make drinks."

Pavel nodded his approval. "Smart Khae. Smart. Why thanks to me?"

"She's the girl you told me to get off the last truck. You know, the one you sent a picture of? She looks Vietnamese—says she is—but she acts and talks American. Why you not tell me she's experienced? She was out there shaking her ass first day she got here."

"She was?" Pavel was surprised. He'd assumed the girl was a spoiled American innocent, attending some fancy academy. "You sure you got the right girl?"

"I'll go get her. You'll see. She works hard, causes no trouble. Screw her yourself if you want. She won't care."

Later, Pavel thought that as soon as he heard this story he should have known something was wrong. Certainly he should have figured it out half an hour later when Khae hadn't come back. But he got sidetracked watching the girls perform and talking to the bouncer, and it was more than an hour before he decided he'd better find out what could have distracted Khae from her main mission of pleasing her boss.

He never found Khae. She was a smart businesswoman, and she knew what was going to happen to the employee who lost the girl the boss had flagged as "do not lose." As soon as Khae discovered Michelle was gone, along with her best performer Vanida, she didn't waste any time. Khae grabbed as much money as she could carry and disappeared into the night.

Pavel turned the place upside-down looking for Khae, and then for Michelle once he realized what must have happened. He talked to enough flustered employees to figure out this Michelle, whom he'd specifically asked be placed under special watch, was gone along with another girl. No one knew how or when they'd left, but the girls had at least a couple of hours' head start and maybe more.

Pavel made a tactical decision to let Khae go. She had too many friends and family members nearby, and trouble with her would only draw attention to his status as an outsider. He opted to focus on the missing girls, who no one would care about. He alerted all of his business contacts, which included the local police, insisting the girls be returned promptly if they surfaced. Pavel knew his clout in the city was enough to ensure his request would be honored.

However, what he'd heard of this Michelle gave him pause. How many inexperienced teenage girls could pull off the kind of masquerade this one had? She might be too smart and well informed to go to the police or anyone else for help.

Pavel blew out a short, disgusted breath. Okay. First the Indian virgin turned out to be more clever than he realized. Now this little spoiled American had outfoxed him, too. What kind of man gets outwitted by a couple of teen-agers? The anger rose inside him until he could feel it physically. He grabbed the nearby assistant manager.

"You. You're in charge here now. Straighten this place up tonight and get everything back to normal by morning or I'll have you killed. I'll be back tomorrow."

He phoned his driver to come get him. It was high time he hired that expert at locating people he'd been meaning to call. Only now, he had two cases for the man, not one.

******

Amy was proud of her detective work. She learned more about the van; it had allegedly departed from Kolkata with nine girls. A contact of Amy's in Kolkata found a man who delivered supplies to the apartment where the girls were held. This unidentified informant confided that most of the girls were locals, sold by relatives. They'd arrived scared but conscious. He'd been bothered when one girl showed-up in the trunk of a car, and had made a point of checking she was alive. He didn't work with murderers. The girl fitted Michelle's description and that had been enough for Amy.

International organizations working closely with Southeast Asia reported to Amy on the clearinghouse in the Burma countryside and the truck traffic leaving from there to Bangkok. Social workers in Thailand had heard nothing about a kidnapped American, but hoped their agencies would get word of her whereabouts.

It looked like Amy was at a dead end until information had come from an unlikely source. An anonymous tip was passed along by the police in Manali, an Indian mountain resort town almost a thousand miles west of Darjeeling. An unnamed citizen had read of a nationwide search for two students from the Lord Peartree Academy, which this citizen had attended years ago.

She wished to help her old school, but to be discreet. She knew of a powerful local crime boss known to have a taste for unwilling virgins. He'd bragged late last summer about a purchase he'd made from a school over in Darjeeling. Word was the deal fell through because the girl ran away and couldn't be found. The crime boss, a former Russian, was quite unhappy. The citizen didn't know more.

It was all Amy needed.

This morning her contacts verified the name of the buyer. It was lucky there weren't many former Russians making their home in Manali. International crime watch groups provided information on the man's known business interests, which were impressively diversified. He liked pirated CDs, but also dabbled in drugs and loan sharking. He was known for keeping a formidable army of thugs—both Russian and Indian—and he rented them to anyone who wasn't a competitor. He handled a little prostitution in India and more in Malaysia and Indonesia. He owned a rather successful brothel in Thailand.

Given that was the van's destination, Amy decided it was time to turn her attention there. Informants in Bangkok confirmed that the business in question bought a few new girls fresh off the truck every couple of months. Had a truck arrived in mid-January? Probably. No one remembered, but one snitch had a contact on the inside who turned out to be happy to provide a description of the five new girls.

As Lhatu and Teddie worked downstairs, Amy sat at her computer reading the report of the five girls Khae had purchased in January. Four of them were terrified locals from tiny villages. The fifth was a hardened Vietnamese prostitute that bore no resemblance to the earnest student Amy had known. Amy scratched her head and realized what could have happened.

Her young friend had plenty of time to analyze her situation, and could have decided to affect a powerful personal makeover. Amy's was sickened that any young person should have to make such a horrible choice, yet if her guess was correct, Michelle's instincts had been excellent. Her chances of survival, eventual escape and even of some degree of ultimate emotional recovery would all be higher if her young friend had found a way to retain some control over her own fate. The more Amy thought about it, the more sure she was.

Amy wanted to burst into applause for Michelle. But first, she wanted to get the girl out of there, now. So she'd stormed downstairs and interrupted a training session with Teddie and Lhatu that obviously had not gone well anyway.

"Let's contact Interpol. The U.S. embassy. Michelle's parents." An excited Teddie didn't know where to start. Before the evening was over they had contacted them all.

Teddie returned to the dorm late that night, happier than she'd been in months. The disastrous trip across the Atlantic was forgotten as she woke Haley.

"We found her! We found her!"

"Michelle or Usha?" Haley was sitting up alert before she got the words out of her mouth. She'd already heard of Teddie's unauthorized trip to the Buddhist convent earlier and so she knew of Usha's relative safety.

"Michelle! They're sending police now to get her. It's early morning in Thailand. Amy's working to get all kinds of international attention focused there so no one will dare cover for these horrible people. They'll take her straight to a hospital. She's going to be fine."

Haley gave Teddie a hug. "Have you talked to her parents?"

"Amy just called Mrs. Tran at work. She cried. Then Amy let me call my mom on her phone too. I don't know when I'm going home or what I'm doing, but I'm at least staying here until I'm sure Michelle doesn't need me on this side of the world."

"Good. I'm not ready to say goodbye to you just yet."

"Amy's been researching this psychopath who bought Usha, and he has a bizarre temper and a cruel streak. Amy's worried he's going to be unhappy when his place gets raided, especially after all the protection money he's paid everyone. I think they're posting extra guards around the school here."

"Wow." Haley hugged her knees in tight to her chest and pulled her blankets around her. "Wow."

******

Keng had gotten the job working for Khae through a cousin who said helping to manage the brothel would be easy money with side benefits. The old lady had been demanding but not totally unreasonable, and Keng had handled the bar for her. He'd supported training the new girl to make drinks because it seemed efficient, and she was friendly to him. It hadn't been a bad existence, until he had the extreme misfortune to be standing in the line of sight of the crazy Russian who owned the place.

Now he was in charge of the damn brothel and had spent hours trying to calm everyone down and see to it that customers were allowed to finish their evening. Half the support staff had fled into the night, fearful the angry Russian was going to punish them for the disappearances. That left Keng working with a mop in his own hand to get things in order before morning.

Keng heard sirens in the distance, and realized they were getting louder and closer, but it wasn't until he saw flashing lights through the window that he realized he was having the worst night of any assistant manager anywhere. It had been nearly two years since police had raided a brothel anywhere in the Patpong area, and tonight, for some bizarre reason, they were raiding his.

Keng looked at his mop. He was a dead man.

March 2012

21. Losing

By the morning of March 1, the police in Thailand were certain no American teenager of any ancestry was working at the raided brothel. Several potentially underage girls were found; the police assured everyone they would be returned home. As the news circulated, various agencies rushed in to help.

The police were holding an assistant manager for questioning as neither the manager of the brothel nor its owner could be located and the assistant manager had begged police to arrest him. Word was a couple of the girls had run off earlier in the evening and the manager was now hiding from the owner, known to have a temper about such things. What a mess.

The police in Darjeeling asked for details about the two women who'd run away and were assured they were of no concern. One was a well-trained local named Vanida, who was a favorite performer in the floorshow. Indian authorities asked if she was a singer or a dancer? The Thai police weren't sure. The other woman was a Vietnamese-American who used the Vietnamese name Lan. She was an experienced bartender who worked willingly. Clearly not the high school girl they sought.

The police in Bangkok added their regrets that the original tip was faulty. It happened. However, they'd continue to look for the American student and would notify India immediately if she was found.

******

Michelle's mom had gone from giddy happiness to surprised outrage in a matter of hours and she wasn't handling it well. She couldn't stop crying. In her heart she believed these people had no idea where her daughter was because her child couldn't possibly be impersonating a bartender and acting like an experienced prostitute. That meant her baby was lost somewhere, as the odds of finding her grew less every day. Michelle's mom rocked back and forth on her couch as she cried, wondering how much of this was her own fault.

Michelle's dad had a different reaction. He'd been irritated with Michelle for letting this happen in the first place. He'd taught her to be more savvy and had been rehearsing lectures to her in his head regarding being smarter about protecting herself. This sort of incident was an embarrassment to the entire family.

However, when word came from India that no American high school student had been located, he considered how his daughter could have engineered her own escape. While his wife sobbed like a ninny in the middle of the living room, he decided it was likely his daughter *was* one of the two run-aways. This idea made him proud, even if it meant she was masquerading as a prostitute.

******

After the lead in Bangkok turned out to be a failure, Amy grew more frustrated each day with Lhatu and his sessions with Teddie. She knew many people would have written them off as a waste of time from the start. However, Amy prided herself on being open minded. She had odd beliefs of her own, and she didn't put down others for having theirs.

It had been a relief to discover the gentle giant from Bhutan wasn't a predator of young girls, but it had been a mistake to hope he was a metaphysical hero of some sorts. What had gotten into her?

Well, there had been Teddie's odd insight into Usha's trip to Gangtok. Then there was the fact that Teddie's mother, a well-educated and sensible woman, had accepted Lhatu and his abilities and had been able to persuade her husband to do the same.

There was more that was odd. The woman had a Nigerian friend who was supposedly watching out for Teddie's safety, yet Amy hadn't caught a glimpse of his cadre of bodyguards. Was Lola Zeitman being bamboozled as well? Or was there something more to Teddie's mother and her collection of friends than Amy knew? She needed to learn about this Nigerian who'd been in the restaurant on Christmas day and was supposed to be coordinating Teddie's protection.

As to Lhatu, the one fact Amy had was that Lhatu and Teddie claimed to have traveled into her room, and yet had failed to see the poster board and note she left for them. The best explanation was they only imagined they traveled, and imagined it so convincingly they believed it.

That meant Teddie was wasting her time and had put herself at risk for ten weeks by remaining in Darjeeling for no good reason. Amy took a deep breath. It had been a week now since Michelle had disappeared into the night only hours before the police raid that would have saved her.

Really, it was time to put a stop to this out-of-body nonsense. Teddie needed to go home. If Lhatu wanted to help find Michelle, he could join Amy in making phone calls and sending out emails, things that could produce tangible results.

******

After it became clear Michelle had disappeared into the streets of Bangkok, Lhatu tried to console Teddie. He worked to convince her to pull herself together because Michelle needed her now more than ever.

"She didn't wait for someone to rescue her, she rescued herself. You must be happy your friend is so resourceful, and glad she is well enough to do what she did. Now, she is hiding in a strange country with no resources. If you can find her, we can get her help."

"I don't understand why she doesn't just go to the police? Why hasn't she shown up yet at the American embassy?"

"She's being smart, Teddie. Police in Southeast Asia are known for returning girls to the brothels they escape from. Some do it for monetary rewards, others prefer an ongoing free pass to the brothel's services. Strangers are most likely to turn the girls over to the police. Getting into the embassy would force her to reveal she has no passport or entry visa, and she risks being detained for entering the country illegally. Some detainees face more sexual abuse while in custody."

Teddie looked almost ill at this news.

"I'm going to teach you better control of where you go. You need to learn how to seek. Focus with me now."

An hour later Teddie was so anxious to try what Lhatu had taught her that she wanted to start seeking as soon as they entered the mist world together. She didn't care if Lhatu approved or not. She wanted to know if his mental approach would take her to Michelle.

The center of consciousness of her traveling body hovered a foot or two above her resting head, then she started to move out of Amy's apartment. Before she passed through the wall, Lhatu waved farewell, conveying his permission for her to go. She gave him a grateful wave back and she started to move down the street.

As the whoosh of her rapid voyage ended, her traveler's body came to rest in a clearing. Lush greenery was everywhere, and a nearly full moon was overhead. Teddie remembered her mother's incessant lessons in earth science. A full moon was overhead at midnight. It had been about nine p.m. in India. So she was a couple of time zones to the east?

Two girls her age were sleeping peacefully on the ground beneath her. Teddie squirmed at the thought of the bugs under them, but neither sleeper seemed bothered. One girl was Michelle; she looked unharmed.

Teddie gasped in surprise at the second girl's identity. She was the female twin, the sister of the boy traveling with Usha. With her gasp she found herself back inside Amy's living room giddy with joy. She grinned when she saw Lhatu, and once he saw her smile he gave her a wide grin back.

Then she saw what must have prompted her body to make its quick return. Amy was in the room too.

******

Amy walked into the room and saw both Lhatu and Teddie deep in a trance. She was impatient enough with the whole thing to seriously consider shaking them both until they woke up. Well, maybe she wouldn't shake Teddie, but she'd have no problem shaking Lhatu. He needed a good hard rattle or two.

Then she saw a smile cross both of their faces at the exact same time. Odd. They both looked so happy all of a sudden. Amy supposed she could give them a few minutes more before telling them she was tired of having this nonsense in her living room every night. She went back to her computer to do some work.

******

Once Amy was gone, Teddie opened the eyes of her solid body, anxious to tell Lhatu her tale.

"I don't know where she was. She was definitely okay. The moon was almost directly overhead, and aren't there charts and things where we can look that up? I mean right this minute the moon is not overhead everywhere, right?"

"Right," Lhatu said. "We can get a rough idea of her longitude, maybe decide if is still near Bangkok. That was a good piece of observation. What else can you remember?"

"Her friend. The girl she escaped with, the performer from the brothel. It's her. You were right. It's entangled in weird ways."

"It's who?" Lhatu asked, but he thought he already knew.

"The boy's twin sister. You know? The traveling acrobat kids. Your urban legend."

Of course it was. One twin was leading Usha, either to safety or into deeper danger, and the other twin was leading Michelle. Lhatu shook his head. "Damn if it doesn't work this way."

"I don't see why having these twins involved is bad. I mean they seem pretty harmless."

"I'm sure they are. I'm not worried about their intentions. They're probably fine people."

He looked at the girl wondering how much he should explain. "There's so much we don't understand. Once you get this kind of link between two people who've been separated, the universe operates with different physical rules. The laws of nature for entangled beings are complicated and surprising. Sometimes it even seems like there's, I don't know, a sense of humor behind it."

Teddie looked down at her feet. "I'm not seeing anything funny about Usha and Michelle's safety."

"I'm not either, but you don't have to enjoy the comedy for it to be happening."

As Lhatu prepared to take Teddie back to school, he assured her events had taken a hopeful turn. They now knew Michelle was okay and had a friend with her. They knew the friend's name was Vanida, and that could provide more leads.

They left the apartment in good spirits, but Amy was distant and unresponsive when they got to the car and told her about the wonderful events of the evening. Teddie knew something was wrong. Had Lhatu *still* not talked to Amy about seeing the note she'd left them? She couldn't imagine why he'd wait so long. By the end of the ride, Teddie and Lhatu had lapsed into an uncomfortable silence as well, most of their earlier joy having turned into discomfort at Amy's barely polite responses.

Then, once Teddie got to her room and told the exciting story to Haley, her roommate behaved the same way. Teddie wasn't going to let such behavior pass a second time.

"Haley, I thought this was wonderful news. What gives here?"

"You don't understand."

"Try me."

"My problems are stupid compared to yours. I mean, you're trying to rescue people, and I'm just trying to prove how cool I am. Or whatever. So leave me alone." Haley rolled over in her bed to face the wall.

"Problems with the climb? What happened?"

"I'm not going."

"What?" Teddie said it in disbelief. "Not again. This is ridiculous. And it's not insignificant, Haley, it's about you getting to be who you are, and it's about inspiring others too. Why would you not go?"

"My dad wants me to pull out."

"Have aliens taken over his brain? He's your biggest supporter. That makes no sense."

"Someone on the climb—he doesn't know who—has asked that I not go," Haley explained. "They've changed the plan again. It started out as this traditional 'assault' on a mountain, with a big support team working to get a smaller group to the summit, in our case sixteen of us. Last fall, three guys wanted to turn the top half of their ascent into an alpine climb, without support people. Alpine climbers move faster and carry their own equipment. It's how everyone climbs everywhere else but in the Himalayas, where the extreme altitude makes a support team a good idea. Last fall the group decided to let these three break away at Camp Three, with the rest of us continuing on with the support and supplies, making a slower ascent and backing them up."

"So what changed?"

"Guess." Haley said. "The two Japanese guys want to join the Canadians. Now the team of five young guys from India want to charge up the mountain with them. That's two-thirds of the group. So the three older Indian climbers from the school in Darjeeling decided they'd like to try an alpine ascent too. That leaves me and the two guys from Norway, Hans and Henrik, whom I met last November. Three foreign climbers and a whole lot of Sherpa. Hans and Henrik decided that was silly, and they'd go alpine too. Now I have to do the same or back out."

"Your dad doesn't think that kind of climb is safe for you?"

"He doesn't, and he might be right, because of the oxygen tanks. A person can hardly move without supplemental oxygen at the summit, so you have to carry oxygen. It's a whole new degree of difficulty."

Haley put her head in her hands for a few seconds and paused.

"But you climb as well as any of these guys," Teddie said.

"I'm smaller than anyone else on the team. I need less, but I also can carry less, and it's not proportional. There are fixed weights and I come out on the losing end of the equation. Based on the ratio of my body weight to the weight of my pack, someone, I think one of the young Indian guys, did the math and decided I'm a risk. My pack has to be over the maximum recommended weight for my size. They've asked my dad to decline the original offer."

"Doesn't that really piss you off? I can't believe they asked your dad, not you."

Haley laughed. "I hadn't even thought about that. He knows these guys and he handles my climbing commitments, but, yeah, it would have been nice if they'd talked directly to me."

"You could insist on going anyway. You're on the team."

Haley shook her head. "Not really. Kanchenjunga is considered a riskier climb than Everest. I need my dad's support, and I need the team to want me there. Most of all, I need to believe I can do it, and they've got me wondering. So it's not gonna happen. It just isn't."

Teddie didn't know what more to say.

Haley shrugged it off. "Did you know that male elephant seals are up to ten times bigger than females?"

"No, I didn't," Teddie said.

"Yeah and dolphins, cute dolphins? The males get together and gang rape the females. Apparently a male dolphin will hump almost anything that moves."

"You need to get a new hobby, Haley."

"Give up climbing?"

"No," Teddie said. "Stop looking into animal sex. It's tough enough being human."

******

After Teddie was dropped off at the school, Amy turned to Lhatu with words made angrier by having been held inside for so long.

"Why are you putting this poor girl through this? You know this mist body travel is rubbish and I know it too."

"You know this how?" Lhatu asked.

"I left you a note in my room. You were never really there or you'd have seen it and responded like I asked you to."

"I saw the note."

"Bullshit."

"Green marker. On a large white poster board."

"You found it in my front hall closet!" Amy was far from ready to soften her anger.

"I don't look through other people's closets."

"I bet you snoop around a little if you think someone could have left something you didn't see. I should've hidden it under my bed. If you'd really seen it, I'd have heard about it that night. Period."

"It was propped on the little stool that sits in front of the mirror where you put on your make-up," Lhatu replied.

Amy paused, and the expression on her face wavered for a second. "Lucky guess. That would be the most logical place to put it, because except for my bed it's the only empty spot in my room."

"True," Lhatu agreed. "You have an exceptional amount of clutter in your bedroom, but the little stool is where it was."

Amy looked at him. "Why didn't you say something right away? For that matter, why didn't Teddie?"

"I asked her not to. I told her I wanted to discuss it with you alone."

"Why in the world would you do that?"

Lhatu sighed. "Believe me, I want nothing more than for you to believe me. But I also know some uncertainty serves a useful function."

It was Amy's turn to sigh in frustration. "Is what you are doing in any way harming Teddie?"

Lhatu shook his head. "To the contrary, it should be making her stronger. I hope I'm giving her an array of skills to help her lead a happier life."

They were a block away from Amy's apartment, nearing the spot where Lhatu always let Amy off.

"Then I guess I'll refrain from delivering the speech I prepared," Amy said. "The one in which I demand you stop this nonsense and send Teddie back to the United States where she is safer and probably happier."

"Yes, I wish you would not deliver that speech." Lhatu smiled slightly. "We're getting closer to finding both girls and we need Teddie. We need her here and we need her being as strong as she is able. She looks up to you and she—no, make that she and I both—need your support."

"Maybe." Amy said it with reluctance in her voice. "Maybe your closet-snooping has introduced enough ambiguity that I'll put up with this a while longer. But I swear, if I start to think you are harming Teddie in any way, I'll put her on a plane home myself and don't think I won't do it."

"I don't. Don't think you won't, that is." Lhatu was smiling a bit more broadly now, and as Amy turned to open the car door, he reached across her and brushed his hand lightly over hers as he opened the door for her.

"Thank you," he said.

She got out of the car without saying a word and walked away, annoyed with herself at the excitement his light touch seemed to have caused.

Please don't let me be developing a physical attraction for a kook who thinks he walks through walls.

It wasn't until Amy was inside her apartment and headed upstairs that she realized Lhatu had never been to her place when she wasn't there. She'd never had reason to bring him upstairs. Anyone might guess her bedroom was filled with clutter, but she wore such little make-up. How would he even know she had a stool in front of a make-up mirror?

******

The perfect private detective was harder to find than Pavel expected. True, he had unusual requirements. He needed someone who didn't care why he wanted to find these two girls, and a surprising number of qualified men made it clear that the purpose for finding them was a consideration. Who'd have thought?

He also needed someone with no ties to his adversaries, lest this little obsession of his be used against him. Unfortunately, Pavel had amassed a rather lengthy list of enemies and some of them had a considerable number of people working for them. Thus a lot of potential investigators were removed from consideration.

He laughed to himself as he poured a small glass of the scotch he preferred to vodka. Go figure. Capable private investigators with no scruples *and* no underworld ties were in short supply.

Pavel had turned the project of locating this detective over to Samir, a discreet, efficient man who handled many of Pavel's business matters not requiring muscle or physical unpleasantness. Samir was resourceful, and Pavel remained confident Samir would eventually find the right man for this delicate assignment.

By early March, Samir had. Sort of. Samir had found the right woman. A mildly displeased Pavel found himself speaking to a tiny Chinese girl who couldn't have been older than thirty, and for all Pavel knew might have been a seventeen-year-old virgin herself. She didn't weigh more than ninety pounds, and she spoke no language other than Mandarin. She brought her own translator, another Chinese girl fluent in Russian and Hindi, and technically Pavel was talking to this translator, which he liked even less.

Samir had assured Pavel before the meeting that the woman had no unacceptable ties anywhere, had impeccable references, and her reputation for discretion was exceptional.

They exchanged a few basics before she informed him through her translator that she assumed the penalty for failure on this project would be death. She was fine with that because she did not fail. She hoped a mutually beneficial working relationship would ensue once that was established.

"Do you have a problem locating young women for me to use for my pleasure?" Pavel asked. The translator didn't pause. Mandarin was repeated. Mandarin was replied.

"I always meet my obligations. I never make judgments."

Pavel was beginning to like this woman better already. "How soon can you start?"

March 2012

22. Knowing

Vanida never told anyone about her secret brother. Even as a child, she sensed no one would believe she met anyone in a special body that could fly through the air. Now that it had been months since it happened, she wondered if she'd made it up.

Pim always told her to get her nose out of those books, and had often added that Vanida had too much imagination for the life she'd lead. Maybe her longing for adventure, and for family like other girls had, pushed her to invent a brother and a superpower so real she believed in them? Vanida had absorbed enough psychology from her reading to understand how this made sense.

She was scared when the new girl tried to talk her into running away. All her life she'd seen other girls punished, sometimes horribly, for such an offense. She'd decided long ago she had nothing to run to, but this Michelle kept insisting her life could be better.

Once they learned the owner was coming to visit, Michelle convinced her no better opportunity for escape would come along. Everyone would be preoccupied. They could be gone for hours before they were missed. Vanida saw the wisdom.

They were both allowed freedom of movement throughout the brothel and the enclosed courtyard providing outdoor seating for the bar. Neither had ever left the premises, but Vanida had seen a place where two people could get over the courtyard wall if they worked together.

The night before the escape, Vanida was surprised to wake up in her special body for the first time in months. So it was real?

She thought this body was for seeing her brother, but no brother was in sight. Rather, she hovered above the courtyard wall, and saw where one could crawl along a ledge and jump down into an adjoining courtyard. It led to a possible escape route. Vanida let her special body move through the neighboring courtyard to figure out how to best proceed. When she awoke back on her sleeping mat, she decided the vision was a good omen. She would escape with Michelle and see what happened.

The real crawl over the courtyard wall went fast and without incident, and the girls moved on foot after they escaped, keeping to the shadows as they made their way to the edge of the city. They traveled by night and rested and stayed hidden by day, finishing the food and water they'd brought, and then stealing fruit out of yards to stave off hunger and thirst.

After a week they were in the country, and set up a camp of sorts in a small clearing. When it became obvious the clearing wasn't frequented by anyone, they stayed. They snuck a little food and water from the nearby small farms, while they rested and considered what to do next.

After a few days of living this way, the girls wondered if their initial instinct to get out of the city was a poor plan. Sure, hiding in the country wasn't what their captors expected, and they were in little danger of being found. On the other hand, they also had no resources to help them.

Michelle thought they needed to get to the tourist destinations in the southern parts of Thailand. Vanida knew nothing about this part of the country, but Michelle insisted there were beaches where they could seek out English speakers on holiday. They could find someone willing to call Amy to verify their story. They'd have to choose this ally wisely, as being turned over to the authorities by a tourist wary of a scam could land them in trouble as bad as what they'd run from.

Walking all the way to Southern Thailand wasn't going to be an option. They needed normal clothes. They needed food. They needed money. Their most obvious choices were turning to serious theft, or turning tricks. Neither girl was willing to accept either alternative.

******

Usha knew staying at the convent until after the summer rains would keep her out of danger longer, but she felt safer with Jampa than she had with anyone in a long time. If she waited, there would be no knowledgeable Jampa to lead her down the mountain. Worse yet, she feared the hours of chanting each day and the lack of things to read and do would sap her will to leave.

Usha was glad the women in the convent had a place where they could live as they chose. She was happy it was this gorgeous location, because thanks to their lack of greed and love of the earth, this place would remain protected as long as the convent stood. There should be such places, and there should be such people; those who embraced simplicity and found joy in their faith. Usha was all for it and all for them. She just wasn't one of them.

Word was the snow would begin to melt in a few weeks and most of the trails would open. Then, she and Jampa would be able to descend. Usha began counting the days.

******

"I'm guessing Michelle wasn't a virgin," Amy said. She'd invited Teddie over for a few days during her spring break, as Teddie's parents decided having their daughter stay put during the holiday was the safest course of action, and Haley had gone off on a trek. Amy had two items of unfinished business for the two of them to cover. Getting this personal information about Michelle was the easier of the two.

"The police asked me that too. They told me they needed to know because it affected their investigation."

Amy nodded with understanding. "I'm glad they looked into it. A virgin is likely to get marketed separately because she's worth more money."

"Well, she wasn't one. She had a serious boyfriend starting as a freshman. He wasn't bad at first, but after a while he kept pressuring her. Of course," Teddie rolled her eyes. "Finally she did it, but said it wasn't much fun. I don't think the boyfriend got how she was supposed to enjoy it too, you know?"

“Yeah, young boys don’t know much about that, do they?”

“It got worse,” Teddie said. “He got all like he owned her and had to know where she was every minute. Michelle got annoyed and broke it off.”

Amy was shaking her head. “It’s the one part of the human body I don’t understand.” Teddie looked at her, perplexed. “The hymen,” Amy clarified. “A silly little flimsy piece of skin that serves no function and causes women no end of grief.”

“You mean, if there was no such thing then people would never know if a girl was a virgin?”

“Exactly. A girl could make any claim that suited her, just like a boy can. Do you know that in much of the world the groom is expected to show off the bloody sheets from the wedding night to prove the virtue of his new bride?”

“No. That’s ridiculous. And disgusting.”

“Worse than that. If the sheets show no evidence of a hymen, in some places she can be executed. Who knows how many loving couples have snuck in animal’s blood to save the bride’s life? Who knows how many grooms had to make a horrible choice once they were surprised by clean sheets?”

“Maybe doctors ought to get rid of it at birth, like circumcision?” Teddie said. Amy had to laugh.

“You’d go a long way towards eliminating trafficking in young girls if you did that.”

Then Amy changed the subject, hoping to catch Teddie off guard. “Did you see a note in my room when you and Lhatu were transporting around? If so, how did it look and what did it say?”

Teddie hesitated. “Lhatu asked me not to talk about it.”

“Well, I’m asking you to. He and I already talked, if that helps.”

“Okay, it does. He wanted to talk to you first.” After hearing this last piece of news, Teddie described the note in detail. She saw the conflict grow on Amy's face.

“You shouldn’t have left that note, should you?” Teddie asked. “Because now you have to decide whether Lhatu and I are both sneaky liars, or we’re capable of doing incredible things. I mean, if we’re telling you the truth, this is amazing. We could learn all kinds of secrets. There has to be a way to get rich doing this; it isn’t a little thing. If you hadn’t left the note in the first place, then you could just keep wondering.”

Amy gave Teddie a long look. "That's an amazing amount of insight from a seventeen-year-old. Has anyone ever told you you're wise beyond your years?"

Teddie nodded. "I get that sometimes. In this case, it's not so wise. I'm going through the same process. Part of Lhatu's training is teaching me to accept changes in my own idea of reality without losing my ability to function in what he calls the default world."

Amy thought this made sense. She was glad Lhatu wasn't only imparting technique, but was wise enough to give his young pupil other tools.

"Are you thinking about corporate espionage for a career now?" Amy probed a little further.

Teddie laughed as she shook her head. "Lhatu and his people are fairly, well, what I'd call superstitious about this. They're adamant it's a gift one should never use for their own gain. I don't share their fear of cosmic retribution, but I do think corporate espionage is a bad line of work. Once I find Michelle and Usha, I don't see me doing more of this. I want it to end well, and then I want to go back to my own comfy default reality"

******

As days of hiding turned into weeks, Michelle grew more restless. She missed having a bed, she missed real food, and she desperately wanted to contact the people who cared about her.

She began pressing Vanida harder for information on anyone they could turn to for help. Vanida didn't trust people in authority, and those who'd owned her had gone out of their way to nurture this mistrust. When Michelle kept pushing, Vanida finally admitted she'd heard of some national shelters set up by the Thai government for international victims of forced labor and prostitution. Word amongst the girls was that once you checked in, you were a prisoner there until your case was resolved. If it ever was.

Vanida thought such a place might be okay for Michelle, because she had family that could be found and the shelters would probably send Michelle home. However, Vanida was scared she'd end up a life-long resident while social workers tried to track down her nationality and origin.

"Maybe it was a bad idea to run away together," Vanida said, using the English sentence structure Michelle was teaching her in exchange for lessons in basic Thai. "We're not alike. Maybe you should go back to the city and find this shelter."

Michelle noticed how much her new friend's accent had improved, and wished she had half of Vanida's flair for languages.

"I'm not leaving you. We never would have made it out of Khae's brothel if you hadn't figured out how to go over that fence. Besides, I doubt I could get back there by myself and find the place. My Thai sucks. We need another idea."

But Vanida didn't have one.

That night, Vanida was in her special body again, with no brother calling her. She drifted up above their clearing and examined various paths. She figured she needed every scrap of information she could get, so she explored different routes and traveled a considerable distance down several of the more promising roads.

Finally, she found an alternative she liked. She'd discuss options with Michelle in the morning, but she had to think of a way to explain her new-found knowledge. Last time, she'd told Michelle she'd found the route out of the courtyard when a workman left a ladder. How could she explain this information? She'd think of something.

"There's a Catholic church about a day's walk from here. An elderly priest runs it, and he has a housekeeper who cleans and cooks for him. They probably won't turn us over to the police. I say we walk there and ask for help."

Vanida said it as though it was no big deal.

"How in the world do you suddenly know about this place?"

"I dreamt about it. When I woke up I remembered hearing about it. I have an exceptional memory."

Michelle looked doubtful, but she'd didn't have a better idea. "Do you think you can find this church?"

"I do. Before you got up I explored a little on my own. I know I found the right road. It's busy during the day, so we need to travel at night. Can you walk that far?"

Michelle rubbed her feet. The only shoes available at the brothel had been meant for enticing customers, so she and Vanida had chosen to leave barefoot. The trek out of the city proved Vanida's feet to be tougher than hers.

"Sure. Let's take a day to forage some food and rest, and then we'll go."

******

Jampa was world class when it came to waiting. He'd left his monastery on the spur of the moment, fueled by concern for a sister he wasn't even sure he had. Once he realized the folly of his haste, he'd retreated into the patience that was second nature for him.

However, with the spring thaw coming, travel would be better before the summer rains began. It was time to leave. Although his sister no longer called to him, and he had little idea of her exact situation, he knew her life had not been good when he last saw her. It remained his duty to give her aid.

He knew she lived somewhere filled with greenery year-round. Bright overhead sunlight shone on leaves larger than any here, as they exploded into a cacophony of life beyond that found in his serene mountains. He believed if he could get to the land of giant green leaves, he'd find his sister. His plan was simple; he'd accompany this studious girl of India, who also came from a world filled with verdant green.

Usha had been a gift to him. Forced to flee, she was as alone as he and Noom. Jampa understood the world was filled with variety, even though he'd experienced little of it. It made sense to him that Usha needed to find shelter more suitable to her own nature. He would help her find such shelter.

He believed his doing so, his somehow returning Usha to the world of green, would gain him access to his sister and her world.

******

Olumiji knew his personal surveillance project had gone on longer than his small group of volunteers had bargained for. Soon, he was going to need to get them some relief or find another approach to the problem of looking out for his friend's daughter.

Both Somadina and the woman from Kolkata had already cut back their available hours because of their own family's needs, and Mr. and Mrs. Dutta had taken several short breaks due to minor health issues.

The boy Tariq had been the weakest telepath of the six, and Olumiji included the Pakistani teen as much to help him get over the death of his own sister than anything else. However, Tariq had grown mentally stronger over the last two months, his abilities improving with the daily practice, and with something else Olumiji had done his best to ignore.

Tariq had gone from being sympathetic to Teddie's quest to help her friends to being preoccupied with Teddie. It was a normal reaction for a teenage boy, Olumiji supposed, particularly one who was bed-ridden and had little else in the way of pleasant distraction. As the others needed more and more breaks, Tariq filled in for them. Olumiji was noticing that some days Tariq was on duty for ten to fifteen hours a day. It was too much.

Fortunately, Tariq did mind his manners, respecting Teddie's privacy with an almost charming sense of honor. The biggest problem with the situation was the slowness with which Tariq's own body was healing. Olumiji suspected, on some level, the boy was reluctant to recover. Healing meant being forced to give up his duties looking out for a girl who had started to fill his dreams. Olumiji could have kicked himself. He should have seen this one coming.

In his concern for Teddie's safety, Olumiji occasionally allowed himself to probe a bit into her mind, and into the minds of her friends. He would never do this normally, but there were special rules for special dangers, exceptions to be handled with care.

When he felt Teddie's anger at Haley's exclusion from the climbing team, he exited. He sympathized with the girls, but this was not his problem to solve. In fact, it wasn't even his business.

When he felt Amy's excitement at Lhatu's brief touch of her hand, he exited faster. When he felt Teddie's joy as she accepted Tariq's invitation to be his friend on a social networking site, he smiled. They weren't supposed to have such contact and they knew it, but it would be harmless if they were careful. Maybe if Teddie became his friend in real life, then Tariq would heal faster.

As Olumiji let his mind skim through those most closely involved, searching for any scrap to help him, he was surprised to find Amy researching on the internet, and he could feel the anger driving her search. It wasn't anger at someone she cared about, but rather a rage at someone she'd never met. This did sound like it might be his business. Olumiji decided it was no time for playing games. He called Amy.

"Any breakthroughs in figuring out exactly who it is we are trying to keep away from you and Teddie?" he asked.

"I didn't even think to tell you," she said, and Olumiji felt her genuine regret it hadn't occurred to her. He also felt her confusion as to exactly what it was Olumiji was doing to look out for Teddie. "We never see you guys. I didn't know if you were still in town, on the lookout."

Olumiji explained he wasn't in town but was monitoring at a distance. Amy shrugged and filled in the details about the tip that had led to suspicions regarding a Russian who had transplanted much of his crime organization to Manali, India, over a decade ago. She was looking into the man's hometown on the internet, trying to learn more.

"It always helps to know what you're up against," Olumiji agreed. Amy appreciated the lack of criticism in his voice. "My group takes a fairly invisible approach to security," he added. "But I'll see if I can learn anything about this guy and get back to you."

Olumiji sighed. Amy said this man Pavel lived in Manali, on the northwestern edge of India. He'd never be able to establish rapport with a man so different and distasteful without the extra help of proximity and visual contact. It looked like he was going to Manali to see what he could learn.

******

Teddie was restless the day she returned to the dorm after staying at Amy's place. Haley wouldn't be back until tomorrow, and Teddie tossed around in her bed well into the night, bothered by Amy's poster board note. Teddie had been delighted to see it at first, but now she understood Lhatu's concern had been for her wellbeing.

As long as she could compartmentalize her two worlds, there wasn't much dissonance. This strange mist body she was growing to love was, in some sense, a fantasy, a child's playful imagination at work. She believed in it but she didn't. Having a skeptical adult like Amy acknowledge concrete proof that her traveling body was as real as her breakfast, was disturbing. Teddie understood why Lhatu wanted to leave some vagueness, so she could have wiggle room to reconcile the two worlds.

As Teddie started to fall asleep, she felt her own mind asking for permission to go traveling. She liked this new feeling of control.

"Yes. I do believe I would like to check on my friends," she said, preparing to go swirling down streets and over fields. Many minutes later she looked down in exasperation at Usha's sleeping body. "I've got to learn how to do this during the day. All I ever see is people sleeping."

She moved outside. The beauty surrounding this convent remained breathtaking. The moonlight turned the tall pine trees a deep, dark green against the sky and made the snow-topped mountain peaks glisten behind them. Teddie wished she could feel the cold crispness of the air and smell the pines, but such joys were saved for solid existence. Travelers could only look.

She saw the barn. Remembering the boy, she passed inside to see if he was there. The barn held a handful of sheep and a medium-sized dog, all sleeping soundly. On the far side of the sheep slept the boy. Teddie was comforted to see Usha still had a friend with her.

As she moved in to look closer, the dog sat up with a gruff bark. A skittish Teddie sat up in her own bed with a start. While her heart pounded she looked around the empty room for any danger. Nothing seemed amiss.

She willed herself to calm down, hoping she could relax enough to go check on Michelle, who she always found sleeping in the clearing. After being startled, however, the light trance state wouldn't return. Teddie tossed in her bed until morning.

April 2012

23. Urging

The easiest way for Olumiji to connect with Pavel was for Pavel to experience a strong emotion, any strong emotion. Olumiji had been in Manali for two days now and had observed the man three times from a distance. One of those times he ate an entire breakfast seated only two tables away.

Emotionally, Pavel was a closed book, his feelings held as tightly in check as Olumiji expected. Pavel projected a fierce sense of pride, competitiveness and a streak of cruelty. One of the biggest sources of his conceit was how well he controlled his own emotions. Yet even those with exceptional self-control are occasionally overtaken with their own passions.

Olumiji followed Pavel's consciousness, hovering with his mind, waiting for that breakthrough. Late on the second day it came. Olumiji feared the emotion would be rage, or some sadistic urge, or perhaps even fear of Pavel's enemies. It surprised Olumiji when it was surprise.

Pavel was happy. No, make that ecstatic. His expectations had been more than exceeded. Someone he considered trivial—ah, yes, a small young Asian woman—had performed an impressive feat for him. This woman, what was she? Pavel thought of her as a private detective, but of a special kind. He pictured her at a computer screen. She was a computer detective?

As Olumiji's emotions began to move with the rhythm of the man, he felt Pavel's pleasure and then his anticipation. The woman had found something precious to him. Found two things. How wonderful. It would be impossible for any good telepath not to also enjoy the appreciation Pavel was feeling. Then Olumiji got a quick glimpse of what the joyful anticipation was for. His breath stopped.

This was not going to happen.

Pavel believed the young Mandarin woman knew where to find both Usha and Michelle. One was hidden high in the mountains, and the other was on the run somewhere tropical, trying to get to a safe place where people she could trust would help her.

Pavel would send men now to get the one girl, tucked away at a convent where she thought the world could not touch her. He would be ready for the other to surface in Thailand. His Chinese detective assured him she could intercept any message from or about Michelle fast enough for his men in Thailand to get to Michelle before anyone else.

Olumiji had to talk to Amy. What could she possibly do to keep Michelle from surfacing and asking for help? He had to talk to Lhatu. The convent Teddie had been to twice needed to be found and somebody had to warn those nuns.

Yet secrecy could play a big role in staying one step ahead of Pavel. The whole point of being a hacker was no one knew you existed, right? By even learning of the Mandarin woman's existence, Olumiji had gained a big advantage. It only stayed an advantage, though, as long as this despicable man had no idea Usha and Michelle had friends who knew what he was up to. This made it unwise for Olumiji to call Amy, or anyone else Pavel knew about. Perhaps his cyber-detective was monitoring Amy and her staff already.

Who was safe to talk to? There was the elderly couple in Darjeeling, the Dutta's, who were part of the team looking out for Teddie. Pavel would have no way of knowing about them. Their telepathic skills were good, and they were local.

He sought them out mentally. The man was napping, but the woman was baking, and on duty, keeping a vague awareness of Teddie's emotional state as she put pastries in the oven. She responded to Olumiji's mental inquiry, and understood his need to communicate with Amy and Lhatu in secret.

The Dutta's had a videophone account and Mrs. Dutta had a friend in Mandi, a town not too far from Olumiji. If he could get to this friend's house, the two old girlfriends could have a video chat that would raise no suspicions.

Olumiji got in his rental car, and as he drove out of the mountains, his thoughts churned. Things were happening fast. Who else could he contact to help? Maybe it was time to inform Amy about his telepaths in x^0. What more could he do? Could she do? While he was on the subject, wasn't there more the people in c^3 could be doing, too?

******

Lhatu and Olumiji were more colleagues than friends. They had a good deal of respect for each other, but they not only came from different worlds, they lived in different worlds.

Olumiji was not the official head of anything. Rather, as one of the more adept telepaths in x^0, and as a natural leader, he often accepted being in charge. Someone had to do that job.

He was passionate about many things. He loved to travel and to meet new telepaths, and he was glad to see his organization growing as telepathy became more common. He had a reformer's zeal for making the world better, and he believed telepathy, and the empathy that accompanied it, could, would and did make Earth a more peaceful place.

Lhatu came from what could best be described as a monarchy. Tradition dictated leadership be passed across genders and skip a generation. Thus, a grandmother passed the reins on to the most capable of her grandsons. As a grandfather, he would pass leadership on to his most adept granddaughter. The custom had preserved stability while maintaining a variety of perspectives in the organization.

Usually, several candidates with traveling abilities were produced in a generation, and the reigning monarch had a choice. Not in Lhatu's case. He was aware he was his grandmother's only possibility, and he would someday inherit the mantle of running c^3. He and everyone else involved accepted this.

Lhatu traveled in both his physical and his spirit body when he needed to, but usually only within Asia. For most of its existence, c^3 hadn't extended beyond his continent. His grandmother, as a young girl, had been the first to deal with the ramifications of modern society and she was surprised to discover how many travelers there were in other places.

Lhatu wasn't sure if that knowledge was a good thing. It wasn't that he disliked those from other parts of the world, but he often found their ideas detrimental to the calm he worked hard to cultivate. He wasn't interested in c^3 growing its membership or becoming involved in the issues of society. He didn't believe his organization should be finding ways to use out-of-body traveling to improve the world, and he hadn't given thought to how it could.

Not that he lacked compassion. He was a caring person, as he had proved more than once by rescuing a young one from an unfortunate situation. What Lhatu had was more peace of mind than Olumiji, and what he lacked was a sense that the world needed to be fixed.

It was a different point of view, and each man's viewpoint shaped and reflected his group.

Over the past few decades, x^0 had embraced technology and had a thriving website, worldwide meetings, and many members who communicated by telepathy and email, often simultaneously. The younger ones kept migrating to ever-newer technology, bringing their talents for transmitting and receiving emotions with them.

Because c^3 was smaller, more centralized and less modern, communication was face-to-face as needed. There was no gathering of travelers on either plane, and they seldom sought each other out. Telepathy, by its nature, was an activity for two or more people. Traveling, by its nature, was solitary.

The two organizations shared roots going back millennia, so there was contact between them. By custom, it was always cooperative. However, the two organizations had never found themselves joined in a project like this one. Their need to work together was bringing out differences both groups would have rather ignored.

Lhatu was video-conferencing with Olumiji when Olumiji's impatient "Can't you people do more?" irritated Lhatu. He didn't like feeling irritated.

Of course he hadn't bothered other travelers with this. It was Lhatu's issue, and he and Teddie were handling it. Olumiji wanted him to send out some sort of alarm? He should get travelers the world over to form a posse and seek out the missing girls and the goons Pavel had set loose to find them? Traveling didn't work that way. Like telepathy, it was about emotional connection, and Olumiji of all people should understand that.

Lhatu and Amy were at the Dutta's house. The elderly couple who'd been part of the group guarding Teddie for the past three months had sat Lhatu and Amy in front of a computer screen showing Olumiji's face, provided them with a pot of tea and a plate of cookies, and then gone out to their garden.

For the first part of the conversation, Amy stood in the background and listened. In their agitation, the men ignored her and spoke bluntly. It didn't take long for Amy to figure out she had more metaphysical issues to deal with than c^3's members floating through space. So Olumiji was a telepath? As was Teddie's mother? In its own way, this was starting to make more sense.

Amy was sympathetic to Olumiji as he asked Lhatu for more urgency. She'd also wondered why Lhatu hadn't jumped in with all the resources he could muster. She'd even wondered if his mystery organization consisted of only him and his grandmother.

Finally, she interrupted the conversation.

"Look, I don't have any special abilities to offer, but I've got contacts in an extensive network that reaches out to women worldwide. From my office, I can get every group to broadcast a 'do not acknowledge any dealings with these girls in any way' message. I'll keep it vague and imply the man who is after them has ears everywhere. Pavel will get wind of it of course, but so what? He already hates me and knows I'm working on this, and he could get more suspicious if I'm not doing anything."

"That's excellent." Olumiji nodded. "Please do it right away. I can't tell you how sure Pavel is that he will have both girls in his possession in days. They've insulted his pride, and too many others know it. Even sadder, he's more determined to have them because of their resourcefulness. He views them as worthy prey, and he is their hunter. The things he is fantasizing about, well, they are beyond comprehension."

Lhatu answered. "You can believe Teddie when she says Usha is still at the convent. I've been looking into places in Bhutan that fit the description. It's no surprise there are a lot of small, remote Buddhist convents and no centralized records. So far I've learned of over two dozen that fit what Teddie has told us. Each one is difficult to get to and cut off from all outside communication. Usha should have been impossible to find at any of them. All I can think of is this computer sleuth found out something through the family that gave Usha a ride."

"I got information about that from Pavel," Olumiji said. "His detective ran a scan on every email sent in Bhutan, looking for references to a girl from India. Maybe some person wrote of helping an Indian girl, and named the convent they took her to. Such innocent crumbs can be followed."

Lhatu looked sad that even the most isolated places were no longer impervious to prying eyes. "I'll have Teddie keep monitoring both of her friends and report anything."

Olumiji added, "The best we can hope for is both girls act as smart as they have so far, and they lay low until we find a way to stop this man."

Amy looked at both Lhatu and Olumiji, puzzled. She got how both of these men had skills that would amaze the average person. She got how they both had big hearts in their own way and how each one wanted to help Usha and Michelle. However, she didn't get why waiting and hoping was the best approach.

"I have another plan," she said. "How about we try *much* harder to locate the exact whereabouts of both the girls by using means Pavel would never expect and cannot detect." She gave Lhatu a long meaningful look. "And then, once we know exactly where they are, we communicate with helpful locals in ways Pavel cannot possibly hack into," and she gave Olumiji an equally meaningful look. "Then we can have those same locals hide the girls until somebody with serious fire power and authority can get them out. I'll handle the last part."

She gave both men a matter-of fact stare.

Olumiji was trying hard to stifle a smile. "I was considering filling you in more about my organization, but you seem to have deduced plenty. I'd be happy to handle my part of your suggested strategy."

Lhatu didn't respond. He was irritated by Olumiji's uncharacteristic push for him to be more proactive. Now, he found Amy pushing him to be even more annoying.

She ignored what was almost a glare from him and continued. "Doesn't what I'm suggesting seem like a better approach than 'let's wait and hope nothing bad happens to them?' Don't you think?"

Lhatu tried to calm himself. This woman had already caused him more agitation than he'd felt in years. "Perhaps c^3 could provide more resources and put a greater sense of urgency behind our part of the effort."

"Wonderful." Amy had accomplished what she wanted. "Let's get to work."

******

The Catholic nun who greeted Michelle and Vanida inside the simple chapel took one look at their skimpy clothes and reached out her hands in warmth. "Girls, you have come to the right place," she said. And they had.

Sister Teresa Marie helped the aging priest care for his small parish just outside of Bangkok's furthest reaches of urban sprawl. She was a sister of the Good Shepherd, a group of Roman Catholic nuns dedicated to helping prostitutes and victims of human trafficking throughout the world. Besides helping Father François, she volunteered in Bangkok three times a week, working to aid and comfort the willing and not-so-willing workers in the city's famous sex trade. She assumed these two girls had sought her out.

"Come," she said in English after she heard Michelle speak. She gave them water and food and pulled assorted ill-fitting clothes out of the bin of lost and donated goods. Then she showed them where they could bathe, and where they could rest for a while if they wished and sleep later that night.

She listened with surprise to Michelle's story of a distant kidnapping and with sorrow to Vanida's tale of life in the sex trade. She nodded and patted their hands and gave them more to eat.

"I need to contact my parents. I need to get ahold of my friend's organization in Darjeeling. I'm hoping I can bring Vanida with me, maybe as a refugee seeking asylum. Oh I am so, so glad we found you." Michelle sat at the wooden table finishing the last of the rice in her bowl, and she looked like she was ready to cry.

"Father François left this morning. He's gone until tomorrow, visiting an ailing brother in the city. You're welcome here for as long as you need to stay, but let's begin by letting your family and friends know you're safe."

Sister Teresa Marie walked over to her desk and wiggled her mouse to bring her computer back to life.

"You use a computer?" Michelle said.

The sister laughed. "Most of us work a little on the side, to raise money for the order and the women we help. Quite a few of us do graphic design, including me. Some create greeting cards, and we even have a few nuns who compose advertising jingles."

The screen opened to her mailbox, and at the top of the page was a message marked as extremely urgent.

"That's odd. Let me read this real quick." She held her breath as she read.

"Well, this is incredible. Did you girls know you are the object of an international manhunt? I guess I mean a woman-hunt. Anyway, you've made news. Here's a bulletin from the Mother Superior saying you're being hunted down by some crime lord who is more powerful than previously thought." Sister Teresa Marie sucked in her breath as she kept reading.

"This man owned the brothel you ran away from. He's described as now being obsessed with you, Michelle, and with a friend of yours. Usha? My heavens. There is great concern any attempt on your part to contact anyone could be intercepted and place you and those helping you in considerable danger."

She turned to the two girls, almost amused. "And you found your way to my doorstep! Aren't I the lucky one?"

Sister Teresa Marie didn't mind a challenge. "It says anyone who encounters you should provide supplies, then move you out of their residence as fast as possible, without alerting anyone. I don't believe I've ever gotten a message like this before."

She called the two girls over to the computer so they could see the photograph of Michelle and read the entire message.

"I guess we have to thank the Lord you didn't show up yesterday, don't we? Or even this morning. You know, my order would never send something out like this unless you two were in considerable jeopardy. I'm so sorry, Michelle, but I don't think we should contact your family or do anything else to let anyone know where you are."

Sister Teresa Marie shook her head at the two girls as she considered what to do next. "I don't care what they say, I am going to have you stay here long enough to get a good night's sleep. Then I'll get you out of here before Father Francois gets back in the morning. The less people who know you were here, the better. Do you think either or you could drive a motor scooter?"

"I've driven one," Michelle said. "My ex-boyfriend had one."

"Good. You're going to get up early in the morning and steal mine, and then get as far from here as you possibly can."

"We can't run from this guy our whole lives," Michelle said.

"No, you can't. But you can run for a while longer, until somebody in authority puts a stop to him."

She opened a draw filled with tape and string and paper clips. In the back was a small envelope holding a crumpled wad of Thai Baht. She pressed the money into Vanida's hand.

"It's not much, but take it."

Then she turned off and unplugged her computer, and turned off her cell phone too.

"We'll just have a nice quiet evening here while you rest up and eat your fill. Maybe we can play some cards."

******

Teddie was restless again and she tossed around in bed unable to relax. She'd been expecting to go over to Amy's after dinner, but Lhatu called to let her know something urgent had come up, and he and Amy would be in touch tomorrow. Urgent? And she was supposed to wait until tomorrow without knowing what it was?

She willed herself to calm down, and then to relax enough to travel. As she often did now at night, she wanted to get a glimpse of Michelle or Usha, to reassure herself they were safe. Tonight was Michelle's turn.

Because she was worried, her trance state wouldn't come. Once she relaxed, she fell into a deep, hard sleep, and didn't wake up until she saw the first light of dawn through the window. Feeling rested, she found herself following the dawn's faint glow as she went out through the glass in the window. She wasn't surprised when she began rushing down the street and her mist body spun onto a busy highway. She closed her eyes as she sped along the shoulder. Occasionally, she felt the annoying sensation of a bug passing through her and squirmed.

When she opened her eyes she was whooshing through the air along the top of a stream. Lhatu had been teaching her about this—how to let her energy-self seek out those she was connected to without the interference of her solid mind. Her travel body seemed certain of where it was going, so Teddie closed her eyes to wait until the journey was over.

Only it didn't end. She kept moving and after a while Teddie opened her eyes again, discovering it was a bright sunny morning and she was traveling down a highway, although she was moving at a more normal speed, like maybe the speed of a car. She seemed to be keeping pace with two farm girls on a motorbike. She looked over at them, then looked at them again.

The one driving the bike was Michelle, dressed like a local peasant. Riding behind her was the other twin. Neither girl had a helmet. They were unharmed, and both grinning at their freedom.

Teddie glanced up to see a truck coming straight at her and in a second of panic she forgot she could pass through the truck as easily as she could bugs or a wall. She started to scream and sat up in her bed with a shriek. Haley rolled over.

"Teddie? You okay?"

"Yeah, I'm fine. Everybody's fine. Go back to sleep."

The next day Teddie skipped class to go over to Amy's place and find out what was happening.

"There's a new urgency," Amy said, and Teddie couldn't help noticing how Amy had taken charge. "The creep who bought Usha is back in the picture, and he's decided he wants both of your friends. He's found a detective with impressive internet capabilities to work with him."

"How would we even know such a thing?" Teddie asked.

"Your mother's friend, Olumiji. I guess the man does read minds, and he managed to read Pavel's. This woman is pinpointing Usha and Michelle's locations now."

"This woman?" That surprised Teddie.

"Females can do anything." Amy laughed without humor. "The point is we no longer need you to check on your friends and make sure they're safe. We need you to figure out *exactly* where they are. "

"But when I go to them, I don't know exactly where *I* am."

"So I've been told," Amy said, gesturing to Lhatu. "But it looks like you can be taught to do more. This group of telepaths watching you—yes, I got to learn all about them yesterday too—they can probably do more as well. We have to assume Pavel will soon have eyes on all standard means of travel and communication. That would make him almost invincible."

"Only we have access to non-standard means of travel and communication that he's not likely to consider in his wildest dreams," Teddie said.

"We do." Lhatu said. "Only I'm going to have to teach you much more for you to be able to do this. It's not our way to push a young one like you, but I have been persuaded" — he gave Amy a look — "that circumstances require even more deviation from our normal approach. We start today."

The Abode of Light

April 2012

24. Bringing

Shortly after dinner Haley called Amy's apartment from the school phone, hoping to talk to Teddie. "She's working with Lhatu; can I help?" Amy said.

"Maybe. I just wanted to talk through something. I have to make a decision, and, I don't know …"

"No problem, Haley. I can't do anything to help them here, so let me come over."

Haley cleared off a spot on her bed as Amy came into the room. All of the remaining surfaces were covered in books, climbing gear, workout equipment, and maps and notes belonging to both girls. They'd filled a room designed for four. Amy smiled at the mess. Girls after her own heart.

"Teddie told me about your being pushed off of the team, Haley, and I'm really sorry about it."

"Thanks," Haley said. "I guess other people are, too. I heard today from Hans, one of the other climbers. He calculated the ratio of my body weight to my pack and then did the same for the smallest guy on the climb, his own buddy, a hundred-and-forty-five-pound male whom nobody is questioning. Hans figured if he carried four pounds of my gear, I'd be even with his buddy."

"Wow. In a world where every pound matters, isn't having another climber offer to carry anything rather amazing?"

"It is," Haley said. "My first reaction was I wouldn't dream of putting another person at risk just so I could do this thing. Hans is six-two and strong as an ox and he says the few pounds won't matter to him. He has some other arguments, too."

"I'd like to hear them."

"Basically, he's close to his godchild. He says he wants to live in world where people get to chase their dreams. He wants his goddaughter to climb mountains if she wants to, and to have women to look up to who've done it. He said he doesn't want little Elsie growing up in a world where guys find ways to keep girls from doing things instead of finding ways to include them. He says the world of excluding sucks for him, too."

"Wow," Amy said. "Can I meet this guy?"

"He's already got a girlfriend." Haley laughed. "I do like what he says, too, but ... "

Amy understood. "But you want to do this without any special favors."

"Exactly."

"You know, Haley, everybody needs help once in a while. Here, let me show you something,"

She typed a few words into a search engine on Haley's open laptop. "You ever heard of Kathrine Switzer?"

"The marathon runner?"

"That's right. In 1967, she was the first woman to run in the Boston marathon as a registered participant. She used her initials and they thought she was a man. When they learned otherwise during the race, they tried to force her off of the course. Look at this picture. What do you see?"

"An official charging at a woman runner."

"What else?"

"Well, there's another guy trying to push him away and several guys surrounding this lady so she can keep on running."

"That's exactly what they did," Amy said. "At the expense of their own finish time, and even their own ability to stay in the race, they surrounded her so she could keep going. Do know what reason the Boston Marathon gave for their behavior? They said it was medical fact that women would injure their delicate inner parts if they ran farther than a mile and a half."

"No." Haley said. "In the 1960s, right along with Woodstock and landing on the moon, they believed a woman couldn't run farther than a mile and a half without hurting herself?"

"That's right. Now I'm guessing Kathrine and others like her wanted to run without help from anyone. Suppose she'd told those men surrounding her to get lost?

Haley understood. "She wouldn't have been able to finish. She wouldn't have had the chance to prove women can run far."

"I keep a copy of this picture on my desk," Amy said. "It reminds me men aren't the enemy. Decent people everywhere work to allow opportunities for everyone. It's not male versus female, it's the reasonable people of the world versus the assholes. Both sides come with penises and with vaginas."

"Yeah," she laughed, "they do. It's just having a guy carry something for you is so trite."

"If there was a larger woman on the climb who offered to carry four pounds of your gear so you'd qualify, would you let her?"

Haley nodded. "I might."

"Then maybe you shouldn't deny this reasonable man the chance make the sort of world he wants to live in, just because he's a guy."

Haley gave Amy a heartfelt hug. "Hans said if I gave him an okay tonight, he'd talk to the other climbers and call my dad. I'll set this in motion and see how it goes."

******

"Are you sure?" the oldest nun asked Usha, her voice so ancient it was a whisper.

Usha nodded. "I am forever grateful for your asylum, but it's time for me to go."

The nun nodded too, without argument. Usha gathered up her only possessions: a small flask of water and a few rice cakes they'd given her. She put on the thick shawl one of the younger nuns insisted she take.

"I'll tell the real world you all say hi," she said as she turned to go.

"This is the real world," she heard one of the nuns answer, and for a second, as she crossed over the door's threshold, she wondered if the nun was right.

******

When Olumiji returned from Manali he decided he needed to be with Teddie and Amy.

"Staying away from you makes it harder for us to communicate," he said. "If I'm here, I stay off Pavel's radar because I'm not running around trying to get in touch with you."

Amy agreed this made sense, so Olumiji set up camp on Amy's couch, as Teddie's instruction intensified.

Teddie understood she was now Step One in a search-and-rescue mission with more urgency to it than ever. The limits of her own energy made more than one trip a day impractical, so she had to make the most of every visit.

There were two sources of information about her friends' locations. The first involved the question of how she was finding them in the first place. Lhatu kept insisting her spirit guide was taking her, and this guide was nothing more than a higher manifestation of herself. This frustrated Teddie. She didn't think she had a higher self, frankly, and she didn't think anything had manifestations.

Olumiji weighed in on the spirit manifestation issue. "Lhatu, you have a semantic problem with Teddie, and the translation into Western thought is working against you. Can I take a stab at explaining this?"

"Sure."

"Teddie, please touch your nose," Olumiji said.

She gave him a funny look and touched her nose.

"How did your hand find your nose? It's pretty incredible it could do that, don't you think?"

"Of course not, I know where my nose is." She almost giggled.

"You're sure you didn't have a spirit guide taking your hand to your face?"

"I'm sure," she said, and Olumiji laughed with her.

"Just like your brain has learned how to take one thing, your hand, and bring it to a connected thing, your nose, so has your mist body learned to bring connected things together. In what you call the mist world—and by the way I think it is an excellent name, only because it doesn't carry any connotations for you—anyway, in the mist world, things are connected that don't appear to be so here. It's a universe of relationships. You can go to Michelle or Usha because they are of you, in that realm. It's what makes you important to their rescue. It's also what makes it so easy for you to find them that you don't even know how you're doing it, much like you can't explain how you touch your own nose."

"Oh, okay. That makes sense." Teddie gave him a grateful smile and Lhatu actually rolled his eyes.

"Got it," he said to Olumiji. "No more spirit talk for the cynical offspring of the Western world."

"So how do I get my brain to understand how my hand is finding my nose, so to speak?" she asked Lhatu, not wanting to disrespect her friend.

"Do you ice skate?" he asked.

"I'm from Texas."

"Okay, other sports must work this way too. You learn to do something complicated, and you can analyze it before and after, but if you think too hard about it while you're doing it, you can't."

"Serving tennis balls."

"Good. For the same reasons, we don't want to analyze either. You're better off going to Usha or Michelle like you have been, but paying attention to your surroundings as you travel. Slow down if you can. The two worlds are exactly the same, so if there is a street sign here, there is a street sign there. Make an effort to notice and an effort to remember."

"The memories are blurry as is," Teddie said. "What's my other choice?"

"Once you get there, be more observant. Look for any detail identifying a town, a street, a store, anything. Make an effort to notice and an effort to remember."

"I think I see a theme emerging here." Teddie grinned.

But observing and remembering was more of tall order than she realized. The first few nights she tried, and she came back with more details, but none were useful. Lhatu suggested she travel during the day. Teddie gave it a try. The additional people and commotion was disorienting, but she did learn more.

Usha had just left the convent, and was traveling with the twin boy. The path was icy and they were moving with care. Teddie saw them look back up the path often, and guessed they were considering returning.

The next day Teddie was able to report that Michelle and Vanida stopped to put gas into their motor scooter. What did the place look like? It looked like a gas station with two pumps painted red. The only sign Teddie saw wasn't in English, and the local writing looked like squiggles to her. After they had more gas, the girls went back to driving. The road looked like a road. The countryside all looked alike.

"We're getting nowhere," Olumiji said.

"Teddie, I know you're trying and it's hard to bring back concrete memories, but we've got to have more."

"Why can't you go with her?" Amy asked.

"It doesn't work," Lhatu said, becoming frustrated. "It's like swimming together in heavy currents or group skydiving. I could stay with her for a while, but it would take all her energy and mine."

"What if there was another way for someone to go with Teddie?" Olumiji asked. "Not because they were a traveler, but because they rode along in her mind?"

"Hell no," Teddie said.

"Teddie, if it would find your friends, surely you'd do anything," Amy said.

Lhatu shook his head. "She could pretend to be okay with it, but if she isn't really comfortable she could never relax enough to travel. Besides, I'm not even sure if the telepath would go with her. They could be stuck back in her slumbering heavy brain instead."

Olumiji looked at Teddie. "Do you think you could relax enough to take me along with you?"

"Can I be honest?"

"I think you have to be," Lhatu said.

Teddie took a deep breath and looked Olumiji in the eye. "You're scary. You're really nice and I get how you'd do anything to protect people, but you're still scary. At least to me."

Olumiji nodded, and Teddie realized he'd probably picked up what she said before she got it all the way out, which was why the man was scary.

"How about your mother?" he asked. "She's a strong telepath too and a very good person."

"God no. I mean yes, she's a good person, but can you name any human alive who'd want their own mother in their head while their most personal thoughts were rattling around uncensored?"

"I see your point. Is there anyone else you could trust? How about Somadina? She's part of the group protecting you."

"I know. Somadina's nice, but she's mom's friend and I don't really know her."

"How about the other folks who've been looking out for you?" Olumiji tried.

"I know them even less. I mean, I'm sure they're good people and all, but..."

Olumiji kept thinking. "How about Maurice?"

"Uncle Maurice is a telepath?" Teddie went from polite to outraged. "No. This is too much. He is the sweetest man ever and one of my favorite people. He can't be part of some weird group. No offense."

Maurice, in fact, was an eighty-seven-year-old from Lola's hometown who developed telepathy late in life after his wife passed away. Olumiji had trained Maurice a decade earlier, and then, a couple of years ago, Maurice had trained Teddie's mother. Maurice visited the Zeitman house regularly now and had been made an honorary uncle in Teddie's eyes.

"I give up. My whole world sucks. I don't even know who in my life does what." Teddie looked to be on the verge of a mini-meltdown.

"I promise no one else in your family or your life is a telepath," Olumiji said.

"I promise you are the only traveler in your kin," Lhatu added.

"So, like, are there other weird abilities I don't even know about that are going to start popping up in everyone else I know?" Teddie asked.

"I doubt it," Olumiji said. "How do you feel about Uncle Maurice?"

"I love him to death. I don't really want him inside my head either, but I guess by his age he's probably heard everything. Can he do something like this all the way from Texas?"

"Most telepaths aren't that good," Olumiji said. "But Maurice is, and he knows you well enough to make it work, I think. It would be better if he knew more about Asian geography, or read

Thai, but at least he could be a second set of eyes. We've nothing to lose by trying. Let's see if he'd be willing."

******

"Oh, poor Teddie. She's got to hate this idea," Maurice said. He'd listened to his good friend Olumiji explain about c^3 and its out-of-body travelers. As a scientist, Maurice found the idea of journeying through another plane of existence hard to believe. Then again, he'd found the idea of telepaths difficult to accept until he became one.

He'd heard from Lola about the nasty business with Teddie's kidnapped friend, and he'd do anything to help, of course. He'd do anything to help Teddie, period. He thought of the girl as part of his own family.

"You should talk to her and make sure she's comfortable with this. She doesn't want to try it with me or her mother," Olumiji said. "Her teacher, Lhatu, says if she's not relaxed she won't be able to travel."

"I'll talk to her," Maurice said. "I think I can reassure her."

That's how one lovely evening in mid-April Maurice settled onto his couch to try something that had never been attempted. Teddie's mother Lola was with him to make sure he remained physically well. She'd sworn to remain mentally removed.

Maurice took a long swig of the sweet iced tea he loved before he leaned back, closed his eyes and prepared to ride along in a young girl's mind as she left her own body behind in the Himalayan dawn. He'd join her as she danced into the air to travel through what Olumiji called the abode of light. In this world, incredible as it sounded, she could find a friend hundreds of miles away. Then she and Maurice would look for clues to the friend's location.

******

As Teddie settled onto Amy's couch, she felt funny knowing Maurice was there but not being able to sense him. "I speak for him," Olumiji told her. "As you relax, if you have a question or a concern, you think it. He'll hear you and answer, and I'll hear his answer and tell you. You don't have to open your eyes or say a word, as long as you're in your solid body. He says to tell you right now that you're doing great. Okay?"

Of course it was okay. What else could it be?

It took Teddie longer than usual to get into her trance state, but she managed. After her mist body rose up at last, she could hear nothing, including Olumiji, as she hovered for a moment in the silent living room. Lhatu, who had stayed in his solid body, could not see her. Amy was sitting, trying to stay calm. Teddie waved to them all before she left, feeling oddly alone as she realized none of them could see her wave.

******

"Wow!" Maurice chuckled as he found his eighty-seven-year-old self hovering in the air, moving through the wall, and dropping from the second story down to street level. "I sure hope my heart can take this excitement."

Teddie couldn't hear him, of course, so Maurice focused on the world around him. What direction were they going? How fast? Maurice wondered if this group looked into having Teddie carry any kind of instrumentation. Could she strap a compass to her arm?

Teddie was focused on what was around her, and Maurice could feel her trying to slow her movement as she scanned for landmarks. He could only see what she saw, so he tried to remember things she might overlook or forget.

Once Teddie arrived at her friend's location, Maurice tried to maintain his touch with Teddie, while reaching out to get anything he could telepathically from Michelle or Vanida.

Vanida was exhilarated; she'd never experienced the kind of freedom she had now. It seemed to Maurice her plan consisted entirely of doing whatever it took to survive, and never being owned by another human again.

Michelle was scared and Maurice thought she understood the dangers of their situation better. They'd arrived wherever they were with nothing other than their motor scooter, and they dare not contact anyone they knew for help. They had to avoid arousing suspicion in the strangers around them. Even showing up in the background of a photo texted home could trigger facial recognition software.

The girls had changed into their original clothes, doing their best to turn hooker's apparel into swimwear, which turned out to be easier than one would think. Maurice kept looking for useful information as Teddie followed her friends for about an hour as they wandered the beach, cleaned up a little in the ocean and lay down on the sand to sleep without interruption before they tried to find a way to eat.

Once both girls were sound asleep in the noonday sun, Teddie sighed in exasperation. *Humans spend a ridiculous amount of time sleeping*. Maurice had to agree.

Teddie decided to wander the beach to see what she could learn. It was filled with local vendors and foreign young people. Maurice felt Teddie's longing for her other senses as she imagined how the surf would sound and the suntan lotion would smell. She made her way up to the highway separating the large, crescent-shaped beach from the town itself, and she froze. There in front of her was a highway sign, one she could read. It said 4029 in the clearest of numbers. *4029. Please let me remember this.*

4029. Please let me remember it. Maurice repeated it twice.

******

Teddie's journey took hours, and before it was over, Lhatu became concerned. Lola, who was watching over Maurice, was worried as well. They were operating in unknown territory, and Lola wanted to take no chances with her courageous elderly friend. She continued to make sure his breathing and pulse remained steady and kept a fresh glass of tea waiting for his return.

In the end, both Maurice and Teddie sat up at the same time, and the first thing each one said was "4029."

Then they both started talking. Lola took notes as fast as she could, while Amy got information from a tired but elated Teddie.

Lhatu checked Teddie for signs of physical stress as she talked, while Olumiji joined Maurice and Lola telepathically to garner any information they might have missed and to pass the main points back to Lhatu immediately.

Twenty pages of combined notes made it possible to figure out much of the physical route Teddie had traveled.

"This is amazing," Lhatu exclaimed. "We've never gathered this kind of detail on how a traveler moves. "

"Have you ever tried to get it?" Amy asked.

Lhatu smiled at her implication. "No, I don't think we have. Not like this, at any rate. You're right, my group is more inclined to accept what we can do, than to dissect it."

After all the notes were compared, there was no question that Michelle was in Southern Thailand, traveling with Vanida. They had a motor scooter. They were in a crowded place, filled with tourists.

"4029?" Lola said to Maurice as he finished his narrative. "You're sure?"

"4029?" Lhatu asked Teddie as her recounting of events ended. "You're positive?"

Amy had an old atlas open to Thailand on the table. The effort to do less online had forced everyone to be resourceful.

"The good news is 4029 is a short highway and it pretty much goes through one place," she said. "The bad news is the place is Patong Beach in Phuket, probably the most popular beach in all of Southeast Asia. At any given time, there are thousands of vacationing, partying kids there."

"So from their point of view, it was the perfect place to go," Teddie said.

"I'll get a telepath over there right away to start looking for them. It won't be easy. The ambient noise will be excessive and both girls are trying to not calling attention to themselves. They're the opposite of victims calling for help, but we could get lucky."

Lhatu turned to Teddie. "This is a huge breakthrough. You did an amazing thing."

Yes, Teddie realized with a bit of satisfaction, she had.

April 2012

25. Connecting

There are difficult places to get to in this world, even today, but no place is harder to enter than the isolated mountain nation of Bhutan. There are only two roads into a country surrounded by formidable mountains. There is one airport. Every foreigner needs a visa, granted only after providing proof of enrollment in a government-approved tour. Each tour is led by a Bhutanese guide who will do his or her best to see you have a wonderful time, cause little disruption, and leave.

Pavel thought his new detective, Mei, did an excellent job finding the email referring to the Indian girl dropped off at a convent on the side of a cliff somewhere east of Trongsa. How many girls from India had hitched a ride from Gangtok into Bhutan about that time? He assumed storming the silly convent with his best muscle would be a non-event and he'd have his unwilling virgin plaything within days. He thought wrong.

Pavel was surprised to learn helicopters struggled to make it over the treacherous high peaks, and the Bhutanese were surprisingly vigilant about unauthorized flights. Entry on foot required a damn mountaineering expedition, and his unescorted group would be detected the first time anyone local saw them. Little villages and farms were everywhere.

Thanks to the skittishness of the Chinese and Indian governments, borders were well watched on both sides. The more he studied the situation, the more it appeared the Bhutanese had created the ultimate gated community.

Meanwhile, officials from Bhutan were ridiculously difficult to bribe. After a couple of attempts, he had to get Mei involved as the Bhutanese placed him and anyone known to be in his employ on some list of undesirables.

He was lucky his new consultant was up to the job. Mei created four fake men seeking to go trekking in the remote regions of Bhutan. She got them permission to join a three week adventure during the high-trekking season in May, when sufficient snow had melted and the summer rains hadn't yet begun.

The bad news was he needed to find four of his goons capable of hiking in the Himalayas and with the patience and finesse to spend days visiting temples and taking pictures without raising suspicion. Once they got near the remote area of Trongsa, they needed the skills to break away from the group, get to where they needed to go, improvise well enough to get the girl, and then get back out of the country. Pavel was thinking if they could get past the most dangerous high areas, he could use choppers for the last bit. It would be easier to run and hide at the end of a mission.

This was going to cost a damn fortune. Good thing he had one.

He considered consoling himself by buying a dozen virgins somewhere else. It would be cheaper and far less dangerous. It would also be far less fun. Face it, he could buy anything he wanted. He did buy anything he wanted. It was the shit he couldn't buy that kept things interesting.

Besides, this had turned into a hunt. If he walked away from this, then the little bitch would win. She'd prove there was something a powerful man like him couldn't have, and he wasn't willing to let that be true. So, if he needed to find four men he could trust, he'd find four.

Then it occurred to him. He only needed three. He didn't have to trust them that much, either, because he'd be there with them, figuring out how to get the job done. He could do this. It would be a real hunt, and he'd have the fun of finding and bringing down his own prize.

Could he sneak in hunting gear? Maybe he wouldn't have to. Didn't the tour descriptions say archery was the national sport? He could be an archery enthusiast without even having to pretend. He could purchase perfectly legal equipment once he arrived. Then after he found his prey, he'd let her run from him. He'd chase her down, and shoot her with arrows treated with some sedative. He'd pick up her unconscious body and carry her out like the trophy she was. Now *that* would be worth the ridiculous time and expense this would require.

Better yet, he could make it this year's hunting expedition! He'd tell his family he'd changed his mind about the Japanese whale thing. He was going to stalk a rare Himalayan primate instead.

He checked his calendar. He'd have to be gone for three weeks. Could Samir handle matters for that long? Sure he could. Samir could work with Mei and find the other girl hiding in Thailand. Maybe he'd come home to two prizes, and have to figure out which one to do first.

The idea was invigorating. Pavel found himself whistling as he wrote Mei an email about the change in plans regarding the four trekkers who needed papers to visit Bhutan.

******

After her travels with Maurice, Teddie went back to school and tried to stay awake through the rest of the day's classes. Most of her life she'd been a good student, but not this year. While kids back home were stressing out about college applications, Teddie was hoping her sense of adventure in spending a year abroad would count for something.

She wanted a nap before dinner, but Haley was already in the room, singing along to one of Teddie's favorite country songs. It was impossible not to ask what was going on.

"One blogger called it Barbie climbs Everest." Haley laughed. "You know what? Even though I'm not climbing Everest, I wasn't offended."

"You're part of the expedition again?"

Haley's wide grin was answer enough. "Cami girl — that's my other name — set to climb Kanchenjunga. That was the other blog's headline. I can't believe it's really going to happen. You do know this means I am out of here in less than a week?

"What? Why? You don't climb until May," Teddie said.

"I know, but I've got to spend time adjusting to higher altitudes. We're only at 6,700 feet. My dad's coming and we're going to drive to this town that is supposed to be gorgeous, and it's at nine thousand. After a few days, we'll drive up to Thangu at thirteen-thousand, and I'll live there until the climb. I'm even going to let my dad do all the last minute coaching he wants. I figure I've got to stack the deck every way I can."

Haley gestured to the pile of schoolwork on her desk. "I'm bringing assignments with me, even though I'll probably have to take incompletes in everything." She looked hard at Teddie. "Are you going to be alright here alone?"

Teddie had to laugh. "Haley, you're about to do something where people actually die. You're worried about me?"

"Well, there's a lot going on here, too."

"I know, and we're going to fix that while you're gone. Meanwhile, you go show the world how strong a seventeen-year-old girl can be."

"Wait," Haley said. "You're about to turn seventeen. I'll miss your birthday. But I do get to have a cell phone again. Now that you've got one, we can text. We'll celebrate remotely. I'll text you straight from the mountain. I'm told there's reception."

"I'd like that. Send pictures."

******

The next evening Amy invited Lhatu over for dinner before they went to get Teddie. She knew he was staying with a local family and often took his meals at a restaurant to give the family some time alone. As the quest for the two missing girls dragged on, she was sure restaurant food was getting expensive and repetitive. She could see that under his outward calm he was becoming irritable, and her impatience with him and his methods wasn't helping. The home-cooked meal was meant as an olive branch, perhaps long overdue.

"How have you handled being gone from your responsibilities back in Bhutan for this long?" she asked by way of making neutral conversation.

"I've made a few short trips back. Others are picking up what I'd normally handle and there is a lot I can to do from here. But your concern is well founded. I can't keep this up indefinitely."

He sampled her homemade chicken noodle soup and nodded in surprised appreciation. “My biggest worry isn’t having to stay here. Unless we locate our two missing people soon, the man who’s hunting them will find them. I don’t think either one will live long in his possession.”

Amy knew it was true. “What turns a man into such a monster?”

Lhatu shrugged. “He has no control over his worst urges. He allows his basest instincts to dictate his desires.”

Amy shook her head. “I know plenty of people with bad self-control. They binge on ice cream. On a really bad day, they yell at other drivers. They don’t kidnap and abuse people.”

“The urge for sex leads to such aberrations,” Lhatu said.

“I don’t believe that. Sex is pretty damn wonderful if you ask me.”

Lhatu smiled. “It can be channeled into less destructive and more enjoyable paths, but at its most basic, the urge for sex isn’t loving. It wishes to take pleasure with no regard for the welfare of another. It is not a spiritual urge. Holy men, and for that matter holy women, of all religions have tended to abstain from it.”

“I think sex can be loving and even holy,” Amy said.

“I think it’s a dangerous instinct best avoided by the soul seeking enlightenment,” Lhatu replied.

They looked each other in the eye, and neither blinked.

“Don’t you have to reproduce to keep your royal c^3 lineage going?” Amy asked.

“Yes. I’ll break my vow at least once to produce one or more children. Under my circumstances, sexual activity for procreation is an acceptable exception.”

“Wow. Bet that lucky lady gets fired up. Nothing turns a woman on like a man forced to break a lifelong vow to do something he views as disgusting.”

Lhatu actually sighed and rolled his eyes. “The act of sex is not disgusting. It simply is. However, it appeals to disgusting urges within the human psyche. There’s a difference.”

“I don’t see one.”

“Are you blind?” Lhatu’s cheeks started to turn reddish, and Amy realized this was the first time she’d seen Lhatu angry. “Take a good hard look at what you fight every day. Every facet of sexism, rape and abuse stems from the inherent nature of the sex act. Half the species is more biologically prone to crave sex, and because of some perverse cosmic joke that same half is capable of forcing it on the rest of the species. Some have even developed a taste for doing so. You look me in the eye and tell me the world wouldn't be a better place if all men didn't take a vow of chastity, and make the rare exception to procreate."

Amy paused, and Lhatu thought this was the first time he had ever seen her at a total loss for words.

"You have a point," she said. She looked for a second like she was going to add more, but she didn't.

"Let's go get Teddie."

"Sure."

******

Sister Teresa Marie didn't know what had gotten into her. She didn't mention the girls' visit to Father Francois for his own protection and for theirs, and after that small indiscretion she couldn't stop thinking about the unlikely pair trying to get by without being able to ask anyone for help.

She was sure her priest and friend knew she was lying when she told him she'd found her motorbike stolen the next day, but he kept quiet about his suspicions. It wouldn't have been the first time she'd given away possessions to a young woman in need.

She kept checking her email for further news about the two girls, but there was nothing. She couldn't inquire personally—that would be the worst way to bring attention to the area—so the next day she asked Father Francois to drive her into town for her normal shift at the women's shelter.

"If you think you'll be okay, I'd like to stay in town for a few days, and then I'll get one of the nuns to give me a ride home. I put a couple of dinners in the freezer for you and the laundry is all caught up."

He smiled. "Thank you, sister, but I'm not helpless. Do what you need to do."

She nodded her thanks. The good Father didn't need to know that what she needed to do was get another motor scooter, and get her hands on one of the small emergency loans her order worked so hard for. Then she needed to head south to the big beach on

Phuket Island, find the girls and help them. Oh, and she probably needed to go dressed as something other than a nun.

******

The idea of being alone in the room every night bothered Teddie more than she wanted Haley to know. The empty beds of Usha and Michelle were an eerie reminder of the dangers around her and of her own inability, so far, to help her friends.

Besides, Teddie could look things up on the internet as well as the next person. Junga was considered one of the deadliest mountains to climb in the world, with a higher death rate than the more famous Mt. Everest. Knowing another bed was empty, because a third friend was off doing something almost one in five people died attempting, only made being alone in the room even worse.

Teddie pulled her favorite green fuzzy blanket around her shoulders and shivered as she closed her eyes tight to keep the tears from coming.

******

Lola was brushing her hair when she felt Teddie's loneliness from thousands of miles away, and the sudden sharpness of it broke her heart. At the insistence of those in x^0 and c^3, she'd done her best to stay on the periphery. Teddie, in her own way, was being a hero and she could be saving the daughters of others. She needed the room to do that, without Lola's worry. So Lola had kept her mental touch with Teddie quick and light, like the soft brush of a mother's lips on her sleeping daughter's cheek.

But this pang was impossible for a mom to ignore. Lola reached for her cell phone, thinking maybe a call of encouragement was in order. Then she jumped in alarm.

******

Teddie hoped she would fall asleep fast and not wake until daylight, so she was annoyed when Teddie the traveler had ideas of her own. Awareness of her travels was now her default, and tonight she envied people who could simply drift off to sleep.

Teddie the traveler headed out of the school with a purpose, and Teddie the tired and scared girl stayed half asleep as her mist body made its way down the street. She expected to find herself checking in on Haley, and realized that was a good idea. It might ease her own mind.

Only once she stopped moving and her consciousness centered fully into her mist body, she wasn't in Haley's hotel room. She'd traveled much further, all the way to her parent's bathroom in Texas. She watched her mother run a brush through her hair while she looked in the mirror with a sad expression. Then she saw her mother twitch in surprise.

******

Lola was looking at herself. Or, to be more accurate, she was watching herself look at herself in the mirror. Teddie, whose mind Lola had entered for a second, was there, in the bathroom in Texas. She was invisible, floating somewhere behind Lola. Lola was now in Teddie's head.

This had to be a new one for a telepath, and for a mom. Not knowing what else to do, she looked into the mirror and gave her daughter's invisible body a hesitant little wave.

******

Teddie froze. Her mother knew she was here. She'd never had a solid detect her presence before. But of course, her mother wasn't a normal solid and she knew that. Had her mother been reading her mind? She'd promised Teddie she didn't. What if she lied and did it all the time?

Teddie forced her fear and her anger to subside. Her mom had also said she heard her children when they were upset, and it was a call no mother could ignore.

So maybe her mom was only guilty of caring about her. Did that mean her mom could hear these thoughts? Okay. Maybe she could. *I love you, mom.* Teddie thought it as clearly as she was able.

******

Lola was trying to get back out of Teddie's mind but the whole experience of seeing herself through her daughter's eyes was so fascinating. She looked older. But she also looked skinnier. Interesting.

Then she heard Teddie loud and clear. "I love you, mom." Lola's eyes filled with tears she couldn't control. "I. Love. You. Too." She mouthed the words slowly, hoping Teddie could see what she was saying.

******

Teddie saw tears in her mom's eyes and she didn't know what to do. Then her mom said something and Teddie had no problem reading her mother's lips. "I love you too" is pretty easy to recognize if it is said slowly.

Teddie felt her own tears start and then she was back in bed in India, pulling the soft quilt tight around her body.

That was really weird, but it was exactly what I needed.

******

Lola felt the warmth of Teddie's bed and the easing of her daughter's sadness. She tiptoed back out of her daughter's mind.

That was really weird, but it was exactly what I needed.

Vanida and Michelle were sleeping by day, and going to parties in the evening to forage for free food. Then they would disappear into the shadows during the wee hours before dawn.

Food and drink could be had if one flirted and looked like one belonged. The girls picked up the knack. Occasionally, a fashionable piece of clothing or a little make-up went missing when they were nearby. They felt bad about it, but they had to survive.

Vanida got them food several times by surprising street vendors with her fluent Thai and offering to help out in a rush in exchange for a meal. There were water fountains and public restrooms and occasionally even decent food in the trash. They were careful and discreet and they got by.

Conversations were the worst because all answers had to be bland and forgettable. They'd settled into being cousins. Vanida, who still had a heavy Thai accent, was a girl from Bangkok showing her homeland off to her American-born kin. What was the name of the hotel they were staying at, again? They both perfected a vapid giggle.

A lot of boys were happy enough to buy them drinks they barely sipped and appetizers they scarfed down. All they had to do was dance with the boys and look sexy.

"So you're in college, right?" one unusually curious English lad persisted with Michelle.

"That's right. Our term just ended. I'll be a senior next year." Michelle thought it was better to stick to a half truth.

"What are you studying?"

"Whatever. Classes." Michelle tried to steer the conversation away with her best *I'm too stupid to care* look.

"No, I'm serious. If you're a junior you've got to be studying something. Is it like, embarrassing? Women's studies? I bet it's women's studies. I bet you're a feminist doing some kind of paper on us, aren't you?"

Seeing the glimmer of concern growing on Michelle's face, he got louder. "You *are* doing some kind of study, aren't you? I knew there was something not right about you two."

Vanida saw several heads turn their way. Not good. "She's studying pharmacy, asshole," Vanida hissed. "She doesn't like to talk about it because half the guys end up wanting her to get them drugs."

Michelle rolled her eyes without thinking, and it lent an accidental air of credibility.

"Well, that could be a drag, I suppose. No class at all, some people." He turned his charm towards Vanida. "So how about you? Are you in school, too?"

"Not now. I want to go someday, but I'm working on other stuff."

"Like what?" The boy just would not quit.

"I'm a writer."

"Really? That's so cool. I always wanted to write a book. About my life, you know," he said. "Are you good at writing?"

Vanida smiled. "I've had people tell me I'm one of the best."

Michelle covered her mouth to hide her laugh, then rubbed her left eye and announced she was going to the ladies' room. That was Vanida's cue meet her in a few minutes on the left side of the building where the girls could make their escape to a louder party with less conversation.

April 2012

26. Deciding

After giving Lhatu a hard time about lacking a sense of urgency, Olumiji wanted to waste no time getting telepaths to the beach in Thailand where Michelle and Vanida were hiding. A couple from Tokyo, both strong telepaths in x^0, agreed to go on an unexpected holiday to Patong Beach and scan for the two girls visually and mentally.

Knowing that brains working to remain hidden won't be transmitting well, the couple sought out others who'd noticed the girls. They got lots of fleeting information. Apparently pairs of young women with a Southeast Asian appearance were not uncommon. People were noticing several all the time.

The first breakthrough came when the Japanese woman sensed outrage while she was in the ladies' room at a popular hotel. The emitter of the emotion was a middle-aged British lady who'd been touching up her makeup. Her eyeliner and mascara disappeared off the counter when she went to get a paper towel. Two Asian girls had been near the sink but they denied taking anything and left.

The lady was sure the girls took her things, but what could she do? You don't call authorities over ten dollars' worth of eye-make-up. Still, she was annoyed.

The Japanese telepath recognized her good fortune. Of course the girls needed to steal supplies. She ran out of the restroom, calling to her husband telepathically. The girls had likely left the hotel to avoid trouble. He agreed, and each of them took off in pursuit. He went left down the street; she went right.

He thought he saw them about a block away, two girls walking fast towards the more thickly crowded streets leading to the beach. He followed them, but they were walking faster. He started to sprint. One of the girls noticed a man running towards them and said something to her friend.

Damn it. He wished he had a way to tell them he was trying to help them. He caught a bit of a plan made between them and they split up, each one making her practiced way through the crowd. The telepath had no idea which girl to follow, but it didn't matter. Soon both had vanished, and his head was filled with the surprised annoyance of all the people who'd been jostled in the process.

******

"You won't be able to get near them again." Olumiji had a headache from trying to transmit ideas with a clarity seldom used in telepathy. A phone call or email would be so much more effective, and good telepaths knew better than to waste energy communicating this way. If only normal forms of communication weren't being monitored by this super sleuth Pavel had found.

"Keep looking for thoughts of minor theft. It's a good angle. Your wife will have to approach them next time." Olumiji signed off when the man acknowledged the general ideas back.

"Be careful," Olumiji added. That was an easy emotion to send, a relief after all the complexity he'd tried to convey.

"I will," the other telepath replied. His own relief at ending the strenuous conversation was apparent.

******

Maurice agreed to a second journey with Teddie, in hopes of identifying the specific convent Usha had visited. He and Teddie took a few days to rest, then each put the same support system into place.

“How is Teddie doing with all this?” Maurice asked Lola as he sipped some water before he settled back onto his couch. “For that matter, how are you doing with all this?”

Lola sighed. “She’s holding up better than I would have imagined. And you know me. Staying one step removed has been the hardest part.”

“I’ll bet it has.” Maurice was sympathetic.

“Then this happened. It helped a lot.”

Maurice was invited into Lola’s recall, sitting in front of a mirror brushing long coppery hair, the likes of which he’d never had. As the poignant memory played for him, he smiled too.

“I bet that exchange is a first for x^0 and c^3.”

“It made me think I could see more of the world if I were less scrupulous about entering the minds of those close to me.”

“But you don’t want to be that person, do you?”

“No, I don’t,” Lola said. “Did you know I’ve always wanted to go trekking in the Himalayas?”

“Why didn’t you go while you were over there?”

“No one else in the family wanted to, except for Ariel, and she wanted to take this trek where you bungee-jumped off of a cliff at the end. Anyway, we didn’t have much time, and after Michelle was kidnapped we cancelled most everything anyway.” Lola shrugged. “What I really wanted to do when I was young was climb Mount Everest. Then as I got older I wanted to make it to the main base camp.”

“You could still do that. Isn’t one of Teddie’s friends over there climbing one of those really high mountains right now?”

“Haley. She’s starting soon,” Lola said. “Teddie said she’s going to check in on Haley until she gets high up the mountain. Teddie’s not that comfortable with heights. Jeez, I hope Haley makes it up that mountain and back.” Lola’s worry was interrupted by Olumiji’s voice letting her know Teddie was ready to go see Usha.

“Showtime,” Lola said.

******

Usha had new shoes. Teddie could tell because she was having trouble walking in them. She and the boy were still high in the mountains. Teddie watched them walk for a while, but it was hard to stay focused because they traveled so slowly. Teddie decided the pace was only partly dictated by the shoes, because she had never seen two people in less of a hurry.

Everything they passed looked the same. There were no street signs. How could there be? There were no streets! How in the world could you pinpoint a specific mountain path? It was all gorgeous.

Maurice agreed. He felt guilty getting to be part of this trek knowing it would delight Lola so much, but he focused on trying to see landmarks. Teddie had a good point. Besides the phenomenal views that came out of nowhere, there were trees. And rocks. Occasionally there were small shrines and rock walls and buildings in the distance that all looked alike. Nothing was distinctive to Maurice.

However, these things could be distinctive to someone who was Bhutanese. Wasn't it a shame no Bhutanese telepath knew Teddie Zeitman well enough to accompany her in her head? And no Bhutanese travelers knew Usha or this boy well enough to locate them while traveling? They were stuck with Teddie and Maurice.

If only there was a way to take a picture of the little rock shrines. Was there?

******

Olumiji kept his distance from Teddie, respecting her privacy. However, he maintained loose touch with his friend Maurice, just enough to ensure he was unharmed by the experience. In the odd way telepathy had of coming and going, he suddenly heard Maurice's voice loud and clear. He stopped and repeated the question out loud.

"Lhatu, have you guys looked into a method for recording an image of what a traveler sees? Is it possible?"

Lhatu stared at him, roughly the way someone might, Olumiji supposed, if he'd been asked if he had sex with birds.

"There are those in the organization who've made unauthorized attempts to look into such abominations," Lhatu said.

"We've chosen to ignore them, because it's not our way to prohibit. We can't imagine any good coming from such a thing."

"In other words, maybe?" Amy said.

"There's a place in the physical brain called the occipital lobe where images are received and processed before they're stored. The eyes of a traveler deposit their images in this location just as solid eyes do. Memories of a journey are preserved in the heavy brain," Lhatu said.

"Yes, but we can't take pictures of the images in anyone's brain, no matter how they got there," Olumiji said.

"That's not entirely true." Amy had moved to her computer. All searches related to the missing girls were inadvisable, but searching on esoteric topics was good because a lack of internet activity would be suspicious. She started typing.

"I read something about this. See, it says here the U.S. military has worked on this for years. Images we see are neural signals in our mind, and this group wants to develop technology to process these signals into photographic style images. It's like your TV takes electrical impulses and turns them into something you can watch." Amy turned to Lhatu. "Is this what you're talking about?"

"Yes. The U.S. was hoping for a spy technique to use brain photos to capture details not remembered. I think they're probably still working on it. About a decade ago, one of the research assistants in the lab you're reading about elected not to re-enlist in the US military. Her mother in Bangkok was ill and she was needed in her parents' homeland. Her name was Lawan and the U.S. army confirmed her story. Satisfied the woman had no intention of telling tales, they let her go. There were two things they didn't know about her. One, Lawan is a traveler, and has been since she was thirteen. Two, she was more informed and observant than the average lab assistant."

Lhatu looked pained. "Once her mother passed, Lawan became obsessed with capturing images from a traveler's journey. She gathered a group of traveler rebels in Bangkok, and a good bit of equipment, and they continue to investigate this possibility in spite of our discouragement."

Olumiji understood the importance of the question he was about to ask, and he sympathized with Lhatu's reticence to answer it. "Have they had any success at all?"

"Yes. Recently." Then Lhatu looked at Teddie as she lay in a trance, her consciousness somewhere on a mountainside in Bhutan. He saw Olumiji's questioning look.

"Absolutely not," he said.

"If you had clear images of Usha's surroundings, and if I had pictures of Michelle showing what part of Patong Beach she was at, we could end this thing now. We could get two humans to safety before a monster destroys them."

"Teddie would need this experimental device implanted into her brain," Lhatu said. "They don't know if it's safe, and sometimes they don't even understand the images they get. I wouldn't ask this of anyone, not even to save others."

Teddie started to stir. She was returning.

"She'd only have it in for a day or two," Amy said, trying to be helpful. Lhatu turned to her.

"No, she wouldn't. They can put the device in with no problem, but it blinds a person when they try to take it out."

"Huh?" Teddie sat up confused. "Who's blind? What's going on? Is everything okay?"

Three adults were all giving her strange looks.

"I'm ready to tell you about everything I saw," she said, "but I don't think it's going to be helpful. Damn, if I just could bring my cell phone along on these things. One picture of those little rock shrines we passed could make all the difference." Teddie paused. "Why is everyone looking at me like this?"

Amy said it. "She needs to know. It should be her choice."

******

Teddie was scared as soon as they started to explain it, and she didn't bother to pretend otherwise. Besides, she figured lying to a telepath about your feelings was a colossal waste of time.

Lhatu had barely finished describing the device before he tried to talk her out of it. He was all about dissonance, and interweaving two planes of existence, and how the general destruction of the universe could ensue if people who moved about on the plane of light suddenly started sending photographs back to the solid world. Teddie had to admit she didn't follow most of his arguments, but his point about charging into the unknown without adequate information was well made.

Amy was worried about long-term health issues. The lab in Thailand had proved they could insert the device after two workers agreed to have the tiny gadget implanted. They had both gone blind after the device was removed.

Three dogs had been given the tiny mechanism as well. There was one device-free blind one, and two healthy animals who'd had the equipment in for over a year with no loss of vision or other problems. They were dogs, but Amy agreed it boded well.

"Are you willing to leave this little apparatus sitting in your brain for the rest of your life? Even if it is safe?" she asked Teddie.

Maurice interrupted the discussion. He was insisting Olumiji tell the group Maurice wanted to undergo the procedure instead. It made much more sense for him to take health risks at his age.

Olumiji relayed the message as requested, but added his own observation. There was no evidence the part of the brain receiving images was where telepathic transmissions were going. They could lose precious days operating first on Maurice, and then have to start over with Teddie anyway.

Finally, the group quieted down. It was Teddie's decision, and everyone knew it.

She thought of Usha, hunted with nowhere safe to run. She thought of Michelle, trapped in a nightmare world and unable to call for help. She thought of the other girls back in the brothel, tied to their beds, violated in what should have been the safest of fortresses, their own cozy shelters filled with soft blankets and stuffed toys. She tried to imagine the men who profited from this pain, growing richer and more powerful because no one could find a way to put a halt to what they did.

"I'll do anything to stop this man," she said. "You can put the device in today."

There were so many details to be arranged. First, the renegade lab had to agree. With Lhatu's travel and communication being traced, Olumiji opted to communicate with a member of x^0 in Bhutan who could contact Lhatu's grandmother Yuden directly.

Word came back a few hours later. In an unexpected turn of events, Yuden would leave tomorrow on a plane out of Thimphu, on a mission to make peace with and enlist the help of the researchers in Bangkok. Hopefully her presence would sooth any bad feelings.

Olumiji mentioned the need to consult with Teddie's parents.

"Of course. They'll need to sign forms so I can have the surgery," Teddie said. Olumiji had to laugh.

"Teddie, this research is being done in a country once known for removing people's kidneys without their permission. I don't think your parents' signatures are an issue. You do turn seventeen soon, right?"

"In three days."

"Well, this is going to be quite a birthday. You're almost an adult and you're making your own decision, but I think it's right for you to talk to your parents. Unfortunately, we have to assume your communication is being monitored."

Teddie sucked in her breath. She'd forgotten about that.

"I'm going to let your mother know by the only safe means. I know she'll be unhappy she can't talk to you, and perhaps talk you out of this, but I also know how proud she's going to be."

"So how are you going to get me to Thailand without sending up some sort of alert to Pavel and his super-hacker?"

"We can't. We have to bring the renegade c^3 lab and its key people here. Pavel has no reason to be paying attention to them, so we'll find a way to do this thing in Darjeeling, under Pavel's unsuspecting eye."

Teddie looked at Lhatu. "You think your grandmother can talk a half-dozen people into coming here and doing this?"

Lhatu actually laughed. "You haven't met my grandmother. It won't be a problem."

Two days later, on her last night of being sixteen, Teddie couldn't stop fidgeting. Since she'd arrived in India, she'd become something she didn't understand. Tomorrow, she'd become something no one understood, and she'd be that for the rest of her life. Scared didn't even begin to describe how she felt.

May 2012

27. Recovering

Once the morning of May 1 dawned, Amy was in charge. The scenario in Darjeeling was complicated, and efforts to save Usha and Michelle needed a leader, not a committee. The person in charge had to know the town well, be able to make quick and sensible decisions, and be able to keep the safety of three girls, in vastly different circumstances, a priority over everything else.

Lawan and three of her co-workers were in route to India, and would arrive that morning carrying massive amounts of disassembled equipment. They were being accompanied by Lhatu's grandmother Yuden, who had informed everyone she would be present for this unprecedented procedure.

Amy watched Lhatu as Olumiji conveyed the news. "You're *afraid* of your grandmother!" she said to Lhatu with sudden realization.

"I am not. She's an imposing and sometimes demanding woman, because she sets high standards for me. She wants c^3 to be well run once she leaves this world. It makes for a certain amount of stress on my part. It's not fear."

"Right." Amy knew when not to say more.

All communication with those outside of the city was now handled by Olumiji, as he worked with his x^0 contacts in Bhutan and in Bangkok to keep updates away from phones or the internet. Olumiji was overwhelmed by the group's communication needs, and Amy wondered how soon his role as human network router would wear him out. She noticed he'd been popping analgesics for two days, and she made a mental note to insist he take breaks at regular intervals.

He'd already told Somadina, the Duttas and Tariq to stand down in their efforts to ensure Teddie's day-to-day safety. Only Tariq had objected, insisting he could still help. Olumiji conveyed how the situation had changed, and promised to keep the boy apprised. Later, when this was all over, Olumiji knew he had to deal with the situation with Tariq.

Lhatu moved into the role of security advisor. He was confident Pavel had no one in Darjeeling trailing Amy or Teddie. It made sense; as far as Pavel knew, Amy and Teddie had no means to stand in his way. Lhatu did assume, however, that Pavel was keeping tabs on them through his professional sleuth and would do so until he collected both of his prizes.

Amy's small apartment was deemed a bad choice for six more guests and a surgical procedure. Mr. and Mrs. Dutta, who had been part of the team watching over Teddie since January, offered their home while they went to stay with their son for a few days. Lhatu worked to get everyone there safely and discreetly, and to notify Teddie's academy she'd be gone for several days.

Once Amy, Lhatu, Olumiji and Teddie were all in place at their new location, Amy propped up a giant white board from her office and started to list the known facts, the way she'd seen countless people do in crime dramas on television.

On the left was Michelle, her name written in bright red marker. Below it Amy had started a list called *things we know.*

at Patong Beach in Thailand
has companion – Vanida – traveler w/ twin brother
Vanida – prostitute at same brothel, escaped w/ Michelle
escape happened night we convinced police to raid place
timing sucked
Michelle/Vanida are surviving, use petty theft,
Michelle/Vanida seen recently by Japanese telepath

Amy stopped writing and looked at her amused audience. "Hey, I've watched a lot of shows. Making a list like this is a good idea."

"It is." Olumiji agreed with a laugh. "I was just thinking how weird some of this stuff would look at the average police station."

Amy shrugged and went on.

What we don't know:
If M/V know how much danger they are in

"Of course they know they're in danger," Teddie said.

"I don't agree. Maybe they just headed south to the beach, thinking they're runaway prostitutes needing to get out of Bangkok. Michelle could have no idea her kidnapping and Usha's situation are related. We can't know how much they know."

"I'm with Teddie," Lhatu said. "I don't think Michelle goes this long without letting people know she's okay, unless she's got good reason not to. They must have tried to make contact somewhere, somehow, and got told to disappear."

"You're right." Amy shrugged as she erased. "The only thing we don't know about these two is exactly where they are at any given moment." She looked at Teddie. "Hopefully with your photos and the two telepaths we've got there, we can fix that."

She started a new list under Michelle's name.

What Pavel knows.

She hesitated. "He knows a lot less than we do. He knows Michelle ran away from his brothel with Vanida, and he can guess the girls are hiding in Thailand, but unless this hacker has gotten more information, that's all he knows."

"Advantage us," Teddie said.

Amy nodded. "For now, anyway."

She wrote *Usha* on the other side of the board in bright blue. She kept writing.

What we know.
Hid at convent in Bhutan since Oct.
don't know which convent
there are a lot of them
has companion, he is traveler and twin brother of Vanida
Lhatu: cosmic connection
Amy: weird coincidence

As Amy struggled with the spelling of the word coincidence, Lhatu interrupted. "Do you know what the Bhutanese expression for a weird coincidence is?" he asked.

"No, but please tell me."

"We refer to them as cosmic connections."

Amy rolled her eyes and continued to write.

Her companion: tried to communicate with Teddie, appears friendly

Teddie says they've left nunnery

"Pavel has the more impressive list on his side," Olumiji said.

Amy agreed. "Based on what you learned, his technical expert knows which convent. He doesn't know Usha has left it, and he won't know her speed or direction once he finds out, but he's ahead of us."

"We do have one advantage here," Lhatu said. "It's difficult for outsiders to get into Bhutan, and even more difficult for them to get up into the remote mountain regions. That's probably slowed him down."

"Okay. So our top priority is for Teddie to get pictures of Usha, and for you to get her location identified."

Lhatu agreed. "We must get to her first. Once we know more, I'll get someone over to the convent also, to talk to them about safety. However, some of these nuns are considerably better at defending themselves than you'd think."

Amy left her white boards up and moved on to her next project, checking on transportation from the airport in Bagdogra. The housewife from Kolkata, another member of Teddie's group of telepathic guards, had volunteered to bring Grandma Yuden, the equipment and the lab personnel three hours over mountainous roads to the Dutta's home.

Olumiji offered an explanation for her generosity. "She's been listening to Teddie's worries and fears for months now. She feels like she knows Usha and Michelle, and she fears for their safety. It's the downside of being a telepath. Let her help us."

Amy was willing to accept this much-needed chauffeur, but she needed two cars. Up to now she'd resisted involving her own staff, not wanting to put them in more danger. Then Ana had insisted she'd pick up the remainder of the equipment and Maurice.

Oh Maurice. That was another delicate situation.

Once Teddie's parents had learned of the procedure, they went from an outraged "no" to insisting they'd fly to India to be with Teddie. Olumiji pointed out how such travel would alert Pavel and draw his attention at the worst possible time.

Then Maurice chimed in. Pavel had no reason to be watching him. If he couldn't have this operation instead of Teddie, then he'd be present, holding her hand and sending telepathic reports back to her parents. Olumiji started to argue, then realized if Teddie had someone she knew and trusted with her, this would all go better.

So now Maurice was on a plane, too, arriving several hours after the Bangkok contingent. Amy guessed international travel would be difficult for the elderly man, and had arranged for him to have his own room in the overcrowded house, so he could rest as he needed.

The final component was finding a local nurse who could be trusted, and who could start preparing Teddie for the surgery to be performed that evening. Lawan's team included two medical doctors, but Amy wanted more. Rather than risk using a phone, Amy went to the nearest hospital.

Sanjana was one of the girls Amy had rescued years ago, armed with mace and outrage. Today, Sanjana was a nurse in the local emergency room, working to save others. Would Sanjana assist with a possibly illegal operation being performed in a local home that evening? Could she furnish a few medical supplies for it as well?

For Amy? She could do anything.

******

They'd been part of the tour group for five minutes when Pavel realized how long the next two weeks were going to be. The actual hiking wouldn't be bad; fresh air and pleasant views were better than sitting at a desk. It was just that he was on a hunt. He wanted to shoot at things.

The list of acceptable travel gear made it clear weapons of any kind were not permitted, but it was true the Bhutanese loved archery. As he'd hoped, he'd been able to purchase a couple of fairly impressive bows upon arrival in Thimphu, and over the objection of his guides he'd insisted on transporting his purchases with him. As the trip went on, he hoped they'd let him practice a little for fun.

Meanwhile, the fast-acting sedative for the tip of a special arrow remained concealed in his toiletry kit. He hoped he'd be able to take down his prey with a single well-executed shot. That would be a worthy victory.

As to the rest of their travels, it looked like there would be little liquor, repetitive food, no entertainment he cared about, and temple after damn temple, apparently even in the middle of god-forsaken nowhere. Hell, these Buddhists made the Russian Orthodox look like lightweights, and Pavel knew that was no small feat.

His men looked to him for guidance. They were being well paid for taking this vacation, but he knew they'd make the extra effort to be more convincing tourists only if he did so. Very well, if he was going to do this, he had to do it right. Nothing worthwhile came easily.

He picked up the oversize camera he'd brought as a prop to amuse himself while he covered up his boredom. He motioned to two of his men to stand in front of the little rock shrine their guide had been going on about.

"Smile," he said, and he clicked the shutter.

******

"You'll have to click the shutter," Lawan explained to Teddie. "It is the absolute simplest of cameras. No video. Black-and-white stills with poor resolution. Military intelligence was hoping for more, but this much, of course, is nothing short of a miracle given how little we understand the human brain."

"So what does it do when I click it?" Teddie asked.

"There is no storage capacity. This had to be as small and simple as we could make it, so it transmits the image instantly to a receiver near your head."

"How am I going to manage that?"

"Your real head," Lawan said. "The image in your traveling brain is stored in the occipital lobe of your solid brain, and the picture is taken there. The receiver sits outside of your resting body while you travel."

"If I carried the receiver around, could I take pictures of what I see with my solid body, too?"

"Of course. But why would you? It's a big bulky receiver and it takes bad pictures. If your solid body is going, why not use your cell phone?"

"I see your point." Teddie thought a second. "Could I use it to take pictures of my dreams?

"We think it's possible," Lawan said, "but so far no one has been able to remember to click the shutter while they were dreaming."

"So how do I click? I can't move anything in my solid body while I'm traveling."

"How do you lift your arm?" Lawan replied

"Not that analogy again."

"Because it's a good one. After the surgery, it'll take days for your body to learn how to take a picture. We'll use biofeedback and you'll figure it out as you watch the receiver for results. See that short guy sitting over in the dining room? He's Awut, my expert. He'll teach you and, when you're ready, he'll help you learn to do it while you travel. He's a traveler, too, and he'll stand next to you while your spirit body watches the screen and practices. It takes time and effort, but we think anyone can be taught."

Teddie shuddered.

"It's a small device," Lawan reassured her. "The procedure for inserting it has to be precise, but your recovery will be minor."

Teddie didn't care. This whole process sounded miserable. She wished Maurice would hurry up and get here.

******

Sister Teresa Marie was on the beach. The swimsuit she'd been able to find on sale was not as modest as she'd have liked, but she was a practical woman and knew she needed to blend in.

She didn't think it was a good thing skimpy clothes were required to look normal these days, but it was what is was.

She started off by seeking out crowds of partygoers, and asking about two younger friends she'd become separated from. Luckily big sunglasses and a hat helped her look anywhere between twenty-four years old and her actual thirty-six. No one had seen her friends, but she kept describing the two girls to anyone who'd listen.

Finally, a Japanese couple approached her.

"We've seen your friends," the woman said. "It's important we talk to you, now, before you ask anyone else about them."

******

Maurice was holding her hand. The small bedroom reeked of the disinfectant used to turn it into an ad hoc operating room. The two doctors and nurse wore surgical masks. Teddie felt a flash of panic as she saw their half-hidden faces, then the nurse said "Count backwards from one-hundred." Teddie thought she made it as far as ninety-eight before she blacked out completely.

******

Haley was uncomfortable with the sad looks her father kept giving her.

"Dad. You've taught me well. I can do this."

"I know, Haley. And I want you to. I'm incredibly proud of you. You have to know that.

"So why the sad eyes? I've spent the last week at thirteen-thousand feet and I've never felt better. Tomorrow, we head towards the base camp. We'll be part of a real expedition blessing ceremony! This is a happy time, dad."

Her father nodded. "I know. I wish my good friend from Canada hadn't gotten hurt last week. He wanted to make this climb so badly. I don't know his two friends as well, and I'd feel better if he could keep an eye on you."

"Dad, I know some of the climbers myself and we're all going to watch out for each other."

Her dad didn't respond. When he finally spoke, he looked at the floor, not her.

"This is going to sound stupid, because it is, but dads aren't supposed to send their daughters off into danger. At least not good dads. It's hard for me not to feel like I should go with you. Be there to make sure you're okay."

"Hey, look, if you're having issues with my getting to climb this peak instead of you," Haley was irritated, but her father cut her off.

"Haley, I'll say it again. I couldn't be more proud of you, but I'm also worried about you. That's normal. I'm having issues with being the kind of father who lets his beautiful young teenage daughter go into danger while he sits by. These are social issues I'm trying to deal with, so don't get mad at me because for once I'm telling you how I feel."

Haley paused. Her dad hardly ever told her how he felt about anything, and he was entitled to his feelings. Hers weren't always noble or correct, so why should she expect his to be?

"I think it takes a special kind of dad to let his 'beautiful teenage daughter' pursue her dreams, no matter how dangerous they might be," she said. "How about instead of giving you a hard time, I thank you."

"I'd like that. Just recognize this is more difficult for me than I thought it would be. I'll be a happier man when I see you running back into base camp in a few weeks."

******

When Teddie came to, she blinked a couple of times, thinking her eyes were playing tricks on her. Could this device force her to hallucinate?

Then she wondered if she'd gone traveling while she was under for the surgery. But no, there were sounds in the room, not the least of which were those coming out of the mouth of her sister Ariel, standing over her bedside.

"Thought maybe you could use another friendly face," Ariel said. "Not that Maurice's isn't friendly enough."

"I thought my family was supposed to stay away?" Teddie whispered, realizing how thirsty she was.

Ariel smiled and handed her an ice chip. "They told me you could start with these. Everyone decided your sister in Ireland could visit you for your seventeenth birthday without arousing suspicions. It's normal behavior. Unfortunately, you've only got about ten minutes of your birthday left, but I've taken vacation for the rest of the week. By the time I leave, you might be in shape for some light celebrating. Happy birthday munchkin. Get some rest."

The next day, Awut started training Teddie as soon as she woke up. After a while, she heard Ariel in the dining room visiting with Amy. It sounded like Ariel knew what was going on, because she was talking about out-of-body traveling with surprising calm.

Of course. They could hardly have sent Ariel here without giving her some explanation.

Teddie motioned to Awut to give her a minute, and headed to the dining room, wondering how her logical sister was going to react.

"So these people go flitting around on some energy plane that mirrors this world, and they come back with usable memories?"

Amy shrugged. "It is hard to explain any other way."

"Wow. That's a kick. And my little sister does this shit?"

Amy shrugged a second time. "Apparently she does it well."

As Teddie sat down at the dining room table to join them, Ariel looked at Teddie with new-found respect. "I'll be damned. It does explain a lot."

"What do you mean?"

"The way you were always telling on me and Zane. We could never figure out how you saw us."

"I hardly ever told on you guys! Anyway, Ariel, I learned do this in India."

"Okay. But you were good at spying on us back then, too."

"I was not."

"Girls?"

Teddie and Ariel both gave Amy a sheepish look.

"Sorry. It's easy to revert to being children when you're with your siblings," Ariel said

"So did mom talk to you about all this?" Teddie asked, making an effort to sound more adult.

"Not mom. Apparently this creep Pavel has our family under radio silence. She had a friend from London come over to Dublin to talk to me in person. He suggested I go see you for your birthday and he explained why. It sounded like a good idea anyway; I felt bad I hadn't thought of visiting you myself."

"Did this guy happen to mention how he communicated with our mother?" Teddie was trying to feel her way through this.

"Yep, I've been read in. My mother is a telepath with a whole bunch of telepath friends, and my little sister goes around spying on people." When Teddie started to object, Ariel raised her hand laughing. "I'm kidding Teddie. I'm envious. It sounds like an incredibly cool thing to do."

"So you're not upset about mom?"

Ariel shrugged. "Not really. I mean, she always kind of seemed like she read our minds anyway, you know?"

"Yeah." Teddie had to laugh. "She did."

Awut poked his head into the dining room.

"These first few hours are critical," he said. "I know seeing your sister is exciting, but I have to ask you, please, come back to work."

Teddie gave Ariel her most grown-up, sophisticated shrug. "Duty calls."

******

Samir respected his boss, Pavel, but to be frank it was nice having the man out of the way. Pavel was impatient and prone to angry outbursts, making progress twice as difficult. With Pavel almost incommunicado in the mountains, Samir could apply calm logic to his assignment to find Michelle Tran.

That was the girl's name. Samir found Pavel's refusal to name his prey understandable, but it was an obstacle to the search. One needed to know everything possible about Michelle if one was going to find her in a country of seventy-million people. Pavel could think of her any way he liked while he enjoyed her later, but for now, she was a human. Where had she grown up? What kind of child had she been? What did she like to do?

Samir assigned Mei the almost trivial task of producing a complete dossier on Michelle and her family, while he read what was known about the other prostitute. She was called Vanida, a Thai word for girl. She had no last name, and had been sold to the brothel as an entertainer. So they really did have camps in Thailand where they trained young girls to perform tricks with their private parts? Amazing.

Mei emailed Samir the information on Michelle mere minutes after he requested it, so Samir gave Mei the more daunting assignment of learning everything possible about Vanida.

"She says Vanida will have no footprint," Mei's translator told him by phone.

"True, but ask Mei to look into what camp Vanida came from. Maybe we can learn if the girl knows the countryside, or has any family to run to."

As Mei went to work on Vanida, Samir turned to Michelle Tran's photos, skimming through them, trying to predict where Michelle the human would choose to hide. Not a lot of camping. A little time in the city. More than half of her photographs looked like they were taken at one beach or another.

So you like sand and surf. That's your happy place, isn't it?

He called Mei. "I'll be in the air tomorrow," he told the translator. "Tell her she'll be able to reach me at my hotel by tomorrow night. I'm taking two of Pavel's men and heading to Thailand." He heard an exchange in rapid Mandarin.

"She thought you said it was pointless for you to go until we had a better idea of where to look."

"It was. Thanks to Mei, I'm pretty sure these girls headed to the beaches, at least if Michelle is calling the shots. I'll start at the south end; they'd want to get as far from Bangkok as they could. I'll go to the busiest beaches first. If Mei gets evidence Vanida had someone to run to, we'll change our approach."

More rapid Mandarin followed. Then the translator said in Hindi, "She says she'll get back to you in a day or two."

******

"You don't think I should even be looking for them?" Sister Teresa Marie was upset. At first she'd considered not talking to the couple, thinking they were working for the man chasing the girls. She relented when their knowledge of the girls seemed so thorough and their concern so evident. "They've got no one. They can't ask anyone for help."

"Exactly," the well-dressed Japanese women explained in her carefully practiced English. "If you catch someone's attention so they tweet or text or chat to help you find them, the message could be intercepted."

"Can I at least drive around and look for my old motor scooter?" the sister asked.

"They have your motor scooter?" the equally well-dressed Japanese man asked with obvious interest.

"Yes, that's how they got here. I went and put the keys in it and filled the gas tank and told them to steal it when they left in the morning."

The nun noticed the Japanese woman had a far-away look in her eye, and she was holding on to the man for support.

"Is your wife alright?"

"She's fine," the man said. Then, turning to his wife, "Let's go back to the room dear and you can, uh, rest there."

He turned back to Sister Teresa Marie, keeping his eyes on her face. Now that he knew she was a Catholic nun, it seemed wrong to glance below her neckline. "Do you have a place to stay?"

"Yes, I'm at a hostel…"

"No, that will never do," the man said. "We'll get you a room near ours and start working on finding your scooter."

So Sister Teresa Marie checked into a room at the luxurious Le Méridien Phuket Beach Resort. She consoled herself that the couple's generosity would leave her with more money to give the two girls. Meanwhile, her room had a mini-bar. She'd never seen a real mini-bar. How much could one of those inviting little cans of soda cost? Surely not much.

May 2012

28. Going

Amy thought the drama being generated by the group at the house on the outskirts of town would make either a great master's thesis in psychology or a killer one act play. There was the changing sisterly dynamics between Ariel and Teddie. There was Maurice, who kept trying to help Olumiji, while Olumiji tried to protect his elderly friend from too much stress.

Then there was the rebel leader Lawan and her devoted group of scientists in an unspoken stand-off with the purists Lhatu and his grandmother Yuden. Both factions faked acceptance of their new alliance, but Amy suspected their philosophical differences ran deep. There was the demanding granny herself, and her odd relationship with her anxious-to-please grandson.

Yet, there was begrudging respect growing all around as everyone worked toward a common goal.

While Ana ran the office in Amy's absence, Amy decided it was time to send some people home. She guided the two doctors into making arrangements to return to Bangkok, assuring them local nurse Sanjana could handle any remaining medical issues. She sent the helpful telepath from Kolkata out for one last grocery run, then had her take the doctors to the airport and head home.

That left eight people, including her. A quick run through the list—Amy, Ariel, Awut, Lawan, Lhatu, Maurice, Olumiji, and Yuden—showed none of them were going to leave any time soon.

Then an unexpected dynamic appeared. It was an interaction Amy could only categorize as flirting. Normally, that would be the last thing such a group needed, but under the circumstances she was reconsidering.

Yuden was demanding, but she brought out her softer side any time Maurice was in the room. Maurice, who was feeling less needed than he liked, seemed soothed by Yuden's attention.

Talk about a relationship with nowhere to go, Amy thought. But that wasn't her problem. Lhatu seemed amused and relieved to see his grandmother distracted, and as he lightened up, so did Amy. As Amy relaxed, so did everyone. So goes the nature of a group.

Meanwhile, Olumiji received some helpful news. The Japanese couple at the beach in Thailand discovered a Catholic nun who helped the girls escape by giving them her motor scooter. She'd chased after the girls a couple of days later, hoping to give them more money. She'd been going up and down the Patong Beach looking for them.

The Japanese couple convinced her to stop her inquiries. Once they learned the nun was the one who'd warned the girls about Pavel's search for them, they moved the nun to their hotel.

"We're still ahead in Thailand," Olumiji said. "And we're so close."

Meanwhile, Teddie kept trying to figure out how to click the shutter. Ariel kept encouraging. Awut and Lawan kept instructing. But no matter how hard anyone worked, the solid real Teddie couldn't find the muscle needed to snap a picture.

That night, Ariel got word from work that she had to leave a day early for a business meeting in Germany. Teddie went to bed sad and woke up a couple of hours later, filled with worry. On Lawan's advice, she'd refrained from traveling in her mist body after the surgery, and she was growing more concerned about Usha by the day. She looked down and saw Usha, and thought she was dreaming. Then as the absolute silence sunk in, she realized she'd gone traveling without meaning to.

Usha lay sleeping on a mat in someone's kitchen. She seemed fine, but Teddie thought there'd be no harm in looking around to make sure.

Teddie entered each room. Usha was in a home with two parents and three children. It was small, but clean, cozy, and well decorated with children's art. Teddie was guessing the mat in the kitchen constituted the family's guest room. These nice people must have taken Usha in for the night.

Teddie felt an odd pang. For all the much-touted hospitality of her home of Texas, no one she knew would dream of providing lodging to a traveling stranger.

She tried to see any detail to identify whose home this was. She studied the children's art, the handmade furniture, even the pile of shoes by the door. It was true, if she could bring back a picture of any one of those, it could be circulated around and somebody somewhere would recognize the place. Teddie stared hard at each scene, wishing she could memorize and redraw it. What a crying shame she couldn't.

She woke up with tears of frustration in her eyes and as she rubbed the water away, she knew. She knew how to do it. She crept into the den where Lawan and Awut both slept, and she shook her trainer awake. Awut took one look at her face and he could tell.

"Come on," Teddie said. "I need you to help with the receiver thingy. I don't know why, but I think I've got this."

After seeing sixteen blurry black-and-white photographs of the room they were sitting in, everyone agreed. Teddie had found the button and figured out how to push it while in her solid body. Ariel gave her a grinning thumbs-up, Maurice shook her hand ceremonially, and Yuden walked up to her and gave her a big kiss on the cheek.

"This is wonderful," Lawan said. "Learning to do this while awake is step one. You are on schedule. Now get some sleep. In the morning, you travel again."

******

Amy needed to run home and get fresh clothes and clear the junk out of her mailbox. Lhatu, in his role as chief security officer, deemed the group had left no footprint to arouse the suspicions of Pavel's cyber sleuth. Having Amy make an appearance at her office and be seen around her apartment building would be good if anything did prompt the man to send someone to snoop.

"You don't need to drive me," Amy said.

"It's no trouble. I'm seen driving you around a lot, and I'm taking Ariel over to Lord Peartree anyway because that's where her driver to Bagdogra is picking her up. She thought it made more sense to be coming and going from the school instead of here."

"Good call."

"Hey, I could get the into this spy thing." Ariel laughed, and said her goodbyes.

"Thanks for coming. I really appreciated it," her little sister said.

"Next birthday, when you turn eighteen, we'll do some real celebrating, okay? No surgeries beforehand." Ariel waved to all as she left.

Teddie sighed. It had been wonderful to see Ariel, but this was one time she could have used a hug goodbye. Too bad her big sister wasn't better with the touchy-feely stuff.

******

"We start with just going," Awut instructed. "You go where you go, I won't be part of it. Just reconnect to the idea of traveling."

Teddie lay down and began the familiar exercises. She expected to find herself with either Usha or Michelle, but to her surprise she was hovering off of a steep hillside covered in ice and rocks. Shit.

Then she saw Haley next to her, adeptly making her way up the slope, grinning from ear to ear. Her friend had started the climb! Teddie felt guilty for not remembering sooner that today was the day.

Go, Haley, go. She wished she had a way to convey the message. She hovered over the rocks for a few minutes, trying not to look down, as Haley fell behind the group. Once the girl knew no one was watching, she turned and waved to the land below. That wave had to be to her dad in the base camp. Then Haley turned, looked up and waved at the sky.

Who is she waving at now? Wait. I told her I'd check in on her as she started. She's waving at me.

I wave back! I wave back! Then she remembered she could do better than think it. She came back to her solid body with a snap.

"You traveled okay?" Awut was concerned.

"Yes. Just a second." She ran to get her phone. Reception would remain good for halfway up the mountain, Haley had told her, even though to conserve her battery she'd have her phone off most of the time.

Teddie looked and saw she already had a message from Haley. The girls had been told to never mention Usha or Michelle and to keep messages short. Haley had complied.

"A bird called a chimney swift mates while flying through the air," Teddie read.

"Let the animals alone and keep your head in the game," she typed back. Then she held her phone out and snapped a photo of herself waving and sent it. Her friend would understand.

******

Amy pulled things out of her cupboard for the group to use, then grabbed a laundry basket and started filling it with clothes for the next few days. Lhatu was in good spirits as he carried supplies to the car. Amy figured he was relieved by how well the renegade researchers had worked with the rulers of c^3. Desire to help a third party does much to mend differences, Amy thought, hoping the split in the group might heal after this. In her opinion, c^3 would benefit from more modernization.

Grandmother's good mood had to be helping Lhatu's disposition as well. Lhatu was playfully trying to tug the laundry basket out of her arms, claiming she had plenty of clean clothes in there already, when Amy pulled back, lost her grip, and landed on the carpet.

"I'm sorry." Lhatu got serious as he reached down to help her up, but Amy was laughing now. He helped her to her feet using both of his arms, and there she was, inches from his face with his arms around her waist.

It was he who leaned forward first. She was sure of it. She only responded. But whoever was to blame, the kiss started and it didn't stop for a while. For a long while.

"I'm sorry," Amy said, pulling away. "I don't know what got into me. I know you don't like to do this sort of thing."

"You're wrong," Lhatu said, pulling her back towards him. "I like to do this sort of thing very much. I choose not do it. That's different."

"You choose not to because?" Amy asked, thinking a second kiss would feel nice now that he was holding her so close.

"Because if I start kissing, I have a hard time not kissing again," Lhatu said, and he demonstrated the problem.

"What else do you have a hard time not doing?" Amy asked, a little breathless from the second kiss, which had gone on longer than the first.

"Oh, there all kinds of wonderful things I can't resist once I get started." Then he did something Amy thought happened only in the movies. He picked her up, all one-hundred-and-fifty pounds of her, carried her into the bedroom like it was nothing and tossed her gently onto the bed. She thought she was going to melt into the mattress.

Then he lay next to her and began to demonstrate the things he liked to do once his vow was broken anyway. After a while, she did melt into the bed, and then she melted again like she never had before.

******

Once the climb started, Haley was pleased with how she was part of the team. Well, maybe team wasn't quite the right word. There were fifteen climbers attempting to summit, eight of whom were from India. Three of them were older, spoke several languages and seemed comfortable with all the foreigners. Haley knew she'd seen each of them at the climbing school as instructors. All three made a point of welcoming her and wishing her luck with the climb. The other five from India were younger. They seemed to know each other well, and kept more to themselves.

Hans and his friend Henrik socialized with Haley, as did the two climbers from Canada who knew Haley's dad. As Haley suspected, the five of them fell into a routine of looking out for each other. Two remaining men from Japan were cordial, but kept to themselves. Haley guessed much of the group's divisions had to do with language.

The initial group also included a dozen of the local Sherpa who accompanied any expedition from the area. These trained men assisted with cooking and camp set-up, cared for the animals hauling the supplies, and tended to first-aid, all while directing the outsiders to the best routes. Like good white-water guides back home, they did everything from the most menial tasks to the most crucial and demanding.

The climb would take the route followed by Kanchenjunga's first successful climbers. The base camp was located at about seventeen-thousand feet on the southwest side of the peak, and this first segment was taking them up the Yalung Glacier.

Haley had studied the maps until she knew them by heart. The full group would be setting up two more camps, where they would pause for rest and acclimation before they hit the Great Shelf, a large, steeply dipping plain at about twenty-four-thousand feet. The Great Shelf would mark the change over from the slow group ascent to the faster individual climbs. Haley learned the two Japanese climbers hoped to make the ascent without supplemental oxygen, an even more difficult feat.

******

Teddie and Awut were a pair, standing side-by-side next to the receiver six or seven times a day in the silent world of the traveler. When they weren't in the abode of light together, Awut worked to teach Teddie sign language. She learned the English alphabet, so she could spell words, and then he taught her basics for international communication and some specific signs borrowed from divers or designed by travelers to meet their own needs.

Lhatu didn't join them, although he often kept watch over their solid bodies so nothing would disturb them. He'd been Teddie's primary teacher up until now, and recognized he'd trained her to be a traditional traveler, solitary and almost spiritual. Awut's approach was pragmatic. Lhatu didn't object, but he also had nothing to add.

Amy took her turn watching over the two travelers also, and she bristled every time Lhatu greeted her with the coolness of a man who didn't intend to repeat what had happened between them. Finally, she broke the silence as they passed each other in the hall.

"You can be nice to me, you know. I won't misread it and think you ever want do *that* awful thing again."

Lhatu's expression went to one of pain. "It was not awful. It was wonderful. Don't you see that *is* the problem?"

Amy kept walking.

The next time they passed each other it was in the kitchen, and Amy whispered. "Then stop being afraid of me. I promise if you act nice to me I won't try to seduce you."

Lhatu kept walking. "I am being nice to you," he said after he'd passed her.

"No, you're not." She said it louder as she walked away.

Later, they passed in the hall again. "Can't we at least go back to the way we were? I get this was a one-time thing for you. You've got vows to keep and breaking them once doesn't mean you're willing to break them again."

"Yes." Lhatu started to answer when he paused at a familiar sound. It was coming from behind the door to the small guest room Amy had given to Maurice. There were moans from a male and moans from a female, and both were getting louder. It sounded like Maurice was using his privacy for something other than naps. Amy and Lhatu looked at each other in disbelief. Then Amy stifled a laugh.

"Your grandmother is having more fun than you are."

Lhatu put his hand over his own mouth and walked outside.

He and Amy met on the patio a few minutes later. His mood was more lighthearted than it had been since two days ago at Amy's apartment.

"I'll do better," he promised. "I think the world of you, Amy, and that's part of my problem. But it shouldn't be your problem. You deserve the best friendship I have to give." He reached out his hand to take hers. "I know you don't agree with my beliefs."

"I don't understand them. But I will respect them."

"I believe you will." He dropped her hand awkwardly, and they looked at each other for another minute, before they both turned away and walked into the house without saying anything more.

******

Samir was in his hotel room when he answered the call from Pavel's Chinese cyber sleuth Mei. "Where are you?" the translator asked.

"Patong Beach," he answered. There was a short exchange in Mandarin.

"You're in the right location. Remember how you asked Mei to check police reports for anything unusual. Turns out a nun in a little parish outside of Bangkok reported her motor scooter stolen a couple of weeks after your girls went on the lam. Mei's been running the scooter and the nun's name through the database in case more activity shows up. We got two hits today. A parish priest who shares residence with the nun sent an email to a friend, concerned that sister what's-her-name was acting odd and now has gone missing. Meanwhile, her scooter got a parking ticket, and it's sitting at Patong beach."

"Excellent. Give me the license plate." Samir wrote it down and scratched his head. "So what am I looking for here? Two prostitutes and a nun?"

There was a surprising flurry of giggles on the other end of the line.

"Mei says you are lucky. The combination should be easy to spot."

******

"I say we kill them all," Vasily said.

"You always think we should kill everybody," Gleb replied.

"He has a point this time," Pavel told his men. "If we disappear from the group, they'll come looking for us. That complicates things."

"Yes, but if our group doesn't show up where it's expected, they come looking for us, too," Gleb argued. "These people are damn tenacious about caring for us. If they suddenly find a lot of dead bodies, then they're both tenacious and pissed."

"Okay," Pavel said, "here's the plan. When we get to Trongsa in two days, I'm giving you poison." He pointed to Gleb. "Relax, not enough to kill you. You'll be fine. But you'll get good and sick, and the three of us will insist on staying behind with you. If they leave somebody with us, that's fine. Either way, we wait a couple of days, and then we get away from whoever they've left to watch us. It can be with or without killing. We improvise. You got that?"

"Yes boss. Three voices said it, but Gleb's carried the least enthusiasm for the plan.

******

Teddie was discouraged by her inability to click the shutter in her travel body. She marched into the living room and declared, "I get it. Thinking about not-thinking-about-something does not constitute not thinking about it. Okay? But I still can't click the stupid shutter." Awut, seeing how frustrated his student was, decided to focus on her accomplishments.

"Look at what you learned to do in only a few days," he said, flipping back through the grainy black-and-white photos Teddie had produced while looking at various items in the living room. They'd practiced having her take photos of people, of views, and of written and typed material. The pictures had become less blurry as she practiced. Awut flipped back to her first efforts. "See how far you've come?"

He kept flipping back. There was a pile of shoes, children's art, some lovely handmade furniture. "What are these, Teddie?"

She was staring at the receiver screen as well. "That's where Usha was staying! I went there the night I figured out how to push the shutter. But I had no idea I took pictures there."

"Wait, you traveled the night you woke me up to tell me you'd figured out how to do this?" Awut asked.

"I did. I mean, I traveled without meaning to. Then in all the excitement of figuring things out I forgot about it."

Awut was shaking his head but smiling. "Apparently you can take perfectly fine images while traveling, but only if you want to. Why don't you stop wasting your time here? Go. Go find Usha and bring back photos. I'll tell Lhatu what's going on."

Half an hour later, a groggy Teddie sat back up on the living room couch.

"You didn't find Usha," Lhatu said to her.

"How'd you know?" Teddie asked.

"Because you've been sending images back like the Mars Rover. We've got every square inch of that convent photographed. It was the perfect place for you to go."

"I didn't choose it," Teddie said. "It's just where I went."

"The really good news," Lhatu said, "is I recognize the place. I've never been inside it, of course, but the barn and setting are quite distinctive. Olumiji will get someone over there now.

Teddie was nodding. "I need to rest for a few minutes. Then I'm going to go try to find Usha and Michelle both."

"No, you need to take it easy for longer than that," Lawan said as she entered the room. Teddie could tell from the expression on her face that something was wrong.

"We need to start pushing you less. Immediately."

Lhatu disagreed. "If there ever was a time to push, it's now."

Lawan shook her head. "No, there's something new. It may be nothing relating to Teddie, but we can't ignore it."

"What?" Teddie asked.

"You know how we have two dogs in the lab with this device still in their brains? Well, neither is young and they could have health problems we don't know about."

"But?"

"But Olumiji just got word one of the dogs died. So until an autopsy is done on the animal, Teddie needs to rest."

Teddie was glad there weren't any telepaths in the room to hear how loud her heart was pounding.

May 2012

29. Ascending

There was a minor incident at the beginning of the climb. All twenty-seven people seemed fully acclimated as they left base camp at seventeen-thousand feet. They stayed together as they headed a thousand feet up the glacier, hitting the highest altitude at which a human can live indefinitely.

Halfway to the first night's camp, one of the younger Indian men became dizzy and nauseous, and got worse as he climbed. An instructor from the climbing school took him aside, and, after some argument, he bid the group farewell and headed down the mountain alone. Haley knew it could have been her or any one else on the climb instead. As the group continued upward, she was thankful random misfortune had spared her.

After two nights at eighteen-thousand feet, the climbers moved on to a prominent rock buttress and set up what they named Camp One, where they planned to spend a few days acclimating. One can safely live for weeks at nineteen-thousand feet, so six of the Sherpa would stay at Camp One with food and supplies, maintaining it as a base for possible rescue work or other needs.

In spite of Kanchenjunga's reputation for fierce sudden storms, the group experienced only a little light snow while they rested at Camp One. The forced descent of the lone young man was brushed aside, and spirits were good.

******

The young woman named Usha was trekking through some of the most beautiful scenery on Earth. She bore little outward resemblance to the earnest but shy girl who'd fled from her boarding school eight months earlier. Fresh air and exercise had given her a healthy glow, and months of quiet meditation had left her calmer and more sure of herself. She'd even learned to speak some Bhutanese, though she primarily spoke English with her companion. The affectionate attention of the boy traveling with her was not detracting from her self-esteem, either.

Though the two violated social norms with their un-chaperoned journey, Jampa was quick to explain their situation in acceptable terms to all they encountered. As is the way of the Bhutanese, they were offered food and shelter without exception.

While Usha had itched to leave the convent, once she was on her own she was in no hurry to complete the trek. The trip from somewhere east of Trongsa to the Bhutanese capital of Thimphu was only about eighty miles as a crow would fly, but they weren't crows. Jampa thought it was a two-hundred mile journey on foot, winding through several difficult mountain passes.

They spent nearly a month making their way to Trongsa, a mere forty-mile walk from the convent. Many helpful people insisted they stay over for two or three nights, and they often did. Several gave them better clothing, food for the road, and even camping supplies. The generosity of these people astounded Usha, who was beginning to appreciate why the Bhutanese government restricted travel.

"I think the Bhutanese would give their whole country away before they knew what happened," Usha said.

Jampa shook his head. "It's normal to be giving to strangers, but people here aren't naive or stupid. They are choosing to be kind to you."

As they walked into Trongsa, the main city in central Bhutan and yet a town of less than three-thousand people, Usha felt like she was walking into Mumbai. Months of isolation can do that. All the white buildings with their red roofs seemed like an overwhelming imprint of humanity, and the large dzong dominating the town stared down at her with its red and gold trim.

"How long do you want to stay here?" she asked.

"Not long. I wish to check in at the monastery, in hopes they'll arrange suitable lodging in town for both of us. I want to send word to others in Thimphu who can make arrangements to help us once we arrive."

"Yes, of course." Usha wasn't anxious to be situated at a local convent, which seemed inevitable, and she was even less anxious to arrive at Thimphu. But the generosity that was keeping her alive was predicated on the idea that she was on a journey, going somewhere. If you are going somewhere, you have to eventually get there.

"You really think the government people in Thimphu will grant me asylum here?"

"I do," Jampa said. "You snuck in, in the back of truck, but you were running in fear. My countrymen tend to be sympathetic to one in your plight."

"I'm so lucky the man they sold me to couldn't follow me into Bhutan. By now he must have forgotten about me."

"I'm sure he has," Jampa said. "If your uncle no longer causes you worry, you can return to India instead. The Bhutanese will also help you with that." With this last observation, Jampa had become more formal.

"I don't think so," Usha said. "I don't belong in a convent, but I have begun to think I may belong in Bhutan. I would like to be in contact with my family, though, and be able to visit them…"

She stopped as they approached a large white building with ornate blue trim and a sign saying "Trongsa Medical Shop" in English.

"The local hospital," Jampa explained, as a large European man stood doubled over in front of the door, moaning in pain. Three other well-built men stood with him, trying to get their friend some help.

"Trekkers," Jampa said. "Hardly any of them make it this far up into the mountains, but May is the biggest month for it."

"Poor man. I hope he's okay. Something sure ruined their holiday."

As they walked on, Usha noticed one of the men giving her a long, intense look.

"I forgot how creepy it is to have strange men stare at you like that," she said.

Jampa turned and gave the man a glare back, and the man started to laugh. It was a deep belly laugh, but it lacked the infectious quality humor usually has, as though the joke was his alone to enjoy.

******

Camp Two was established above twenty-thousand feet, after the group followed a narrow rib of rock up the edge of the main icefall associated with the glacier. Kanchenjunga is known for its ongoing avalanches, and although the group had kept to the safest routes, Haley began to find the constant thunder of falling snow unnerving. She knew no route was completely safe, and she also knew she needed to maintain a good mental attitude in spite of the disturbing sound.

So she was distressed when, after leaving Camp Two, she discovered her two closest climbing companions, Hans and Henrik, at odds with each other. She knew how friendships could wear thin under the hardships of cold, fatigue and discomfort, but she expected better from the two men who had been mature enough to argue for her inclusion.

She hung behind, hoping they would work through whatever the issue was, and heard more than she meant to about what seemed to have set off the problem.

"No, I don't want to let anyone else know," Henrik said. "That's why I kept it in three separate places to begin with."

"Well, now you have twice what you need, in two places. And it's not like the bag I left behind is going anywhere. We'll descend down this same ridge and you can pick it up on the way." Hans was trying to sooth his friend.

"I intend to. I just figured I could count on you to carry my backup."

Hans hung his head in obvious frustration. "Look, if you want me to, I'll go back down and get it. It'll only take me a day and a half, and I'll catch up with you guys when you stop to camp on the Great Shelf."

"You know damn well pushing yourself like that would be a bad idea." Henrik didn't seem consoled by the offer. "I don't want that on me. No thanks."

Haley pretended like she hadn't overheard the conversation, but it bothered her as she climbed. So Hans had left something behind, something important to Henrik. It sounded like medicine. Insulin? Was Henrik making this climb as a diabetic? If so, Haley hoped having twice what he needed would be plenty. She wanted to see her friends make it to the top and, more importantly, she wanted to see them make it all the way down.

******

The young woman named Michelle was living as a homeless person on one of the most popular resort beaches in Thailand. She bore little outward resemblance to the calm and confident American who'd arrived at her boarding school eight months earlier. The horrors she'd seen had left her shaken, and she feared she might never find a way to return to her old life.

What remained from her past was an inner core of strength and a practical nature not prone to self-pity. She and her companion eked out survival by living half in the sun and half in shadows. They both avoided any kind of sexual contact with men, and neither felt a need to explain it to the other. They did, however, exchange stories.

Michelle was incredulous to learn of Vanida's bizarre upbringing, owned by two women and taught from a young age to use her vagina to do tricks. Fed on romance novels and promises of being rich, she'd perfected a skill most women wouldn't be able to describe without blushing.

Michelle shared stories of her family life, and they fascinated Vanida, who longed for parents and a sibling. Vanida heard about life at Lord Peartree and the four misfit roommates who'd entered the school at the start of their junior year.

"Usha? That means 'dawn' in Hindi," she told Michelle. "I feel for this Usha, and for you too, because you both lost something. I can't miss what I never had. I'm more free now than I've ever been."

They didn't talk much about the bogeyman they were running from until a man tried to chase them down in the street one day, yelling at them to stop. It scared both of them to their core. Huddled together in an alley afterwards, Vanida pressed for more information.

"Last I knew, Usha's uncle sold her to pay off her father's medical bills. God, that sounds so terrible."

"Why?"

"Because I live in a world where people don't do that. It would be considered so horrible that all but the most psychotic wouldn't consider it."

Vanida thought a minute. "Do you think people would sell off their young female relatives if it was something that happened fairly often? If no one thought it was a big deal?"

"Yeah." Michelle was surprised at how certain she felt. "I'm pretty sure plenty would. Then again, I don't have all that high an opinion of humanity at the moment."

"What do we know about the man who bought Usha?"

"Not a lot. Before I was kidnapped, Usha ran away to stay with a family friend in another city. This man sent people up there to get her, which I thought was kind of excessive. So this agency hid her family so he couldn't use them to find her. We thought that would be the end of it; she'd hide for a while and would turn up somewhere. Then I woke up locked in a closet."

"You didn't think it had anything to do with your friend Usha?"

"At first I thought so, but after a while it was hard to see a connection. I mean, no one even asked me about her. They just shipped me off here. I finally figured I was an unlucky random victim. Otherwise, why do this to me?"

"They'd probably have let you go if he found Usha and got what he wanted," Vanida said. "This latest hunt for you means this man is still pissed. He hasn't gotten Usha, and now he's lost you."

"You think I've gone from collateral damage to being part of his obsession?"

"Yes, but I also think the fact that he is chasing you is proof he isn't as powerful as he thinks he is."

******

The group planned to make Camp Three at the base of a large sloping plateau located a thousand feet below what is considered to be the death zone. At the rarified air above twenty-five-thousand feet, the human body is dying, and the only question is how fast.

As the air became thinner, the group climbed more slowly, and it was a relief to stop for their last real rest before each one would don the gear they needed and attempt to summit. The remaining Sherpa set up this final camp for them, and cooked them one last meal—a hot lunch. They stored extra dried food, ample climbing gear and more oxygen tanks for use by those making the full ascent.

Two more climbers had been forced to head back down after leaving Camp Two. One of the Canadians broke two fingers when a falling rock landed on his hand, and one of the young Indian men injured his ankle and deemed it to too tender to continue. These two were now descending slowly with the help of a Sherpa.

As the remaining group made their way onto the plateau for Camp Three, one of the older climbers from the mountaineering school began to cough up blood. When pressed for information, he admitted he had been breathless most of the night, and knew he was showing symptoms of high altitude pulmonary edema. He left with the remaining Sherpa to head back to the base of the mountain.

The two Japanese climbers wanted to make the full ascent without any supplemental oxygen, which meant they needed to keep going so they could get up and back down without any more time elapsing than necessary. They wished the rest of the group well, and did not even stay for lunch.

That left nine climbers that night at the camp on the Great Shelf, pausing for a brief rest as they stared in wonder at the magnificent hanging glacier above them. Haley looked at the eight men with her. There were three young Indian men she'd hardly spoken with, and who were only a few years older than she was. Two of the veteran climbers from the mountaineering school remained, and they were the group's unspoken leaders.

Hans and Henrik seemed to have put the unfortunate incident with the lost medicine behind them and had resumed their former camaraderie. The remaining man was the Canadian. He'd been less warm to her than his companion with the hand injury, and now that he was alone she got the impression he hoped she wouldn't slow him down. Well, she didn't intend to.

The weather stayed beautiful for the two days spent resting at the camp, and then their luck changed.

******

Lhatu drove Teddie over to school so she could go to classes while they waited for details of the dog's autopsy to come back from Bangkok. Olumiji put an enthusiastic Tariq back on temporary duty, to keep mental watch over her while she was at school. Amy called the academy and secured permission for Teddie to stay off campus at night, so Lawan could monitor her health. Teddie squirmed with restlessness each evening while she paced around a house that seemed smaller every minute she was there.

"I can't get exactly what killed the dog," a frustrated Olumiji confessed two nights later as he held his head, "but it doesn't really matter, because I'm sure it wasn't the device. More importantly, *they're* sure it wasn't the device."

He turned to Teddie and smiled weakly. "Young lady, you have been cleared for takeoff."

When she only gave him an odd look back he added, "You're from Houston, right? A little humor from home?"

He's trying. He's exhausted and he's trying to help me relax.

"Thanks," she said, managing a chuckle back. "I'm glad it's launch time."

May 2012

30. Descending

"Who do I check on first?" Teddie asked, talking more to herself than to the other people in the room. Lhatu answered.

"Remember my telling you there are three kinds of travel. Do you remember the first one?"

"Of course," Teddie said. "Wandering. The only method of the untrained beginner, and a form of relaxation and exploration for the adept."

"Exactly," Lhatu said, pleased. "And the second?"

"Seeking. You've trained me in this, and now I seek my friends who need me."

"Perhaps," Lhatu said. "Seeking is the second method, but we didn't talk about the third. It's known as 'answering a call' and I believe it's what you must do now."

"You think whichever one of my friends needs me most will call to me? How will I know which one it is? How will I answer?" Teddie was not happy about having this last minute information foisted on her.

"Trust your higher self," Lhatu replied. "Be open. Go where you go."

Teddie suppressed an eye-roll. "I'll do my best. I *can* promise I'll go where I go."

She shook her head at the vague instructions and then concentrated all of her efforts on entering the trance state that had become almost as natural to her as being awake. As she left her solid body, she wondered for a brief second which of her two friends was going to need her first.

******

When the group heard the characteristic rumble high above them, most had time to act. The ensuing plop of falling snow was small; it barely deserved the name avalanche. Most of them already had their gear on, and supplies were piled at the edge of the small camp. Only Henrik, who was moving slowly that morning, was sitting on the ground far from the group, sorting through things in his backpack.

It fell such that it only half-covered their gear, but totally covered Henrik, who hadn't even stood up to run. Hans hurried back to where the top of his friend's hat was poking through the snow and started digging. Part of the group moved to help him while the rest worked to pull the gear free from the edge of the snow, all praising their good fortune it hadn't been worse.

Henrik was frantic as his friends pulled him and his backpack out. Haley was amazed a veteran climber would be so agitated. A second, louder rumble let them all know more falling snow was coming. This time they ran, with two of the men dragging a resisting Henrik and his backpack to safety with them.

The falling snow exploded into a white fury as it landed with both a beauty and a roar. The nine climbers turned to watch in wonder. Once the noise subsided, Hans asked Henrik "Where is your medicine?"

"I've been trying to tell you. It was laying next to my backpack."

"So now you're down to one portion?"

"No. Now I'm down to nothing. I'd been pulling from both sets, so I took out the two caches to see how much was left in each. I wanted to divide it up evenly and give you half to carry. It was all spread out on the ground when the avalanche hit." Henrik gave Hans a look of desperation as he pointed to the fresh pile of deep snow. "Now all my medicine is buried under there."

"He's diabetic?" Haley asked.

Hans shook his head.

Henrik looked over at her. “I have something called Addison’s disease. My adrenal glands don’t work right, so I take medicine every day for them.”

“What are you doing climbing a mountain?” the Canadian asked.

“Climbing mountains is what I do. This disease is no issue. John Kennedy ran a country with it, and all kinds of people with Addison’s do strenuous things.”

“So how long can you go without your medicine?” asked one of the climbing instructors.

“Normally a couple of days. I brought three times what I needed and put it different places. I’m no idiot. Then one bag got left at Camp Two with the supplies.”

“So get down to Camp Two,” the Canadian said. “You can get there in two days.”

“Yeah, if I was doing okay.”

“But you’re not?” Haley asked.

Henrik shook his head. “I’m moving into what they call an Addisonian crisis. Probably set off by dehydration—I knew I needed more fluids last night but I was too tired to bother. That’s why I was sorting through the medicine this morning, to see what I had left. This crisis isn’t a crisis, as long as I take my medicine; but I do go through medication faster once I’m in it.”

“What happens without your meds?” Haley asked.

“My blood pressure and blood sugar levels drop. It becomes life-threatening within hours.”

“God knows we’ve all kinds of meds on us. Do we have anything that will help?” the Canadian asked.

“Not that I know of, and I’m not about to start swallowing random pills. Salt, sugar and fluids will stave it off for a while, and I’ll take them, but within hours I’m going to need my shot. I carry syringes ready to go, of course. There’re two of them buried under the snow.”

The other instructor shook his head. “We could look for days and not find your medicine under all that. Our best bet is to get you back to the Camp Two where you’ve got your extra medicine waiting.”

“That’s at least two days of walking. He told you. He won’t make it,” Hans said.

"Can we radio back and get one of the Sherpa to bring it up to us?" the other instructor suggested.

"That's two days away, too, if a Sherpa climbs almost continually," Hans said.

"You're toast man," the Canadian said. "I'm sorry to hear it. But I'm not doing you any good standing here at twenty-four-thousand feet talking about it. No offense, but I've got a mountain to climb."

He looked around. "Anyone else ready to come with me?"

Both mountaineering instructors nodded.

"Helicopter?" one of the young Indian men said pointing to the sky?

Hans shook his head. "Most can't fly over eighteen-thousand feet. Kanchenjunga is so remote; we couldn't get a capable one here in time."

One of the mountaineering instructors said something to the three younger men in Hindi. The young men talked among themselves, gesturing and raising their voices. Finally, one of them uttered a single syllable and turned and joined the three older men preparing to move on up the mountain. The other two young Indian men moved over and stood next to Henrik. Their intentions to stay and try to help were clear.

Hans turned to Haley. "You'd best go too. You and these two boys as well. I'll stay here with Henrik and do everything I can to make him comfortable, and then I'll head down the mountain once… once…" He couldn't finish the sentence.

Haley shook her head as she waved the anxious foursome on. "You guys go ahead. It doesn't look like we've got a third avalanche coming, so I'm just going to poke around in the snow a little before I give up. Who knows? It might be my lucky day."

"Me too," the quietest of the Indian youths said.

"Me too," the one who had asked about the helicopter added.

"Suit yourself," the Canadian said with a shrug, and then he started upward.

One of the instructors gave Haley and the two boys a stern look before he left. "Do *not* give this heroism of yours more than a day. You must choose to ascend or descend by tomorrow morning. Do not needlessly add yourself to the death toll."

"They will all be leaving in the morning," Henrik said. "Don't worry. The death toll for your climb should be no larger than one."

******

Teddie seldom stopped mid-journey, but this time she did deliberately. She didn't know what she was heading into. Knowing where she was going could help her prepare. She looked around for either the lush greenery of Thailand or for the sparkling white of Bhutan. The glisten of snow met her eye. Very well. She prepared herself for Usha's world.

******

Hans and the two boys were still digging around in the area Henrick had been pulled from, but Haley had stopped and was sitting on her backpack thinking. She loved maps. She'd loved this mountain since she'd first heard of it, and all the more so since it had become the most beautiful sight to greet her every morning in Darjeeling. She'd memorized the tales of every climb and those of each attempted one, and she knew of every inch of this mountain for which information was available.

"There is one way to get down to Camp Two where the medicine is and back here in four to five hours," she said.

"No there isn't," Henrik said.

"Yes. It's an easy half-hour hike down to the top of that huge cliff. It drops over sixteen hundred feet straight down onto the small icefall that leads right over the ridge we camped on.

"Are you nuts? Winds off the side of that cliff could be up to a hundred miles an hour, and it's coated in ice. Climbing up or down it would take days. It might not even be possible."

"And repelling down it would take maybe an hour. I know we have a climbing harness. How much rope do we have with the supplies?"

"Rope that needs to hold a grown man?" Henrik asked.

"No, just a hundred-and-twenty-pound girl."

Hans had started to overhear the conversation and moved towards it.

"No. The wind could be too strong. You could get smashed to death against the rock face before you got half-way down.

Haley nodded. "That's true, except today the winds are coming from behind the cliff. Right now, it's possible to repel. It might not be in a few hours."

"Once you made it down, you'd have to cross through the edge of the icefall, and that's way too dangerous," Henrik said.

"The faster and lighter you are, the less dangerous it is," Haley said. "It's not far to the ridge and I'll be descending, which is quicker and makes it easier to see a safe route. The hardest part will be coming back up, but I can retrace my previous path and twenty-thousand feet ought to feel like sea level to me now. I should be able to get back to the base of the cliff in a little over two hours."

"Yeah, and then it takes you three days to get back up it," Henrik said.

But Hans was way ahead of him. "No, it takes me and my two helpers here maybe an hour to pull her and your medicine back up the cliff face, which can be done if she doesn't plant any anchors while she's going down. No real climber would ever descend that way, of course, but Haley can because she's not going to repel. She is going to let us lower her down while she uses her feet to protect herself, and then she's going to let three strong men pull her right back up to the top. Aren't you Haley?"

Haley was nodding, glad Hans understood. But Henrik was shaking his head. Haley noticed that he was fingering a photo of his own three-year-old daughter he had pulled out of somewhere in his bag. "There is no way I let anyone's daughter take a risk like that."

"Excuse me," Haley said, "but people's daughters take risks all the time. If you're lucky, maybe your own daughter will save somebody's ass someday."

She took a breath and tried to let her frustration go. "Look, you want all the people with the upper-body strength up on top doing the pulling," she said. "You want the lightest person possible on the end of the rope. Lucky for you, somebody's daughter is willing to be that person, so your daughter doesn't grow up without a dad."

"You're determined, aren't you?" Hans said.

"It's that or let somebody's dad die. And there is no way," she looked at Henrik for emphasis, "I am letting anyone's dad do that."

Henrik was silent for a few seconds. "Thank you," he finally said. He handed her his daughter's picture. "Tuck it in your pocket for me while you do this, okay? Maybe it will bring you luck."

Haley wasn't a big believer in lucky charms, but she knew enough to humor a man facing death if she failed.

"I'll be back with the stuff before you need it," she said.

As she walked away, she smiled when she heard him say, "And I hope she grows up to be just like you."

The rope had more knots and clamps in it than Haley would have liked, but it was the safest adequate length they could put together fast. Not many people can throw themselves off of the equivalent of a hundred-and-sixty story building, knowing their life depends on a dozen knots, a lack of jagged outcrops, and the wind not changing direction. Haley was one of those people. She leaned back into the climbing harness, placed her boots against the cliff wall and let her instincts take over.

By the time her feet hit the ground almost an hour later, her legs were tired, having fought the whole time to keep her body a safe distance from the irregular rock wall. She had lost sight of her helpers half-way down, but she turned on her cell phone hoping for the last bit of remaining reception, willing to use precious battery to let them know she was okay. Ravi, the more talkative of the two, had turned his phone on also. "Safe," she typed. "Good," he replied. She paused a few minutes to rest and regain her strength.

Hans pulled out his binoculars and looked for the slender figure as it moved toward the treacherous icefall. He was concerned her rapid descent might have left her ill or too exhausted to make her way over to the nearby ridge of land.

He laughed when he saw her. He needn't have worried. Haley was skipping her way over the ice, graceful and surefooted, looking like a ballerina dancing her way along the roof of the world.

******

Teddie sucked in her breath in sheer terror. She was hanging in space, somewhere off of a cliff. What had gone wrong? She turned to see Haley next to her, secured in some device as she lowered herself to the ground.

So her higher self had decided she ought to be here? Teddie lowered herself alongside of Haley, moving down the cliff face until her friend was standing on solid ground. Teddie watched her type "Safe" into her cell phone and take a few minutes to rest. Had she come all the way down this huge cliff? No way.

Haley didn't rest for long before she turned and headed into a field of ice blocks behind her. These irregular chunks of blue and white were different shapes and sizes, and often had big cracks in-between them. Haley was skipping over the cracks, headed towards a ridge of land only a few hundred yards away.

Teddie moved ahead to look around. In the direction Haley was going was a large fissure stretching further than the others, and it was at least five-feet wide. Teddie willed herself to rise a bit higher, to see in what direction the fissure disappeared most quickly. If Haley went right, the fissure grew wider and was filled with snow. Could she walk on the snow? Or would she try to and sink into it? To the left, the fissure began to heal, and before she went too far out of her way Haley would be able to jump it easily.

If I could talk to her, show her what this thing looks like. Then she realized it. *Wait, I can.*

******

Hans hardly took his eyes off of Haley as she crossed the ice field. He was hoping he would have a clearer view of the ice from above and be able to offer her some guidance using Ravi's cell phone. But the field was too far away for him to be see anything useful, even with the high-powered binoculars.

So he was doubly surprised when Haley stopped walking and took something out of her pocket to look at it. Her cell phone? She studied it for a minute, and then she started to backtrack and head off to the left. What the hell was this? Who else in the world could possibly be sending her directions?

******

Haley expected to hear from Ravi. When the message said, "Go left," she didn't think twice about it. When a grainy black-and-white photo followed the text, she was more puzzled, until she looked and saw she had received both from Teddie. Haley smiled. So her friend was checking in on her, using that weird shit she did.

Well, weird or not, Haley could recognize a picture of a dangerous crevasse when she saw one, even on a bad photo. Going left was definitely the best option.

******

"What's going on?" Lhatu asked when Teddie returned suddenly to her solid body. "Are you okay? Are they okay? Why are you sending back pictures of snow?"

"I have another emergency my higher self thinks I need to deal with first," she said as she grabbed her phone.

"Go left," she texted as fast as she could type.

Lawan had the picture of the crevasse on the screen.

"Send it to me," Teddie almost barked at the confused woman. "Sorry, I didn't mean to order you around, but I need it now."

She hit a few more buttons on her phone and turned to the room full of people who were staring at her.

"Gotta go. Higher self thinks I've got two more emergencies, and it looks like I'm going to have to go back and forth between them, and do some calling of my own."

With a deep breath and a visible tremor running through her body, she relaxed, and Teddie was gone.

******

Four hours after they left Henrik, Haley was back at the base of the cliff. She knew it had taken longer than she'd figured, but they'd be in time to save Henrik. She pulled out her phone and typed. "Ready." The next thing she knew, she was off of her feet, ascending up the cliff face. Legs out. Brain on. The ground receded below.

May 2012

31. Calling

Jampa hadn't been in his lighter body in weeks. He felt guilty when he thought of his sister, whom he'd intended to find and help well before this. Instead, he'd chosen to stay with the real girl Usha, while deciding the mysterious Noom, who had troubles he could only guess at, could wait. But what if she couldn't?

Jampa was self-aware enough to know he was attracted to Usha, and his infatuation could be turning into love. It was hard to tell how much his growing affection had affected his decision. Jampa suspected he'd always choose to help a flesh-and-blood person in need over a mirage he didn't understand.

Usha had been lodged at a home in Trongsa, while Jampa was given shelter at the monastery. His time with Usha had convinced him he would not become a Buddhist monk. He had no problem with most of the eight precepts, but he'd decided he was meant to be a husband and a father. At least, he felt driven to do what husbands were expected to do. Lately, he felt highly driven to do a lot of it, preferably with Usha, but if not, with any suitable partner who'd have him. The strength of these carnal desires surprised him.

He fell into a restless sleep on the floor, yearning for the privacy to relieve his urges, when he was surprised to be in his light body, moving down the steep, narrow streets of Trongsa. He assumed he was seeking Usha, and he laughed at himself. Bodies of light, as far as he knew, were incapable of doing anything to alleviate the cravings compelling him.

To his surprise, he didn't seek out Usha. He felt the difficult-to-describe, but unmistakable tug of another. Not his sister. The only other he knew was Usha's American friend, and he agreed to go to her. The speed at which he began to move let him know the journey would be long, and so he allowed his consciousness to relax while he traveled.

The girl greeted him with a friendly wave, but seemed surprised. Had she called his sister instead of him? She kept looking around, but when no one else appeared, she shrugged and motioned for him to follow.

******

Vanida fell into a restless sleep, considering plans to thwart the first-class creep who was chasing them. How could she use his power against him? Instead of hiding, maybe she could get Michelle's picture plastered over the internet, posted from many locations? Maybe she could do the same with Michelle's friend Usha? She was considering how to do this when she felt the gentle tug of another. It wasn't her brother, so it must be the Western girl. No one else had interacted with her.

The call came from far away—she was certain. Very well. She'd once enjoyed traveling far to play in the white powder up north. She hunkered down for the journey, and was soon moving down the steep, narrow streets of a mountain village. She entered what appeared to be a monastery, and found the Western girl waiting for her in a room full of sleeping monks.

At first, the girl gave her a look of confusion and even exasperation. Had she not been called? Then Vanida saw the girl was floating over the sleeping body of Pêe chaai, the brother Vanida had not seen in months. Perhaps the girl had expected her brother?

The girl shrugged and motioned for Vanida to follow. Moving with the girl was difficult, but Vanida managed the short trip as they moved down one narrow street and up another.

They came to a place of lodging, passing through the outer walls and into the room with four men in boots and hiking gear, dressed to go out. They had a disturbing number of bows and arrows lying around the room. They seemed in good spirits.

She wondered why the girl had brought her here until she saw the girl look at a photograph lying on the table. The Western girl's eyes went wide when she saw the picture. It was a portrait of an Indian girl, and written across the bottom in blue ink were Latin letters spelling the name Usha.

Vanida sorted through the information. Usha was the name of Michelle's friend. There were plenty of Ushas in the world, of course, but Vanida found coincidences to be rare in the trips her special body made. The Western girl appeared to know this Usha. So, the Western girl was the other friend from Texas, the one Michelle called normal?

Well, you never know who is normal and who isn't, Vanida laughed. The girl caught the mirth in her eyes and nodded. She pointed to Usha's picture and put her hands over her heart. *My friend.* Vanida wished she had a photo of Michelle to offer back, but it wasn't necessary. The Western girl's expression made it clear they both knew who each other was.

Vanida looked around for more useful things. She recognized the Russian alphabet on many items. It wasn't difficult to guess what was going on.

Michelle called the Western girl Teda, or something like that. Teda motioned for Vanida to follow. They moved towards a small house and Vanida followed her inside.

Usha was sleeping on the floor, looking like she couldn't have been safer. More heart gestures. Vanida nodded—she got the idea.

What kind of man hunts down such a defenseless girl? A man who was enjoying the chase, Vanida decided. The good mood of the men in the other room made it clear they thought the hunt was almost over. Vanida realized with a chill, it probably was.

She wanted to return to her solid body in Thailand, to the body in which she could do something to warn Usha. But of course her solid body was hundreds of miles away.

Teda had been staring intently at things for the last few minutes and now she waved a farewell. Vanida couldn't imagine what this Teda could do to help Usha either. The only one close enough to be of any use was her sleeping brother Pêe chaai, who had no way of knowing what was going on.

If only she could tell Pêe chaai. Talk to him, write him a note. Then she had another idea.

******

Jampa followed the girl into a nice hotel and had to laugh when she chose to drift up the stairway all the way to the eighth floor. He would merely have risen in the air where he was, but perhaps she didn't like heights. She led him to a room with three men. One, a small man from India, sat hunched over his laptop. Next to him was paper on which he had written a series of five numbers. Phone? Address? It had a letter prefix. License plate?

He was copying the numbers down and giving them to the two other men. They were large Europeans, and they nodded as though they were being given instructions.

The man from India motioned to them to come look at the screen. It showed a small motor scooter, its license plate visible. So it *was* a license plate. The scooter was parked in front of a small shop and the name of the store was visible, too.

They nodded and smiled. Find the motor scooter.

The Western girl—Jampa thought Usha called her Tehdu or something like that—Tehdu motioned for him to come. He'd never followed anyone but his sister, and following this other traveler was more difficult. Using all of his concentration he trailed along behind her until she stopped in front of the little store, and pointed to the motor scooter. Then she moved into the adjacent alley and gestured to the two sleeping female bodies.

One he did not know, but he could guess it was the other Texan friend he'd heard of. Tehdu made a hands-over-her-heart gesture and pointed to the girl. Yes, this was her friend.

The girl sleeping next to the friend needed no introduction. Jampa recognized the sleeping body of his own sister. Now it was clearer. While he'd accompanied Usha, his sister Noom had been involved in this as well.

Such a connection might have baffled another, but Jampa's philosophy of life embraced cosmic connections. What puzzled him was that the two girls were sleeping in an alley, while anyone in town could have provided them with lodging. And, why were two rather unpleasant-looking men coming for their motor scooter?

He suspected this was tied to Usha's troubles and thought the girls needed to be woken and warned. He looked up to see Tehdu play-acting all sorts of symbols of danger. She pantomimed choking, stabbing and throat-slitting like a mime on a killing spree.

Jampa nodded, in part to get her to stop. Danger. He got the idea. He would warn them. But how?

******

Teddie was back in the living room in Darjeeling, and everyone could see the panic in her eyes.

"I hope I set a new record for sending photos," she said.

"You did," Lhatu said. "But you must explain them. And you need to calm down and take a few deep breaths."

"I don't have time for deep-breathing," she said. "Listen. I've got a group of Russians in the middle of Bhutan about two-hundred yards away from where Usha is sleeping."

She pointed to one of the first pictures she'd sent back.

"One of those men is Pavel," Olumiji said. "I recognized him as soon as this picture arrived. I can't believe he found a way to get there. Why in the world does he have archery equipment with him?"

"Judging from their other gear, it looks like they're part of some trekking expedition," Lhatu said.

Amy interrupted. "You need to find out which one. We need to know where this hotel is. You're finally off the hook for sending messages, Olumiji, because this is going to happen way too fast for Pavel's detective to have any effect on the outcome. Lhatu, you've got to call Bhutan now and get these guys arrested."

"It's the middle of the night over there." Lhatu thought that was a reasonable objection.

"I don't care. By morning they'll be gone and Usha will be gone with them. I promise you they have a plan for getting out fast and they're going to be remarkably hard to find once they leave with the girl. There has got to be a police station in Thimphu that is open all night. Please start there. Maybe someone can figure out the home Usha is at and warn them. Lhatu, they could kill everyone in that home."

Lhatu nodded and headed to the next room with his phone.

"Amy, there's more," Teddie said. "Keep flipping."

Teddie had sent back a dozen photos of the Russians in Bhutan and another dozen of where Usha was sleeping. Then the scene changed. It was a large, modern hotel room where a man from India was hunched over a computer. The screen showed a motor scooter.

"We checked the license plate. It's the scooter the nun told the girls to steal," Amy said.

"Where is the nun?" Teddie asked.

"Safe. She's at the hotel with the Japanese telepath couple looking for Michelle."

"Okay good, because I didn't see her anywhere," Teddie said. "But I did see this man give the information about where the scooter is parked to these two guys."

"I recognize the small Indian man," Olumiji said. "He's Pavel's assistant. The other two look like the muscle Pavel keeps around."

"That would make sense," Teddie said. "These next pictures show Michelle and Vanida, sleeping about twenty yards away from their vehicle. They are about to get found as well."

Lawan spoke up. "I know Thailand. If we're past staying under the radar, I'm on the phone now getting these girls some help."

"I'll get word to my telepaths at the beach, soon as I can get one of them to wake up enough to hear my telepathic request," Olumiji said.

"Why don't you call their hotel room?" Amy said.

"Good point. Calling now."

Awut turned to Teddie. "You did great, and now these very capable people will move as fast as they can to save all of your friends. Will you take those deep breaths now?" he asked.

Teddie looked at him, and her eyes started to fill with tears. "No, I did not *do great.* I did okay. Great would have been getting them some local help right away."

"There was no way for you to do that, Teddie," Awut comforted her. "A traveler has no way to ask for help."

"I had a way. I tried, Awut, I tried, but somehow I screwed it up. I called for both of the twins to come see, so they could each wake up and get help. But they got switched. I ended up with the boy in Thailand seeing the danger Michelle is in. Vanida came to me in Bhutan and saw Usha's predicament. Neither one will be physically close enough to help once when they return to their solid bodies. So I did have a way, and I couldn't make it happen." The pools of water in her eyes were threatening to overflow.

Lhatu came into the room and touched Teddie on the shoulder.

"You did not fail. The universe engaged in the sort of confusion I talked about with these entangled twins. You did what you could, and by trying to bring in another traveler at both locations, you did considerably more than anyone I know would have managed. That was a great idea. Don't fault yourself for what you can't control. Wait and see how your efforts work out."

"Did you get a hold of anyone in Bhutan?" Teddie asked

"No, but I left a lot of good messages. I may get a call back before morning."

"I don't think anybody is going to make it in time to warn either of them," Teddie said with her head in her hands.

******

Jampa wanted to return to his solid body in Bhutan, so he could try to call someone to help his sister and her friend in Thailand. He couldn't imagine how, but surely someone at the monastery could help him figure out a way to get assistance to someone far away.

He tried to snap back into his body, but instead he found himself moving out of the abode of light and even further from the solid world. He was being called by something familiar.

He heeded the call. The first thing he noticed about this new world was that it was various shades of green. Jampa felt the energy of the earth and growth and life all around him. Although the world of his light body was soundless, he heard a distant heartbeat, slow and deliberate. Maybe, he thought, he was only feeling its rhythm in his bones.

Noom stood facing him. He knew she'd called him. He half-expected her to berate him, to demand to know why he'd gone elsewhere instead of finding her and giving her aid. But of course she had no way of knowing he'd ever intended to help her, and no way to berate him if she had.

He looked at her more closely. She'd changed. There was nothing of the child left in her face, but she was also no longer the angry young woman who'd caused him such concern. She looked determined, and afraid. Her look said she needed his help.

Jampa wanted to help her with all his heart, but he couldn't imagine how. Noom reached out and touched his hand. In a world where he'd never felt the sensation of touch before, he felt her fingers as firmly as he'd ever felt anything. He understood it was because, on some level, he and Noom were one and the same.

With that knowledge, he entered his solid body.

As he sat up, he was surprised to notice he'd been sleeping in the dirt. He wiggled his toes awake and looked down to see bright pink nail polish. Who had done such a thing to him? Then he saw his toenails were attached to delicate feet attached to a shapely pair of female legs. He had on a miniskirt, a halter-top and a lot of cheap jewelry. A dozen years of training in meditation was not sufficient to calm him down for the first few seconds.

After that, he shook his companion awake. He was surprised at his light sweet voice when he spoke.

"We've got to run. Now!"

He grabbed the girl's hand and pulled her along as he—no, as she—ran down the alley and onto a side street looking for a better place to hide. As Jampa tried to adjust to a gait made different by a strange new set of hips, he could hear footsteps gaining behind him, and ahead he saw a motor scooter speeding down the little street toward them.

"Sister!" The girl with him yelled in surprise to the driver of the motor scooter, a woman in a sparkly cocktail dress. She brought her scooter up next to them with an abrupt stop.

"Get on fast and hang on tight," she said. "I knew I could get here faster than they could." As she sped into the night, with both girls squished onto the passenger seat and hanging on for their lives, Jampa blacked out in confusion and fear.

******

Vanida was trusting her instincts, believing her own fate was intertwined with that of her brother's. Perhaps Pêe chaai's consciousness was now present in her solid body, but she wasn't sure. If not, she hoped his heavy mind would continue to slumber, while Vanida directed her brother's body's actions in the physical world.

She forced his large body to stand, getting used to its size and different weight distribution. She considered checking out the other main difference, but gave herself a mental slap. No time for such nonsense. She needed to find the house where this Usha was staying and lead the young woman out of danger.

Vanida made her way down the dark street, taking pleasure in being able to travel at night inside a large male body. What a different life it must be, to feel so safe all the time. Vanida wondered if her brother might be willing to exchange bodies more often.

She got to the home and stopped short. Now what? She was in a physical body that didn't walk through walls. She could pound on the front door, but this large male body might provoke fear, a problem she didn't have in her own body. So, there were two sides to this issue.

She opted to climb in a window. The longer legs were helpful; the bigger size was not. Usha gasped when she saw the body of her male friend.

"We've got to run," Pêe chaai's deep voice said to Usha in a hoarse whisper. "Your crazy obsessed man has found you and he's on his way." Pêe chaai's hand took Usha's, and Usha followed along as Vanida led her back out the window and into the trees behind the house. Now what?

******

Vanida slammed back into her own body with a ferocity she'd never experienced. She was fighting to keep from sliding off the back end of a motor scooter speeding down a dark highway. Her arms were wrapped tightly around Michelle, who was hanging onto a woman in a sparkly evening dress, who was driving like a madwoman.

I think I might have missed something important.

She hung on tighter, hoping the woman would stop soon and somebody would explain what the hell was going on.

******

Teddie thought about Lhatu's words and decided to go back to Usha's side. No matter how exhausted she was, at least she could track where Usha was taken and improve the chances of eventually rescuing her friend. Before she tried to reenter her trance state, Amy came in and gave her a hug.

"I don't know how you did it, but I've just gotten word from an agency in Thailand. They've got a Sister of the Good Shepard and two human-trafficking victims at a shelter in Phang Nga, and the three are demanding immediate protection from men they say are chasing them. Well, to be more precise, the nun is demanding the protection. One of the girls is fascinated by the library and the other hasn't stopped crying and hugging everyone since they got there. Police are on the way, they've contacted the U.S. State Department, and it looks like the story is about to break on CNN. I think we've got Michelle, and Vanida."

Teddie gave her a grin but Amy kept talking.

"Olumiji has managed to wake a telepath near Trongsa. He's trying to get more people, to organize a crew to find and protect Usha. It would help if he knew more about where she was.

"I'm on my way," Teddie said. "Watch for photos."

******

Jampa came to consciousness hugging a tree, holding on to it for his life. Then he remembered he'd been on a motor scooter. He wasn't on one now. He let go of the tree, feeling a little silly.

He looked around. He was standing the middle of the woods, with a frightened Usha at his side. What was this about? Last he'd known, they'd both been sleeping safely.

I think I might have missed something important.

"Come out, little girl," a voice said in English. Was that a Russian accent? Jampa peaked through the branches to see a grown man wearing night vision goggles and armed with a bow and arrow. Jampa motioned to Usha to hold still, but he needn't have bothered. Usha was motionless, holding her breath.

"I've got heat sensors," the man said sweetly. "It won't take me long to find you, my little one. My nice darts will make you fall asleep in my arms."

Wasn't this the trekker they'd seen a couple of days ago standing in front of the hospital? Jampa was putting two and two together, and he had to believe Usha had done the same. They were out of options.

******

Teddie's sense of urgency propelled her to Usha's side faster than she'd ever traveled before. What was the real speed limit, she wondered? The speed of light? Probably.

She looked around the dark green forest behind the house where Usha had been staying. The girl had gotten as far as the woods before her hunters arrived, and by some miracle the boy was with her. Teddie thought the man in the goggles with the bow looked ridiculous, but that was from the perspective of not having a real body that could be shot. Three more men with bows kept their distance behind him, being careful to let the big game hunter be the one to take down his prey.

Teddie felt certain she was catching more activity out of the corners of her eyes, but every time she looked closer she couldn't see a thing. Finally, it occurred to her. The woods were filling up with other travelers. How many lived around here? Well, this country was the home of c^3. She started to count the beings of energy. Some seemed like smoke, some like flickers of lightning bugs, others were translucent, glowing creatures.

Perhaps because these travelers were more advanced they were able to modify their appearance to suit their whims? A twinkling creature resembling a White Dragon took its place in the front, and Teddie stared at the shimmering beast, thinking there was something familiar about it. Of course. It was the creature found on the flag of Bhutan, the land of the thunder dragon.

This particular thunder dragon looked right at Teddie, then morphed for a second into the face of Yuden, Lhatu's grandmother and the imperial sovereign of c^3. The dragon gave Teddie a playful wink, then returned to directing her royal court.

One large group of travelers congregated off to the left. Teddie watched while one of Pavel's men started talking and pointed to the group. Did travelers give off heat? Lhatu said travelers were beings composed of energy. Energy could be heat. Maybe a whole group of them gave off enough to be detected?

Another man interrupted. He had infrared goggles and was pointing in the direction of a dozen or so travelers off to his right. Teddie noticed another group had clumped near, but not right in front of, Usha and Jampa, and it looked like that's where Pavel thought they were.

Then all of the travelers gathered together far off to one side, and the men picked up that reading. At least, they seemed to be congratulating themselves as they took several steps in the wrong direction into the trees, while Usha and Jampa did their best to not move a single muscle.

When no one was found, Pavel spent a few minutes checking his equipment. Teddie watched, amused, as all of the other travelers now clumped together again in a new position even further into the woods, and the men moved off again several feet in the wrong direction. This time they went far enough that Usha and Jampa could back away further under cover of the men's own noise.

So it went for a few more times. The men moved further in the wrong direction while the hunted two moved to safety. Finally, Pavel put a halt to it all by throwing his goggles on the ground.

That's when the newly formed Trongsa Commission to Protect the Innocent and Disarm Deceitful Visitors Intending to Do Harm arrived on the scene. Sixteen men, seven women and two children armed with axes, pitchforks and kitchen knives made their way into the clearing. Pavel laughed as he came out of the woods with his bow raised. Then he saw the cameramen who'd arrived behind them, broadcasting live by satellite. He lowered his weapon, with a gesture of apology.

Teddie could do no more, so she headed back to her own solid body to rest. She was relieved, even ecstatic, but she was also exhausted. She curled up on the living room couch and her friends in Darjeeling let her lie there for as long as she wanted. Before she was ready to wake back up, she received one last call. She chose to answer it and after that, nothing disturbed her slumber.

******

Once his medicine took effect, Henrik decided he'd pushed his body far enough. After thanking his four companions several times, he made the difficult decision to descend alone the next morning.

Haley and the three climbers with her assessed their own physical and mental conditions and decided they were fit to keep going. They knew the path. The weather was good. They had enough supplies. The top of the mountain was waiting.

In a slow, dream-like drama, the quartet made their way upward, breath by deliberate breath. The sky glowed blue and the snow was blinding. They climbed, each knowing sooner or later their bodies would say enough. Each wanted to have made it to the top when that happened.

Later, Haley would have little memory of the final ascent. Her thoughts became fuzzier as she climbed, and each member of the group began to use their four carefully rationed bottles of oxygen to increase their energy.

The last hundred feet or so was mostly a stagger. The group stopped a few feet short of the top, in respect for the beliefs of the Sikkimese, who still hold the exact summit to be sacred. Most climbers have done this.

Local legend says the top of Kanchenjunga won't be well remembered by those who see it, and photographs of it will vanish along with the memories. Haley pulled out her camera for a quick group shot and was sad to see her battery was dead.

Hans and Rajat shook their heads. Neither had his camera anymore. Ravi pulled out his phone with a grin, set his timer as he placed it on the ground, and the group waved. Haley hoped the picture had taken. Then they began the slow descent back to oxygen and life.

June 2012

32. Answering

Pavel would have found a way out of his predicament, if it hadn't been for the damn Chinese girl. He and his men had committed no serious crime by hunting in the woods at night to amuse themselves. One phone call the next morning to his lawyers would have taken care of everything.

Well, everything but the damn Indian virgin who insisted to the Bhutanese that Pavel had been hunting her down for months, but she had no proof. The monk kid with her claimed it was true, but when pressed to explain how he knew, he resorted to mumbo jumbo with no legal validity.

Their claims were unfortunate only because they meant Pavel would have to walk away from this virgin for good, and lay low in general. Otherwise, though, he'd have been fine.

Then, the one link Samir insisted was secure broke. While the Bhutanese were holding him to examine the situation, copies of emails, recordings of phone calls and even recorded live conversations with his Chinese hacker appeared on the desks of both the Bhutanese and the authorities in India. Pavel and several of his key men were on record as not only pursuing two under-aged girls across half a continent, which would have caused enough problems, but they were also documented discussing assorted other business matters linking them to prostitution and human trafficking in multiple countries.

Armed with this evidence, the nation of India demanded extradition. Efforts kicked in to apprehend Pavel's more unsavory employees, who in aggregate had caused a good deal of harm all along the Himalayan foothills.

Bhutan was happy to send the men on to justice elsewhere. After his extradition to India, Pavel learned the Indian government sought his cyber sleuth Mei as well.

"I thought she could be trusted," he barked at his team of lawyers. "I'm glad they're going after her, even though she cooperated with them."

"She didn't," his chief counsel said. "She was true to her word. She had nothing to do with the evidence being sent."

Pavel gave the man a disbelieving look. "How's that possible? There was no one else in the room during some of those recorded conversations."

"Yes, there was. It turns out Mei's translator didn't share her flexible moral code," the lawyer said.

Pavel tried, but he couldn't recall what the tiny, indistinguishable Chinese woman translator looked like. He didn't think he'd ever bothered to ask for her name.

"Mei's own background checking wasn't as good as she thought," his lawyer said. "After your arrest forced her to re-evaluate her only employee, she discovered her translator's older sister was sold into slavery as a child two decades ago. It appears the woman worked for years to put herself in a position to get even."

"Against me? Why?" Pavel asked. "I had nothing to do with this sister."

"You could have." His lawyer shrugged. "Apparently the translator objects to your line of business. She not only provided an impressive amount of evidence against you, she single-handedly brought down Nandi, the procurer who sold you Usha to begin with. You weren't even the only client of Mei's she took an interest in. She produced data against several others engaged in similar questionable activities."

"You mean she went after *everyone* who dealt in girls?"

His chief counsel nodded.

Pavel understood the desire for revenge, but damn.

******

The last thing Teddie wanted to do was to go back to school. She'd missed over two weeks now and was so far behind she couldn't imagine she'd ever catch up. But it was time to leave the home Mr. and Mrs. Dutta had lent them, and Teddie's real home was, for the time being, over at the Lord Peartree Academy.

The school took a flexible approach to her situation, and welcomed her back as they made arrangements for her to have a few private tutoring sessions with her instructors before taking her final exams a week late.

She had happy video-calls with her parents, rearranged her ticket home and settled into some serious studying while she waited for her roommates to return. Well, mostly she studied. She did do a little online chatting with Tariq, who wanted to know how the whole adventure had ended. Hearing of Usha and Michelle's safety seemed to bring the boy so much joy that Teddie couldn't resist telling him every bit of the story.

******

Haley caught her breath as she saw her dad's figure waiting for her outside of the base camp. She broke into a trot, the rich air of seventeen-thousand feet filling her lungs as she ran. A surprise snowstorm had delayed them for days on the descent, and their remaining cellphone had exhausted both of its batteries, so the foursome had been unable to let the camp know they were on their way.

As soon as her dad realized who was making her way down the slope, he let out a whoop and began to make his way up towards her as well. Her descent was faster, and they met about a quarter of the way out of the camp, exchanging an embrace that spoke a thousand words.

"Henrik told me what you did," her father said as they made their way back to camp together.

"He made it back? "

"Just yesterday. He rested at Camp Two for days. They've transported him on down for medical attention. He's probably fine but is getting a thorough look. Haley?" Her dad didn't know whether to scold or praise his daughter.

"I know, Dad. Somebody wise once told me to do the best I can under whatever circumstances I find myself in. That's all I was doing."

"I figured you'd see it like that," he said. "By the way, Abe Lincoln said it, not me. So, can I ask you what the very top of Kanchenjunga is like?"

"You can." She grinned. "It's beautiful. Unbelievable, actually. I know a lot of it was the altitude, but even the memory of standing there sort of feels like a dream, but a gorgeous one." Then she got more serious. "Did the others make it? To the top? Back down yet?"

"Well, yes and no. Five of the climbers quit early, as you know, and the two Japanese men trying to ascend without oxygen made it to the summit, but got stalled out in the same storm you did, and both got pretty ill. They've both been hospitalized."

"That's too bad."

"The four climbers who left you behind got here two days ago. They ran into nothing but problems after they left you and never made it to the top. I can't believe they went on without you."

"It made sense, Dad. At the time we separated we had no plan for helping Henrik. Hans was staying with Henrik while he died, and I guess Ravi and Rajat and I were giving Hans some companionship at the start of his grim vigil."

"It was really that dire?"

"Yeah, it was. Nobody faulted any of them. It wasn't going to take eight people to hold Henrik's hand."

Her dad let out a long sigh at plans gone awry. Having Haley back safe was what mattered. "Haley, this thing you did is part of you now, and it always will be. You need to rest, and then, I hope you'll be ready to head down. I'm eager to go home."

"I'm ready too, Dad, but only if we go by way of Darjeeling. There are a few important loose ends in my life I need to take care of."

******

Usha came back to Darjeeling two days after Pavel and his men were apprehended, and at her request Jampa was allowed to come with her. She greeted Amy and Teddie with hugs, thanking them for all of their efforts.

The next day, Usha's mother Ashmita and her sister Diya arrived by car, with all kinds of good news. All of them were safe and grateful for the asylum they'd received. Where? They couldn't say. They'd worried horribly about Usha, and couldn't believe she'd managed to elude for months the awful man Uncle Jeet had sold her to.

When Usha asked what had happened to Uncle Jeet and Aunt Riddhi after Usha's disappearance, Ashmita replied that she neither knew nor cared.

Ashmita did know the agency would help her get to Mumbai, where her own family would help her establish a new life. But maybe not Usha? For while the academy couldn't give Usha credit for her junior year, given she'd missed most of it, they were willing to offer her a second scholarship starting in September. She'd be a year behind others her age, but she could finish high school there if she wished.

"Usha, you should consider this," her mother said. Then the woman noticed the way Jampa and her daughter were looking at each other. "Then again, maybe you should come with me."

"Mother. This is Jampa, and he helped save my life. He is my friend and a respectful one."

Ashmita turned to the young man. "You're Buddhist? You're from a monastery?"

"I once was. I was sold to them when I was a small child."

"Oh." Ashmita's face softened. "I'm sorry. No child should be sold."

"I never knew my own mother," Jampa said "so I don't know what happened, but I like to think she loved me like you love Usha. In the end, I was lucky. The monks were mostly good to me and taught me much."

"So you're going back?"

"No, the monastery is no longer my home. I'm hoping to work with a friend of Amy's. His name is Lhatu, and he and I have much in common."

"You'll work in Bhutan?"

Jampa nodded. "Yes, I'll be in Thimphu. I'll work with an aid organization of Lhatu's, and I also hope to get into the tourist industry in Bhutan. It's growing and they need Bhutanese who enjoy working with outsiders. I seem to make a good guide." He smiled at Usha, "Because of both, I'll get a chance to visit India often."

"I see," Ashmita said. Wisely, she said no more.

******

Teddie enjoyed seeing how happy and healthy Usha was, and meeting Jampa turned out to be a delight. It was nice to know his name, and to know someone her age who understood the weird phenomenon of traveling. She wondered if he'd talked to Usha about it. Yet. She couldn't help noting the two of them were cute together. Maybe something was going to come of this? Teddie hoped so.

The next day, an ecstatic Haley came back to the academy for a few days to make arrangements for the various incompletes she would need to handle. She had already texted Teddie about her successful climb, but hearing the story in person was far more thrilling. The three girls sat huddled together in their old room as Haley talked.

"You really went over the edge of a sixteen-hundred-foot cliff?" an incredulous Usha asked.

"Yes, yes I really did."

"Weren't you scared?" Usha asked.

"Weren't you? With all you did?" Haley replied. "Look, I figure there must be a thousand ways to soar like an eagle. You and I and Teddie, we all found one of our own. It's scary up there, but beautiful, right?"

"I want to hear about the top of the mountain," Teddie said. "Do you have a picture?"

Haley shook her head. "It turns out two of the other people at the summit didn't have cameras by the time they got there. My battery died, and my friend Ravi thought he snapped a photo, but it never took. Legend says the summit can't be photographed. Who knows, maybe it can't."

Teddie smiled to herself. She had a surprise for Haley, but it could wait.

The three girls fell back into conversation, with Haley describing her unexpected friendship with the two young climbers from India and Usha giving highlights of what she'd learned in a Buddhist convent. Only Teddie felt she had so many secrets to keep about telepaths and travelers that she had to watch what she said. Haley noticed her growing quiet.

"Hey, did I ever tell you about the sea hare?" Haley asked.

"Oh no. Not more animal sex, please."

"You'll love this one. It's a kind of underwater slug," Haley said.

"Ick." Teddie was not interested.

"No listen. It turns out slugs have both male and female parts. So sometimes, well, a whole group of them get in a line and, you know, with the guy parts doing the guy thing and…"

"Yes, we get the idea," Usha said.

"So sea hares, they do this on the ocean floor. Only instead of standing still, they move along making a kind of parade of it. Seriously. They do this giant sex conga line."

Teddie giggled in spite of herself. "Okay. That is your best one ever, Haley."

******

Vanida had options, and the idea of choosing her own future was the greatest delight she'd had in her young life. She learned her brother's real name was Jampa. He was ecstatic to have found his only family member, and he hoped she'd seek refuge in Bhutan. Michelle's friend Amy was eager to help Vanida find a new life in India. Both ideas had appeal, but Vanida realized she was Thai in her heart, and she wanted to stay there.

Luckily, there were those in Thailand willing to assist her also. The renegade c^3 group wanted to give her a job while they studied her innate abilities. Lawan offered to help her find housing in Bangkok and get her started on a new life.

Better yet, the Sisters of the Good Shepherd were willing to get her certificates of study to enable her to enroll in college classes. They'd even help fund her studies. Vanida made one visit to the campus library. She could study here? Read all these books? Vanida eyed shelf after shelf, and she didn't know whether to laugh or to cry. She'd never be able to read them all.

Maybe someday, she'd write a book of her own and it would sit in a library like this. She felt a happy rush go through her body at the thought of it.

The invitation to work with Sister Teresa Marie in her programs to help the prostitutes of Bangkok was equally appealing. The intrepid nun was delighted at the thought of having Vanida join her, and Vanida saw how she had a unique vantage point from which she could reach out to the numerous nameless girls and women who had nothing else working in their favor.

Her decision was made, and in the end, deciding wasn't difficult at all. However, Vanida enjoyed every minute of making the choice.

******

The relief agency in Thailand kept Michelle for a couple of days to make sure she was physically and mentally ready to make the long flight home. Michelle insisted on traveling by way of Darjeeling. She wanted to revisit the school and even the mall where she was kidnapped. She explained to her mother on the phone how it would help her find some closure. Her mother agreed to meet her there.

Mrs. Tran, a small woman with a bewildered look on her face, arrived in town first. The woman was exhausted after the trip but anxious to settle various matters with school officials and to collect Michelle's things before she went to a hotel to await her daughter's arrival. Teddie ran out to meet her.

"Do you think Michelle could stay here in the dorm with us just for a night?" Teddie asked.

"I assumed she'd stay at the hotel with me," Mrs. Tran said. She looked a bit hurt. "Don't you think she'd prefer that?"

"I don't know," Teddie said honestly. "But there's a good chance one night here on campus might help her to say goodbye to this place and all that happened. Then it might be easier for her to move on."

Mrs. Tran nodded and gave Teddie a small smile. "You always were good at knowing these things. I'll ask Michelle what she wants."

The Michelle who arrived hours later seemed to only want everyone to leave her alone. "I don't need your sympathy," she told her three friends before any of them could start. Then to her mother, as she shrugged off a hug, "I'm fine." Teddie couldn't help exchanging a look with Mrs. Tran that said, "Give her time."

Michelle opted for dinner out with her mother and then a night at the dorm. As the four roommates got ready for bed she said, "I don't want to talk about it."

"Of course you don't," Haley said. "No one in their right mind would want to."

The room was quiet for a few seconds.

"So, now that you made it to the top of the mountain, are you committed to showing off your underwear in public for the rest of your life?" Michelle finally asked, filling the silence.

"I might have dodged that bullet. Turns out my discomfort at the original ad got some press and a company that makes outdoor gear for women wants to use me in their ads."

"Haley, that's perfect," Teddie said.

"Yes and no." Haley shrugged. "I mean, I've already been told the ads are going to center around things like 'these hiking boots are great for girls' and 'I'm so glad I get to model them for you instead of my underpants.' You know, a little humor sells a lot."

Michelle giggled in spite of herself.

"I think your friend's brother is my new boyfriend," Usha said.

"You mean Vanida? Yeah, I guess she's my friend."

"Did you guys part poorly?" Teddie asked.

Michelle shrugged. "No. I mean, she's all happy about how great life is, and she's got this wonderful future ahead of her and you know…" Tears were starting to form in Michelle's eyes.

"And you don't have the exact same wonderful future ahead of you?" Usha asked.

"No, not really. I go home to being the poster child for human trafficking. How many news outlets carried my picture? My story? Like every guy I go out with now is going to wonder exactly what happened."

The little pools in her eyes overflowed and the tears began to turn into sobs.

"I don't have a future anymore." She said it between sobs, but every one of them heard her.

Her friends let her cry. Sometimes self-pity is warranted; sometimes making no argument to the contrary is the best a friend can do.

"You're a hero for surviving, Michelle," Haley finally said.

"Yeah, well, I don't want to be a hero. I want my life back." She gave her nose a hard unladylike blow as she said it.

Teddie chimed in. "What you did, Michelle, living through the kidnapping ordeal, faking them out in the brothel so they didn't drug you or hurt you, and then surviving off the land and on the street while you were hunted down—jeez, it's like secret agent stuff. You were cool beyond belief."

Michelle laughed a little in-between sobs. "I came up with good ideas for getting by."

"I told Usha and Teddie that the three of us each found ways to soar like eagles this year," Haley said. "Michelle, you figured out how to fly higher than any of us, and to do it in the middle of an awful storm. You did something amazing."

"I just kept wanting to have everything be like it was. Have me be like I was. Now I understand that's not gonna be possible."

"So you have a new you. Michelle, the smart, tough lady who doesn't take any shit from anyone, and yet has a heart of warm gold inside," Usha said.

"Yeah okay. Smart. No shit. Warm gold. Maybe I'll figure out how to be the new me."

"Of course you will," Teddie said. "And when you don't want to be that, you get to go ahead and cry." All of her friends agreed, and to prove it every one of them started to cry with her.

Then the tears turned to giggles, and the giggles turned to shared stories, and the long process of healing began.

June 2012

33. Departing

When Lhatu learned of the pivotal role his grandmother played in keeping Pavel from completing his bizarre hunt, he knew how uncharacteristic it was for her and the c^3 organization. The more he thought about it, the more he realized her entire trip to Darjeeling had been unprecedented. When she called to ask him to return home after Michelle's safe arrival, he wasn't surprised.

"You're dying." he said.

"Yes. We're all dying; some of us faster than others. I don't expect *my* death soon, but I do think it's time for me to hand over the reins of c^3. I'm hoping you'll decline."

"Decline?" Lhatu was aghast. He'd trained his whole life to succeed her. She had no other heir. Was he so unworthy?

"I couldn't ask for a better grandson, or for a more adept traveler as my successor," she said. "But the world is changing faster than it used to, and this organization can't survive as it is. Your leadership would be similar to mine; you'd basically do as I've taught you."

"This is not what you want?"

"No, it's exactly what I want. But I can see how what I want is not what's best. Best for c^3 is to retain its most essential traditions, while finding a way to embrace the whole world. The traditions of travelers elsewhere, the openness of today's communication, and scientific knowledge are all going to find us. We could fight this for another generation, maybe two. But why? It's best to flow with the river, and you've not been trained to do that. In fact, you've been trained to resist it, and that's my fault."

"Then I decline, as you wish."

"Good," the woman said. There was a bit of a twinkle in her eye. "I thank you for your obedience to my wishes. To whom do you plan to give your responsibilities?"

"To whomever you wish."

"There is this wonderful man in Thimphu named Lhatu who is an adept traveler, knows the organization well and would do a wonderful job."

"I'm sorry, grandmother, but I don't understand. You wish me to hand the reins over to myself?"

"No." The woman smiled. "I wish for my heir, the next in line, to turn the reins over to the human named Lhatu. Without all his baggage, perhaps this human will see his way clear to learn new ways. My advice, if asked, would be for him to consider choosing two close advisors to help him steer c^3 into the future."

Close advisors? Lhatu was puzzled. "Do you have two others in mind?"

"I do. We've recently accepted two amazing young twins into our midst. Jampa brings fresh energy and yet has many of our traditional values. He could maintain the core of c^3 here in its home, allowing you the time and the energy to reach out more and perhaps live elsewhere."

She seemed quite pleased with herself as she continued. "Vanida, his twin sister, brings none of those traits. She's independent, even rebellious, and is connected to our renegade scientists in Bangkok. She brings balance. She'll help heal rifts within our organization, and will help us embrace the modern world."

"Yes, grandmother. I know of these twins, and I can see how including them as my assistants could benefit c^3."

"It could also benefit this man named Lhatu. An old woman's observation is Lhatu is steadfast in his loyalty to his family and his obligations, but his interests have strayed away from those who'd have once been considered acceptable consorts for him. Perhaps under this new plan, he will no longer feel the need to suppress his desire for the comforts of a mate for whom he yearns."

"Oh, I couldn't possibly consider…" Lhatu sputtered.

"Of course you could," his grandmother said. "Though she is a Westerner who shares none of our beliefs, she's a wonderful woman and your happiness and hers are already intertwined. You are an idiot if you don't at least consider it."

With that conversation, the possibilities in Lhatu's world opened up in ways he'd never dared hope they would.

******

The flowers were a charming, old-fashioned gesture, and Amy wasn't sure what to make of them. Lhatu had called to let her know he was in town and wished to ask her out to dinner. He mentioned a nice restaurant, something fancier than where they normally ate. She dressed up, so as not to feel uncomfortable, thinking this was a celebration of Usha and Michelle's safe return.

Then, he met her at her door with these flowers. They were a wild array of types and colors creating a bouquet that made one blink in wonder. She smiled as she realized the bouquet looked like her.

"I love them."

"I thought you might." He sat at her counter and smiled as she put them in water. She studied his smile.

"You've only been gone a week, yet you seem different."

He responded with a look somewhere between hunger and pleading. She understood it right away, but wasn't sure how she ought to respond. Did she want to play more games with him? Yes, in fact, she did, but she also knew she probably shouldn't. She reached out and tentatively put one hand on his to suggest he reconsider, but at her first touch he was up out of his chair with both arms reaching for her.

"You don't want to do this. I say it as a friend." She started to push him away but didn't quite get the word friend out before he started to kiss her.

"Yes I do." He pulled away to say it, and then went back to kissing. "I'll want to again tomorrow," he added the second time he came up for air. The kissing began to include fondling before he added, "And the day after. And the day after that."

This time Amy pulled away. "Changing your philosophy of life all the sudden?"

"I'm surprisingly open to that at the moment."

"Okay. It's nice to know what to expect."

"Oh, you have no idea how good this will get," he said.

Over the next several days, he proved to her he was right.

******

Teddie was happy Lhatu and Amy were going to pick her up one last time and drive her to the airport in Bagdogra. She could sense as soon as she got in the car that something had changed between them. Before long they were holding hands and giving each other smitten kitten looks when they thought she wasn't looking. She smiled to herself. Grown-ups in love were so sweet.

She'd already said her goodbyes to the school, the town and the mountains. Her last final yesterday went okay. Her grades wouldn't be great, but she'd pass everything. She was ready to get home.

"Have you heard from Michelle yet?" Amy asked.

"Oh yes. She got home two days ago. She was nervous about seeing her dad. She thought he was going to blame her for letting this happen. I can't imagine he's that insensitive. He didn't, though. She said he seems oddly proud of her and her mother keeps looking at her like she's the most precious thing in the world. Their family dynamics have definitely changed."

Amy nodded. "Usha is doing great as a temp in my office. I'm going put her on fulltime for the rest of the summer, so she ought to have some savings by the time school starts."

"It's nice Ana needed a roommate so Usha has a place to live. Haley's back in Denver and happy, so, I guess the year ended a lot better than it could have."

"Much better," Lhatu said. "Did you know Vanida is working fulltime now with the lab in Bangkok? And Jampa has gotten an internship with a tour company in Thimphu? They both said they want to concentrate on those things before they get more involved in c^3, but I think they'll become my management team eventually."

"About that," Teddie said. "I need a break too. Like, to sort of be a normal person for a while. You know?"

"I know exactly, and you should. We do need to monitor the implant in your head, though, so you'll have to let us do check-ups once in a while."

"Of course." Teddie had expected as much.

"But a break is good," Lhatu continued. "You learned so much so fast. Now, travel outside your body for fun. Contact c^3 if you ever want to learn more."

Teddie smiled. "I will. For the next few months, though I'm going places in my pick-up truck, with my country music playing, as loud as I want. It's going to be a nice way to travel."

A Thousand Ways to Soar

July 2024

34. Being Helpful

Twenty-nine-year-old Teddie Zeitman had five or six years left before she lost her ability to use the chip implanted in her occipital lobe in 2012. Lawan, researcher for c^3, hadn't told her many of the components were slowly biodegradable and the implant would someday become useless. Teddie wished she'd known it sooner.

In Lawan's defense, she assumed Teddie would only use the chip to find her missing friends, and then wait on research to provide a safe way to remove it. That *had* been Teddie's plan, at least at first.

Twenty-year-old Teddie, however, began to appreciate the possibilities. She traveled more, both in the solid world and in the abode of light. She was studying international relations in college by then, and with some reservations she signed up for a course on ways to address the problem of human trafficking. During the first class, memories from 2012 came flooding back with more force than she expected, and she left the room nauseous and almost dropped the course.

But she didn't. By the fourth week of class, she knew what she had to do.

Research on the chip had been stopped in 2014, after several more animals died or went blind due to the device's placement or its removal. Lawan and her staff believed Teddie's body had accepted the device, and she'd be fine, but they were unwilling to take a similar chance on another human. The situation left Teddie as the only traveler who could bring back images of where she'd been.

Teddie began by going after the most horrific of sex offenders. Pictures of missing girls began arriving, along with photographs identifying where they were. Businessmen and women who facilitated the trade were likely to show up too, their complicity made obvious by a series of images. Torture and abuse? You and what you were doing could be on the internet tomorrow. By the time Teddie was twenty-four, the grainy black and white photos were everywhere.

Of course, there were backlashes. Those concerned about privacy, as well as those concerned about merely protecting their financial interests, sought to prevent the pictures from being used in court or even by law enforcement. They were somewhat successful, but not completely.

Many sought to trace the origin of the pictures as they showed up randomly in the mail and online. All that could be determined was the information originated somewhere in the nation of Bhutan. The Bhutanese responded saying they didn't condone human trafficking, and while they were unaware of who was sending the information, they were also disinclined to make efforts to locate the source. Due to the difficulties in entering the country, that was the end of that.

Those who knew Teddie well were concerned about her safety and her well-being as she forayed further into a slimy underworld. Her family and friends, and, in fact, all of c^3, provided support for her as they could. The telepathic organization x^0 was not far behind them. Teddie's mother and her friends stayed true to their word and didn't enter her mind, but they ran interference for her, their efforts often led by an aging but tireless Nigerian man determined to right the wrongs he'd witnessed as a youth.

One telepath in particular insisted on being part of Teddie's mission, and knowing of the sad loss in Tariq's past, Teddie included him. At first it was more out of sympathy, but over time she learned to enjoy his quiet wit when they spoke. He became the only telepath she trusted to ride along in her mind the way Maurice once had. After a while, she felt safer and foraged further when he was with her.

By the time Teddie was twenty-six, a subtle change had occurred. No man or woman who engaged in acts that took away a young woman's right to her own body could live without looking over their shoulder. Who was taking these photos? How was this person finding them? Why did no one ever see the photographer?

It turned out many bullies and most cold profiteers didn't appreciate being shown in the act of committing their sins, whether or not it resulted in jail time. Some sought other outlets resulting in less unfavorable publicity. Others took a more offensive stance, defending their actions as legitimate business concerns or as a time-honored expression of women's natural roles. This last group faced the wrath of a world being made more aware every day.

These days, when Teddie had trouble sleeping, she made the rounds to check on her friends. She'd become adept at journeys far longer than most travelers made, moving in the world of mist at near light speed. Tonight she was restless, and made her usual first stop. A quick pass by Pavel showed him to be safely confined in his small cell in an Indian prison. He was pacing uncomfortably. Good. No more attempted jail breaks. She'd keep checking.

Then she made a pass near Amy and Lhatu in Darjeeling. It was the middle of the day in India, and Amy was at work, running the office with more passion, more plants and more colorful clothes. Her three-year-old daughter played nearby on the floor, and the new baby slept in his swing. Their five-year-old son must be in school, or maybe he was with Lhatu.

These two had persevered through a rocky start. They'd been two such independent people, with separate missions in life, different backgrounds and little previous experience in how to make a relationship work. Today, they seemed more in love than ever.

She gave Lhatu a call to meet her, but when he didn't come she wasn't surprised. Travelers seldom could drop everything in the middle of the day to come wave hello. She'd give Amy and Lhatu a video-call tomorrow. That worked better for exchanging news anyway.

Next stop was Bhutan, and a quick peek into the secret office that processed and distributed her pictures. No longer only a quiet intellectual, Usha had embraced the strong examples of powerful Hindu women and female deities. She took what Teddie provided, and she sent information to the world with the skill and passion of a warrior. Teddie often thought her photos would have made little difference without Usha's shrewd dissemination.

Jampa spent much of his day helping Lhatu and Vanida run c^3, but also spent time assisting his wife. Teddie wondered what they would do once the pictures stopped coming. She hoped Usha would find new ways to fight crime.

Teddie kept traveling. Vanida was sitting on her porch, high in the hills of north Thailand, working on her fourth novel. Teddie knew Vanida was at her happiest when she was writing. She thought about calling out to her friend, but Vanida was hunched over her keyboard with such a fierce look of concentration that Teddie decided not to interrupt her. Vanida had confided that this fourth book would be her most intense yet. Best let her write it.

The next stop was Michelle's place along the coast of Northern California where she and her boyfriend were renting a cottage together. He was an artist, and Michelle modeled for his sketches by day, and worked on her own fashion designs. Teddie had seen the drawings Michelle did late at night, once her boyfriend was in bed. Simple black-and-white art drawn in bold angry strokes, the sketches captured the plight of the victims Michelle had seen and refused to be one of. Teddie hoped someday her friend would grow comfortable enough to share her amazing drawings with the world.

The last stop was Denver. Haley was sleeping of course, but Teddie made a quick pass by the office where Haley ran her mountaineering school for children. Even in the moonlight, Teddie could see the walls and study the grainy black-and-white photograph that brought her back here so often.

It showed four smiling people in parkas and hoods with goggles and breathing apparatuses hanging around their necks. Behind them was the sky, a spectacular view, and the very tip of a mountain that had allowed itself to be photographed, just this once.

Anyone who studied it would noticed the photographer was slightly above the people in the picture. No small feat for capturing a group standing at the top of a mountain, yet as far as Teddie knew no one had ever asked Haley to explain. Teddie hoped it would stay that way.

She returned home with a snap. Something had disturbed her solid body. Damn, she'd left her phone on and now it was ringing. It was Tariq.

"What's up?"

"Teddie. I have a chance to come to the United States! It's for a medical conference in San Diego, near where you live. I wondered if, well, maybe, if you wanted to meet."

Oh my. All these years and phone calls and emails and time spent with Tariq, and she'd never once set foot in her solid body in the same room with him. He'd listened to her thoughts, watched out for her, and even gotten help when she found something truly awful. He was a medical doctor now, yet he always found time for her and her cause. Of course she wanted to meet him.

"Tariq, that would be wonderful."

July 2045

35. Dancing Forward

Teddie hadn't wanted to go to Chicago for the celebration, but it was one of those family times. Her brother Zane was getting an award from a company he'd helped shape decades ago, and he deserved having his family there to cheer him on. She'd get to see her parents, too, and her dad hadn't been doing all that well lately.

Tariq was in Pakistan now at his mother's bedside, and she missed him. His gentle humor kept her own disposition sunny, ever since that lucky day twenty-one years ago when she'd walked into a hotel lobby in San Diego and saw him for the first time.

His absence meant she'd have to bring their fourteen-year-old son with her; he was too likely to get into trouble staying at the homes of any of his buddies. Did the kid own something suitable to wear? She didn't think so. At least her nine-year-old daughter could stay in San Diego with friends.

Once Teddie arrived in Chicago, she was glad she came. Her shy son sat at the end of the table alone, but her dad plopped down next to him and starting talking. Given the boys animated response, they had to be discussing sports.

A man stepped up to the mic. As the first tribute began, Teddie slipped into a light trance. Years of practice had honed her ability to leave an alert looking body behind, and had given her the confidence that, if she stayed close, she could make an instantaneous return if she had to. She headed off exploring, intending to be back in a few minutes, well before the introductory speaker was done.

Looked like there was a prom going on in Ballroom B. The young men and women were dolled up, sipping fruit drinks and flirting. Some things never changed.

Some did. Boys' attire had more flexibility these days. The girls' dresses were different than those of years ago, but the young ladies appeared to have tried as hard as Teddie's friends once did to show off as much skin as their school would allow.

She lingered longer than she meant to, enjoying the energy and beauty of the young people. She was about leave when she noticed two of the boys exchange a knowing wink.

Hmmmm. What was this about?

She watched with growing alarm as one boy got two girls to pose for a photo, while his friend dropped something into the girls' drinks. Little white tablets. In the drinks. Teddie looked on in outrage.

She couldn't knock over the drinks; she couldn't warn the girls. Her traveling body was mute and useless, and had lost its photographic abilities years ago. No wait. This time she had a perfectly good solid body on the other side of a hotel partition. She snapped back, ready to get up and invade the prom.

Teddie mumbled something to her family members about the restroom and made her way into the lobby as another speaker took the podium. She marched straight over to Ballroom B, only to be told no one but high school students were being admitted.

Great. She could hope to intercept one of the girls in the lobby bathroom, but that was too undependable. Worse yet, it could lead to her getting thrown out by hotel security if the girls didn't believe her. There had to be a better idea than pulling the fire alarm or screaming she'd seen a bomb, both of which were a criminal offense.

Maybe her family could help. She went back to take her seat, trying to come up with an idea, and saw her brother Zane speaking.

Damn, she'd missed his introduction. Zane was accepting a plaque, saying a few vague words about how happy he was. Teddie felt sorry for him. If anyone in the world hated public speaking, it had to be Zane. Then, his voice grew stronger.

"You know, when you're a little kid you have no idea how your life is going to turn out," he said to the crowd.

Isn't that the truth. For example, you don't think you're going to change the world because you've been turned into the greatest weapon ever developed for exposing pathetic behavior.

Zane paused in his speech, reached for a water glass, and surprised the crowd when he raised it high over his head.

"To each and every human being getting to joyfully do the dance of life." Zane paused and smiled. "I don't mean just a couple of quiet toe taps, people. I mean twirl-around-in-circles-while-pumping-your-fists-in-the-air dancing. Get your feet moving, because whether you dance with fire or polka bands, with drums or a full orchestra, no one can do your dance better than you. So dance it with joy."

The applause started and grew in enthusiasm and Teddie's mind flashed back to her old friend Haley's bizarre fun facts about animal sex. Why was she thinking of that now? Why was she remembering the sea hare, an underwater slug that had sex in a conga line?

Then Teddie saw the opportunity. She hopped up to her feet as her fourteen-year-old son looked on in horrified embarrassment.

"To dancing for joy," she yelled back at her brother. He gave her a single raised eyebrow as she twirled around pumping her fists in the air. Her father looked confused, but her mother picked up something was amiss and Teddie needed help.

Lola stood up, gave a loud hoot and repeated Teddie's little dance. It was kind of cute when done by an eighty-five-year-old woman, and a few others laughed and stood up and repeated the motion as well. Then a few more, and a couple dozen more after that.

It was exactly what Teddie hoped for. She turned her little jig into a walking movement and her helpful mother joined in behind her, forming the happiest little two-person conga line seen in a while. A few others added themselves on, and pretty soon an impressive group was kicking and shaking its way out of Ballroom A, all dancing for joy just like Zane had extolled them to do.

It's one thing to tell a fifty-year-old woman she cannot enter a school event. It's quite another to stop a two-hundred-person conga line hell bent on joining your party. The doorman picked up his radio and was about to call for backup, when he noticed the dancing and laughing group seemed so harmless and happy, he decided to give it few minutes and see how things went.

Joy is contagious. At first the kids laughed at the adults crashing their prom, then after a few minutes some shrugged and joined in. Then pretty much everyone did. Teddie's mother was having the time of her life, so Teddie let her lead the happy group out of the prom and right into the wedding reception being held in Ballroom C.

After many of the wedding guests joined in, Zane was coaxed to the front of the line and he took the fake sea hare orgy on through the lobby and out into the streets of Chicago. Thanks to modern communication, people were waiting outside to join and dance music was blaring. Before long, traffic was rerouted and a parade permit was filed by the city while the spontaneous dance progressed. By the year 2045, the city of Chicago had learned how to be helpful.

Teddie took the opportunity to put two woozy girls in a cab headed home, glad to have made more of a difference in their young lives then they'd ever know.

Before it was over, the sea hare boogie was estimated to have included over six-thousand dancing humans, leaving on-the-scene-reporters to speculate Zane had inspired the world's longest conga line.

Teddie watched the dancers, thinking this moment was perfect. It was how the world should be, it was the way people should behave, and it was the way every story should end.

March 2064

36. Being Brave

Teddie held her mother's hand as her brother Zane left the hospice room. They both knew the end was near, but Zane had been here for hours and needed a break.

Teddie had made sure everyone knew she wanted to be called in time to say a final goodbye. She knew others thought she was being difficult, but she had her reasons. Yes, she'd said her farewells to her mother more than once, but not in the way she planned to today. If she could get herself to do it, that was.

******

Lola was enjoying a warm feeling of contentment, filled with the recent comfort from her husband and son. She was so lucky to have people who loved her help her through this, life's most difficult rite of passage.

Then she saw little Teddie in her mind's eye, a four-year-old dynamo of emotion and curly black hair. The child was squirming with excitement and nervousness.

"Mommy? Mommy. Come with me. Come see," the little girl said, tugging on her hand.

"I'd love to, but I can't go anywhere, sweetie. Mommy's sick right now."

But she was wrong. She *was* going; she was leaving the hospice, moving down the hall, and going right through the wall.

She looked around in a panic for Teddie and didn't see her anywhere. Lola realized with a sinking feeling that she was lodged deep within Teddie's own mind, traveling with her. It was something she'd sworn never to do.

"I'm so sorry, honey. It just happened. Mommy's weak right now, I guess she doesn't have much control anymore."

"Mom, everything's okay." Grown-up Teddie thought the words clearly. "Listen. I can't hear what you're thinking, but you should be able to hear me. I've invited you into my mind. You've accepted. I won't keep talking, because I have to concentrate on what I'm doing. I'm taking you for a trip, and then I'm going to bring you back. Stay calm, and enjoy the ride."

A trip. How nice.

Ever since the odd telepathy exchanges she and Teddie had shared decades ago, Lola had known Teddie wanted no part of interchanging the strange gifts the two of them possessed. Lola respected Teddie's wishes, and they'd loved and supported each other, but kept their distance. Lola thought Teddie's desire for independence was grounded in wisdom. A child needed a certain amount of distance to grow.

So what was different about today?

Oh that's right. I'm dying. This is a farewell gift. I wonder where she's taking me.

Lola saw the glimmer of dawn in the east over a mountain range growing larger and she knew. With all that had happened in her life, she'd never gotten back to the Himalayas. Never made it to the base camp at Everest. Never even taken a flight over the great mountain range defining so much of the world's largest continent. How had she gotten too busy to do that?

She'd looked at a lot of pictures though, so she recognized Sagarmāthā, Mount Everest, before Teddie was even close. Up they went to the base camp, slowing down so Lola could see it well. Then they flew up over the Khumbu Icefall and on to the summit. The peak was cloud-covered, and Lola could feel Teddie's disappointment. "On to Junga then," Teddie thought with determination.

They flew like the wild geese did, right through the rarified air, with thousands of feet below them and the peaks spread out underneath, sparkling in the coming daylight. Lola thought she had never seen anything so beautiful.

They landed on the top of Kanchenjunga the way a bird would, and Lola took in the view through Teddie's eyes. Her daughter didn't rush, but lingered so Lola could enjoy each direction and each scene to its fullest. Finally, Teddie took to the air, and as Lola followed along she made a slow flight to the west, staying over the beautiful mountain range for as long as she could.

As the flight neared its end, Lola heard her daughter think "I did it. I really did it. It was even kind of fun. I hope she liked it."

Then Lola was back in her own aching body, in her own hospice bed.

"I've gotten braver, Mom, haven't I?" Teddie asked.

Lola wanted to thank her daughter, and say so many things. Instead, she managed to whisper.

"Always loved you. You were always so brave."

She couldn't keep from feeling how surprised and pleased the words made Teddie feel. Then she heard Teddie's thoughts.

"Okay Ariel. Now it's your turn."

Really? Now what?

More

Layers of Light is part of 46. Ascending, a collection of interrelated novels about five family members who discover they can each do the extraordinary when they have to. These books are designed to be read as stand-alone stories or in any order.

If you enjoyed *Layers of Light,* consider *Flickers of Fortune*, the story of Teddie's older sister as she learns how difficult it is to be precognitive. You might also enjoy *Twists of Time*, the tale of Teddie's father as he learns to use his ability to warp time to protect the students at his high school. You may prefer to start with *Shape of Secrets*, the story of Teddie's brother as he learns to alter his appearance, or *One of One*, the story of Teddie's telepathic mother as she finds herself the unlikely hero in a rescue mission in Nigeria.

You can also go directly to *One of Two*, the last book in this collection, in which the Zeitman family combines their skills to prevail over the most dangerous threat they've faced.

Thanks

I have relied on many people to help me weave this tale, and am particularly indebted to seven women I've never met. I mention only a few of their contributions here. I am grateful to:

- Dhivya Balaji of India, for the Sanskrit name Jvalalaya along with her aiding my cultural sensitivity in telling this story,
- Dorottya Bacsi of Hungary, for her encouragement of Haley's character and accomplishments,
- Judith Ludlow of the United States, for her guidance in making this book more accessible to a wider audience,
- Mellissa Barth of Canada, for her encouragement to rework Michelle's back story,
- Michelle Willms, a sociologist/psychologist from the United States, for her insights into trauma
- Sophie Robinson of England, for her fine sense of detail, and
- Shree Janani of India for providing facts about and perspective on her home country.

Thank you ladies, for reaching out across divides of age, culture, location and philosophy to help me make this a better book!

Thanks to my sister June Hanson, who provides me with notes as she reads. Thanks to my daughter Shenandoah, who ensures my stories are free of holes, and to my son Casey who helps me better understand my own novels. Thanks to my husband Kevin, who helps me research, who proofreads and encourages, and who holds me at the end of the day.

For this particular book, my heartfelt thanks go most of all to my daughter Emerald, who allowed me to borrow from her knowledge as a budding social worker and from her own personality and hopes, as I created the characters Teddie and Amy and their struggles to improve this world. This was an emotionally charged subject, sometimes difficult to write about and difficult to read. I thank Emerald for sticking with me, and I hope in the end she and I will have touched a few hearts and minds.

Additional Information

Although this book is a work of fiction, where news items, cultural information, and scientific facts are included, it was my intent to be accurate. I would like to express my thanks to the following sources for information and background material used in this book. Any misrepresentations of information from these sources is unintentional and regretted.

Links to websites I used in my research and the nine songs woven into the original story can be found at my blog *Leaving the Nest to Touch the Sky* at https://ctothepowerofthree.org.

Astral Dynamics: A New Approach to Out-Of-Body Experiences by Robert Bruce
Beyond the Sky and the Earth: A Journey into Bhutan by Jamie Zeppa
Buddhism For Beginners by Thubten Chodron
Girls Like Us: Fighting for a World Where Girls are Not for Sale by Rachel Lloyd
Half the Sky: Turning Oppression into Opportunity for Women Worldwide by Nicholas D. Kristof and Sheryl WuDunn
How Animals Have Sex: A Guide to the Reproductive Habits of Creatures Great and Small by David Strorm
Illustrated Atlas of the Himalaya by David Zurick, Julsun Pacheco, Basanta Shrestha
Kangchenjunga: A Trekker's Guide (Cicerone Guide) by Kev Reynolds
Kangchenjunga The Untrodden Peak by Charles Evans
Married to Bhutan by Linda Leaming
Not for Sale: The Return of the Global Slave Trade and How We Can Fight It by David Batstone
The Road of Lost Innocence: The True Story of a Cambodian Heroine by Somaly Mam
The Secret Sex Lives of Animals by David Lambert

About the author

Sherrie Roth grew up in Western Kansas thinking there was no place in the universe more fascinating than outer space. After her mother vetoed astronaut as a career ambition, she went on to study journalism and physics in hopes of becoming a science writer.

She published her first science fiction short story and then waited a lot of tables while she looked for inspiration for the next tale. When it finally came, it declared to her it had to be a whole book, nothing less. One night, while digesting this disturbing piece of news, she drank way too many shots of ouzo with her boyfriend. She woke up thirty-one years later demanding to know what was going on.

The boyfriend, who she had apparently long since married, asked her to calm down. He explained that, in a fit of practicality, she had gone back to school and gotten a degree in geophysics and had spent the last 28 years interpreting seismic data in the oil industry. The good news, according to Mr. Cronin, was she had found it at least mildly entertaining and ridiculously well-paying. The bad news was the two of them had still managed to spend almost all the money.

She was now Mrs. Cronin, and the further good news was they had produced three wonderful children whom they loved dearly, even though to be honest that is where a lot of the money had gone. Even better news was that Mr. Cronin turned out to be a warm-hearted, encouraging sort who was happy to see her awake and ready to write. "It's about time," were his exact words.

Sherrie Cronin discovered that over the ensuing decades Sally Ride had already managed to become the first woman in space and done a fine job of it. No one, however, had written the book that had been in Sherrie's head for decades. The only problem was, the book informed her it had now grown into a six book collection. Sherrie decided she better start writing it before it got any longer. She's been wide awake ever since, and writing away.

Places

Bagdogra: nearest airport to Darjeeling, 3 hours away by hired car

Darjeeling: Mountain resort in northern India

Gangtok: capital of Sikkim, a country formerly between Nepal and Bhutan and now part of India

Kanchenjunga: third highest mountain in the world

Lord Peartree International Academy for Exceptional Students: fictional school in Darjeeling India

Manali: picturesque Indian resort town where Pavel lives

Mishmi Hills: in India's Arunachel Pradesh district bordering China and Burma

Patna: town in northern India where Ashmita and Usha's siblings live and Usha's father is from

Patong Beach in Phuket, Thailand: most popular beach in all of Southeast Asia.

Patpong district: area of Bangkok notorious for sex shows

Trongsa: Bhutanese town nearest to the convent that offers Usha shelter

People

Alex: Teddie's father
Amy: social worker from Chicago
Ana: employee in Amy's office
Ariel: Teddie's older sister
Ashmita: Usha's mother
Awut: Teddie's photography teacher
Bela: Ashmita's friend in Gangtok
Chakor: Usha's deceased father
Diya: Usha's 11 year old sister
Duttas: elderly telepathic couple from Darjeeling
Haley: mountain climber from Denver
Hans and Henrik: Norwegian climbers
Jampa: young monk living in Bhutan
Jeet: Usha's uncle in Patna
Khae: manager of bar in Bangkok
Lawan: ex-US military researcher and rebel within c^3
Lhatu: man from Bhutan
Lola: Teddie's mother
Maurice: old family friend of the Zeitmans
Mei: expert cyber detective from China who asks no questions
Michelle: Teddie's closest friend
Nandi: procurer of young girls for exclusive clients
Noi: One of Vanida's trainers at a camp in the Thai countryside
Noom: name Jampa uses for his sister
Olumiji: Nigerian telepath
Pavel: the man who purchases Usha
Pêe chaai: name Vanida uses for her brother
Pim: One of Vanida's trainers at a camp in the Thai countryside
Riddhi: Usha's aunt in Patna
Samir: Pavel's go-to man for delicate items
Shawna: a childhood friend of Teddie's
Sister Teresa Marie: a Sister of the Good Shepherd
Somadina: Nigerian telepath and close friend of Teddie's mother
Tariq: Pakistani boy who aids Teddie telepathically
Teddie: high school student from Houston

Uncle Steve: Haley's agent
Usha: high school student from Patna
Vanida: trainee in the sex industry
Vasily: Pavel's old friend and assistant
Yuden: Lhatu's grandmother
Za: murdered mother of two unusual twins
Zane: Teddie's older brother

www.ingramcontent.com/pod-product-compliance
Lightning Source LLC
Chambersburg PA
CBHW020904200626
46814CB00001BA/163

* 9 7 8 1 9 4 1 2 8 3 3 6 3 *